**PAUL S EDWARDS** is a deb[...] of England. Ever since queuing to see Star Wars at the cinema aged five, he's loved Science Fiction. Inspired by his Uncle Bill feeding him battered paperbacks from Clarke, Asimov, and Herbert when he was too young to properly understand them. It was only a matter of time before he decided to turn his hand to writing himself.

*The Triton Run* is the first part of a space opera duology.

Follow Paul on X/Twitter @LovelessAge

# THE TRITON RUN

## PAUL S EDWARDS

Northodox Press Ltd
Maiden Greve, Malton,
North Yorkshire, YO17 7BE

This edition 2025

1
First published in Great Britain by
Northodox Press Ltd 2025

Copyright © Paul S Edwards 2025

Paul S Edwards asserts the moral right to
be identified as the author of this work.

ISBN: 9781915179579

This book is set in Caslon Pro Std

This Novel is entirely a work of fiction. The names, characters and incidents portrayed in it are the work of the author's imagination. Any resemblance to actual persons, living or dead, events or localities is entirely coincidental.

All rights reserved. No part of this publication may be reproduced, stored in a retrieval system, or transmitted, in any form or by any means, electronic, mechanical, photocopying, recording, or otherwise, without the prior permission of the publishers.

This book is sold subject to the condition that it shall not, by way of trade or otherwise, be lent, re-sold, hired out or otherwise circulated without the publisher's prior consent in any form of binding or cover other than that in which it is published and without a similar condition including this condition being imposed on the subsequent purchaser.

TBD

# 1

## WILDING

*The Dark*

When her left eye started haemorrhaging blood, Dee Wilding knew her time was nearly up. The warm drops of blood on her cheek and a crushing headache stirred her awake, as she realised she'd lost consciousness again. Soon, the effects of hypoxia would be irreversible.

It was almost completely dark now. The EVA suit had long since run out of power, shutting down the AI and HUD, followed by basic functions like life support and heating. Whilst well insulated, she was feeling cold, *deathly cold*, she noted with a perverse sense of amusement.

It would've been easier to remain where she was and drift off to permanent sleep. However, this had been a journey of incredible experiences, so she might as well go out with another one. It was a pity that none of her colleagues or friends were here. Eventually, her body would be found, of course. There was too big a prize waiting to be seized. Though there wouldn't be too much concern for a dead war criminal. After what she'd done at Buchanan, they'd say she deserved to die alone, cold, and scared.

Before the suit's lighting failed, Wilding decided what she was going to do. For as long as she was capable, she'd patrolled the vicinity of what felt like a tomb. As none of the corridors led anywhere, she concluded there was no chance of finding safety. She'd pressed every switch, button, or flat screen; hammered at them even, to no effect. She'd not attracted the attention of any unseen residents of the alien ship. Her screams and tears only served to waste vital oxygen and energy.

The suit's exoskeleton had long since powered down. So it took all her will to pull herself up from the hard floor to her feet. She rocked, struggling to get her balance, as weak limbs burned with the strain. She grabbed onto a guard rail for support. It would be an unfortunate end if she slipped and fell to her death in the darkness below.

Trying to take a breath reminded her there was none left to take; her air tank depleted.

She swayed again, relieved to see some of her platoon coming out of the darkness ahead of her. Powell, Parynski, Garraway, Squire, and Dunk all looked concerned, presumably wondering why she'd not kept up. They wore the same Martian orange spacesuits, with black helmets, backpacks, and front storage pouches. That confused her. She didn't think she was on Mars. Dunk carried a huge rifle over his shoulder, while the others held smaller side arms. Despite their transparent visors and name badges, she'd have known them from their size and gait. She'd lived alongside these guys for years. Of course, they'd come back for her.

'You were lagging behind, Ma'am, you ok?' Dunk asked.

A wave of confusion. Perhaps she'd suffered a head injury during the assault. 'I'm ok, Dunk. Sitrep.'

'The Ambassador's entourage are ok. Can't say the same for the Martians. Still waiting for pickup, we've set up a perimeter, and can exit to the surface when ready. Need anything else, Ma'am?'

She thought hard, but her mind was blank. 'It's ok. Proceed.' A pause before asking the question she feared would make her look stupid in front of the group. 'Why'd you come back?'

Dunk half-turned to go, before turning back with a reply. 'To check you're ok?

Some pretty bad shit happened back there.'

And with that, they were gone. She was about to say something else, though the thought felt muddled.

That was it. Time to go. Wilding looked around and the darkness consumed her. Nothing to see bar a slight glow from the wall panel. She remembered and her heart broke once more. She'd been hallucinating. Powell was long dead and had never left that Martian base. She'd not seen Dunk for years.

With no power in the suit and little strength left, she dragged herself along the rail until she reached the illuminated glass panel. She'd seen similar panels when her torches had worked. Even then, they'd been dark with shadows inside. Struggling to separate grim reality from her imagination, she resolved to stick to the plan. As Wilding had known it would, pressing the small tab next to the glass panel, it slid aside. She desperately wanted to sit down and rest, though knew she was about to take a permanent rest, well unless... It was too optimistic a thought to be serious.

Wilding pulled herself into the opening, turning to face the way she'd come in. The panel slid closed, blocking her exit. The alcove was to become her coffin. Her chest burned with pain, desperately seeking air that had long since run out.

She tried to find the source of the glow. It seemed to be all around her, inside the cubicle. Her vision blurred further; the other eye had started to bleed, too. Sensing movement, she noticed a slime starting to fill the chamber, sloshing initially over her boots, rising rapidly. As it went past her eye-line, she clamped down on the fear that embraced her. She was a tough fucker in battle, and she'd die one too. But the Butcher of Buchanan wouldn't survive this one.

When the chamber was full, Wilding leaned against the back wall and fought away another blackout. She yearned to see her mother, the memories now so vague nothing materialised. The platoon had become her family. She'd do anything to protect them and done something that most thought unthinkable to protect them.

Wilding's final act was to release the helmet, and the liquid flooded her suit. She tried to keep her eyes open, dropping the helmet onto the floor beside her. It filled her ears and nose.

Unable to resist, she gave in and opened her mouth, letting the fluid engulf her. Everything went black.

# 2

# SQUIRE

*Onboard the BSV, Neptune Orbit*

Chris Squire listened to the message twice, skimmed the supporting text files, and slumped back, resigned in his chair. Not again.

The traumas that haunted him never really went away. He waited for the inevitable wave of intrusive flashbacks and anguish to wash over him. He could suppress the memories with medication, at least temporarily, after assessing what he needed to do. He shook his head, trying to shake away the guilt that accompanied him.

He'd arrived too late to save anyone on the Trike habitat. They were dead, all of them. Thousands of bodies were strung out before him, like a macabre necklace.

Scanners revealed a long trail of frozen corpses, some wearing their day-to-day attire, some helmeted in EVA suits, some without. Many of the suits had holes torn in them. Squire thought they were the lucky ones. A few had been forced out of the airlock in fully functional suits. They suffered worse, facing the horror of seeing their hopes for survival dashed. A couple of bodies appeared naked, with layers of frost enveloping them. He made out large patches of frozen and congealed blood.

His shipboard AI, Paisley, tried to break him out of his reverie, but Squire angrily chided it to leave him alone. This pain was his alone. Most who died in space that day, trailing away from a triple ring habitat, were women and children. The corpses of the men who had died in the doomed fight to stop the massacre were also in orbit. They had died earlier, cut to pieces in the rear-guard action, their bodies expelled in bulk from the docking bay. Millions were escaping Earth to avoid the horrors of war, starvation, and dictatorships, only to suffer a worse fate in space.

Squire had engaged the scoop and sent out drones to hunt for survivors in vain. He hadn't expected the scale of the carnage he discovered. The BSV wasn't equipped in terms of storage, despite using the expandable trailer and nets he carried to collect the human ejecta strung out across tens of thousands of miles.

So there the dead remained, while the murderers had managed to escape. The owners of the habitat had immediately filed for protected bankruptcy before vanishing. Nobody was willing to put up the funds to retrieve the bodies, though Orbital Security had later sold the structure and, though damaged, it had been delivered to Jupiter.

Even during waking hours, it didn't take much for his mind to return to those events. Reminding him of the hour or so he'd spent in the cargo bay; examining and imaging the collected corpses before depressurising the bay and returning them to their icy tomb. He'd concluded, regretfully, that it had been better not to recover a single body than just a few.

In his nightmares, the corpses spoke. The little girl in the pink coveralls begged him not to send her back to the cold, her frozen pigtails jutting from her head like frayed ropes. The woman in her gym gear asked him where her husband was. He couldn't see her face behind the visored helmet of her space suit, but the woman inside spoke to him, nonetheless. Squire couldn't bring himself to remove the helmet, torn open at the back. She begged him to find a sealant pack and repair the puncture.

Trying to chase the ghosts away, he raised the cockpit lighting. Only Zefyrex cleared his mind, which he was working with Paisley to reduce his reliance on. It was risky, if not suicidal, to heavily sedate a ship's only pilot. The night before he'd skipped it, struggling to sleep, disturbed with visions of the events from a decade earlier and a million leagues away, every time he drifted off. He'd given up on sleep and had patrolled the ship listlessly, reviewing system updates, before finally slumping into his command chair and turning off the artificial gravity to save power. He'd dozed off just before the urgent instructions had arrived. On waking, the flashbacks subsided, retreating to return another day, leaving him exhausted and sweating. His new mission brought it all back.

Paisley filtered the news feed to Squire's pad, prioritising a message from Scott Arden. Shocked, Squire did what he often did to calm himself. After telling Paisley to restore artificial gravity, the wraparound screen facing him lit up, showing live footage from exterior cameras and sensors. Beautiful Neptune rose before him, her pale globe shimmering a slight greenish-blue hue as clouds tore around it at thousands of miles per hour. His attention initially drawn to the great storm, a darker shadow dominating its equator. Squire personalised the image, working to zoom in and enhance the view, identifying some of the pale sets of rings, small icons appearing to name the moons that were visible. Despite their distance, he could see several dark flecks against the blue, small spider-shaped habitats hanging in low orbit at the top of the clouds. He queried the lack of activity around them with Paisley. Some had been evacuated overnight, their mining operations suspended whilst the storms subsided to safer levels.

After a few minutes and some deep breaths, Squire reconsidered the instructions. It was to be a major excursion, to intercept a vehicle in distress, the Kuiper Scout. It would take months. He assessed the mission whilst releasing the straps across his legs and chest. No other ships currently in Neptune-space had the range, besides automated kites and a supply ship on its way to Pluto and Charon, which had developed a serious fault and was now limping home for repairs.

In addition, no one this far from Earth had the extreme rescue and repair experience Squire had for such a mission.

# THE TRITON RUN

Had Arden known, or cared, about Squire's struggles, he'd have not been sent. However, Squire was never going to publicly admit to his internal battles.

The casualty had sent out an automated collision detection signal, which had been weak, before abruptly cutting off. No further communications had been received since, despite hailing. The exact collision location was uncertain, such were the distances involved, and more accurate co-ordinates would follow once he was en route.

Squire went to the galley to collect some fresh coffee and returned to his seat. He could predict how this was going to go, and it wouldn't be beneficial for his mental health. Though he'd not yet received a crew manifest, a U-net search made him fear the worst. He was certain that Dee Wilding, his old platoon leader, was on-board. She'd suggested she had taken a position on-board the last time they'd exchanged messages.

Wilding wanted to take the role without fanfare, getting as far away from what had happened on Mars as possible, relieved she could even get work. The appointment was to look after the researchers, scientists, and officials on board the Kuiper Scout. Despite being overqualified, Wilding was not on-board as the pilot, rather in an advisory capacity, to ensure the scientific mission ran smoothly. The Scout was to navigate close to some of the objects at the near edge of the Oort Cloud without putting themselves in danger. He wondered what the public reaction would be when it was revealed Wilding was on board.

He felt the slight vibration of the engines coming back online, slowing the ship down for a course change. They were headed away from Triton One and beyond the end of the line. With a friend out beyond the edge of the system, there was no way Squire would refuse Arden's request; he wouldn't even wait for their conversation. Arden would leave the finer details of the salvage mission to him, anyway.

Squire double checked the pre-flight routines which Paisley

had started, as well as the capacity of the hold. Still full of debris from a collision clearing near Neso between a reckless pleasure cruiser and a satellite. His external scoops had gathered large chunks of flotsam and jetsam, while the AI operated lasers incinerated other remains. He'd have to transfer the job to one of the other Scoopers. Whilst the remaining debris presented a risk to local traffic, their simulations suggested that standard shields would cope with most of it.

He set a course to loop away from Neptune, where he could empty his hold beyond the no-fly zones surrounding the planet's rings. They'd then shift into a slingshot orbit using the planet's gravity to provide a speed boost as he powered towards his new target. Paisley had already requested a supply ship intercept them before they accelerated and left the Neptune system.

He called up an image of Dee and himself from the last time they had been together. As usual, they both looked drunk. Back during Marine training, she'd saved him plenty of times, usually from catching a stray bullet in the war games. Squire doubted he'd be able to save her life, but he felt a duty to bring her body home.

'I'm coming buddy. I'm coming.'

# 3

# ZANDER

*New York Underground Transit Station*

Theodore Zander, President of the UN Senior Chamber, and de facto President of Earth, clasped his hands behind his bald head and sighed. His private hyperloop car was due any minute, and he could not wait to get away. It would take him and his entourage south to Sao Paolo. Groups were scattered around the large underground chamber. The vaulted ceiling ensured there were no feelings of claustrophobia, despite being many floors below ground level. Other dignitaries and their staff milled round, some giving interviews to the smattering of press lucky enough to get a pass. Others were engaged in a heated debate about the morning session. Everyone was heading off in different directions, back to their homes or constituencies.

The session had been a disaster. They had kicked the one piece of legislation which needed passing into the long grass as scandal had dominated the debate. Hopes of approving the appointment of a Special Envoy to negotiate a cease fire in the conflict around Saturn had been dashed until the new year. At least the scandal hadn't personally affected him, a nice change.

Zander was tired and ready for home. Not that much awaited him there. He closed his eyes and tried to relax, focusing on the aroma of strong coffee from the jug on the table nearby. Just as he felt he was drifting off, an aide gave him a nudge and whispered that their car was due any minute.

Trying to shake any drowsiness away, he took a final swig from his cup, tossed it into a recycling bin. The motion of finishing his coffee sent out a signal to the rest of the room, who had given him some space. He was immediately surrounded by a swarm of minor state leaders, all desperate to be seen to associate with him. The press scrum followed them. He raised his hands to get the throng's attention.

'Not tonight. It's been a long session and my ride's here. Today's events clearly need consideration and when I'm able, I'll make a statement. I've some private commitments over the next few days. I'm afraid you aren't invited! Goodnight.'

"Private commitments," was political jargon for "I want to be left alone."

Putting on a polite smile, he pushed through the crowd, shaking hands, and acknowledging those leaders who got to him in time. He paused to exchange pleasantries with a few of them, suggesting future meetings, and feeling guilty at having to put off one of Europe's state representatives. Zander promised to call them the following morning.

Two agents flanked him, and there were other agents in the crowd. His security chief, Reuben Volchik, took him by the elbow and directed him through the crowd towards the loading room on the far side. Reuben looked younger than he was, still appearing fresh faced, barely out of college, and built like a heavyweight boxer.

As he scanned the room, he noticed another slight figure weaving their way through the throng, slipping silently through gaps that weren't there. Without fail, she always caught up with him.

He put on his most diplomatic smile as Chen Yang stopped in front of him, bowing slightly whilst keeping her steely eyes incongruous with her thin, almost fragile, figure, always directed at him. Her own security detail remained a few steps behind her. Reuben stepped to one side so that he had an unobstructed view of Yang and the President's eye while his other agent stood behind Zander. Reuben's glance at her security told them to stay where they were. It was a regular dance.

'Representative Yang. I regret I didn't get to speak to you personally earlier, though my offer of an official visit still stands, if we can fix a mutually acceptable time.'

Her skin was pale against a black, formal dress suit with her dark hair tied up behind her, the complete opposite to Zander's colourful couture.

She spoke efficiently, in short, clipped tones. 'President Zander, I must insist on an urgent, private discussion regarding the relaxation of the visa requirements for the outer Cities. We're so overcrowded. The economy in our bloc is static and we need the assistance you pledged.'

Zander gently shook his head.

'This is best discussed at length, with your Prime Minister, in a conference call, don't you think?'

The conversation went nowhere for a little longer until Reuben leaned carefully between them, avoiding touching either delegate. He was a good actor, as ever, 'Excuse me President, Representative, I'm sorry to interrupt, however the President's car is ready to load.'

Volchik stepped back, standing to attention, arms clasped behind his back. Zander tried not to smile too obviously. Reuben was well trained.

'Representative Yang, I'm afraid it'll have to be another day. Forgive me.'

As Zander moved to step away, the short figure stepped across his path. A clear breach of etiquette and if she weren't a Representative, his team would have taken this as an act of aggression and intervened.

'This isn't acceptable,' she said in a quiet, but firm, voice. 'We can't cope much longer. People are starving.'

*And if your government didn't spend so much on unnecessary military hardware, you wouldn't be in this position* he wanted to stay. Instead, he was polite, though firm. 'I hear what you say. You know my views. I'm afraid I must go now.'

She let him start to move away and finished the conversation with the barbed criticism that was always used against him.

'Not caring about citizens isn't new, is it? You haven't forgotten about the Trike? Not content with refusing them citizenship, you voted against even sending them supplies.'

She paused, clearly for dramatic effect. 'There will be a reckoning.'

With that, she bowed, spun on her heels, and moved away into the crowd. He sighed.

That criticism always hurt, though he'd paid the price many times over. Those who had been listening in all looked awkwardly away.

Many of them agreed with her.

# 4

# ROO

*Triton Observatory Mobile Operations Centre*

The geyser warning had abated, and the red alert cancelled. Caterpillar tracks that had been extended from the edges of what was effectively a small town on legs were withdrawn and the base rested once again on the cold surface of Triton. It was soon back to business as normal.

After spending the afternoon in the emergency Ops room planning routes out of the ice flats where they had been for the last three months, Roo was pleased to be released to her main duties. She'd headed to her 'tank' where she'd prepared to start work.

Three sides of the room were utilitarian and dark, the other containing an enhanced image of the base's exterior. The ice flats continued towards a protracted line of cliffs punctuated with gaps and ramps, some of which she'd been assessing for use as an evacuation route. An aerial rescue was feasible, expensive, dangerous, and would take longer, as the base would need to be broken into modules. It would've been far easier if it could move together. The sky would ordinarily be dark, with no sign of Neptune, which permanently overlooked the other side of its largest moon. She'd enhanced the image to where she could make out the trails their vehicles had made across the ice, the occasional crater, and a slight reddish haze in the sky.

Roo sat down, drew her hair into a ponytail, pulled a headset over her face and placed her hands on the arms of the chair.

'Load.'

She relaxed, becoming one with her Chip, mentally flicking through her work diary, reminders, and messages.

Whilst Roo replied to some routine messages, she switched to her private drive and messaged her mother. She responded to a query from a colleague and reported to Legal - some information she'd picked up from the news that might be relevant for a judicial inquiry they'd been tasked with supporting.

Her awareness became engulfed by her augment chip, synchronizing with the headset and its additional processing power. Whilst Unet chips were common, few were able to cope with and utilise the additional processing the augmented system offered. A blessing and a curse. Whilst computers could easily outperform their human counterparts, artificial intelligence still couldn't use instinct or apply a gut feeling to data in the same way as a trained Tapper. Her work was as much art as science.

Roo was surrounded by a bright space field. Her various feeds appeared as floating icons all around and she set to organizing them. Roo was just about to start on the oldest task in the queue when a ping came from Teresa Garcia, Lead Scientist at the Ops centre.

'Got an urgent alert for you. An SOS from the Kuiper Scout. I'm uploading the data to you now. Try to get a fix and extract what might be out there that can help? I've found nothing. Arden is granting access to all systems.'

'As if I need permission,' muttered Roo.

The name, Kuiper Scout, meant nothing to Roo. She waved a hand, and an icon appeared in front of her containing the file from Garcia. On her instruction, it expanded and morphed into an old-fashioned view screen. The file was bugged, so she set about trying to stabilise it for extraction. Even before she opened it, Roo assessed it as an emergency signal. It had come from Outer Sentinel 6, tight beamed and bounced into Triton One, repeating for 2 hours before stopping. It had been with them for over a week, using a recognised, though antiquated, emergency code. Seemingly, it had been inadvertently quarantined by their own systems in fear of a cyber-attack of some sort.

Roo made a note to reprogram their auto assessment bots so that any message flagged as an emergency, even using old code, would be referred immediately onto a human user. The SOS message was limited, a standard broadcast with the casualty's ID code. Roo would need to trace its origin, so scrambled was the location. Tapping into the Sentinel's own systems, she directed all other messages using the same ID code or vicinity to be diverted to her personal message account.

Within minutes, she was in the groove, assimilating and assessing all that was received and allocating tasks to various parts of her Chip's AI. She set tracers running through the Sentinel's com network, accessed several local telescopes, scanners, and sensors. She was pleased to see Arden had some of them looking for the Scout already. Unfamiliar with the ship, Roo ran parallel searches on make and model. The more she knew about it, the better chance there was of tracing it. It might give off some discrete signature.

Roo lost all track of time in the tank and chose to ignore the alarm reminder to take a break. Immersion time in the Tank was carefully controlled, but this was urgent. She'd seen the crew manifest and there were about twenty crewmembers onboard.

She stood back from her screens and took a deep breath, feeling pleased with herself as a new data packet arrived. It was almost certainly from a location close to the origin of the SOS. She messaged Garcia. 'I think I've got something big. Have got it in full and its accessible. Looks like a visual file. The quality might not be great as there's a lot of interference. I'll clean it up and send it you stat.'

Garcia replied that she'd be waiting for further news. Roo concluded that whoever'd sent the SOS and the data package knew exactly what they were doing. It was a strange format;

however, the sender knew the Unet6 protocols were defunct and that the Sentinel firmware was out of date. There just hadn't been the inclination to update it. The sender had worked out that a message on the latest format would've generated an error and bounced back. Someone was clearly very innovative; and it was likely, therefore, that there must've been at least one survivor.

Whilst she had the footage metadata analysed and cleaned, she checked its veracity. It appeared to be genuine, a broadcast from an EVA suit. The packet contained some suit diagnostics, so she set a separate analysis up for those.

Roo messaged Garcia again. 'Find somewhere private for this, Teresa. It's from an EVA suit and I think we've several hours of footage, it's cut into many chunks, and I think…. think there are at least five hours between the start and end, though it was all sent at the same time.'

Roo waited until her Chip had done all it could, and Garcia had indicated she was ready to watch the footage. 'OK, let's play.'

# 5

# YANG

*Onboard a Shuttle, Earth Orbit*

Despite the delay and the crackle, the audio was clear. 'Sarah, you'll get caught. Please back off. I can't lose you, even for this…'

Chen Yang stared at the monitor impassively. She nodded ever so slightly, unsure if her husband would be able to see it amongst the pixelating image. The reception was often poor due to the distances involved. Here it was exacerbated by the shuttle's journey through Earth's outer atmosphere and into orbit. They'd been talking for a while about everything except the elephant in the room. The cause.

She hated him calling her that name, though she knew why he did it.

'Please don't use that name. She's gone. It's now or never, my love. We've lost so many good people trying to catch him. Finally, he's there for the taking now.' Her voice was deliberately calm and quiet, so he had to listen attentively to hear it through the static on the call.

Whilst her husband tended to ramble, to fill the awkward gaps caused by the delay on the link, with Chen there was rarely a word wasted. She paused for her message to reach him in his quarters out at Neptune, for his reply to find its way back.

Her chair rattled slightly as the shuttle accelerated further. They were running behind schedule, and she wanted to be on her interplanetary cruiser before everything happened. Adjusting her sitting position and straightening her jacket, she sighed inwardly. Their relationship was strained. With three years apart, save only a week or two together every now and again, the emotional gap between them was becoming wider. For their regular, three times a week, face-to-face engagement, they'd resorted to using antiquated channels to reduce the chances of discovery. She'd changed shuttle in low orbit to hide her tracks and all coms were scrambled. Chen was willing to die for the sake of the Exiles and the mission; she wasn't sure he still felt the same.

A crackle and the pixelated mess that showed his face moved. 'At the cost of innocents being killed. I know we need restitution, but is murder really the answer all these years later?'

She remained still whilst the com system cleaned up the message as best as possible, and after a moment buffering, it continued. She knew there was more he wanted to get this off his chest.

'Do we even know what they'll do when we have him? I know we need to make a statement with them both. Personally, I think showing mercy would be a PR dream. It'd force a settlement. I don't want to see an execution.'

His mouth tightened. He was hoping for reassurance.

She couldn't give it. She lied to him to keep him onside, in the fading hope that they'd get to make the future together they'd always wanted.

'I don't know what the plan is. Let's see what happens when we get him.' She didn't want to say his name.

She paused before continuing. 'You've lost sight of how many we lost, how the survivors were treated. We've been ostracised, made homeless. How can that be forgiven?'

He looked stressed, nervously pushing his blonde hair out of his square face. 'Well, we aren't homeless, are we? You've become a Representative. Nobody from the old days would even recognise you. You can do what you want.'

The delay on the line meant she could clamp down her rising anger.

'Hiding is not freedom. You know if they discovered my true background, I'd be arrested. Anyway, why aren't you committed anymore?' Her response was pointed.

Chen didn't think he'd betray the cause, though she resented how he loved his new career, his life, his friends and didn't want to lose them.

He was undeterred. 'We gain nothing if we kill people linked to events long since forgotten in the media. There have been other disasters on habitats since. Think about what's going on at Saturn? I'm scared I'll never see you again. Do those in charge have an exit strategy to all this?'

Chen shook her head, her short, black hair barely moving. She lied again, wanting him to think she wasn't behind all this and redirect his anger elsewhere.

'My security clearance is as high as it'll get since I was elected. The intelligence I can gather means we're nearly there. We're ready to pounce. Then we can move on.'

She wanted to focus him on the future, however she needed to keep him in line. 'Your commitment concerns me. You were only there to deliver us one of the targets, or at least monitor him. You've become comfortable, pretend not to remember that ten thousand people, three huge mixed and happy communities, were just abandoned. Your family. My family. Don't forget they put me on the last shuttle to get out before the massacre. They played God when they had no right to.'

She knew that the firmness in her voice shocked him. She also knew that he knew she was right. He was happy with his lot now, save being apart from her. He didn't reply. She could see he was dumbfounded, not sure what to say to avoid her anger. Weak. The silence allowed her to conclude the conversation. Chen's voice softened again.

'I have to go now, to transfer to another ship. I hate it when we fall out. I'm heading out to the belt. If I think we can, I'll arrange for us to meet. See if you can get some time off. I'll try really hard, I promise.'

He nodded. 'Good, I'll look forward to it.'

'I love you.'

He smiled. He usually did when she told him.

# 6

## JUDE

*Porto de Santos*

Jude Parynski and her father had both booked up-trips from the same space elevator. The Tsiolkovsky was sea based and the oldest remaining elevator on Earth. It was co-incidence they were going up well at a similar same time, so they'd arranged to catch the same ferry and meet for food.

They met at the port terminal in Santos. Despite the worries hanging over her, regarding her job, she'd managed to sleep much of the seven-hour hyper transit journey from the New York office. The journey was less than five thousand miles and the car hit a thousand mph for some stretches. Her father, Bruce, had been in the car just before her, having travelled down from Brunswick, Maine.

It was late by the time they'd boarded and found their cabins on board the overnight ferry that would take them out to the Tsiolkovsky. The ferry was teeming with people, all booked to head upwards. Jude had booked ahead, so they'd got a table in the Italian restaurant situated at the prow of the ship. They got window seats and ordered pizza and beer.

She looked out across the port, which dominated the skyline. Dozens of cargo vessels were moored offshore and beyond them towers of cargo containers, awaiting transfer. The sun was setting, its red haze casting shadows across the scene. The panorama was temporarily blocked by a dirigible drifting down the estuary, the two-storey gondola underneath encircled by a balcony full of travellers, all snapping away. The dirigible was destined for the landing deck a few miles away, from where the passengers would likely be headed for a morning ferry.

Even late at night, the port was busy, congested with ferries, pleasure craft, and two submarines with their hatches open to the surface. The vessels weaved their way through traffic, returning commuters from the offshore colonies and bringing a small number who had travelled down on the elevator.

Jude and her father had eaten in silence largely, only making small talk. It was the first time they'd been together since Mary's funeral.

She watched him as he ate. He'd clearly not rested on the journey down. They were both of average height, slim with shaggy, dark hair that was hard to control, though Jude had hers cropped short. They shared a strong chin, prominent nose, and blue eyes. The main difference between them were the wrinkles that were starting to appear on the older man's forehead, the crow's feet round his eyes and the slightly paler skin tone.

While Bruce went to the washroom, Jude watched the news on a screen. She found political shenanigans dull but noted that the newsreaders seemed to take the new threats against President Zander more seriously than before. Jupiter was again in conflict. The latest strikes in the gas mines had turned violent, the war around Saturn rumbled on, and there were reports of pirate activity near Mars. As her father returned, he waved over the waiter to order another beer. Getting drunk again. He rarely drank off planet and his tolerance was low. She decided that they needed to tackle the subject of her mother, his wife, before they became inebriated. Jude knew that if she got drunk, they'd end up in a fight.

He found his seat again and took another sip. He looked tired, unbelievably so. She grabbed his hand.

'How are you?'

He avoided eye contact, staring at his plate. Taking a deep breath, he shrugged. 'I'm fine. Just a pity I couldn't get to see where, you know?'

Jude leaned in so he couldn't avoid her gaze. 'Dad. I know.'

She could see he was trying to hold back tears. He was a strong man who had been putting on a brave face for too long.

'I tried, fuck, I tried. They've even closed the freeway out of Brunswick, so unless you go cross-country, there's just no way of getting to Jackman. They've just abandoned the town to the Outsiders. I couldn't get home.'

'I understand, Dad. It's not safe out there. I wish Mum hadn't been so stubborn.'

'If only I'd been around, I could've made her move!' Bruce snapped back, shoulders slumping. He felt as guilty as she did.

'It's not your fault. She married you, knowing you'd be away for long periods.'

'And that's why the marriage failed.'

They were interrupted as the public address system informed passengers that they would be casting off imminently.

'You'd got back together. She was so excited that you were coming home. It's just awful timing that the town fell whilst you were away.'

The conversation went round in circles, both punishing themselves for something Jude knew in her heart was out of their hands. She repeated, 'It was just awful timing.'

Jude kept telling herself that. She should have done more herself, but she was too wrapped up in her work, her undercover investigation.

'I was a fool, and when I finally sort myself out, the only thing I ever wanted was taken away.' Bruce stared into the depths of the fresh drink that had been delivered.

'You sure you're ready to go back to work? You don't have to go back into space. If you aren't right, it won't be safe.' Jude knew he was going to set off on a long trip to get away from everything and everyone, yet he hadn't begun to grieve properly and was in no rational place to start.

Mentioning work seemed to lift him. His shoulders straightened, and he looked directly at her. Right now, she just wanted him to take care of himself, so perhaps, for him, work was the answer. Since he'd left the forces, he'd struggled to settle down, to stay still. He was a good man, though after what he'd seen and done, she understood.

'Maybe... yeah... hopefully. I've turned lots of work down. I don't need to be *here* anymore,' he waved his arms around. 'Flying is the only thing I am good at, and being a

Ferryman is something I am the *best* at.'

Jude tried to take a different approach. Money was never important to her father. 'Why do you need to take the dangerous jobs now? Set yourself up in business or take a low-risk job. McGraw said he'd always take you as a shuttle jock, you'd find that a doddle.'

He stroked his chin, ruminating, then looked up at her and smiled. 'If you mean boring, then yeah. It's not me.'

That was the answer she expected. She sensed he was trying to lift his mood, or perhaps it was the beer. She tried to explain that she just wanted to know he was safe.

He reached out and playfully slapped her leg. 'Anyway, this one should be easy. Let me clear my head and we can discuss your mother when I get back. You'll know what's happening to you by then?'

Jude tried to avoid him steering the conversation onto her. 'So, what's this job you've got?'

'The Triton Run again, to the end of the line. Been a while since I last saw Neptune.

They barely need us on the newer yachts, it's so much cheaper to send them unmanned. Ships are better equipped for longer hops and with so much more traffic out there than when I started, even a serious failure shouldn't mean a loss. So many salvage companies out there too…'

'Pity they are mainly dodgy, practically pirates,' Jude added.

He smiled, for the first time since they'd sat down. 'I can handle them. What about you? You were going to tell me about what's going on. We didn't get time at the funeral.'

She sighed. Best to get it off her chest now.

'I'm not sure I'm going back. That last job was bad. They've put me on leave pending an inquiry.'

An awkward silence followed. Nobody could have missed the investigation that had been all over the news, where following an undercover operation and an assault by enforcement teams, a large number of women and children were rescued from sex slavery on a habitat in one of the outer orbital groups.

'You ok about it?' Parynski reached over and touched her wrist.

She shook his hand off, realising her tone revealed more. 'Not really. The assault should've been sooner. They wanted to wait until I'd got clear. We lost people by waiting…'

'I'm sure you couldn't have done anymore?'

Jude shook her head. She'd still not got over it, and the loss of her mother had compounded her distress. 'I failed some of them. When I was being pulled out, we were discovered. I got a bit trigger-happy.'

He nodded. 'I can understand that. What next?'

She shrugged. 'No idea. I'm going to visit Mel on Grissom base for a while. I could be on desk duty for some time whilst the dust settles. I just hope they don't hook me for my… aggressive tactics. Hopefully, the inquiry will clear me.'

Parynski mumbled his agreement and took another mouthful of beer, wiping his mouth on his sleeve. They'd finished most of their food and Jude was now aware of the feeling of movement as the Ferry moved from the mouth of the estuary out into the sea.

'You won't be safe to fly if you keep drinking at this rate,' she said. 'Come on, let's settle up and walk the deck. We both need all the fresh air we can get. Us off-worlders can't take our beer.'

He gave her a weak smile. 'Good idea. Let's get a coffee before we head back. I believe the cafe above the bridge does a great one. In space, good coffee is one of the few things I miss…'

# 7

# WILDING

*The Dark*

All around her, and inside, darkness enveloped her entire being. As her consciousness stirred, she concluded that she must either be dead or waiting to die. Her thoughts were scattered, shattered as if by a hammer and with shards strewn across the floor, all independent and with no logic to them. Wilding remembered bits here and there, felt some sensations, but not others, unable to put them back together. It could've been a headache, though she couldn't place her head. All she had was thoughts removed from reality. Nothing physical, just thoughts. Perhaps she was dead, and this was it. Was she waiting for judgement? Then she remembered, a bit at least. It was likely there was only one way she was headed, if there was to be a reckoning.

Whether she'd remained in this state for hours, days, or years, she had no idea. She drifted in and out of consciousness, though gradually the headache dimmed, and a feeling of panic faded. Hypoxia. Perhaps this was brain damage. That might be it. She could be in a coma, perhaps an induced one. Then more memories came back, a deluge that swamped her mind. She remembered the accident, what happened to her ship and the way it had ended.

Even though she couldn't feel her body, she felt a strange sensation as she shivered. Something was happening. There was a presence nearby, though she couldn't sense what it was. If she was in a coma, perhaps it was the Doctor, or even a friend. Whilst she'd not been aware of a warmth previously, she suddenly felt cold sweep over her. Her eyes suddenly flicked open.

To her surprise, she could see clearly.

She screamed.

# 8

# SQUIRE

*Onboard the BSV, Edge of the Kuiper Belt*

The Blue Sky V, or BSV as it was known, was easily the ugliest of the hundreds of space craft Squire had ever piloted. As far as he was concerned, it was also the safest, and it was home. The B class "scooper", and its pilot, had been chosen because of their experience of rescue and salvage missions. The fact he knew someone on board the casualty was an unfortunate coincidence, one that he had to put from his mind.

Even in an era where space travel was common, accidents were still a sensitive issue, and the loss of a ship came with huge implications for owners and charterers alike. Arden hadn't personally been interested in the science mission itself, but some of his investors were, and so he'd put the money up for the project.

The BSV had always reminded him of his first summer job, at his uncle's golf driving range where he learnt to drive, powering round in a battered old tractor collecting golf balls whilst balls rained down on the vehicle, usually by accident. The tractor had been equipped with scoops that dragged on the floor and collected hundreds of balls, depositing them in a crate at the rear for tipping back into the ball dispenser at the range. To protect the tractor, and more importantly himself, from the deluge, it was covered by a homemade cage, with a small opening at the front so he could see. He'd been shown how to ensure he never presented the front of the vehicle towards the players on the range, some of whom in mischief were inspired to try and hit the most unique of moving "holes in one".

The BSV was like that tractor in that its shape was purely utilitarian. It had a relatively small nose that contained a scoop that could be extended like a snout or trunk to collect debris, followed by a huge storage area that flared out behind it with further extendable scoops, particularly underneath. Hidden away was a compact living module and then to the rear came the main engine block. Each component was detachable, though it was hard to tell, as most of the exterior was covered by a metal web; a shell of pieces comprising extra layers of protection that could be adjusted at short notice to cushion any impending impact. These hundreds of scales were a variety of colours, some gleaming and clearly new, some pitted with small craters (and a few holes) and others appearing decayed. They seemed to be fabricated out of different materials, many ceramic or metal. At present, most were aimed forwards. Capable of being extended from gaps in the scales were dozens of arms, all multi-limbed and with multiple purposes, some containing claws, cutters, scooping devices and yet more with sensors and camera equipment. Other attachments contained defensive weapons, including lasers and missiles. Additionally, the ship was protected by largely invisible deflector shields. The rear of the vessel usually saw extendable clamps holding a trailer in place and additional netting. Having been recently emptied, they were now stowed away.

Squire and the BSV had been together since he'd picked up the contract for keeping Moon orbit clear of debris. Over a century of traffic and the destruction of the Epsilon Express in low orbit had temporarily made the Moon a dangerous place to visit. Squire had bought some decommissioned orbit scrubbers from the UN and had gone to work. He liked to tell people that his success, patience, and reliability had drawn him towards the wealth the outer system could offer with contracts in the asteroid belt, the Jovian system and now out at

Neptune. In reality, it was his desire to get away from his past.

The BSV was ugly on the outside and untidy on the inside.

He spent his free time in the lounge area, strapped into a comfy chair, surrounded by everything he needed to entertain himself, plus a small console to keep him in control of the ship. Only when he was working did he retreat to the cockpit. He finished his dinner and tossed the empty sachet towards the bin, missing, as usual. He'd collect it later if Paisley didn't. He finished his daily health check reports, checking that Paisley had stripped out all mention of his Zefyrex use and submitted them.

The BSV had been a seven-man ship, though he had configured it so that he could do most of the tasks and rely on his AI for the rest. Being on his own meant he was in charge and earned more, not that he ever spent much of it. Except on the ship. Having completed his reports, he grabbed another drink pouch and took a sip. He sat back and closed his eyes. Stimulated by his Chip his mind swam with the latest news, sports results, and the latest technical updates on his ship whilst at the same time he was able to focus enough of his consciousness to reply to U-messages from his few friends, family, and work colleagues. Once done, he allowed the latest hockey game to dominate his sub consciousness. He chose to watch as a spectator rather than the more tiring options of viewing, as if he were a participant.

He snapped out of his daydreaming when the console next to him flashed and pushed an alert into his Chip. A data packet from the Triton Observatory had been received. They were leading the search for the Kuiper Scout. He sat up and adjusted the angle of his seat to prop him up at the monitor he wanted to review the report from.

'Paisley, you seen this?' he asked in the knowledge that, of course, the AI had already reviewed and analysed the report better than he could ever hope to. Concentrating on the screen, he shut down the sports feed that was distracting him.

'Yes, all reports have been opened and considered. Unfortunately, it doesn't assist us.

I can guide you through the most pertinent data and can skip what you aren't interested in.'

'Thanks, for now just let it play through and add it to my mission database,' said Squire.

'Already done.'

Squire smiled to himself. Was it possible for a machine to be smug?

Paisley understood him probably more than his friends did. His work was lonely, and whilst most of the time Squire preferred it that way, it was a relief to have someone to talk to without the time delays space coms encountered. Paisley put up some of the most relevant images on the screen and zoomed in, various statistics appearing overlaid around the centre. A small 3D hologram also sprang into life to his right. Perhaps unsurprisingly, yet frustratingly, the latest images didn't help at all. In fact, they were less clear than the images from yesterday. As Neptune continued its slow journey around the sun, it would gradually move further away from their target, so until they were close enough to scan it themselves, he wasn't expecting too much. He hoped that within a month or so they would have more accurate data to plot the exact location of the Kuiper Scout.

All there was for him to see was a dark smudge, a long potato shaped object with a spike coming out of it. Their working theory was that the Scout was the spike and that it had hit the larger object. As he approached, his own sensors would provide more information. Until then, it was largely guesswork. The report he received included a short news report, which he watched. Word was out.

Whilst no local asteroids or large ices had been recorded in earlier observations of the area, it was presumed that there had been an unexpected collision that had rendered the ship disabled. The Scout had been there to investigate clouds of ice and other debris and he expected that on arrival he was going to find a mess. It was the likely prospect of a cloud of debris that had led to the BSV being the sensible option to investigate.

Squire stared at the smudge for a few minutes, almost willing it to sharpen before his eyes. He spoke out loud to Paisley.

'Could that smudge be something we already have on the charts? Presumably, the Scout would have taken some images? Apart from Dee Wilding, is anyone else on board any good? Assuming they just lost coms and propulsion, what are the chances they'll still be there waiting for us?'

Squire knew that Paisley had heard these questions every day since they had disengaged the refueller that had intercepted them just before they left Neptune behind.

'I think you're tired with the fitting out this week. You've seen the manifest three times, you were taken through it before departure. As for what we face when we reach the Kuiper Scout, it's impossible to be accurate in any prediction. It's unlikely in my view that just those two systems will have failed in isolation. We are due to arrive in nine weeks at current progress and within three weeks, our own sensors may be able to start providing more practical data.'

Squire needed a hit. He slapped the arm of his couch in frustration and clicked off the display. 'We've been together longer than my marriage and you still don't understand that half my questions are just when I just want to talk to someone.' A statement rather than a question.

There was a pause. Squire knew Paisley could reply immediately; however, he was programmed to insert pauses into conversations to make them more natural.

'I am sorry I cannot be more help. What else is on your mind?'

'Do we know if they managed to launch any of their payload? They were due to launch a probe into the belt and a half dozen 'U' connectors, weren't they?'

The connectors were satellites that linked the Unet. Something that originally started as an Earth-wide network now spanned much of the solar system, though the further out one went, the slower the connection. Squire yawned, overwhelmed with tiredness and impatient at the time it would take to reach his destination. It had been a long day, and he'd done a lot of work kitting out their storage areas, in case it was needed as a sick bay, accommodation or most likely a morgue. The 3D printer on board had enabled them to put up some partitions and even build some simple bunks. He switched off the monitor and slumped back in his seat. Paisley lowered the ship's lighting in response, hoping that his master would fall asleep before resorting to medicating himself.

'They weren't scheduled to launch anything around the time of the collision. Their itinerary involved a further four weeks' travel before the first launch, which was to be followed by another four weeks before the second and third launches. There should be more than sufficient provisions and power for those on board. If they weren't killed at the time of the disabling event, they are still possibly waiting for us.'

Squire manually lowered the lighting even further, shutting off some of the console lighting. As was common, he'd decided he wouldn't bother unstrapping himself and heading to his bunk.

'I just don't see how they hit something big enough to disable them. I never worked with Captain Ibrahim personally. I heard he's good. If it's a big rock, how did they miss it… well, they didn't miss it, you know what I mean. Either way, it's going to cost a fortune one way or another to sort this all out.'

He adjusted his straps and the back of his seat moved further towards the horizontal.

'Paisley, I'm calling it a day. Do some more analysis of all the images, search for any imaging taken of the sector in question. Wake me if we get any transmissions, though ignore any personal calls from Arden. Were my daily reports ok to be filed?'

Efficient as ever. 'Yes, double checked and submitted. Apart from the slight coolant venting from the reserve bay, all systems are satisfactory. Is there anything I can do for you before shutting down?'

'No, that'll do. Goodnight.'

With that, Squire flicked off the lighting and the anti-grav. He cursed as the wrapper from his meal floated past him and he swatted it away. He'd grab it tomorrow.

# 9

## ROO

*Triton Observatory Mobile Operations Centre*

Roo's heart leapt as the footage crystallised.

The view came from a helmet cam, and showed little, save a grey metal bulkhead wall. A red-cheeked face appeared. Roo knew Wilding was mid-to-late-fifties, though she looked younger. Her short, dark hair dripped wet with sweat, and her piercing, tear-stained eyes dominated the image.

Roo recognised her from news reports of the trial. She'd regularly stared at the camera whilst in the dock, protesting her innocence. Dee Wilding. She grinned, leaning close to the camera, seeming to adjust something on the helmet. Then the camera lifted, turned, and dropped. She'd put the helmet on. The view remained equally uninspiring, what appeared to be a dark science bay.

'Well, I didn't expect this. It's working,' came a voice. A slight *whumph* accompanied the suit, sealing itself to the helmet.

'This shit is some macabre message in a bottle, I guess. But while I'm broadcasting, I may as well tell you what I can. I know there's no help coming in time, so don't be feeling guilty.'

'I've only sent this to Outer Sentinel 6, unless Alpha Centauri is listening, and I've had to use the old protocols. Also included are my co-ordinates and what I think is our trajectory. We're moving surprisingly slowly, so there're no excuses for not finding me… eventually.'

Roo set off a tracer to analyse the packet of data for the co-ordinates. The sooner she could get them to Squire, the better. An early change of direction could save days of travel time and fuel. The camera angle changed, and Roo heard Wilding catch her breath. She was hurt. The room was a mess, the artificial gravity was off, and flotsam floated around her, gently bouncing off the walls and ceiling.

'Okay, this is what you need to know, the 'story so far'.' She chuckled grimly, then adjusted her position by lowering herself to the floor where she tethered herself down. She scrambled round inside a nearby locker, extracted what looked like a cutting torch, checked it and then it vanished out of sight. Roo guessed she was attaching it to her pack. The screen went dark as the lighting went out for a second before coming back on. 'It does that a lot,' confirmed the narrator.

The voice continued '…I'm Officer 2nd Class Dee Wilding, qualified EVA, and Pilot. Flight authorisation number 443256 dash 2. Who am I kidding? You all know who I am, what I did. Well, tough shit, I'm the only narrator here and no, this is not all my fault. It wasn't my fault back then, either. I'm assigned to the Kuiper Scout as Chief Astronaut to help investigate some of the ice balls out here. I guess we found one, though it's not made of fucking ice!'

The footage cut out, being restored to give Wilding's view as she pulled herself along various holding rings towards a sealed door. The lights flickered off and on again and a helmet torch came on to illuminate Wilding's direction of transit. She started to open the door, struggling with the manual controls.

'So … after we were hit, the whole ship went to shit. Power pretty much died, and the atmosphere vented through a rather large hole. In many ways, it was a relatively gentle, slow collision. If it weren't, we'd have been vaporised. The central column of the ship collapsed on itself, and we lost structural integrity. I'm the only survivor because I was on an EVA trying to investigate some weird sensor readings we got. Maybe we'd detected this alien object. I'll send those. It looked like they needed a fix of some sort.'

The use of the word alien piqued her interest, so she messaged Garcia to see if she had also picked up the reference.

With her suit pressurised, Dee opened the door and moved into an area without atmosphere, pulling herself out of the way to avoid any objects that may have been inbound.

'If you are wondering why I'm so cautious, it's because this is my spare suit. The one I was wearing sustained damage when the Scout was breached. My legs took some shrapnel too.'

Entering the next room, she looked right to search out places to get a grip. 'You should see the view! I'll keep the surprise for later.' The EVA suit was augmented, so she made relatively quick work of traversing what was quite a long chamber.

The footage stopped, so Roo used the natural break to run some reports. Voice recognition software confirmed that Wilding was who she said she was. Passenger lists, specifications, ownership records and blueprints all flashed up. Roo scanned a 3D plan of the Scout that hovered to one side. She concluded that Wilding must have been towards the rear of the ship, in the main module that was long and narrow. She must have just left the storage and accommodation section and was headed to the nose where the command capsule would be, if any of it was left.

The footage came back briefly, showing Wilding's view as she struggled with another door that was at the end of the corridor. It cut out again. More updates flashed before Roo. The distress signal had broadcast 2 days before this footage was filmed. Based on the footage Roo knew there was little chance of the salvage ship Arden had dispatched reaching the Kuiper Scout before it was too late.

The image came back on. This time Wilding was strapped into a navigator's chair, facing the camera. She'd taken the suit off and was in a light blue jumpsuit. The helmet cam must have been wedged on the console facing her. Roo immediately spotted the dark patches, almost certainly extensive bloodstains, on both legs below the knees. The legs bulged, suggesting there were bandages and wound sealant packed under the suit. Wilding winced whilst adjusting position.

She was drying her face and hair with a towel.

"Ok, here, for now, is the only safe place to be. The first collision disintegrated the cockpit, and as we became impaled, the side was ripped open.'

Wilding winced again and looked away from the camera. She knew her fate, and for a moment, looked ready to crack.

'I've done some tinkering and all the juice that's left is routed to this section. I estimate I've got a day or so left of power, plus the suit will run just fine for forty-eight hours and I've oxygen for similar. I've added a second oxygen tank to the suit, and I've also put another three tanks and packs on the outside of the Scout, so when I evacuate, I can keep exploring as long as I can. You'll wonder why I need to? Well, I've no food or water save my suit's recycled supply and one ration pack in the suit backpack…and it's out of date!'

She grinned ruefully 'At least it won't kill me. When I next EVA I don't expect to come back on board.'

The image was lost again, so whilst the screen remained blank, Roo messaged Garcia. She'd just started watching. 'I think we have a fix, within a margin anyway.'

'Anything I can do to help?' replied Garcia.

'I've already bounced it onto Squire. It won't make a difference.'

Silence. There was nothing else to say.

Wilding was back in the suit, helmet on. The room was darker now. The running lights were off, so the main illumination came from her helmet light.

'Welcome back. It's too dangerous to stay in here, I can hear funny noises. I think the superstructure might tear itself apart. Before I show you where I'm going, and you should be getting excited, I wanted to inform you that this packet also contains some private messages. There is a message to my old platoon, some of them anyway. I'm sure you'll watch it anyway and see me cry. Parynski and co…I hope you are listening.'

Roo knew that Parynski wasn't that common a name, and she wondered if it was her friend Jude's father. Whilst she watched the rest of the footage back, a search confirmed that it was indeed Bruce Parynski. Now a renowned Ferryman he'd served in the same platoon on Mars as Squire had, both led by Wilding. Assuming he'd kept the same Unet ID, Roo guessed she could contact him as she'd used years ago when arranging a surprise party for Jude.

'Next is the technical bit about the way I'm broadcasting. All coms went down, the mayday systems failed. I tinkered with some gear I could get powered up to make a beam transmitter and took a temporary power pack outside with me. The way we collided and our current position… the whatever it is, blocks my direct view back in-system. I walked all over the hull. I couldn't signal directly home, so I had to search elsewhere. Only receiver I could detect is the Sentinel, so there you go. It was still running on defunct software. Hoping I did the reconfiguration on the signal right or I'm talking to myself.'

'We hear you, Dee,' Roo said out loud.

The data revealed that more than an hour of real time would pass during the next break in the footage, though for Roo it was a matter of moments. Wilding had moved to another part of the ship. The speaker was filled with Wilding's laboured breathing, the background hiss of the life support and the hum of the suit's motors.

Likely for dramatic effect, Wilding had steadied herself in the new room, camera focussed straight ahead. It was the long corridor she'd been in previously, some fifteen feet in diameter, something over seventy feet long. It ran between the bridge and living quarters at the front and the storage hubs and engines at the rear.

The port side of the corridor, the blueprints told her, served as an observation deck, long panes of space toughened glass running much of the way along it. Wilding turned her head, and the camera panned along the previously hidden side of the corridor. It was missing. The observation panes were gone. The edge of the gap was sharp, torn and in one corner looked almost cauterised. Wilding gave them time to take in the view.

'Viewers! It's incredible. Sorry it's not that well-lit. This hole is the reason there is nobody else left. Our systems were scrambled, so everyone gathered here to watch me do my first EVA since we'd set off. Still not sure how this all happened? ... well, you'll see. They didn't stand a chance.'

Wilding sniffed, holding back her emotions. Looking out through the gap, hard to make out in a darkness and punctuated only by a handful of beams from the Scout, at first glance, there was what appeared to be part of a spaceship. Roo struggled to enhance the imaging.

'What the fuck is that?' Roo whispered.

As if she had heard her Wilding spoke. 'It's not recognised on any of our records, not even any of the extract we can see. Those pipes look like some sort of exhaust, but no idea from what ship.'

'No fucking kidding.' Roo answered. She felt excited, confused, helpless, scared.

It was huge, bigger than any ship she'd seen before. Her Unet analysis quickly informed them that projections were that this was comparable to the Ark class carriers that went on their one ways trips to colonise Saturn's moons. The object disappeared into the darkness beyond the range of the torch beams.

The Scout appeared to be speared into the side of the object at an angle approaching 45 degrees. The position of Wilding at the top of the 'spear' was not far enough away to give a true image of the size of what they were looking at, such was the difference in size between the two ships.

Roo thought it looked like an asteroid that had a space craft sprouting out of it. A rocky exterior covered the mid-section of the craft. Toward the rear, the rock gave way to machinery and huge metal panels. The rocky areas were unforgiving; hills, canyons and other more mysterious areas were covered in shadow. Where the ship poked through its rocky shell, it did so in a very utilitarian way, lit only by the Scout's exterior lighting that Wilding had rigged.

It was almost as if Wilding had known they'd need a few minutes to take in what they were seeing. Eventually, she continued.

'Quite something, isn't it? It's as exciting as it looks - and scary. I have been over, or should I say down, there twice. First time to the nearest bit, which was the middle of the rocky section. It's huge, and dangerous.'

She laughed, breaking off as she winced, feeling the pain from her wounds. 'Ha, of course it's dangerous it's an alien spaceship.'

Swinging from handles in the ceiling, Wilding manoeuvred nearer to the exit to give a better view. She looked left and right so viewers could see more of the bulk of the ship. There were no signs of activity.

'The second place I visited was more interesting. I headed towards what looks like the nose, if you can call it that, but I was running low on air so had to head back. Definitely looks like whatever or whoever built this dug out an asteroid or moon and put a spaceship inside it. Probably quite practical, the rock will act as a shielding system against most impacts and radiation. I don't know if they had deflector shields, but if they did, they weren't working or weren't strong enough to stop us hitting them.'

Whilst struggling, Wilding seemed to be enjoying the drama of the footage. 'Yeah, I know I'm dragging this out, but what else do I have left to do? At least this'll make me famous, well, *more* famous. I didn't film the earlier trips. To be honest, it didn't cross my mind. I was still thinking of survival then and spare suits don't always carry on board cams as standard. I had to cannibalise my old suit for it. Luckily, my spare was in my lab as it needed a repair itself.'

Her breathing again registered loudly in the speakers, taking a deep breath to control the pain.

'The maddest thing is that this is a fucking alien spaceship, a first contact of sorts…'

Wilding paused again, Roo unsure if it was for dramatic effect or because she needed another breather.

'I've one more trip left in this suit and time to explore. I'll head over there again and keep going till either ET decides to look after me or kill me, or more likely until I run out of air. Anyway, keep tuned to Dee Wilding TV, presented by me, the Butcher of Buchanan.'

# 10

# ZANDER

*Airborne, en route to the Tsiolkovsky Space Elevator*

Zander and Volchik sat in neighbouring acceleration couches in the rear lounge of the Flyer, on final approach to the landing strip on an atoll near the base of the Tsiolkovsky Space Elevator. Zander had tried to tie up some loose ends following the end of the Senate term, had been frustrated again by Deputy Lindstrom. He was on the way to the Moon for a family break, a location chosen deliberately because it wouldn't be expected by the media. He was meeting his sister there, the only member of his family left. At least the only one who still spoke to him. There'd been many threats on his life recently, and he needed somewhere safe and quiet for a few days to reassess things. It would also give his security team chance to review arrangements.

He messaged his sister, advising her that he was currently on schedule. He'd not seen her in two years, said he'd call once he was at the top of the elevator. She wouldn't reply. She'd always been frustrated, during his marriage, that the job had interrupted family time and liked to remind him that, before the bomb, she didn't know how his wife had come to tolerate it.

He'd met his wife, when, as a charity magazine editor, she'd been granted an exclusive interview with him. Zander had been in the World Senate for eleven years, the last eight as President. He had always promised he would give up politics whilst he was sane and before he was corrupted. Opponents unfairly said it was too late for the latter. In the end, he'd not got out quickly enough and had lost what he loved most. He'd be glad to leave the job behind if he could find another purpose.

Volchik politely coughed to disturb him.

'Sir, Joe Dubovsky is online and waiting to speak to you. Says it's urgent.'

Zander looked at him, raising an eyebrow quizzically. 'Must be. Isn't he on holiday?'

Volchik didn't reply, not knowing the answer.

'Ok, put him on.'

An image appeared in front of them, alongside a solid hologram of Dubovsky.

Dubovsky looked like he had not long got out of bed, which bearing in mind the time where he was probably was the case. His shirt was open at the collar and his mop of hair wasn't its usual carefully organised self.

'Apologies for disturbing you, Sir, but there's news of an interesting casualty out beyond Neptune.'

Zander leaned forward to get a better look. Immediately the blurred image alongside Dubovsky sharpened into a 3D model of a long, thin space craft that rotated in front of them.

Its front section was square, followed by a thin midsection before the rear flared out beyond the engine blocks.

'That's the Kuiper Scout or something, isn't it? Owned by Arden. The stupid bastard invited me to its launch ceremony years ago, was never sure why. What's so interesting about it?'

Dubovsky nodded. 'Watch this data feed. It's not very long.'

The image of the ship vanished and Zander watched two minutes of chaotic images, co-ordinates, some garbled radio messages about a collision, large runs of numbers that Zander guessed would be on board technical data, one static image from an exterior camera looking down the hull that seemed to suggest a huge breach, a dump of data pertaining to the health of the crew and a shot that seemed to show an object close to the ship. That shot lasted only a second or two, with the whole presentation concluding immediately afterwards, replaced by a standard SOS message. The 3D, shimmering display vanished and then reappeared, just showing that final shot.

'Where did this come from?'

'Neptune. Arden has registered the casualty as required under the Outer System Aid Agreement, though that far out there is not much anyone else can do to help. I've offered our expertise should it be needed. He's sent a recovery vessel to the scene and cancelled charters on a few other ships, which could've been sent for a follow up mission of some sort. The reason I thought you'd be interested is because it appears that this is not just a tragic accident. I've had the images checked out. Can you see the metal framework? Well, whilst it could be the Scout, I believe that some of that metalwork is not the Scout-'

Zander had little interest in anything to do with Arden and his business affairs. It suited him that the man was now based at the edge of the Solar System. Dismissively, he said, 'That's got to be the most likely answer. The collision messed the ship up, so it's not recognisable. Unless there's someone else operating out there we don't know about?'

Dubovsky grinned like a naughty schoolboy. 'There's no way there is another scientific mission out that far. Indeed, no ships at all. So…' Dubovsky shrugged and almost looked embarrassed.

Zander caught on, rolling his eyes. 'Oh, come on, not little green men? How many years have we been looking and now you tell me we might have just crashed into them!'

'Sir, we've no idea what it is. The distress message could be faked, so we should keep all options open. Arden obviously is in the box seat to lead on this, though we should keep an eye on it. And… what if it is something alien?'

Zander looked at Reuben. In the unlikely event, this was a first contact. He couldn't be seen to have done nothing, and if he could do anything to lean on Arden, then it was worth considering.

'Ok, so we can't send any practical assistance, even if we had any. We could move some of the first contact team we have out to Uranus, just in case. Don't tell Arden, he'll think we're interfering and might shut me out, however he might be grateful for some help later.' The President sat again. 'I want a full history of the ship and its crew. Let's see if it could be something more mundane.'

Dubovsky was as efficient as ever. 'I've run some initial checks and will upload the data. All looks to be what it says it was. A science trip. Dee Wilding was on board. Remember that name? The crew and passengers were all pretty much scientists.'

'Ok, thanks. I'll take a look. How is Arden doing these days? Thankfully, I have nothing to do with him.'

Despite being dragged out of bed, Dubovsky had clearly been working hard in preparation for this briefing. Whilst on the face of it this collision was innocuous, he'd treated this news as if it were something big and had entered crisis management mode.

'Arden's ok, his business has been tanking, albeit he's still the richest man outside of Jovian orbit. Half his gas mines have been shut for a month due to dangerous storms and he's lost a lot of men. He'll be keen to get this rescue right if he can. He's promised he'll keep us up to date, though it's strange he kept this quiet for a week or so.'

Zander shook his head. As ever, he spoke carefully and calmly. 'A casualty and dead passengers are always going to look bad. I bet he's desperate. What about the strategic angle? Let me humour you. What if this is little green men? Does he want to make friends with them first? He'd be willing to take some risks if he thought there was a big enough gain personally.'

Dubovsky agreed. 'He's not stupid, but yeah, he'd want to maximise any opportunities out of this.'

Zander drained his water. 'OK, this could be something or nothing, probably nothing. Let's keep calm. Get the first contact team on the move. Make sure we are getting everything he gets. I want access to all his data and get some of our own scopes looking. Update me when I get to Grissom.'

'Will do.'

As Zander shut the connection down, their pilot warned them that they were now authorised to land, so he checked his straps. He could hear the rest of his entourage strapping themselves back into their seats and chatting in the next cabin.

Zander sighed. 'Let's hope it isn't little green men, anyway. We've enough on our plate.'

Reuben looked at his boss. Though his job was security, not policy, Zander enjoyed his company and trust. 'How well do you know Arden?'

Zander scratched his nose. 'Not that well. It's fair to say we don't like each other. His kid was kidnapped. Never turned up. Not even a ransom demand.'

'Shit, that's terrible.' He sighed as memories came back.

'He was punished for the same reasons as I was.'

# 11

# JUDE

*En Route to the Tsiolkovsky Space Elevator*

Jude and her father sat on a bench at the front of the observation deck. She peered towards the horizon, where she could now make out the imposing sight of the space elevator surrounded by a swarm of black dots, service flyers, drones, and other small aircraft. There was a no-fly zone in the immediate vicinity, but from this distance, they looked as if they were landing on and swarming around the tube that went upwards, vanishing into the sky.

With no large transports allowed to fly near the sea-based elevator, thousands had taken the daily ferry, essentially a repurposed cruise ship, from Sao Paolo. In the early morning sun, Jude could see that flanking their vessel were two large cargo carriers stacked with containers. Many simply contained supplies or machinery for the elevator island complex they approached or luggage to be transported up the cargo elevator with the passengers. The growth in sending machinery into orbit had slowed with competition from factory and mining complexes on the moon, Mars, and the asteroid belt. The growth area of traffic was in people. Thousands were heading out into space, seeking the opportunities that the colonies presented.

Jude wished everyone really knew what it was like out there. She'd seen both sides of life off Earth. There were some making a lot of money in developing industries, far more were being exploited in places where nobody could shout for help and human rights were worthless. Hundreds vanished, with no prospect of being found. It was too tempting for some employers or landlords to simply open the air lock on nuisance staff or those who couldn't pay their bills. Despite the risks, she understood the desire, or desperation, which led to the decision to take the gamble.

She was disturbed from her reverie as first a drone and then an unmarked flyer swooped low overhead. The flyer swung low behind the platform that housed the elevator and vanished, landing on one of the series of nearer islands that made up this chain of atolls. 'You see that?'

'What?'

'Might be wrong, but I think it was a UNS drone and an unmarked flyer. Must be a VIP taking a ride up the elevator. Can't remember the last time I heard of that.'

She pulled her pad from her bag and logged into a news portal to see if she could find out who it was. Based on those markings on the drone, there would only be a handful of people to whom it could relate.

Within two hours, the ferry had reached its destination and cast into shade as it briefly swung underneath the raised superstructure of the tower base. It resembled an old oil platform, save it must have been a dozen times the size.

After passing many docking points, from which cranes removed crates of cargo from tankers and placed them on ramps that delivered them to be loaded in turn onto the elevator, they emerged into bright sunlight, slowly pulling up alongside a concrete harbour built into the side of the small island that housed the reception complex. Beyond the reception island was another island linked by a series of bridges that housed a holiday resort. Gleaming hotels emerged from the green forest that covered the atoll, surrounded by a silver strip of beach.

Thousands of people came here for breaks, just so they could say they'd seen the elevator.

Many paid for a 140 hour round trip, just for the experience.

As they waited for the ferry to dock the cargo raft, they'd towed was disconnected and drawn away to be unloaded. They took their time getting up as crowds swarmed to the outer rails to take photographs and videos. Her father dozed off again, still worse for wear after the previous night's drinking. Jude swung her bag over her shoulder and kicked her father's shoe to wake him.

As Parynski wiped the sleep from his eyes away, they talked again about his plan to meet his three crates of personal belongings before they were loaded onto the ship. He was hoping to create a few hours' grace in case he needed to buy any extra supplies or equipment.

'I thought this ship you are delivering was so amazing it'd be fully kitted out with everything you'd need, anyway?' Jude asked.

He laughed, 'It should be! Compared to taking wrecks from one planet to another, this should be easy, even if the distance is huge. The Triton Run, to the end of the line and back.'

Jude linked arms with him and pulled him close. She looked up at him. 'Not like you to get a straightforward charter. Is it safe?'

'Yeah, it's her maiden voyage, though. Should take me just over 6 months full speed, there's no longer trip. Will take me longer coming back. Might try and catch up with Squire if he's about and on Triton One. For the return, I'll hop on various transports that are as cheap as possible. After all, their cost comes out of my bottom line.'

'So, I'll be ringing you on your birthday, again, as usual. Why didn't they at least ferry the ship out to the 'roid belt?' asked Jude. 'It's as good a starting point as any.'

Parynski shrugged. 'Yeah, it's a long, long way. I'm doing it because I'll be discrete. Don't think the owner even wants some of his own people to know about it. Strange one. Plus, this isn't a usual pleasure craft. She's too big to fit into a tanker, and only an earthmover could house it, and that would risk attracting too much attention.'

Jude was intrigued. 'Why so secretive though?'

## THE TRITON RUN

He leant closer to her. 'She's only registered as a short-range pleasure yacht. Owner doesn't want anyone to know she's capable of flying herself to the end of the line and back and could take on half of the Martian Orbit Force on her own...'

Jude realised her snort was the reaction he wanted before he continued.

'Now I'm exaggerating a little, but she looks well specced out. Shouldn't be a trip where I'm inside the engines doing running repairs, shutting off the life support for half the ship as it leaks, or where I go hungry!'

They joined the back of the throng, filing down the stairs towards the exit ramps.

She looked at him with a smile. 'I think I know who is paying you. Only one person out that far could afford a ship like that.'

He put a finger on his lips and jokingly shushed her. The smile then slipped from his face. 'I've worked for him before; I was on a retainer. This was booked a while back. The plan had been to do this and come home and live happily ever after with your mother.'

She reached an arm around his back and squeezed him tight. 'I know.'

# 12

# ARDEN

*Triton One Habitat, Triton Orbit*

Scott Arden preferred face-to-face meetings. It was easier to read people and get what he wanted. Whilst unavoidable due to the distances involved, he never enjoyed meeting with CGI avatars or holograms, especially when the individual was so far away that AI took the lead on behalf of some of the attendees, making them harder to influence. AI logic kicked back against emotional pressure.

Arden's boardroom, despite his immense wealth, was spartan. Neptune was rich, dominating the market for accessible helium-3 and ongoing research into engine development for interstellar vehicles. Business had been tough over recent months due to natural phenomena, heavy storms in Neptune's upper atmosphere, but it would bounce back. The boardroom was plain, no different to all the other meeting rooms his Habitat contained. The only exception being a series of images that primarily displayed pictures of his fleet of space craft and an exterior underwater shot of a home he still owned on Earth. He'd not been back for years. It was empty without his girls. The largest image was a portrait of his wife and daughter. He now spent most of his time on Triton One, the management habitat located near his shipyards, a safe distance from the gas mines that hung in the Neptune atmosphere.

The habitat comprised a rotating central tower, which formed a core out of which sprouted dozens of long arms of different lengths that ended with small spherical docking ports and reception areas. The area was congested with a constant flow of ships of all sizes coming in and out. The larger, more utilitarian craft usually docked at the shipyards and tenders brought crew, guests, and other visitors to Arden's hub, Triton One.

All eyes around the boardroom table were on Arden whilst he checked a data feed on his wrist. He knew what they were seeing, what they were thinking. He didn't care. He didn't care for much apart from business.

The data band hung loose on a thin arm, protruding from a plain set of work coveralls that matched the style of the majority of his employees on board. The outfit was too big for him because he was unnaturally thin. He was pale, deathly so, and with a face that was little more than a skull with skin pulled tightly over it. What little hair he had was limited to a few wisps of grey at the top of his forehead. His eyes were black dots, hidden away at the back of deep sockets, lips thin and pale. He took a swig from a tumbler in front of him, then cleared his throat. He faced a tricky situation, though one that could have incredible potential.

'OK, let's start. What we're here to discuss is important. The Kuiper Scout, which some of you will recall was launched from here on a scientific mission, has sent out a distress signal. Squire has taken the BSV, but he's so far out it's going to take a long time to get there.'

As he started to speak, a display unit set into the centre of the table put up rotating 3D images of the BSV, the Scout, and a real time map of their projected relative locations. All eyes moved immediately from Arden to the images.

'Casualties out beyond Saturn aren't that unusual,

however we really can do without losing the passengers and payload. I've got others involved, but I want this group to act as a steering committee to manage the situation. What I'm about to show you is truly remarkable. We need to establish its veracity and respond to secure the situation before hell breaks loose and half the inner solar system sends out people to investigate. I've asked for some help. We'll need lots of it, but I've given us a head start. What I don't want is every privateer coming and sticking their noses in. Particularly, I don't want Zander and his cronies getting involved.'

He waved around the table. 'This is quite a large group, though I suspect most of you know each other.'

They all worked for Arden. As Governor of Triton and CEO of Neptune Helium, he ran the entire Neptune system. It was all he had to live for these days. He owned or managed a significant percentage of the habitats in orbit, as well as the gas mines. The biggest and best equipped shipyard was also his.

There were over a dozen in the group, most attending in person. They included PR representatives, engineers, his Chief Medical Officer, IT specialists and Security.

Nearest to him was Hans Muller. An impressive physical figure, he was his Shipyard Manager. Arden struggled to bond with him as he kept himself to himself, but his performance as an engineer was unrivalled. Muller made it clear that he didn't have the time or inclination to mix with those he didn't need to. Arden believed his efficiency and ability to ensure complete flexibility with their facilities had dramatically increased revenues from the renting of berths and from repair and servicing.

He'd spoken to some in the group before the meeting, and he invited one of those to speak first. She was appearing via Avatar, dressed simply in an orange jumpsuit. She was about fifty, olive skin and dark hair swept up into a bun.

'Hi, Teresa Garcia, lead scientist and Director of the observatory and coms centre on the ground on Triton. We've two 'scopes currently directed to assist. Unfortunately, our most powerful array is inner system, on Oberon, and offline whilst it gets an upgrade. We've sped up the programme and hope to have it online in a fortnight. Current scans of the target are being circulated and uploaded to the BSV every six hours. We've logged about 20,000 objects in the Kuiper Belt and estimate there might be over 100,000 overall. Though the Scout could have hit anything, the footage we have is remarkable.'

Arden sensed some of his staff mentally switching off as a long discussion ensued on how to control the inevitable media fallout. 'The biggest aspect to the media interest is the presence of Wilding on board.'

Arden took a slug of his drink. Wilding was the elephant in the room. 'Well, that's just the way it is. She was cheap, overqualified for the mission, and wanted a chance. Let's not allow prejudice against one person to affect what this is all about. We've a suitable ship en route. The BSV will be capable of assisting the passengers on the Scout if they need it and can either effect repairs or tow it onto a return vector for retrieval. Salvaging her could prove to be a huge task.'

Arden turned to Garcia. 'I appreciate the technical struggles we have. Let me know if I can divert any other resources your way. I know she can't make it today, but your Tapper has been of great assistance.'

'Roo lives for emergencies like this,' smiled Garcia.

Arden could see that Garcia was energised by the situation. Though fearful of the market's reaction to another loss, he appreciated the potential of the situation and was equally excited. He indicated for her to continue.

'Roo managed to retrieve an SOS data packet and some

other messages we'll look at in a moment. She's also narrowed the search area. There's no catalogued object in the vicinity of where our data tells us that the Scout might be.'

Muller leaned towards the image in front of him to get a better look. 'If we can see a smudge already from this distance, then it can't just be the Scout because it's too small to see? It must have collided with an 'ice', an asteroid or something bigger?'

Arden knew what was coming. Garcia regularly complained about Muller and his views. She'd decided to play with him. 'Well, what else could it be?'

'Pirates.' As soon as he said it, all eyes fell on Muller. Arden snorted disdain and Garcia shook her head. Despite being quiet, Muller was known as a conspiracy theorist, to the amusement of some colleagues. He was serious.

'We know there's some. Ok, most are asteroid hoppers, but their ships are getting bigger and they're getting more confident. Everyone knows some raided Ganymede hard, and we had the attack here last year, stealing fuel and supplies. They're getting ambitious. The Kuiper Scout is a valuable piece of kit.'

'You are wrong about the attack here. That was fake news.' That was his PR Chief defending their reputation to the death, even when he knew it wasn't true. Arden knew that this wasn't the venue for blanket spin.

Hans slammed a hand down on the table. 'That's crap. Scott knows it too. I know what happened here when they attacked. You want the facts?'

He looked around the table, daring them to challenge him, his eyes wide. For such a usually mild-mannered man, Arden was sure most found it funny.

They allowed Muller to continue. 'I was working at the shipyard when they docked, took ten hostages, killed twenty-three. They did so much damage. If they're out this far, then there's only so far they can go and limited places to visit. They'll struggle to get inward past the Jovian sentries, in the event they even had the inclination. They know Neptune space is the place to be since the gas mines took off. Even though it's a long way out, they could be interested in the Scout.'

Arden raised his hand for silence. 'OK, look, it's an interesting theory and worth considering Hans, though I think when you see what we have, you'll change your mind. If it's pirates, then this is a new MO for them.'

'What do you have?' Muller asked.

'Let's watch the footage we have. Roo recovered it and is scanning for more. I'm going to need your collective views on what we've got and believe me, nothing is off the table. The main thing is that we need to get on top of this and secure the casualty.'

And with that, the room darkened the image from Dee Wilding's helmet cam appeared before them.

# 13

# JUDE

*Top of the Tsiolkovsky Space Elevator*

Once the carriage reached the end station in upper orbit, the passengers unstrapped themselves. Before disembarking, they were given some time to recover and were visited by the on-site medical team to ensure there had been no adverse reactions to the journey up.

The top of the elevator looked, from above, like a bicycle wheel. The central hub housed the tether and several levels of storage bays where freight cars were emptied and loaded. The upper levels contained accommodation, restaurants, and a hotel. Radiating outwards like spokes were a dozen or so transport tubes that ferried people and materials to and from the outer wheel which contained a variety of docking and repair bays, the facility to launch satellites by 'kicking' them into orbit and an observation deck for tourists. The spindles were covered in solar panels. The top of the facility contained a platform akin to a runway from an aircraft carrier with a small control tower in one corner.

Her father had taken an earlier car up, so she was alone. The facilities looked slightly tired compared to the newer elevators, its lower prices kept it busy with those on a budget. She checked the departure boards to confirm her father's shuttle had left and looked for any unusual departures that were lined up. As she had been coming through security, Jude had bumped into an old

## THE TRITON RUN

flame, Reuben Volchik, who she hadn't seen for years. He'd ended up working in security for the President. He'd seen her and had used his clearance to wave Jude through the faster channel before vanishing into the crowds. She wondered if he had been on the flyer.

Jude did two laps of the wheel, pretending to herself she was stretching her legs, keeping an eye out for Reuben. If only she had his number. She decided to get some food. The restaurant in the central hub was busy, packed with crew and passengers. She grabbed a coffee and sandwich and took a small table. With perfect timing, just as she was about to tuck in Reuben, appeared, struggling to carry a tray of drinks and a bag of snacks. Instinctively, she jumped up. 'Here, let me help...'

Reuben, holding another bag in his teeth, nodded towards a discrete door that was situated on the far side of the seating area.

He mumbled, 'Good to see you again Jude, get that door, please?'

A sealed carton dropped off his tray, and Jude dramatically scooped it up for him.

Realising she was acting like a desperate teenager, swooning over a heart throb, she blushed. Trying to regain her cool, she led the way, weaving through the crowd of other customers, encouraging the throng to get out of their way. When they reached the door, he paused, and it clicked open for him. Jude sensed they were being watched. Jude leaned into the door, and it opened into a small ante room. Reuben stepped in after her and thanked her after putting his tray on a table next to the inner door. The ante room was small, and they were stood close. She couldn't help but confirm that there was no ring on his wedding finger.

'Is the Pres in there?' Jude blurted out when she really wanted to ask how he was and where he was going.

'It's a good job, it's you asking, and nobody else,' he replied, only half laughing. He seemed pleased to see her; she realised her thoughts were all over the place. 'Now thanks for holding the door, but clear off! Catch up soon? I promise I'll be in touch when I'm next on leave.'

She hugged him, startling him initially before he reciprocated. Jude stepped back, feeling all embarrassed.

'Great, look forward to it,' she said, and with that, she stepped back into the food hall, the door clicking shut behind her. Feeling all hot and flustered, her head was full of good memories until she recalled the moment they broke up because they were heading off in such opposite directions it would be impossible to maintain a relationship.

Jude returned to her table and finished her food. Then she headed to the departure terminal, checked her flight was on time and that her luggage had been delivered. Apart from fluttering her heart, seeing Reuben had piqued her interest. She couldn't understand why the President wouldn't take a space plane. Curious, she returned to her seat, pulling out her pad and started searching the news. The only mention of Zander was the attack on his entourage in Berlin. The storm that followed was focussed on trying to identify those behind the attack, with the usual mix of home and system groups mentioned. It was likely to be the Exiles, quite who they were remained to be seen.

Wondering which flight he was supposed to be on, she used her police login to access the passenger lists for the next few flights. It would almost certainly be within the next few hours, though he might be picked up by a private shuttle. Such was the volume of traffic she struggled to spot anything that stood out. She ran some checks to strip out aliases. Everyone checked out as best as she could tell, but then so they should. She noted her flight was only two-thirds full, so likely to be upwards of thirty-five spare seats. That was certainly unusual, so she wondered if they had been discretely reserved by the President's entourage. She was on a flight that would go to a transport hub on the moon.

Jude decided to head to the higher most observation window in the exterior ring and looked towards the launch pad on the top of the central hub. She found a place at the front and took in the impressive sight of a bulk carrier launching itself off and away from the elevator. Within seconds, the platform was a hive of activity.

Two suited figures, secured by tethers, and a swarm of automated drones, appeared from an opening and scoured the launchpad for debris and damage. Within fifteen minutes they had covered the surface and returned inside save one drone that remained deploying what she guessed was a repair sealant to what was likely to be a little bit of damage on the surface. It soon also moved away once its work was done. Two incoming ships were due soon, a small tug for a quick refuel and a private passenger vessel.

She moved to another window and even though she'd been up space elevators plenty of times, she enjoyed taking in the view. Below the ocean was bright blue, reflecting sunlight, her view unimpeded by cloud.

Suddenly, the floor rocked, tipping her away from the window onto the floor. Elevators were designed to move in bad atmospheric conditions, she told herself, though this was too dramatic. There was panic on the surrounding walkway. Passengers sent sprawling were all picking themselves and their scattered luggage up. There was some screaming, shouting and general anxious chatter. Jude helped an elderly orderly up who had fallen nearby. His motorised trolley had spun and hit the wall. She put him back on his way and went back to the window. A siren sounded in the distance.

A second tremor followed. It felt closer. An explosion. She held onto a handrail and looked out the window at the central hub. The site of the damage appeared to be some fifty metres below her current location. Attached to the side of the tube that contained the elevator mechanism and the tether was a track that brought up cargo. The cargo elevator cars were sealed containers attached to the outside to maximise capacity. The container at the front of the train on its way up had blown apart and was venting fluid of some sort. The vehicle had stopped.

The first impact had felt as if it came from above, perhaps

on the landing bay. As she watched, a third explosion followed and the whole of the carriage tore itself apart and away from the track. The uppermost section of track broke into pieces, some falling away and hanging out into space.

The elevator would now be shut down until all was safe. As she recalled the only other occasion, she was aware of a malfunction to this degree was on another elevator where a fire had broken out in the passenger cab. It had killed all passengers on the way up due to smoke inhalation. The inquest had led to a redesign of the cabins.

She wished she had her Chip. It had been removed when she went undercover. It would have been a mine of real-time updates, and she could have tapped into the emergency channels. All around her was chaos as people realised something potentially serious had happened. An automated voice came over the PA, telling all staff to report to emergency stations whilst asking all passengers to maintain calm and head to the main muster point in the waiting bay in the central hub to await further news.

All now appeared calm outside the window. Whilst the top half of the track was missing, the integrity of the rest of the elevator appeared sound. The tether itself was designed to repair itself if it suffered minor damage. She saw a flash and realised it was the lower part of the automated cargo train ejecting itself from the track and hopefully heading for a safe landing in the sea from where it could be recovered. Those in her area of the walkway were doing as they were told, collecting their things, and heading for the central waiting area, a chamber adjacent to the restaurant.

Her inquisitive side got the better of her and she fought the tide of people heading to the muster point, doing a lap of the ring. She pulled her security lanyard and badge out of her pocket and put it on. She wasn't on duty and had no authority here, but it might stop people from questioning her. When Jude had completed her the circuit back round to the side of the tower facing the launch platform, she found a scene of strange devastation. The ship furthest from her had been torn apart, completely shattered. Judging by its size and the shell that remained, she assumed it was the tug. The other ship, a larger, squat craft, sat unharmed. It must have touched down just after the other ship had gone up or it would have taken damage from the debris and force of the explosion. A few drones wheeled around the platform, trying to work out what to do. She presumed the engineers and emergency services on the landing bay were in lockdown. The new arrival would have to wait until it was safe before the airtight corridor was dragged out to link to its airlock.

'You are getting fucking slow Judith Parynski,' she muttered under breath as her heart sank. One accident was extremely unlikely up here, two could only mean one thing.

Zander. Her thoughts turned back to the assassination attempt in Berlin. She had to get back downstairs and see what she could do. If this attack was as co-ordinated as she feared, then the President might need all the help he could get.

# 14

# PARYNSKI

*Onboard the Skydancer, en route to Mars system*

There were tears running down Parynski's face as the first video cut off. He put his head in hands for a moment before taking a deep breath and wiping his eyes with his sleeve.

The video he'd just watched from Dee Wilding had affected him in a way that was only matched by Mary's death. Parynski knew her Platoon was the closest she had ever got to a family, and they'd been split up sooner than otherwise might have been the case, because of what happened at Buchanan. He'd even visited her in military jail before she was belatedly discharged. The stigma had stayed with her, and she'd needed her closest friends. Based on the heartfelt message he'd just sat through, it didn't sound good. It was a mix of goodbye, and a final will and testament.

The messages were sent days ago. He told himself that seeing them earlier wouldn't have made any difference. He could barely watch, yet he knew he had to. He copied the data dump and sent it to Jude. She'd likely still be on the up journey, he estimated, so he'd speak to her later.

Now out of Earth's immediate neighbourhood and on the way to Mars, he finalised the autopilot's commands. The course was set, swinging by Jupiter before heading out towards Neptune. Beyond telling the Skydancer to avoid Saturn in the current climate, he'd not paid much attention to the course. He'd be through the asteroid belt in twenty-one days, though

# THE TRITON RUN

his final destination would take a lot longer.

The Skydancer's artificial gravity was on, and he sat back in the comfy command chair on the bridge. Whilst it was nestled away near the centre of the fuselage, it was dominated on three sides by screens that gave the impression they were viewing external ports. Plush furniture surrounded him, some half dozen chairs and couches that passengers could be strapped into. Each chair was positioned behind raised consoles and screens and 3D projectors. Most were off at the moment. The design of the Skydancer was very much a mix of practicality and vanity. It was the most comfortable ship he'd ever been on, never mind had the task of ferrying from one planet to another.

Parynski had been watching in horror as he realised Dee was almost certainly dead. He selected the second visual file, converted it into a playable format, and got up. He paced the room, gathering his thoughts, before heading to the well-equipped galley for a drink and returned with dread to his seat. He put the footage on the big screen in front of the cockpit, where the forward observation window would normally appear to be.

'Ok then Dee, let's see what happened to you,' he said to himself before speaking louder to the Skydancer. 'Please continue playback, turn off forward and side visual panels.'

The room dimmed slightly as the screen in front of became illuminated.

Wilding was standing on the lip of the gash in the side of the Kuiper Scout, helmet mounted camera pointing out ahead of her into the void. From her position, the Scout was protruding upwards at an angle of 45 degrees from the rocky surface on the top of the thing, the alien craft. She was leaning out from what was effectively the underneath of the carcass of the ship.

'I climbed down to where we collided. There's no way in. The front of the bridge was vaporised, and the rest seems to have been so superheated it turned practically into glass, it's all melted. There seem to be a few deep cracks in the rock further away, but they are too dangerous in a suit to try and get down…'

Dee pulled herself back in from the edge. 'We made quite a bang, as you can imagine. The window I'm stood in was torn open in the collision as the Scout became impaled. The whole frame of this module buckled. It's been seventy-two hours since we said hello and if there is anyone or anything in that rock, then I've not disturbed them yet. From my observations I haven't seen any sign of registration, so I've no idea where this baby is from. My scanners are all long dead whilst I can, I hope, broadcast.'

'They'll never forget you if this is what you say it is,' said Parynski to no one.

The speaker crackled.

'-where I'm going to aim for, I'll boost out as far as I can and then hope I gauge it right to push myself towards the surface and a gentle landing. The jets aren't reliable on this suit, so if I go in too fast, there'll be a big splat. I hope to touch down at the edge of the rock and where the metal exterior starts. Then I'll try to get inside.'

The view changed as Wilding gave the chamber a final scan. She checked her suit's legs, and the helmet mounted cam swivelled as she checked over her shoulder. Parynski could hear her wincing in pain as she stretched. Once the checks had been done, she paused to get her breath and, Parynski surmised, to allow the suits medi-kit to dose her with some more pain killers.

'Ok then, Kuiper Scout, this will stand as your last log. The ship is being abandoned by me, Dee Wilding, last surviving crew member. I'm confident that the rest of the crew and this mission will be remembered forever, and I thank you for your comradeship these last few months. We set out to find something interesting, and that we did. I'm just sorry we all didn't survive until the end of the mission and gain the glory that I hope will be attached to our names. I should have enough fuel to do this. If it doesn't work, I am going to be on a one-way ticket to the Oort Cloud because I won't be able to land.'

And with that, she launched herself into the void.

# 15

# JUDE

*Top of the Tsiolkovsky Space Elevator*

Jude tucked her ID inside her jacket and instinctively reached down to draw her small personal pistol from the holster tucked up her trouser leg.

Shit.

Of course it wasn't there, it was in her luggage. Whilst she had authorisation to carry her weapon in most locations, the elevator was one of the few exceptions and as she was off duty, she couldn't even pull rank over the regulations.

She took a corridor down a spoke toward the central hub. She walked quickly, catching back up with the crowds being shepherded to the central holding area. She ducked away and skirted round the back of the group and headed towards where she had met Reuben previously.

She reached the open centre of the public area, now congested with distressed and confused passengers being directed by staff into groups. She estimated there were several hundred there. The public address system was trying to calm the situation without much success. Those who had seen the lower explosions had now mixed with those from the higher deck and who had seen the tug go up in flames and were sharing their concerns. Jude reached the entrance to the food court, where it opened out onto the central muster point.

She never heard or even felt the bomb go off, only its impact.

Jude came round on the floor, her body wedged against something hard with her ears ringing and her body aching. She coughed, her lungs full of smoke and the smell of acrid, burning plastic. She took what felt like several minutes to gather her faculties and assess her situation.

It took a while for her running eyes to focus through the smoky scene. There had been an explosion, seemingly in the centre of the group of passengers. The walls, floor, and ceiling were covered in blood and body parts. Nobody was moving, though she could make out some whimpering as those who hadn't been killed immediately were now dying painfully from their wounds. She rolled onto her front and took some deep breaths, gulping in cleaner air.

She must have been thrown several metres by the explosion, luckily protected by the crowd between her and wherever the bomb was. Her left eye socket was very tender. There was blood coming from a cut on her cheek and she ached all over. She had done better than most. She hoped that the President, and Volchik, were safe and would stay that way. She had no idea if there was an emergency way off the elevator.

As the smoke cleared, she noted that it was darker. The emergency shutters had come down, so the explosion must have breached the observation windows. That, as well as the initial blast, had caused complete chaos in the structure. The ceiling had come in and furniture was piled against the side where the shutters had come down as the atmosphere venting had tried to push it outside.

She became aware of footsteps.

Jude played dead, cautiously opening one eye as a boot landed next to her. Standing above her, oblivious to the fact she was alive, was a black jump suited figure. The suit looked partially armoured and suitable for upper atmosphere excursions. The visor on the helmet was up and as the figure stepped away to cautiously scout the area, Jude saw a female face inside. A second figure stood near her; rifle strapped to their back.

Relieved no one was paying her any attention, Jude reached out and very gently pulled a tray towards her. More attackers appeared, patrolling the carnage, occasionally putting a blast into a body to make sure it was dead. They were all dressed identically. Jude couldn't make out any details that gave her a clue as to their origin. There were eight of them. One of the figures disappeared, returning with a colleague who was accompanied by two haggard figures wearing Space Elevator Co uniforms. The women were covered in blood, hair plastered across their faces, and were sobbing uncontrollably, clinging onto each other for comfort. They were pushed along, a rifle poking them to remind them to keep moving.

Two of the armed figures hung back, one near Jude, the other retreated out of her view. The others moved cautiously towards the doorway of the seating area where she'd first spoken to Reuben. Their weapons were aimed at the doorway.

The younger of the two women was struggling to hold a pad as her hands shook. She looked nervously back at the figure behind her, who nodded at her to speak. Jude cursed her lack of a weapon, though she assessed she was better waiting to see how this would play out. The longer she dared to wait, the more information she would gather. Right now, the only advantage she had was that nobody knew she was alive. The woman spoke as loud as her cracking voice allowed, quivering and pausing with nerves.

'Hello Mr President. I hope you can hear me. My name is Amber Jones. I'm a boarding assistant here. My colleague is Julie Anne Vasquez. I've been asked to read you a message; I hope you'll do as asked.'

She paused again to stop her hand from shaking. Julie Anne cuddled up to her tighter, giving her support. 'The elevator has been taken over - I don't know who they are. Whilst there has been some force to take control, you'll note that they've taken great care not to destroy the elevator's integrity. You'll know how dangerous it would be if the tether was to be torn. If you do not cooperate, that is the final solution here.'

Jude grimaced. If the tether that hung below the structure tore, it could cause all sorts of damage. Some of it may tear away like a whip into orbit, causing damage to anything that came into its path. That which dropped away and was pulled down by gravity would fall as the earth rotated, landing over an area that could be 22,000 miles long. It would loop round the Earth like a yoyo. Jude knew there were some self-destruct mechanisms designed to split the tether into chunks, but it was such a durable material that, if any made landfall, it would cause considerable destruction.

She had to stop that happening. At present, she had to assume no help was coming. There was no response from the secure room, so the women continued reading the script.

'If the tether is released, you'll have a lot more blood on your hands. We ask that you come out and surrender. We want to take you away and talk to you.'

The speech, such as it was, kept coming with the pad acting like an autocue. Scanning the figures, Jude tried without success to assess who was the leader. There was no clear first target for her. Eventually, after a long pause whilst the women sobbed hysterically, a further message appeared for them to read.

'You have one minute to come out unarmed or both these women are going to be tortured right here.'

The woman couldn't believe what she'd just read, and the two collapsed, sobbing together in a heap, begging and whimpering. Jude noticed the attackers withdraw slightly; weapons still aimed at the door through which Reuben had gone. The attackers all snapped alert as the door opened. Reuben, face showing no emotion, stepped out, arms raised in surrender. He came out without his jacket, shirt sleeves rolled up to show he was not armed. Whilst he kept his eyes forward, Jude could tell he was doing all he could to take in as much information as he could.

'The President will talk, but we need a guarantee of his safety, for his team and any remaining hostages. Enough blood has been spilled.'

Silence. Reuben stood impassive. After a few moments, the nearest attacker approached him, weapon aimed at his chest. The attackers' body language conveyed calmness and confidence. They knew there was no help coming for the survivors.

An arm appeared through the doorway, followed by what Jude assumed was another member of Zander's security team and then the President himself. The two of them walked, arms raised over to Reuben. Zander stood a proud figure, back straight with a poker face that had got him through many negotiations. Reuben was taller, with a solid frame. The other guard was shorter and stockier, with a shaved head. Sweat poured off it. He chewed gum nervously.

One of the attackers stepped forward, voice artificially disguised through his face mask. 'On your knees!' he snapped 'Any deviation from what we say will lead to awful consequences, President Zander.'

The three men did as they were told. Zander looked up at the masked man, speaking matter of factually.

'Set out your demands and I'll do my best to meet them. If you hurt anyone else, I can't promise to help.'

The attacker, who now appeared to be their spokesman, lowered his weapon and circled the three men.

'You'll do as you're told. We're going to need to take you and a couple of others on a little journey so we can have a talk in peace. We just need to decide who else to take with us, to encourage your co-operation. These ladies appear the obvious choice.'

He turned away and waved two colleagues towards the open door the President had come from. 'Where's the rest of your entourage?'

Zander looked at Volchik, seemingly hoping for inspiration.

Reuben cleared his throat and spoke aloud. 'Wright, bring everyone out, arms raised, please.'

'Thank you.'

Jude strained her neck to try to follow what was happening. Hearing the click of the inner security door to the secure room open and swing wide, she hoped a fight back was planned. Two of the attackers approached the door, holstered their weapons, and swung stub nosed weapons from their shoulders, taking aim at the doorway. The guard alongside Reuben read the situation first.

'It's a trap!'

# 16

## PARYNSKI

*Onboard the Skydancer, en route to Mars system*

Parynski watched as, like a diver gracefully leaping from a diving board, Wilding left the Kuiper Scout behind. The image broke up, went black before being restored and then stabilised. Wilding had pushed herself out of the opening and effectively 'flew' approximately one hundred metres above the rocky surface below. She skilfully kept her head down, maintaining altitude and speed, pushed along by small adjuster jets built into the suit's backpack. Dee was very experienced at EVA manoeuvres.

Ahead could be seen a region where the rocky surface was replaced by grey metal. The surface below was clearly not sculpted; it was the exterior of an asteroid or moon. The surface was pitted with small craters and deep gullies. Every now and then, a metallic pipe could be seen snaking out across the surface before heading back underground. Heavy breathing came over the speaker.

'Adjuster jet fuel is running out now, so time to start the descent…'

The camera jolted as Wilding looked round and adjusted the angle of the jets to gradually push her towards the surface, which came into sharper focus. In the distance, Parynski could see where the rock ended and the metallic shell of whatever was beneath emerged.

'I've a better chance of a soft landing on the rock without bouncing off. The rock and ice surface is quite brittle on the top I can get a grip.'

Parynski could feel himself tensing up as Wilding gave a last push from her jets down towards the surface, following by an impressive manoeuvre where she rotated to fire off a jet that slowed her descent. Parynski noted, as he knew Wilding would have, that the landing site was comparatively smooth compared to the area where the Scout had impaled itself; a few small hills and craters, nothing that should be a concern to someone with her expertise.

With a yell, she crumpled, touching down inside a small crater, and bounced away from the surface. The speed was, however, a lot slower than the speed she'd been carrying, and the bounce was relatively shallow. Wilding was ready for that and had angled herself, so she was pushed onwards and forwards, flying a matter of metres away from the surface. Another nudge from her jet made her touch down again, followed by another smaller bounce in which she crossed the border between rock and metal. The next time she touched down she was able to secure herself, magnetic boots working, their grips crunching through a thin layer of ice.

The surface under the dirty ice layer was a battleship grey, mottled with stains and small impact craters. 'Ouch, that fucking hurt…' Wilding laughed, remaining crouched to absorb any residual impact that her suit's exoskeleton couldn't cope with.

The image went black, returning moments later, whereupon Wilding was elsewhere.

'Sorry viewers, just had some admin to attend to. Suit started alerting, had to run some tests and reboot the AI. We seem to be ok now.'

She swivelled her head to give the audience a view of the landscape. It was bleak and dark, illuminated only by the suit's floodlights. 'So, this is it. No going back now. With this video will be another data packet. I took some scrapings from the hull and shot some images as best as I can. Sadly, infra-red is dead, or I'd be able to look for any signs of life.'

Wilding leaned down to look at the floor. 'It's not that different to some of our advanced ships. The hull is various panels sealed together. I can't work out exactly how. I haven't got time to analyse it further.'

She pointed towards the horizon. 'That's the direction I'm going. I circled around here where it's flat and I can't see a way inside. It looks like the terrain changes slightly, so I am hoping there's a hatch, or I'll have to cut my way in. That wouldn't be ideal as I risk breaching any air pockets.'

Wilding started walking, a strange loping style designed to ensure at all times she was attached to the surface. She made it seem effortless, though Parynski knew it was only through a lot of experience that she could move so efficiently.

The footage cut again. When it returned, based on the meta data attached to the file, it was some six hours later. She'd spent days at a time in an EVA suit previously, sometimes in combat situations, but Parynski knew Dee was in a bad way. She was now in a trench, wide enough for two to walk alongside each other. There were rails bolted to each side at differing heights. Dee had extended her own tether from her backpack and looped it through a catch at the end.

The sound crackled and came back on.

'Sorry about that, forgot I had an audience. You've not missed much. I stopped filming to save battery power. I found this opening, and the edge of what seemed to be a sort of cloaking mechanism. It seems to be failing, maybe we did this thing some real damage when we hit it.'

Wilding grunted as she adjusted her suit. 'For the record, I'm feeling remarkably good for a corpse. Probably won't last, well it can't. The suit has patched me up and not seeing the mess my legs are in is making me feel far happier.'

# THE TRITON RUN

The camera moved forward as the floor sloped downwards into the dark, and the walls rose around her. Wilding made small talk to fill the silence. After a few minutes, it became apparent to Parynski that there was another source of light. Dee had spotted it too.

'Oh shit. We have life. Well, we have light.'

She knelt on one knee as best she could, shining the helmet beam onto the luminous strips, which produced a dull glow at ankle level. Having captured the image, she stood and cautiously continued.

Parynski estimated Wilding must have travelled at least two hundred metres horizontally in the trench, more importantly, some twenty metres downward. She looked up to show the ceiling above her, ahead there was a door which looked fairly similar to an airlock. Just before it, the railing ended and Wilding unhooked her tether, checking her boots were working to keep her attached to the surface. She tentatively placed a glove on the surface of the door.

'Looks remarkably normal. What I need to be careful about is causing a breach and emptying the whole ship of whatever atmosphere there might be in there.'

Torchlight played across the doorway, revealing what was some sort of opening mechanism. A thin handle was clearly identifiable within a small circular recess to the side of the doorway. The door itself was solid, with no window.

'There must be some sort of camera here to monitor the outside of the door,' she said as she looked around the area, seemingly without spotting anything obvious. Despite the illumination from the strips, it was still fairly dark. Parynski wondered if the ship was dead, and the lighting was part of an old automated legacy system, designed to respond to activity by the airlock.

Wilding reached towards the handle, gripping it easily and commenting it was surprisingly thin for what could be a physically demanding task if the lock seized up. She pulled it outwards, and it smoothly came away. She then tried to turn it one way, nothing.

'Idiot, I still try to open bottle tops the wrong way!' laughed Wilding before twisting it the other way. It turned easily, supported by some sort of assistance mechanism. After three spins, the door moved inwards and then slid out of the way, revealing a plain metallic chamber inside.

'Ok, I'm into the airlock.' Wilding paused for a moment and then visibly jumped as similar luminous panels to those outside came on, giving the chamber an eerie light. She audibly took some deep breaths and stepped inside, attaching herself to another rail inside.

She had no idea what the gravity situation would be like inside.

Bar the rail the airlock was empty. It was approximately fifteen feet wide and thirty long and on the far side there was another door, wider than the one just entered through. Wilding turned momentarily to check the door she had come through was still open, before crossing the chamber. Just as she reached the far side and stepped towards a small porthole cut into the inner door, the image cut out.

'Fuck!' Parynski jumped out of his seat in frustration. 'Skydancer, where's the rest of that? I need it now!' he bellowed as he paced round the bridge.

The ship responded. 'Captain, that is the end of the visual footage contained in that packet of data. I can provide you with a summary of some of the technical data, but there is no more film at this present time.'

# 17

# JUDE

*Top of the Tsiolkovsky Space Elevator*

The *whump* of the small rocket that one of the attackers fired meant those about to come out had no chance. Smoke rolled out of the room after the impact and a nearby ceiling panel came clattering onto the floor. The guard who had shouted a futile warning keeled over, having taken a shot to the head. Zander instinctively reached to check him, just as three attackers closed in and kicked him away.

Jude had to act now before they were all dead. She gritted her teeth and swung the tray into the ankle of the guard stood by her. He released one hand from his rifle to reach down, but she was already on the move, pulling the leg she had hit from under him. Punches weren't going to work with lightly armoured pressure suits. The man tumbled over, and she grabbed at his weapon.

In a blur, Jude used the rifle to lever herself up, and she then smashed the butt through the face plate before rolling away. She fired off a burst to the attacker nearest Reuben before she rolled behind a pillar for cover, taking a good look at the positions of the other attackers. She wanted to draw them away from Zander so Reuben could get him to safety. Keeping herself low, she ran from the pillar, back towards the counter she had originally been lying next to.

Jude winced as she heard screams, then a handful of shots.

# THE TRITON RUN

The female hostages.

She ran, trying to keep low whilst firing rapidly. As expected, the remaining attackers all directed their fire towards her. She dropped the attacker who had fired the rocket as he was too slow to switch back to his pistol. Whilst she couldn't stop to watch, she became aware that Reuben was also on the move, engaging those near him and grabbing a weapon. She slid over the counter and dropped behind it in a heap. Too slow. She'd taken a shot to the left shoulder. It burnt like a bastard and her face stung with tiny shrapnel cuts. She curled up behind the thickest part of the counter as shots rained around her, occasionally firing off a volley of fire towards where she thought the attackers were.

Then the shots pinging around her stopped.

'Jude, help me secure the President,' came a voice, panting hard. Reuben.

'I think we got all of them,' he said. Her tactics had worked, those she hadn't taken down had been put down by Reuben.

She pulled herself up, peering over the top. Zander was curled up in a ball, with Reuben stood over him. The President was covered in blood; he'd taken some severe punishment. Reuben swung his weapon around as he covered the area. Jude put a shot into the twitching body of an attacker and then immediately admonished herself. She swallowed down the bloodlust, and through the blood and grime, she smiled. 'Never have you looked so masculine, you bastard, but for goodness' sake, take some cover. You're exposed there. There are probably others. I'll cover you.'

Reuben waved her towards him. 'We need to move quickly. Only one got away.' He swung his weapon over his shoulder as he used both arms to lift the President up. Zander was barely conscious. His face had taken multiple impacts and was swelling up. His left leg was a bloody mess. Jude was sure he'd been shot there, probably to restrict his mobility.

Jude cautiously stepped around her hiding place; her view

limited by the smoke billowing out of the doorway where the President's team had met their end. She suspected there was a fire in there. 'We can't be sure help is coming. Let's hide and hold on as we don't know if they will counterattack…'

A bang. Reuben dropped in front of her, a huge pool of red spreading from his back. Jude howled in despair, dropping to her knees by Zander and emptied her cartridge into the smoke. It was the smoke that had probably saved her from being taken down by whoever had shot Reuben. She was hit again in the leg and dropped on top of Zander's prone figure, her weapon slipping out of her fingers. It was all over.

She was only vaguely aware of the figures who appeared around them. A second squad dressed the same as the first. They pulled her off Zander and forced her to stand. Her leg hurt.

'Guarantee you live a bit longer. Pick up the President and help him walk to the launch pad.'

She couldn't fight back. She nodded, pulling Zander up and putting her good arm around him. He came to slightly, eyes struggling to focus. Together, they could limp along, she thought.

'Just so we are clear, you have two uses, firstly to look after him and secondly to make sure he co-operates.'

Jude guessed what would happen if he didn't.

# 18

# SQUIRE

*Onboard the BSV*

Squire had worked hard to kit out the storage bays just in case there were survivors. The chances of finding any were negligible; he grimly acknowledged he'd be better served preparing a morgue. The salvage and recovery gear were all in order, and Paisley had prepared a preliminary salvage plan. They'd got no chance of moving the object on their own. Squire hoped to be able to secure it, assess it and then direct the operation to transport it to the shipyards off Neptune.

With a growing smudge on the scopes, he'd done what he always did to control his anxiety, took Zefyrex. He knew he'd have to address his addiction; it had contributed to a lot of his failings, yet it also provided a solution, albeit temporary, to his mental health concerns. The recent videos of Wilding haunted him, whether awake or asleep, replacing his usual nightmares. She'd been the CO of his Platoon, the "Guild of Defiants" they'd called themselves. It would hit them all hard because of the way she'd been treated after Buchanan.

He'd fallen asleep in his command chair again after another shot. The lighting suddenly came on and music blasted out of the PA to disturb him. He opened his eyes and groaned.

'Paisley, you'd better have warmed me some coffee if you seriously want to wake me like that!' He stretched as best he could in his harness. The com system pinged, and Paisley spoke, knowing Squire preferred speech to subvocalising communications via his Chip.

'I received a message two hours ago from Bruce Parynski wanting to speak to you. He said it was important. Conscious you've not properly slept for days and were in a deep sleep, I've arranged for a call back. I've also a series of reports for you from Muller regarding salvage materials and the intercept courses of a 'roid carrier that's been made available.

Coffee is freshly brewed in the ready room, and I'll put the video link through there.'

Paisley was too efficient, a deliberate plan to get him to pull himself together quickly. By the time he began the conference call, Squire was awake and refreshed. The initial conversation was stilted whilst the com system adapted to the distance between them. It had been a while since they had spoken, but such was their relationship they picked up from last time. Parynski complained Jude wasn't returning his messages. He wondered if she had been sent undercover again already. He was now beyond the asteroid belt and on a heading for Jupiter to get a gravity boost. They talked about the videos from Wilding, both gutted. Parynski noted that it was the first time since Buchanan that they had worked for the same boss. They discussed how the presence of Wilding made the whole event box office, whatever the background of the ship the Scout had collided with.

Bruce continued with small talk. 'Typical that I'm travelling all that way, and you won't even be there to buy me a drink.' They both laughed.

Squire could tell that Parynski wanted to talk about something else, so eventually he chided him. 'Come on then, Bruce, what is it?'

Parynski sounded relieved to be asked. 'There's another video from Dee. She did a respectable job of getting the footage out and Arden's team say they're all over it. It's the last one we think. I wanted us to talk before you see it. It was actually Roo's idea, but she's right.'

'What makes you think it's the last one?'

'I just felt, having seen this, you might want some company. Shit, my job is as lonely at times as yours and you're heading into the unknown here.'

Squire wanted to snipe back about being fine, annoyed he'd been kept out of the loop even if they felt it was in his best interests. He didn't. Parynski knew him too well.

'Thanks. So, what is this?'

'It came in a later data packet, same source and signature.'

'Ok, show me.'

The screen before Squire switched from a split of Parynski's face and a standard info readout for the BSV to a frozen close up of an illuminated metal panel. The image broke up several times before solidifying. The camera then moved and spun to face the helmet of a space suit. Wilding. The heat shield on the face plate had been raised. She looked exhausted, but managed a grin. The image jumped again; she was manually holding the camera she'd unhooked from her helmet.

'Ok, this is the epilogue. Like a Director's Cut of a movie, I've come back to give you some additional footage. I figured I may as well whilst I can. Once I got inside the inner door whilst I was still recording, nothing was being broadcast. I went back to the surface to send you what I recorded. I couldn't record it all as the hard drive played up, and I needed to ensure I could send you what I found.'

Wilding's face dropped; grin clearly forced. 'So, this really is it. I guess I was hoping inside I'd find some walking and talking oxygen breather who'd rescue me…well it's not to be. I feel blessed to have been the first, I better had have been the first, to see what I have seen, and I hope it'll improve my place in the history books. Good luck to whoever comes next…'

Her breathing was erratic, and she winced in pain.

'So… I am going to sit here whilst the footage broadcasts. Then I'll say goodbye and head back inside. There are a couple of other directions I want to try before…well you know.'

The screen went blank before the picture was restored. Parynski confirmed that what came next was the earlier footage that

# THE TRITON RUN

Wilding had taken but which formed the last received broadcast.

Wilding was moving forward cautiously, her suit's floods sending their beams out directly ahead. There was no commentary. The only sound accompanying the footage was laboured breathing and occasional slurping from a water tube in her helmet. For several minutes she moved down the corridor, only stopping once to check the supports in the legs of her suit. Squire and Parynski talked about the implications of the suit running out of power and at what point would the power assisted walking switch off to divert power to the core requirements of the suit?

The corridor sloped away at a steep angle. The ceiling was rock, the walls were the same dull metal as in the corridor outside, with the floor a matt black. It was impossible to get a decent look at it, though it seemed to be a slightly adhesive or padded surface. The luminous strips set near the floor in many places appeared to have failed.

'If you wonder why I'm quiet, it's because I am absolutely shitting myself,' Wilding whispered.

After descending what was the equivalent of two storeys, she came to a junction where the tunnel widened. The chamber had a slightly raised ceiling compared to the corridor and three openings. One went off to each side, the other carried on downwards. To her left was a sealed door of the same style as the external airlock. This time the manual override was missing, and a console of sorts was built into the wall. It looked quite a basic unit, with some forty-eight different buttons. Dee tapped a few of them, receiving no reaction. There were markings on some, so she directed light onto them.

'For the geeks out there, see if you can make sense of this lot. While the buttons are being pressed, there's no feedback. I could've done with Dunk to hack it, but even he couldn't work if there's no power.'

Wilding told them she'd decided to press on deeper into the ship, so continued straight ahead. The corridor widened significantly and there were multiple sealed doors on either side. She looked up and whilst it was difficult to make out clearly, it looked as if above her were wide gantries on either side. She pointed out more doors that were only accessible from the upper level. There were no handholds or ladders that would enable her to climb up, so she carried on her way.

'Clearly, someone or something has lived here. All seems powered down at the moment. These luminous panels, where they do work, may operate off a different power grid. Those upstairs gantries are unusual, as there's no way up for me. Suggests either alien monkeys, birds or they have jets in their suits. Doesn't look like it was a gravity free environment either. There is gravity, slightly less than earth. No idea how it's powered because we aren't spinning.'

The new corridor continued its inward path before levelling out. She passed what seemed to be a storage area containing a variety of sealed units fitted into the wall. Wilding's gloves were too big to get into the handles and lever them open. Using one of her tools, a door set at waist height sprung open. The cupboard was full of what looked like tools an electrician might use. The sizes and shapes of the tools were familiar, albeit seemingly designed for smaller or more delicate hands. There were also tied spools of cable.

Satisfied none of the other doors would open, she continued. The corridor ended at what might have been a lift shaft. There were grooves cut into the walls above and below, though no sign of any cables or a lift car. The torch could only reach so far and all that could be made out was what might have been another opening up above her.

The gap was probably twenty feet. Too far just to jump. The corridor appeared to continue on the other side, with a slightly wider entrance.

Wilding said, 'I've got enough juice in the thrusters to get me across and back again a couple of times.'

Wilding leant out into the chasm, clipping her suit to a pipe, peering upwards. Squire shouted out, as Parynski had done first time he had seen the film, as Wilding momentarily slipped, falling flat on her face, legs dangling over the edge. Just as it appeared as if the weight of her suit would drag her over the edge, the tether held, and she jolted still.

Panting hard, she pulled herself back up and crawled to the wall where she clung onto the pipe, laying there for several minutes, getting her composure back.

'Ok, that was embarrassing.'

With a grunt and without much dignity, she pulled herself up the piping to her feet, where she paused again as her breathing slowed.

'Ok, I think I'm now starting to reach the point of no return, but I don't want to be talking to myself. That would be a waste. So, I think I'll get over the gap and see what I find. I'll then retrace my steps if I can and head back to the surface, where I'll broadcast this footage. If I have any power left in the suit, I will then come back inside and…'

She didn't need to finish the sentence.

Squire watched in equal measures of trepidation and awe as his old leader unclipped the tether, took a run and used her jets to get across the gap. It was no mean feat. EVA suit jets were not designed for internal use, certainly not in tight spaces like this. On the other side, Wilding paused. Squire bit his lip. Dee was getting slower and slower now, though he was strangely reassured. She must have got back to the surface, or he wouldn't be seeing this.

She swung her helmet around, taking in the new corridor. It was similar to the old one, save it quickly widened. Again, there was an inaccessible upper tier.

'I should've taken a look up there.' muttered Wilding whilst the torch beam played over the gantry above her head. The beam flashed over various objects, though nothing appeared out of the ordinary.

Wilding continued walking, the image bobbing up and down. She was limping more now. Eventually the corridor became an opening so wide the sides and the ceiling were hidden in darkness. Squire's stomach tightened as he realised that ahead there was light. The floor again ended, but this time, the view could not have been different.

# 19

# PARYNSKI

*Onboard the Skydancer*

Squire and Parynski repeatedly discussed the part of the video where the central chamber was found. They'd watched Wilding's footage together and independently. After a few days Squire had gone silent, according to Paisley he was busy with the refit. Parynski knew to give his friend space if he wanted it. He had his own routine chores to attend to anyway and was concerned he'd heard nothing from Jude. He asked a friend of Jude's, Roo, to find out what was going on. She was a Tapper and had been liaising with him over Dee. If anyone could find out about Jude, it was her. Even if she were undercover, she'd find out. Parynski had also been distracted by the ship's weaponry AI coming on automatically and targeting a tanker that had been running alongside him for a few hours, unaware of the status and capabilities of the Skydancer. It had then pulled away, heading for a rendezvous elsewhere.

Unable to sleep, he put the footage on again. The chamber Wilding had reached made Parynski think of a citadel dug out of rock. It was still largely dark, though better lit than the previous rooms Wilding had been in. It was dark at present, lit only by Wilding's beams. It was, Dee had estimated, well over one hundred meters in diameter. The camera couldn't see the ceiling, sensors reporting a dome high above her. All round the side of the rocky walls were cut out walkways and shelves, not dissimilar in design to those seen earlier. The far side of the chamber was shrouded in darkness, but Parynski presumed, based on what he could see, that it was circular and that one could almost walk a full circuit on each level. Each level had several tunnels leading off it. Some were simply cave like openings hewn from the rock, others contained closed doors.

The speaker crackled, and Wilding continued. 'Something you won't be able to appreciate in TV land is that it's windy here! Yes, wind inside a spaceship. It's not that strong, but I can feel it, or should I say, see it. Some grit has just blown across my visor.'

The camera came to rest on the centre of the chamber. Wilding looped her tether on a rail and took in the scene. Rising out of the darkness were dozens of stone spires. Made out of the same material as the walls, they were all different. Some had wide platforms at the top, others were pointed with odd places here and there on which someone could stand. It reminded Parynski of the Hoodoos that Jude had seen on a site trip when visiting Arizona's Chiricahua National Monument. The spires varied in height, some carried on upwards towards the ceiling, vanishing into the darkness.

'What?!'

The image jumped as Wilding reacted to something out of shot.

The camera turned to the left, midway across the other side of the chamber the walkways ended. In a gap of about thirty metres, there appeared to be a rising giant red sun. The huge orb looked like it was just starting to rise from an imaginary horizon, and within moments, the gloom in the chamber lifted slightly.

Wilding twisted round, trying to work out where the image was being projected from.

'It's like the bat house at the zoo,' Wilding mused, 'Except without the bats. It's certainly not our Sun anyway, that's for sure.'

Parynski wondered what star it was, and whether it had been studied or viewed before. Wilding unclipped her tether, stepped back from the edge, and cautiously made her way round the circuit. It was solid rock beneath her feet here, inlaid every now and again with the dark panelling she had stood on before. Some of the other galleries were largely metal, scaffolding type structures running from rocky outcrop to outcrop. Inset into the outer wall, at small intervals, were what appeared to be either doorways or windows. A solid opaque material, possibly reinforced glass, formed a black panel that was approximately seven feet tall. The camera moved closer as Wilding leaned towards them. The surface seemed impenetrable. 'The cam probably can't pick it up. I think there's something behind these screens.'

Inset into smaller panels alongside each larger panel was a small control console.

Wilding tapped it with her glove. 'Seems to be no juice in any of these circuits, though there is definitely some power beyond the lighting because that Sun show won't be coming from nowhere.'

The next half dozen panels were the same. Wilding estimated there could be several hundred on each level before turning back to marvel at the image of the sun. Further round the balcony, a light came on behind one of the panels. Wilding was too far away to clearly see what had happened, but the panel had turned transparent, and a pale-yellow light glowed from behind a dark shadow.

The image cut suddenly, and he was back with Wilding stood outside the original entry point, back on the surface of the alien craft.

'Don't mind admitting I pretty much filled my space suit when I saw that. And yes, me, the professional astronaut, the ruthless Butcher of Buchanan, ran like a coward. Please don't remember me just for that.'

Parynski appreciated his friend's gallows humour.

'Well, in a moment I'll click send for the last time and to save battery stop filming. You've seen as much as I have, so whoever comes next should be better prepared… maybe braver.'

Wilding sniffed. For all her false bravado, she had been crying.

'Who knows how any of us would react in your shoes, Dee, who knows?' he whispered to her.

'Anyway, I've got enough air, I think, to get back to the chamber and see what is behind that light. Keep your fingers crossed or pray for me that whatever or whoever is waiting is friendly and can help me.'

The screen went black.

# 20

## ROO

*Triton Observatory Mobile Operations Centre*

Despite their seriousness, Roo was enjoying her new duties, focussed on supporting the effort to recover the Kuiper Scout. It made a pleasant change to the petty commercial hacking that Arden often asked her to do.

In between that she followed the news elsewhere, had spent her break watching the footage from a freighter that was high in orbit above the space elevator attack, relieved to hear that after the attackers had escaped the emergency services had been able to get the fires that were set under control and that the tether had been secured. It was an audacious attack, and the President had been kidnapped. No ransom had yet been requested.

She'd been reading conspiracy theories about how the attack was being used by President Zander's deputy, Lindstrom, to seize power. She was behind it, they said, as she'd already recalled the senate and was seeking to be installed as President. It seemed a big jump to Roo to suggest she was involved in the kidnap. Zander's supporters were suggesting that not enough was being done to trace the President, arguing that though he was no longer that popular, he should be protected at all costs. How could someone so famous, so important, just vanish?

Roo could have kicked herself when the message came in from Bruce Parynski, worried that his daughter, her friend, had gone quiet, hoping that she'd be able to trace her one way or another. Roo had asked when he'd last seen her, heart sinking when she realised she was on the elevator when the attack had happened. All bodies had been identified, so she quickly concluded that Jude must have been kidnapped alongside the President.

She told Arden she'd be off duty for another couple of hours. When she explained it was to trace a friend, he agreed, knowing she'd do it anyway, though grumbled at the link to Zander. 'That bastard deserves everything that comes his way. And don't be distracting Parynski, he's got my new ship!'

She went into the Tank and loaded up her Unet drive. A mosaic of images representing different data sources appeared, forming a wall of sorts around her. It was synchronised footage of the attack from the arrival of the attacker's craft until it launched and escaped local cameras. There were two dozen feeds, ranging from the closest ship where she'd watched the attack in real time, some from the closest habitats and satellites where she'd had the images enhanced and blown up as best as possible. There was also a number of exterior cams mounted on the elevator launch bay itself. Where she felt like there was missing footage, she tapped into local systems to get what was needed. It concerned her that nobody else had seemingly looked at this evidence. To her disappointment, there was only one piece of blurry footage from inside the elevator itself. The attackers had ensured internal CCTV was down.

She set to work, watching the footage and imaging over and over again. The imaging of the attackers wasn't helpful, so Roo set running another analysis of the 3D images against known records for various groups who had been blamed for the other attacks on Zander's avatars.

Struggling to get a useful image of the attackers, she moved onto the ship that had delivered them and then extracted the survivors along with Zander and, seemingly, Jude. The ship used couldn't be easily identified. All indicators of manufacturer, model and owner had been removed. It seemed to be flying with false panelling, added purely to throw the authorities off the scent. Whilst not expecting a response, Roo set off another search for large body parts coming for sale in the scrap market. It was likely they had jettisoned the superfluous bodywork once they were away from Earth orbit.

Opening a screen showing the shuttle as it took off, Roo programmed a Nav AI to run thousands of variations for the course and then set about getting other searches to cross reference the outcomes. Whilst there were infinite theoretical courses to take, what they could have done, in reality, was narrower. They hadn't gone to the Moon; they hadn't gone inward towards Venus because they had they would have been spotted. They hadn't entered the Earth's atmosphere because the ship wasn't capable.

Roo picked up the ship on a path out beyond Mars. The course was unusual, away from the recognised shipping lanes. She obtained access to some inward-looking Jovian Sentinels who had picked up a craft that matched a close enough description. The problem was that this ship had been found abandoned and drifting by a passing tanker. They'd not taken the care needed to identify the craft properly and had simply nudged it out of the way of the shipping lanes after attaching a warning beacon. There was no time to investigate it further.

Roo set an AI to analyse the neighbourhood at that time, and cross-referencing a variety of sources was able to identify two other ships that could well have intercepted the ship's flight path. Chances were that one of them was a decoy, so she had to review both. Both courses ended within the asteroid belt. Hunter apps fed back that one of the ships was almost certainly unmanned due to its dramatic course changes and speed. If there were any humans on board, they would have been killed. Assuming nobody would go to all this effort to kidnap the President to either deliberately or negligently kill him, she dismissed that ship as a decoy.

For the likely suspect craft, she had no detail as to its origin or specification. Based on the one scan of it she had, it appeared to be an ex-military, long-range shuttle. It didn't seem armed. Its course took it into an area of the belt that was no longer known for its activity.

There were no artificial habitats in the area, only asteroids that had been mined or used to house bases.

None of the rocks in the new, narrower, search area contained any inhabited asteroids, though it was feasible that pirates or miners had taken refuge in a mothballed facility. There were an even smaller number of possibilities that could house a suitably sized dock, and which would presumably be of a large enough size to house a terrorist cell.

Roo's attention was drawn to a target that caught her eye. She pulled up a more detailed image to examine, along with a series of schematics for an old mine and its accommodation facilities. Floating in front of her were two similar shaped asteroids that rotated around each other.

'A binary pair! How rare are these?!' she said out loud to herself. She felt pleased with herself, though she had no idea what she'd do next. 'Antiope 90, here we come.'

# 21

# JUDE

*Antiope Mining Facility*

Jude drifted in and out of consciousness numerous times, never quite sure what was real and what had been dreamt. She first came round in pain whilst being dragged, in an EVA suit that barely fitted, through a departure tube and into a shuttle. She'd been dropped on the floor in the air lock and passed out again.

Later, she had woken strapped to a couch, surrounded by space suited figures. She remembered a horrendous pain in her skull and one of them remarking, 'She hasn't got one, she's had it removed. It's empty behind the scar tissue.' She'd blacked out again.

The next time she came to, she was unrestrained. She was in a pitch-black room, curled up on some sort of cot. Even allowing a few moments for her eyes to adjust didn't help. She couldn't make out a thing, and even stretching out into the dark was fruitless. She didn't have the strength to do anything further. She slumped back and tried to calibrate her senses. She was naked but warm. There was considerable background noise, different to before, so she was confident she was now on a different ship. She then realised that she wasn't quite naked, her lower left leg was strapped, and her shoulder wound was covered in sealant. Both areas were pain free, though there was a small burning sensation at the back of her neck, where they had looked for a Chip.

These people were professionals. The audacious nature of

their attack proved that. She tried to go through recent events, and it became too much. Jude cried softly to herself for what felt like an age, crying for her friends who had died and crying in despair at her predicament.

She had no idea where she was, where she was going, or what was intended for her.

Eventually, she ran out of tears and slept again.

She then woke somewhere new. Jude still hurt all over, but slowly her thoughts turned to survival. It was Zander that they had come for and she had to presume he was still alive wherever she was now. A rock ceiling above suggested she was no longer on a ship and there was no background engine noise or vibration. She curled up into a foetal position, trying to listen for any clues that may help. She could hear voices nearby, the sound of doors opening and closing. After the energy expended in her grieving, the concentration needed to try and listen for any detail quickly proved too much and she passed out again.

## 22

## PARYNSKI

*Onboard the Skydancer*

Parynski dropped into a coms chair and flicked on the imager, replacing an enhanced external view with Roo's face. She looked exhausted.

'Unaccounted for? What happened?'

She looked incredulous. 'You've not heard about the elevator? Shit, it was weeks ago,

I presumed you knew. With all the stuff about the Kuiper Scout going on, I forgot to mention it at the time. I'd no idea then that it might involve Jude.'

Parynski pulled himself forward to the end of his seat. 'What's going on Roo?'

She showed him some of the footage she'd access to. Usually, being a Ferryman required every bit of concentration he had to get a ship that was not suited to long journeys to its destination. He'd be constantly fighting with the ship, carrying out repairs and trying to eke every last bit of power he could out of an engine. He didn't usually have time to worry about the outside world. That's why his marriage had struggled.

His stomach turned with fear and guilt. This trip had been easy. He had dropped into his usual routine and spent quite a bit of time watching sims where he could interact with an avatar of Mary. He knew that wasn't healthy, but he couldn't help himself. He'd resolved to try to move on once he'd reached Triton. Most of the work he'd done on the Skydancer had been because he was curious about the ship; it was both luxurious and military spec in equal measure. In fact, he'd never heard of a military vessel that could do some of the things the Skydancer seemed capable of. He was ahead of schedule, beyond the asteroid belt and heading towards Jupiter.

'A rescue team went on board the elevator and identified the dead. Everyone is accounted for except for President Zander and Jude. These attackers did a pretty gruesome job. The only assumption can be that they were abducted.'

Parynski slumped forward, head in hands. He took a deep breath and looked up, looking Roo in the eye.

'Well, if there's nobody, then she must be ok. She's a strong girl. There's no way she escaped with the President?'

She shook her head, 'Sorry. I watched it myself. One ship got away; I think they must have been on board. We've had no demands yet.'

'Ok, what do you know? Where's she likely to be?'

She grimaced. 'This is where you may be able to help. You need to turn around… I'll give you a new course shortly. The ship was discovered abandoned in a shipping lane. I'm working on the idea they switched ships and headed to an old mining habitat on a binary asteroid called Antiope.'

Parynski nodded. 'Ok, well, I'm probably on the right ship to help. Let's find her and then inform the authorities. They'll be better equipped for a rescue.'

Roo took a deep breath.

'I'll send what data I have. The official investigators have gone on a wild goose chase and are now distracted. Seems there were two ships. We tracked the decoy, which headed into a more congested area. It was an automated ship, I think, based on its performance; local enforcement were a bit more aggressive than needed when trying to slow it down. It was booby trapped. Three local ships were lost, plus a local tanker was severely damaged. All sector efforts are being put into the clean-up of the debris. They seem to be taking it all at face value and are likely to announce the President was lost in the next day or so. Convenient for Lindstrom, it seems, not that there's any suggestion she's involved.'

Parynski struggled to keep up, interrupting her. 'What do I do?'

'You turn around and follow a search pattern I send you. We keep our eyes peeled and work out what the hell we do when we find them. I bet we'll end up at Antiope. I'll make sure the authorities know about it and send help; our problem is that there's nobody near in the belt so any help will be some time. At the very least, we can locate them.'

Parynski nodded. 'Wonder how Arden will react to me arriving late and taking his new toy on a bit of a diversion? If I have to, I'll go and get Jude myself. Pity I don't have Wilding with me.'

## 23

## WILDING

*The Dark*

After the scream, a stillness came over her. She wasn't quite sure why she'd screamed, but after she'd finished, a calmness enveloped her. The scream was perhaps a reaction to having tried to hold things together. Wilding was surprised she'd been able to scream, though in this subconscious world nothing felt real.

She was somewhere else.

This couldn't be right. She'd been on board the alien spaceship in that chamber when her air ran out. Maybe this was the first part of whatever was next, the afterlife. She was stood in a landscape she didn't recognise. Alien. It reminded her a little of Mars. The sky was a cloudy orange, dusty. Away to her right was a bright red sun setting, similar to what she'd seen in the chamber before it had gone dark. Across the terrain whirled hundreds, if not thousands, of black specks. They wheeled in circles, driving upwards before swooping down out of sight beyond a rocky ridge. Some sort of bird, she guessed. Wilding could hear a high-pitched clicking and howling. Perhaps they were talking to each other.

As far as the eye could see was a rocky, red wasteland. Away to the left it was dull and flat until, at the horizon, she could make out what appeared to be a city. Tall skyscrapers reached upwards and even from this distance she could see the light pollution.

She turned away from it and back towards the setting sun. It was setting beyond a raised ridge and all the activity seemed to be that way. The city was too far for her to walk to, anyway. She was still in her space suit, minus her helmet. She probably should have felt hot, but she had no concept of temperature. If this wasn't an afterlife, perhaps it was just a simulation. For a moment, her heart leapt. Perhaps she'd been rescued, and this was an induced coma.

She started to walk towards the ridge, picking up pace. Her thick boots kicked up dust as she moved. The chattering and squawking noise grew in volume, drowning out the sound of her own footsteps. She didn't really want to take this route. She felt she had no choice. It was as if her actions here were being driven from elsewhere. Maybe it was a sim.

There was no sign of life to either side, so she focussed on what was ahead. It was hard going because there didn't seem to be a path. After a hundred yards or so, she reached the top of the ridge. The ground evened out, and she took in the scene. If what she'd seen on the alien spaceship was real, and she doubted everything right now, then this wasn't the afterlife. Something else was going on.

Wilding wobbled slightly as she took in the scale of what she found. She took a step backward and dropped onto one knee to maintain her balance. A slight breeze whipped at her face, causing her eyes to water.

Opening up ahead of her was a canyon. She'd never been to the Grand Canyon, but this was what she imagined that must be like. As far as the eye could see was a huge crater. The rim, she estimated from her raised position, ran a mile or so away from her in either direction before curving slightly and spreading out, heading away to the horizon where her focus blurred. She estimated it was many hundreds of metres deep.

The huge opening wasn't empty; there was a river running towards her position before curving away in a U-bend. The river was probably wide, though from her elevated position it looked like a blue ribbon laid out on a dirty orange carpet. Throughout the canyon she could see mesas, cliffs, valleys, and thousands of spires. The spires were all unique, rising hundreds of metres with platforms cut or dug out of them at various points. Some sprouted branches that speared out in different directions.

With the sun going down, it was already getting darker in the canyon. What dominated the view was the swarm. Solid black in places, particularly on the platforms that were built into the spires, whirling flecks of black in the air. There were hundreds of flocks wheeling round in the sky, coming together to form huge black swirls that flew high, as if on drafts of air before splintering into dozens of smaller groups that dived into the shadows. Flocks disintegrated before forming new groups that wheeled across the sky in a ballet. There must have been millions of them.

Whether it was the sudden lack of warmth from the receding sun or something else, Wilding started to feel increasingly cold and isolated. It would likely be dark soon, and there was nowhere to go. The city on the horizon was too far away, and she didn't want to spend the night out in the open. Descending into the canyon made sense.

At this point, Wilding mentally shook herself. This couldn't be real, despite feeling so clear. She concluded that whatever was going on was with good reason, aimed at educating her about something. If she were to remain here, wherever or whatever this was, she needed to find answers, before that she needed to find somewhere safe. Instinctively, she wanted to get away from the canyon and the swarms appeared quite menacing. She couldn't be certain from this distance, but they seemed to be the same creatures that she'd found in the tanks on the spaceship. They reminded her of a prehistoric pterodactyl.

Away to her right was a narrow path that took a shallow route along the canyon wall, descending into the shadow. She took it, her right hand touching the rock as she did. Occasionally, she paused to grab hold of an outcrop whilst she had to catch her breath or to check the stability of the path ahead, which was increasingly hard to see in the gloom. There was still quite a strong wind below the lip of the canyon. No doubt the bird creatures were using it to assist in their efforts to fly.

She'd been travelling downwards for about thirty minutes when she had nearly fallen after being buzzed by one of the creatures. Wilding hoped it was an accident, though had a growing sense it was deliberate. She was being checked out. After being buzzed again minutes later, a wing tip actually hit her arm, causing her to lose her balance. As her left foot slipped from under her, she dropped to her knees. Wilding would have given anything for a rifle at this point. She pushed herself back into the wall, hoping the shadows would give her safety. She should have stayed above ground; she'd made a mistake.

Whilst she crouched there, she spotted a glint of light reflecting on a silver surface. In the distance, at the bottom of the canyon, was a squat silver object with wings. It was hard to judge its size from where she was, but to Wilding it was unmistakably a shuttle of some sort. She resolved to head for that. Her thinking at this point was being influenced by the noise. It was starting to overwhelm her senses. A constant squawking and screeching dominated her. Taking a deep breath, she resolved to keep heading downwards towards the shuttle when she realised how closely she was being watched. There was a swarm, perhaps a dozen or so of these creatures, wheeling around perhaps fifty feet away. They were all watching her. She could feel it. In the deepening dark, it was hard to see their eyes, even though they flew and glided in a way that kept their long faces pointed towards her. There was an intelligence at work here, an intelligence she'd never encountered before. If she was dreaming, this wasn't from her own imagination.

The swarm moved nearer, the creatures performing cartwheels and pirouettes right in front her. She kept her eyes on them, awaiting the next flyby. Her right hand clung desperately onto the wall. She realised it was holding on tight to a small outcrop and was in spasm. If she were knocked off the path, the fall would kill her. Though she might already be dead.

She tried to ignore the pain and her left-hand darted round on the floor around her for a rock or anything she could use as a weapon. She was distracted momentarily as she thought she'd found something before the rock crumbled in her hand. In that second, two of the creatures swooped across to perched either side of her.

There was no escape. They stood tall over her crouched form. They pushed wings out to their full extremes, blocking out most of the remaining light. Long, thin faces loomed close. She saw their eyes. They looked right through her.

Everything went black.

# 24

# ZANDER

*Antiope Mining Facility*

Zander sat alone in the canteen eating breakfast. The rows of benches and tables were mostly empty, except for two men and a woman. They were hunched over their plates chatting quietly, but stopped occasionally to look at him.

The serving hatch was still open and through it, he could hear the busy hubbub of the kitchen. He played with his food, pushing it round the plate. It wasn't that the food was bad, it was that his mind was elsewhere. Zander paused to scratch an itch on his leg where a plastic cast still covered his wound. He also felt discomfort at the back of his skull, where his Chip had once been.

Two weeks after he'd woken here, he was still suffering from what he assumed were withdrawal symptoms to the Chip and the constant flow of activity in his brain. Everything still felt slightly fuzzy, though he wondered if his captors were medicating him.

Zander didn't even know where here was. The medics who had been there when he woke had declined to answer any of his questions. He'd been allowed to potter around the complex, some doors opened when he approached, others didn't. It was quite simple. Outside of his room, he mainly frequented the mess hall and small social room where there was a gym, stereo and 3d viewer that played a huge selection of movies. There was no access to the outside universe.

Despite his presidential entourage, Zander was used to his own company. While he didn't like it, he could cope. All he could get out of anyone here was basic pleasantries. They all knew who he was. He could see it in their faces. Whoever had gone to the trouble to abduct him would almost certainly want to keep him alive, for now at least, which on the face of it was a small relief. Despite a slither of optimism Zander had started to feel defeated, he couldn't see a successful way out of this situation. They were going to win, after all.

Zander gave up on his breakfast, placed the cutlery on the plate and pushed it away. His captors were relaxed in their assessment of what he could do because he was even allowed metal utensils. He received polite nods from others who had taken their empty plates back to the hatch to be washed, and then they headed off through a doorway that was sealed to him.

'Just me and you then, Sir.'

The voice from behind him was female and whilst he couldn't remember if she had spoken to him on the Elevator, he knew who it was. He didn't have a clue who she was, though. Right now, she was the most precious person to him in the universe. His chances of surviving had also increased. He felt strangely confident of that.

He turned. The smile was incongruous to the rest of her appearance. She wore an ill-fitting jump suit, the same style that he wore, unzipped to the waist. Underneath, she had a t-shirt, and her left arm was in a sling. She looked pale, her head roughly shaved round the back, as his had been when he'd come round. She looked gaunt and weary. He smiled back and swung his legs over the bench in order to get up and walk over to her. For strangers, the hug was one you would give to a long lost loved one. She reciprocated the grip, collapsing into his arms.

'Thank fuck you are alright,' she said, head pressed into his chest.

He stepped away, holding onto her one good arm. He felt his spirits lift. 'It's great to see you. I wondered what had happened to you.'

He gestured towards the bench and gently guided her back to where he'd been sitting, noting she was limping. 'Please come join me…' He looked around nervously, 'That's if you are allowed to talk to me, nobody else seems to be.'

She sat gratefully on the bench he had taken her to, nodding with a smile.

'I think so! They told me to ask you what the rules were.'

'Let me get you something to eat. You look like you need something. I can then explain what little we know.'

Despite her weak appearance, her eyes were steely, and she looked him in the eye. 'And then we can start to work out how we fight back.'

# 25

# PARYNSKI

*Onboard the Skydancer, en route to Antiope 90*

Roo had been providing him with all she could find out about the base at Antiope, and he'd been working with the AI to assess it. Needing a break, he'd done what he always did.

He headed back to his room and called up his library of Unet sims. He had something important to do.

The sim had been created by local enforcement agencies, and Roo had managed to extract it for him. They were created as a matter of course on complex crime scenes. The process of 'dropping' into a fully immersive sim tank was always disturbing, no matter how many times you did it. Whilst your body remained in position, the mind struggled whilst its senses were overwhelmed with sensations that screamed against what it knew to be right. The initial booting up process took him into a temporary sim where he was on a beach, able to feel the sand between his toes and a warm breeze. His mind was initially conflicted, wanting to embrace the new sensations that it was being fed whilst fighting sanity checking instincts. Some never adapted to the transformation whilst those with full Unet capabilities learnt to control the urge to fight the ghosts taking over their senses and to relax into the simulations. Parynski knew that a Tapper like Roo would have found the process far more palatable.

It was a winter morning, bitterly cold, and there was snow

# THE TRITON RUN

on the floor and the leaves of the trees that faced him. He was stood in a small knot of trees in front of a darkened hulk of a building. Behind the building, rising towards the top of a range of tall hills, was a snow-covered forest. A road wound its way up the hill through the trees, snow ploughed into large piles alongside it. There was no traffic. Hovering above the road and across the horizon were dark dots standing out against the white, snow heavy sky. Military helicopters. Every now and again, he saw a red flare flash as the helicopters launched rockets into the forest towards an unseen enemy.

The cold hit him and he shivered. It was the aftermath of a battle. He set off towards the building, stepping over piles of broken branches, scorch marks and a whole host of other debris he couldn't identify. The first few bodies he came across were on the floor near the building. They were surrounded by camouflaged troops putting them into body bags before being loaded onto the armed helicopter he knew was in a clearing round the other side of the copse he'd materialised in. There were multiple 'copters in the vicinity, no ground vehicles. More armed soldiers patrolled the area, weapons raised. He knew the area like the back of his hand. He moved past some medics, and out of instinct, stepped out of the way of a patrol marching through the clearing and heading back to their transport. They were pulling out.

A small posse of reporters huddled together, surrounded by a cloud of small drones that created the footage and experience that he was a part of now. As Parynski passed them heading towards the building, their military escort came and moved them back to the ride they had hitched a lift on. He knew how the press had reported this. It wasn't good news. The town had been assaulted from multiple angles. The military had arrived too late, taking advantage of a temporary withdrawal of the attackers to regroup. They'd swooped in to rescue a handful of survivors, collect some of the dead, and assess the situation. It was a battle that couldn't be won without more losses and without flattening the forests for miles around.

The town had been under pressure for months and the state had offered a package to residents, encouraging them to evacuate so it could be abandoned. The government reminded voters that it wanted to focus efforts on defending the nearby cities. If only Mary had listened.

Parynski strode towards the main complex in the town, a large set of buildings linked by bridges and tubes. It housed a shopping arcade and various municipal buildings. As he cleared the trees, it became clear that the building was in a bad state. The roof had collapsed, black smoke billowed out of the hole forming a long plume that trailed away towards the horizon. Flames could be seen at an upper window. There was no effort to tackle the blaze. The town was being abandoned.

Parynski realised there was no sound at all from the sim, so rebooted it. His surroundings shimmered and solidified again. The noise hit like a sledgehammer; the sound of crackling from the building as it burned, lots of chatter from the troops and media, the thrum of helicopter vanes and the regular whump of rockets being launched, all interspersed with the sound of machine gun fire. A temporary perimeter had been set up and soldiers were laying down, suppressing fire to keep the attackers away whilst they attempted to extract survivors and destroy anything that would be of use after they'd withdrawn.

He found a temporary gazebo type structure where a number of officers were gathered round a selection of monitors and a console that had been wheeled off a transport. Roo had hacked the console previously for the all the information it obtained. None of it explained what had happened to Mary.

It wasn't possible to get inside the nearest entrance to the complex. The wide opening that had once been an archway of glass and steel was now a shattered mess. Steel beams twisted into awkward angles, and he could see one of the bridges joining two sides of the complex had come down. It had been a nice enough place to live, cold much of the year but picturesque and with a slow pace of life. That was one of the reasons he'd struggled to settle. Mary loved it. He turned back the way he'd come and caught a glimpse off to one side of a row of two storey wooden houses that had been gutted. The outer walls stood, but the insides hung out like a burst couch, completely shattered. There had been some resistance here, even if it was unsuccessful. Parynski knew his wife would have been at the heart of any resistance.

Out the front of the building was a pile of black debris, wood, ash, twisted metals, and melted plastic. There could quite easily be bodies in there and whilst he'd known the troops had taken limited forensic swabs, they didn't have the time to do a thorough job. Grimly, he knew this extraction attempt was a cynical attempt by the state government to make it appear it still had things under control when the reality was that it was on the run. Its weak borders were shrinking and there were a growing number of no-go areas, held by groups who had no intention of playing their part in a democratic environment. The economy was struggling and anyone with any talent would try to get off planet, seeking high paid work on the Moon and increasingly trying their luck elsewhere.

Parynski reminded himself of the aerial footage he'd seen previously from the lead recon 'copter as it had swooped in, showing Mary's street with HD footage mixed with infra-red data. It revealed little, a few front doors were open, and a couple of driveways were littered with suitcases and other belongings. It looked like attempts to evacuate in an organised fashion had been abandoned.

He strolled up towards the old house. He stared at its front porch for a moment, remembering the times she'd meet him outside when he arrived back from his long excursions. He wasn't sure why, but he explained out-loud what had happened to their daughter and before he left the sim, he resolutely told their house 'I'm going to get her back Mary, I promise she'll be safe.'

He wished he were as confident as he sounded.

# 26

## GARCIA

*Triton Observatory*

Garcia couldn't wait to reveal her findings. She and Roo were in the same room at the base on Triton. They'd logged into the conference remotely from the rest of the attendees. Arden was in his boardroom as normal with others in the group, including engineers and security staff. Some of the meetings had become repetitive and dull, with Squire still not at the locus and with just logistics to talk about. While they were all excited by the implications of Wilding's video messages, they'd exhausted the analysis they could do on the footage. Muller, the engineer, updated on progress of the building of a cradle for the object, assuming they could bring it back to Neptune.

Garcia enjoyed observing the body language of the group. They were bored. As the agenda reached her item, she knew that would change. Roo gave her a wink nobody else would have spotted. Garcia paused whilst the quality of the link stabilised. 'I think my team have traced where the alien ship came from.'

She let the news settle in, trying to control her own excitement. At present, their working theory was that it might just be an alien spaceship, despite the initial cynicism and odds against it being the case.

Arden put down his drink, trying to avoid looking annoyed at not having been warned about this in advance. 'You've tracked its journey all the way out from the solar system? Where is it from, which system?'

Garcia shook her head. 'We spent weeks looking at the work required to project that. Our starting point was to take the course the ship was likely to be on when it hit the Scout and take it all the way out of the solar system, across the Oort cloud and into whatever system it might have reached had it maintained a sensible and consistent course based on our own flight capabilities. Practically we don't know what this ship is capable of, so it's hard to be accurate unless Squire finds a log or something. Also, with all the distances involved, the potential origins are all moving as well, so it's a really hard calculation...'

She took a deep breath and continued.

'Anyway, it's simpler than that. The likely entry course into our solar system is through an area we know little about; however, I think I can safely say that, on its last leg at least, it came from just outside our range of catalogued small objects.'

Garcia pulled up a rough 3D image that shimmered into existence in front of all of them. It showed the assumed collision courses of the two vessels plotted and a line heading outwards, away from the alien ship, to a smudge that had been artificially enhanced, so it was easy to see.

'There,' she pointed, 'The alien ship departed from whatever that is and maintained a consistent course until it hit the Scout. It was headed on an insertion course to join up with Neptune's Trojans. That's all on which I can speculate. Where it came from before this remains to be seen.'

'Wow.' Muller wasn't one for words in these meetings. His surprise reflected the views of everyone watching.

'So, what is it? Another rock, another alien ship, a fleet of them, what?' Arden was already thinking ahead.

'That's what we need to find out.'

Arden looked confused. 'So, what do you mean when you say this is where the object that crashed into the Kuiper Scout originated? How certain are we?'

'As accurate as our projections allow us to be, yes. I've pulled in a lot of favours here ... the eyes of the solar system are on us.'

Again, she was interrupted, this time by Muller. 'Surely this alien...spaceship...didn't actually start out from this new object? Maybe it just used it to stopover en route from somewhere further out?'

Garcia shrugged. 'That may be a correct assumption. I hope we will find answers there.'

She updated the map to include all the catalogued areas of the Kuiper Belt, pointing out that there were many areas that had not been properly mapped. Lots of objects only carried temporary ID tags next to each of them.

'The belt has a lot of ice and rock hanging around, but it's not that congested. Most of it is so small it wouldn't cause them the Scout any problems. Shields would vaporise or melt most objects and they had a few cannons, which would've been able to deflect or destroy anything too big to navigate around. I have no idea why it didn't register the object it struck. It's simply too large not to spot at the range their scanners operate. Also, we need to know why this alien ship didn't alter its own course or avoid the collision itself. They should've spotted the Scout moving, albeit very slowly at the time, because we now know it had stopped for Wilding to carry out repairs. A spaceship is so different to the rest of the crap floating out there.'

'Anyway...' She called up an enhanced image of the object from the direction she said the alien ship had come. Small panes of information flashed all around it, confirming what Garcia had already noted. It was a comparable size to Charon, Pluto's small moon, shaped like a slightly squashed satsuma.

'It's quite big, bearing in mind where it is, though far from unique. We keep finding these sorts of things the further out we look, which is why this all seems so peculiar...'

Garcia allowed the object to rotate.

'…We can't be certain, but if you look at this side of the object, you'll notice one side has an unusual profile. It's funnel shaped. As crazy as it seems, our alien ship might've somehow been launched or expelled from inside that funnel.'

Silence. Garcia saw them react exactly how she'd done on first examination of the image.

Arden stood. 'You're saying you think the object which hit the Scout came from inside that planetoid?'

Garcia nodded. 'I call it "Propylaea". Whatever it is, whatever it's use, it's a monumental gateway in terms of our knowledge regarding what on Earth is going on.'

# 27

# ZANDER

*Antiope Mining Facility*

The only thing imposing any sort of routine on Zander and Jude were mealtimes. So they tried to sleep in advance of the meal closest in its typical content to breakfast, in order to create some semblance of normality. It was great to have someone to talk to. Zander believed residents were under orders not to speak to them, whilst Jude just argued that they were criminal scum and incapable of basic humanity. They were, she said, simply terrorists.

Zander found it hard to disagree after what they'd gone through. He spent most of his time alone, mentally scanning the day's events, looking for clues as to who or what was behind this.

'My life, or at least the last few years, were defined by the impact of a terrorist attack. Now it's likely to end because of another one. I suppose all of this is a cyclical in nature.'

'Your gallows humour doesn't work on me,' Jude replied. It was her determination and spiky nature which kept him going.

A week earlier, when she'd deliberately tried to start a confrontation with a man in the gym to see what would happen, she was quickly dragged away. They'd beaten her enough to make her healing wounds ache for several more days and then confined to her room for twenty-four hours. Despite that, Jude was insistent it was worthwhile to find out just what the regime here was like. Zander wasn't sure if it were just bravado when Jude

# THE TRITON RUN

said she could have killed her assailant quite easily had she wished. She proclaimed that she would save her efforts until it mattered.

Left to their own devices for days on end, they'd spent much of their time exercising and talking. They had no idea where they were, though mutually agreed they were likely to be in the belt where their location could be easily hidden. Their current environment contained a large number of chambers, a level reserved for accommodation with rooms off each side of the passageway and a narrow, circular corridor which ran around its outer perimeter. The corridor was only wide enough to allow the two of them to walk abreast, and they were quick to get out of the way when one of the guards appeared.

Most didn't carry weapons and clearly didn't think that they required them. Some doorways were guarded by men and women, rifles slung over shoulders, tasers strapped to their belts. The guards wore body armour over their coveralls. Occasionally they'd see trolleys of supplies brought through the doors, which they presumed led to a space dock.

The base had no sense of luxury. The food was, from time to time, rationed and of poor quality. Their cabins, or cells, were basic, and from their walks they concluded that some corridors were liable to flooding with waste which stank the whole place out for days on end at times. Even worse was one occasion when the A-grav failed and the detritus ended up smeared across the walls and ceiling.

Zander and Jude came to rely on and enjoy each other's company, becoming each other's therapists. Both grieved heavily for their recent losses. Zander punished himself daily for those killed in his name, not just those close to him that he'd lost. Jude struggled to contain her anger. She wanted revenge. Zander tried to get to her to focus on her immediate safety and her desire to see her father again.

Things changed after several weeks when they bumped into Rebecca.

She stood out because she was at least ten years younger, they estimated, than anyone else that they'd come across. She was a quiet girl who they'd spotted in the canteen. Shy, furtive, and nervous. She rarely made eye contact with anyone.

Rebecca was short and slim with long hair, not quite emaciated, yet all sharp angles, and sunken cheeks. She was a teenager and must've been on board for some time. It was rare to see people with long hair, apart from on the habitats, because of the simple reason that they weren't conducive to wearing a helmet.

She was pale, as many of those who spent most of their life off Earth were. Zander wondered how well she was cared for. Initially, they could only get monosyllabic answers out of her. After a few days of the two of them stalking her, trying to make bumping into her appear accidental, she started to slowly open up. Once she accepted that they were prisoners as much as she was. Jude was initially suspicious of the girl's motives.

'If Rebecca's here to somehow extract information from us, then it's the most elaborate such plan I've heard of, and surely a group as ruthless as those who captured us would have just tortured us from the start?' Jude accepted that he had a point.

Zander was shocked when the girl revealed that she didn't know who she was. She knew her first name, had some faded memories of childhood, and had been on this station and on board a variety of similar bases for what seemed to have been at least eight years.

'What are your names?' she asked.

The two adults looked at each other. 'He's Theo, I'm Jude.'

There was no point telling her who they were. Though Zander was a celebrity, it was unlikely to mean anything to the child. Rebecca smiled, repeating the names back at them, enjoying the interaction. She acted as if she'd received a gift.

Quite quickly, the two of them started feeling protective towards her, though Jude, with one eye permanently on escape, concluded that, 'Rebecca might just have some secrets that might help us. The problem is that she might not know that, yet.'

# 28

# WILDING

*The Dark*

Wilding gained consciousness, if that's what it was, sometime later. The lighting in her tank had now gone out, and her view was limited to shadows, brought to life by the projected sun, which appeared to rise and fall at a regular interval.

She struggled to understand what was happening, but she increasingly felt touched by emotion, by messages that she initially didn't understand. It was *them*. It *had* to be. How, she had no idea, although for now she clung onto the hope that she was still alive, and that this situation was only temporary.

The emotions and messages appeared in a discrete way, gently invading her psyche, presenting themselves as if they were her own. Wilding was aware of the risks of manipulation, though, right now, she wasn't in a position to object to her situation.

Wilding developed the impression that they were trying to apologise for the way they'd been introduced, that the incident in the canyon wasn't intended to scare her. She referred to them as *they*, as she couldn't differentiate between them, at least not yet anyway. She wasn't sure if she was being communicated to by a single entity or hundreds. For a while she'd been too scared to message back, preferring the periods that she could only compare to sleep, where mind exhausted through a mixture of fear and concentration, she drifted off.

The more she responded, the communications developed from simply trying to express an emotion to a mental conversation in English. She wondered if she wasn't just going insane. They were remarkably fluent within a brief period. What began with an exchange of ideas or emotions developed incrementally into exchanges of views and feelings. She couldn't understand how, or why, the Qarti, as she believed them called, could read her mind and to what degree. They seemed to suggest that the substance they were immersed in, as well as keeping them alive, acted as some form of conduit. Wilding could increasingly read their thoughts, though the sensations were cloudy. When they struggled to communicate, she sensed their frustration.

Sometimes there was anger. She was unable to assess who or what the anger was directed toward. Images, sounds, and words all blurred into one. She thought it was comparable to the latest Tapper tech. It took her a while to understand every new idea that was thrown at her, so she presumed to the Qarti, the conversations were extremely slow and difficult.

Wilding got the impression they had been in these tanks for a long time. Whilst in the tanks they couldn't hurt her, she got the feeling that in addition to their curiosity, they were also slightly scared of her. As she was of them.

The whole concept of shared thoughts and memories made her head swim. If she could have been sick, she suspected she would have been had she had a physical shape. For now, she only had her consciousness. Everything else, the real world, where her body hung in a tank of gunge, appeared remote and out of reach.

Her hostage training initially kicked in and though she felt she didn't learn much initially, it was oddly comforting to know they were interested in her. She'd spent hours repeating lessons to herself about how to shut out any intrusion and not give away any information. For a while, the Qarti had left her alone, indicating they wouldn't pressure her and would await her willingness to talk. Or at least it appeared that was what they'd said.

Wilding realised that if she just retreated permanently into her own silence, it would make her go mad. If she was going to survive, she had to engage. For a while, the tranquillity allowed her to relax and rest, trying to consciously lower her stress levels. Even after she and the Qarti settled into regular exchanges of information, from time to time she'd feel fatigued. She'd temporarily retreat into her own mental space and put up the barriers she'd been trained to deploy. She'd only used them once before, when captured by slavers during a botched rescue attempt. Her platoon had been deployed to rescue hundreds of youngsters who had been abducted. The rescue had gone wrong, and she'd been captured. Whilst awaiting backup, she'd been tortured, physically and mentally. She'd refused to reveal the location of her Platoon. She'd suffered immensely, had saved lives in the process.

One day, when Wilding believed she was safe in her own thoughts, a strange feeling of warmth came over her. It was sympathy and a sort of understanding.

The Qarti.

Without realising it, she'd relaxed so much she'd let them into her deeper thoughts, a higher stratosphere of private being. She absorbed their thoughts. They were trapped too, as she was.

They asked her how she had come to board their ship. *Who are you? How did you get here?*

It was a deeper question than on the face of it. She wasn't sure where to begin. The guilt she carried, regardless of how she felt, started to seep through the internal walls she had erected years ago, consuming her. Her thoughts, fragments of memory, all came tumbling out in a jumble.

*I had to save people, important people. I had to slaughter people to get to safety. They were already going to die!*

A voice came back from the Qarti. *We understand. Tell us.*

For a while she was confused, doubting her feelings, her memory. Since she'd started to run out of oxygen, she couldn't be certain what was right or wrong. Her anxiety remained high whilst she doubted herself, but she gradually composed herself to allow the story to come out.

Everyone bar those there that day, at Buchanan Base, had doubted her. They'd objected to her actions. Only her Platoon and those they'd rescued knew the truth. It was only through the passage of time and following a second trial that she was discharged, albeit on a legal technicality. She was commonly regarded as a war criminal. A mass murderer.

Fear hit her like an ice-cold spray of water, shaking her out of the exchange of information for a moment. The Qarti would also regard her as a criminal. They might not appreciate just how desperate she was at the time and that had she not made the decisions she did, all her colleagues, and those they rescued, would have perished. Those who had died at her hand would not have survived anyway, facing a painful and wretched death as it was.

*Tell us… we will understand. We too were wronged.*

A calmness descended on her, a warm comfort. It wasn't from within, she guessed they were projecting it on her. In the knowledge she had little to lose, she told them all she could remember.

# 29

# SQUIRE

*Onboard the BSV*

Before going freelance, Squire had worked for the largest salvage firm operating between Earth and the Moon. He'd been involved in clearing up some pretty horrific accidents, collisions in orbit, system failures and occasionally the aftermath of skirmishes between feuding businesses or criminal gangs. He'd even led the rescue mission when the Jarre, the biggest luxury liner in operation at the time, had suffered disaster en route to Mars.

It was the best job he could get when he'd been discharged from the forces.

Squire hadn't chosen to go freelance. He thought he had a job for life. Well-liked and good at managing salvage projects, he didn't see any need to change at all. The money was good and because he enjoyed it, it was worthwhile.

That was until the Trike. He'd tried to carry on as normal, even saw therapists on the side, however he struggled to move on from it. It haunted his thoughts. That's when the Zefyrex came in. He found he could carry on working despite everything else falling apart as he spent his wages on the drug and became unreliable, never going home when on leave.

He lost the lot. His wife and daughter had both given up on him and they'd ended up nearly bankrupt. He'd not spoken to his ex-wife since the day he'd been kicked out. His own fault.

## THE TRITON RUN

By necessity, he went freelance, taking a contract off Neptune where he was far enough away from all responsibility back home and a long way from the wreck of the Trike. He won a salvage and junk clearance franchise. The few other vessels he ran were decent, and he always led from the front, leaving the tougher tasks for himself. This one was the toughest.

They'd now nicknamed the target the Xenos, the alien, or foreigner. That morning Paisley woke him to see the improved imaging and Squire watched it grow on the main view screen. He'd fired off the last few high-speed drones he'd had on board to get there a few days before he did. On board, 3D printers were capable of making replacements, but for now, he preferred to conserve materials. He couldn't keep his eyes off the images as he floated across the command room and strapped himself into his chair. Even Paisley seemed impressed. 'We've never seen anything as big as this before. I need your instructions so that I can plan ahead.'

Squire shrugged and let out a low whistle.

'I've a few ideas, Paisley, but this is it, though. *IT*.' He let the emphasis hang momentarily. 'The most important salvage mission of all time and potentially first contact with aliens. Fancy meeting some space bugs?'

Paisley replied, 'Personally, I've no desire to come into any proximity with anything that'll put your life at risk. As far as I'm aware, this is not mankind's first encounter with alien life. Technically, life, albeit unintelligent, has been found in several places in the solar system. It's also unlikely that whatever has ownership of this object, they will be of insect background.'

Stirring up Paisley was a sport at times for Squire, though it never ceased to amaze him how quickly he learned from Squire. He pulled the image off the screen, and it grew into a 3D image in front of him. It wasn't quite complete for reasons he couldn't quite understand. The drones should have provided a complete scan. Squire ran some checks and asked Paisley to double check them.

'The imaging we have is correct, although I agree with your assessment. There is a gap in our scanning towards the front, or what customarily appears to be the front. It seems as if that part is subject to some sort of cloaking device that is fooling all of our sensors.'

Squire nodded. 'That's why they collided, I'd bet. The Scout couldn't see it because of the cloak, maybe it was fully operational before the collision, which is why we still cannot see all of it?'

'That theory is logical.'

'It also suggests they didn't want to be seen, so they might not be too happy to see us.'

They both got down to work and within a few hours, they'd had a conference with Muller to update on security arrangements and salvage plans. Whilst Squire was attempting to board what was left of the Kuiper Scout and explore the object, he was going to set up a wide circuit of weapon drones, just in case. They would accompany the casualty back to Neptune if they could indeed move it. A Sentinel had been ordered and would be delivered to Neptune. If this object was as important as they thought, then others might want to seize it.

Over the following days, the Drones reported back with far sharper images of what was seemingly an asteroid which had a ship built in and around it. What was left of the mid to rear of the Scout was impaled on it. The new footage showed areas that Wilding had not been able to access externally and suggested some sort of flickering cloak or shield. Their working assumption was the Scout had caused quite some damage that likely affected the Xenos internally as well as on the surface, and this had led to a partial failure of the cloaking mechanism.

'If the cradle is going to hold this, it needs to be a lot bigger than we thought. We had the diameter fairly well predicted, unfortunately it's a lot longer. I presume there're no signs of life reported yet?' Muller had asked.

'You think I might have forgotten to tell you?' laughed Squire. His voice then softened as he thought about Dee. 'But no, nothing. I'd much rather be approaching here accompanied by all the 'roid carriers and towers you've got on order than alone, sadly I don't really have a choice.'

# 30

## JUDE

*Antiope Mining Facility*

Time spent with Rebecca broke the day up. Jude believed that Rebecca enjoyed it, too. She gave them a tour of the base with nobody paying them much notice. Rebecca wasn't as restricted as they were and she described a town miles and miles away she used to be able to get to, carved inside a huge cavern. For now, they couldn't get that far.

They were sitting in Jude's room on the bed, with Zander on the floor propped up against the wall. Rebecca looked at Jude. 'You keep saying that your father will come for you. Well, how d'you know? Mine never even tried.'

Gradually, Rebecca had opened up to them. She'd been quite isolated bar some other children she'd been allowed to play with from time to time. She didn't know who they were, and she'd not seen them for a while. She'd occupied herself watching films and playing Sims.

'He'll come. I promise,' Jude spoke gently.

'I don't even know who my Mum or Dad are.' Rebecca looked forlorn. 'I don't even know why I'm here, or who I am. I'm sixteen. What use am I to anyone here? I've been here years and for what?'

Tears appeared at the corner of the girl's eyes. Jude grabbed her hand. Rebecca was generally awkward around people, but she didn't stop her. Emotionally and in terms of maturity, there was an innocence there. For a girl of sixteen, her transformation into an adult had been slowed.

Across the base, Rebecca received a friendly reaction from the crew, who clearly didn't see her as a risk. Rebecca told them that she kept herself to herself bar friendships with a few of the mess hall staff and Doctor Howard, who had spent time teaching her maths and getting data sticks with books on them for her to read. Jude remembered Howard. He'd been very friendly and talkative when he was monitoring her recovery from her wounds, save he kept his mouth shut when she started asking probing questions.

'Who is it that's holding us, Rebecca? Do you know who's in charge?' Jude asked.

A pause. Rebecca screwed her eyes up, signifying her trying to collate her understanding of the situation. Eager to help, she smiled at them both, her eyes widening with glee, 'I knew that one day this would help me.'

She started slowly, and when she got going, the information poured out of her like a waterfall. They stopped her and over the next few days resumed the conversation, always in a location where they hoped their conversations couldn't be eavesdropped. Rebecca knew a lot about the workings of the base, though not once had she done anything to jeopardise her knowledge and to put herself under suspicion. She had been a perfect prisoner. She knew so much about the crew; shift patterns, names, and interests of most of them, and weaknesses. For example, the guard who stood by the left-hand entry to the docking bay on every third day regularly drifted off to sleep on duty after his evening meal break. Rebecca had seen him scolded by one of his colleagues on several occasions.

Jude's assessment of the crew was that it was a curious set up. As shown by the ruthless assault on the space elevator, they could be exceptionally professional and ruthless, but at times, they were sloppy. Jude discussed what they learnt with Zander when Rebecca wasn't with them and they concluded, partly by testing some of what they'd been told, that Rebecca was genuinely passing on useful information. It wasn't a set up. They just needed to work out how to put the intelligence to effective use if the plan was to genuinely try to escape. After a week or so, Rebecca, who had been growing in confidence around them, suddenly showed a spark of mischief in her eyes that they'd not seen before. 'So, how'd we put what we know to get us out of here, then? We can't just wait for Jude's father. Surely between the President of Earth, an undercover cop and someone who knows this place like the back of her hand, we can work out an escape plan?'

While this took the pair aback, it was what they wanted to hear. They'd told her about their backgrounds and Zander's job had excited her. They looked wide eyed at each other, then nodded at Rebecca. 'Let's wait and see,' Jude said smiling,

'We will work it out.'

# 31

# SQUIRE

*Onboard the BSV on arrival at the Xenos*

Squire even had a shave in the morning before his EVA. 'I want to look my best if ET is waiting,' he'd told Paisley, though in reality it was the realisation that it was likely the whole of mankind would watch the footage at some point.

Three days had been spent orbiting the Xenos, completing detailed scans and analysing material received back from their drones. Once he'd got over the shock of the shimmering caused by the failing cloaking system, he'd been able to spend time focussing on what he could see. The 'cloak' was better than any he'd ever come across from his brief time in the military. Cloaking technology was banned across the solar system as it created too much of a collision risk. While it was a ban that was impossible to enforce, it was one which he'd never heard of being flouted.

The imaging of the surface was now more accurate and included some internal detail too, particularly tunnels and open areas near the outer edges of the object. The areas where some of the cloaking still worked weren't as accurate as he liked, even though his drones had gone in close and filled in some of the detail. The cloak seemed to work by putting out a false image in a screen around the Xenos, because on the surface, it was not apparent.

There were no signs of life, save what seemed to be some sort of mechanical movement near the end where he assumed the engines were. Examination of the external engine vents would have to wait until the ship was secured.

The unlikely fusion between the two objects seemed secure. Simulations suggested the Scout had rammed the Xenos at such at such a unique angle and speed that the smaller ship had gone in deep, like a spear deep into the flank of an animal being hunted. Much of the smaller ship had simply melted and fused with its new host. There was no way they would ever be separated. One theory was that this fusing was actually a defence, or automated repair, designed to maintain the integrity of the Xenos. One concern was that it didn't make sense that a ship of this technological advancement, as evidenced by the cloaking device, didn't have its own sensors or deflectors. There seemed to be extraordinarily little power coursing round it, save for small traces in isolated areas, and coupled with Wilding's footage, they concluded that deflector systems must have failed.

With the agreement of the team back on Neptune, he'd used a handful of his remaining drones to enter the Scout. Some tried to follow Wilding's route, others had cut their way into other exposed parts. They'd revealed little bar empty corridors and huge storage tanks.

He added an overlay to his own maps, matching Wilding's route to his drone's scans. Wilding had gone deeper than his drones were able to reach. Squire estimated she'd been able to travel about a quarter of the way towards the centre.

Squire had asked Paisley to filter his coms, such was the deluge of messages and instructions. In addition to the steering group, others within Arden's business were now involved, competing interests all pressured him. Some scientists wanted the object recovering as soon as possible, others were concerned over contamination. Nobody expressed any desire to find Dee Wilding. She was a war criminal, they said, she didn't matter.

There'd been media interest from all over the solar system, with Arden's media team muddying the waters, leading to most of the stories from the inner system being dismissed as fake news.

The arrival of an alien spaceship was too far-fetched for some.

After an eight-hour EVA, Paisley and Squire had ensured the BSV was carefully secured to the Xenos by a series of cables. The BSV was near enough to allow for comparatively easy passage down to the surface whilst a safe distance so that it shouldn't collide with either the Scout or the Xenos.

He'd reported back to Triton One and tried to sleep for a few hours. It had taken a level of medication to which Paisley had objected to get him off to sleep. He'd been roused at the agreed hour and was relieved to feel a solid mix of excitement and fear. Squire breakfasted whilst checking the latest updates on the BSV systems and watching a news broadcast. Stowing his breakfast leftovers away, he released himself from his harness and drifted towards the chamber that would allow him access to the airlock on the top of the craft.

'We ready to go, Paisley?' he asked aloud, knowing the answer. They'd agreed to go in via the entrance Wilding had used. It made sense, as they knew it was accessible and it meant they were more likely to find her. Drones had confirmed that the remains of the Scout were empty.

Paisley had now taken control of a human shaped avatar and awaited Squire. It was taller and stockier than Squire with the air tank essentially a spare for use by Squire and with a tool belt strapped across its chest. The robot 'wore' its own white EVA suit, designed for work outside the safety of a ship.

'Your suit has been prepped and checked. The tethers are all holding firm. We're locked in position, and I've updated Triton One. They'll receive a feed from me whenever I can get a signal back to the ship.'

Squire reached the pole that ran between floors and pulled himself into the equipment room to put on his suit. 'Any idea if we'll get anymore instructions?'

'No, I don't think they'll reply now, not with the radio delay.

# THE TRITON RUN

They knew our planned start time and won't want to distract you.'

It would take a while for him to get used to the voice coming directly from the android rather than via the dozens of speakers scattered round the BSV.

'That'd be a first,' muttered Squire as he slid into a recess and pushed his feet into thick leggings. He pushed himself back into the wall and it enclosed around him. Mechanical arms appeared and swarmed around him, pulling the suit into position, and sealing it. The helmet lowered from the ceiling and was promptly sealed with a satisfying thwump. Like Paisley, his suit was white. The suit booted up immediately, linking to his chip and displaying a whole series of menus on the HUD for him to operate via mental commands. The smell of suit air hit him immediately. When the self-check routines were complete, he stepped away from the wall and Squire made small talk whilst they made their way into the airlock, which was a tight fit for two. After double checking all systems, they started the recycling mechanism.

Within five minutes, they were both standing outside the BSV. Squire stared down at the Xenos, reliant on floodlights from the ship and several drones to light up its surface.

'Do you wish me to make the crossing first and secure a line for you?' asked Paisley, as ever putting his master's safety first. Squire took a deep breath and pushed the fear away, asking his suit to do what it could to keep his heart rate low. He grinned and looked across to his companion.

'Fuck off Paisley, as if I'm going to let a robot beat me to landing on an alien artefact.'

And with that, he turned and leapt.

# 32

# WILDING

*The Dark*

She'd lived through these moments often enough. Recall wasn't a problem. She wished she could forget. With the Inquiry, the interviews, the criminal trials, and the court martial they'd been discussed in incredible detail. There were also the nights when that day came back to her in her dreams. Wilding wasn't sure how this all looked to the Qarti, or how her recollections were being accessed. She was an observer, watching herself take the decisions she had needed to. Alongside her, just behind her shoulder, was what felt like a shadow. It was them. She was going to be judged again. Perhaps this time she would be judged fairly.

The view was catastrophic. The city was on fire in places, and they could hear the sound of gunfire. Occasionally a rocket was launched from one of the side streets, taking a shallow arc before coming down a few blocks away, taking with its whole buildings that, along with their contents, were hurled into the air and scattered. Smoke billowed from many buildings, finding its way to the fans in the ceiling of the dome like ropes being pulled upwards.

Wilding scanned the scene using the finder on her rifle. The streets were packed. Many had come to see what was happening, others came to fight. There were thousands down there, blocking their route back to the lifts at the side of the crater. The crater wall wasn't far. Buchanan City nestled into a slight dip near the northern wall, but at present it looked unreachable.

The two sides were identifiable. The smaller numbers belonged to the state government, though they heavily outgunned their opponents. The troops wore green and yellow combat suits, with helmets and visors down. As they pushed their way through the streets, they flanked a column of tanks. The lead vehicle had a squat turret at the front, three muzzles protruding in different directions. Sparks leapt from the largest, where a projectile weapon was showering the crowds with bullets. The crowds tumbled like dominos. The other two muzzles were shorter and appeared inactive however her sight could see across a wide spectrum of light bandings, and she could make out laser fire. It was clearly being spat from the weapons as nearby strategic targets exploded. Walls came down, deliberately blocking avenues so the protestors couldn't escape. A bus that was carrying dozens burst into flame, cooking those inside.

Dunk and Parynski appeared alongside her. They all wore the same dusty red suits, designed to help them get across the exterior Mars terrain without being spotted.

Dunk looked frustrated. 'They're showing no mercy. We've got to do something.'

Wilding kept her view ahead on the slaughter. 'We can't. We have our orders and even if we wanted to, we'd not stand a chance.'

Wilding understood what he meant. She too felt sick at what he was seeing. She repeated extracts from her briefing for their colleagues, knowing the rest of the platoon would hear across the channel.

'There are 40,000 people in this city and just too many well-armed people here to intervene. They've been preparing for an insurgency for years, practically encouraged it.

Now's the time they want to put it down and concentrate their power.'

Dunk wasn't impressed. He turned to face her, too close.

'So, we are doing nothing? We could put down some of those tanks, at least slow them down. I've been watching the tank movements, and they don't really make sense. They are slaughtering people, but I don't understand what they're up to.'

Wilding spun, waving at him to back off out of her personal space. 'Our first priority is to get out of here alive with the ambassador. In case you'd forgotten, this is a rescue mission. We aren't supposed to be here, and we can't get involved. Let's just hope the protests don't escalate. They risk breaching the dome and if that happens, we'll be fucked.'

She gave them a moment to accept her authority before giving orders. 'Dunk, go get everyone ready. We need to get out of this tower while we can. We don't want to get the attention of some of those rocket launchers.'

Dunk nodded reluctantly at them and went back inside. That left Parynski, Wilding and Squire on the balcony.

They were twelve storeys up, on a balcony that was attached to the guest quarters of the main Parliament building. The building was built around a column that rose from the Martian floor up to support the largest dome of the city. There were half a dozen of them, situated across the crater floor which housed the city. The building spread out below them like a star fish with the lower levels containing administration blocks. While the tower contained media suites and accommodation for the government and visiting dignitaries. It was in one of those suites that they now waited.

The timing of the public protest and their charge against the seat of government had been eerily convenient. Wilding's team had just been on the outskirts of the city centre when chaos ensued, and they were able to follow the crowds before sneaking away and entering the Tower. Gaining entry had been straightforward, just before the whole building was subject to a lockdown. They'd taken control of the elevators and headed up to the suite where the Ambassador and his family were being held. The Buchanan administration had refused to release them until Earth had backed down and granted the city independence.

There had only been one brief shoot out on the floor where the suite was situated, routine for a group as professional as hers. Most of the guards had retreated fairly quickly and Mack, their Coms Chief, reported that local coms were calling for an evacuation of the building and wider area by all Government troops. As ever, when the going got tough, those in charge acted like cowards and ran.

Whilst her team rounded up the Ambassador and his family, hurriedly dressing them in temporary EVA suits, Wilding assessed their options. It was at this point that she reminded herself that she was no longer in control of her destiny here. She was an observer, watching herself. The Qarti were engrossed, assessing and trying to understand every bit of her memories. No judgement, just curiosity.

They reached the ground floor without much trouble. The elevators were disabled due to the alarms, so they had to take the stairs. Dunk took point and Wilding had accompanied the Ambassador and his wife. Parynski had carried their little girl in his arms, so they weren't slowed down. The building had been evacuated. They only came across odd staff members who had neglected to leave or had been unable to do so. Most were unarmed and were ignored. Guards who tried to stop them were killed. They'd hoped for a relatively discrete mission, in and out, without causing too much trouble and avoiding a gunfight. Any battle was, they'd thought, likely to be against the Government troops.

Even whilst watching past events from this new viewpoint, Wilding started to feel anxious about what was about to happen. She implored the Qarti to understand this was not her fault. Circumstances had conspired against her. If only they'd arrived before the protests had got out of hand and before the Government had temporarily evacuated.

# 33

# ZANDER

*Antiope Mining Facility*

A loss of the sense of smell was something that many who spent a long time in space reported. Zander wished he'd lost his, struggling with the overall stench of the people around the base. Water was precious and whilst the habitat was supplied with ice from somewhere, the laundry they used work on recycled urine. The laundry consisted of a small room with rock walls and four machines that both washed and dried. Warning notices covered the devices, advising users not to overload them and to be aware of the fire risks. Fire in space was never a good thing.

The three of them sat on the floor, staring at the washers, willing them to work faster. It had become part of the routine, every few days they'd come and wash their clothes. It was something to do. The machinery was noisy and the room warm despite various fans and tubes trying to take away the heat the machines produced to recycle it.

Rebecca sat in the middle of them. As usual, they chatted, joked, and tried to entertain themselves with games. The mood had, however, dipped a little as the repetition of their routine and the helplessness of the situation over recent days had become apparent. Even with Rebecca's wealth of intelligence, they couldn't see a way that gave them a chance of escape. Jude kept talking about wanting to go on a sortie behind some of the sealed doors. Zander said that whilst they might be able to work out the codes or break a lock, the chances of getting caught were too great.

Rebecca enthused again about the part of the base that was seemingly luxurious compared to the utilitarian area they inhabited. Though she'd not been there for some time, she was still able to enthusiastically describe huge chambers with large arched ceilings above a town that was surrounded by fields and a farm. The town had been well inhabited and contained a school, shops, and a bar. She'd been allowed to go to the school for a while.

'This is getting on my nerves,' said Jude, getting to her feet and pacing up and down.

She kicked out at the nearest machine in frustration. On arrival, all machines had been being used, so they were waiting just to start to wash their clothes.

Zander was struggling to get her to contain her aggression. She carried a bruise on her left cheek from an incident when she'd been trying to get a male orderly in the canteen to engage in conversation and when he kept replying with monosyllabic answers, she lost the plot and started shouting at him. Zander was reassured by the fact that she'd hurt the guards who intervened more than they had her, and that there had been no retribution since. The following day, a sheepish Doctor Howard, accompanied by a guard, had stopped them in the entertainment room and asked them to stop asking questions because they were wasting their time. Howard had been the only person on the base that Rebecca had built a relationship with. He was quite furtive and tried to dismiss the questions this intervention had created. Zander felt he didn't belong here with the others. 'Look, for your own well-being, please just relax and accept the hospitality for now,' he'd said.

The 'for now' spooked Zander, despite Jude reminding him that there had to be an end game to all of this. He pulled his legs under him to make space for Jude's pacing around the room.

Zander understood her frustration but didn't think it helped. He'd been struggling for the last few days, unable to sleep and frustrated at their predicament. He'd breached his security protocols by sharing some of what he knew about the earlier attacks against him, partly to fill the time and partly to see if they could produce a link.

Zander had no real idea how he was linked to Rebecca; he had many enemies. It came with the territory of being a political leader. He wondered what was going on back home, whether he was missed. Lindstrom would be loving it. Bitch.

Rebecca looked fearful when the black clouds gathered round Jude. She'd confided as much to Zander when they'd been alone. She'd been more withdrawn since the confrontation that had led to Jude being beaten.

'Wonder if we can remove some of these loads, do ours, and then put theirs back on?' Jude asked, thinking aloud. The machine in front of Jude stopped with a clunk as she pulled the power mid cycle.

'Don't risk pissing anyone off, Jude,' said Zander, sensing Rebecca's unease. Ignoring him, Jude opened the door to the machine and started pulling clothes out. The load was a mix of utilitarian jumpsuits, underwear, and sports gear. She suddenly lifted up a blue sweatshirt in front of her and stared intensely at a badge sewn on it. It contained three rings.

She broke out in a rueful grin, turning it to show the others.
'Recognise this logo?'
Zander got it straight away.
The Trike.
'Exiles…'

# 34

## SQUIRE

*Inside the Xenos*

Progress was slow as Squire and Paisley traced Wilding's route into the heart of the vessel. Their scanners found occasional residual traces of her suit, where she'd touched something. They also detected ice and rock dust that her boots had shed. The only evidence of power came from the occasional strips of low-level lighting that Wilding had also seen, though some of these had gone out.

Squire followed Paisley closely. Paisley was accompanied by a small drone that hovered just in front of him, glowing like a miniature sun. Every time they reached a turn, or a crossroads, Paisley would despatch it ahead of them to confirm if it were safe. The drone applied real-time updates to their own 3D mapping and on several occasions, they paused to review footage it had taken. Paisley also kept on putting up short clips of footage from Wilding's suit-cam on the HUD to help them decide what to do.

They managed to open a few side doors. Others remained sealed and short of trying to hack the dead electronic pads next to them they weren't going to get in without having to cut through it. They'd leave any exploration that required damaging the Xenos, well alone for now. He was to try and minimise any contamination of the ship.

Paisley was able to use brute strength where some manual mechanisms were stuck, and over the course of an hour, they opened half a dozen doors. None led anywhere exciting. Some opened up new corridors that the scout drone explored before coming back, having not found anything of interest within close range. Others were store cupboards containing sealed boxes and pieces of machinery to which they could not attribute a use.

Squire struggled to settle with the constant fluctuation in lighting as the drone moved away on reconnaissance and then returned to its master, shadows dancing up the surrounding walls. He was constantly twisting and turning to get a look at whatever creature he imagined he saw scurrying off into the dark. Squire had sound piped in from external microphones they wore. The only noise was their footsteps on metal or from time to time the crunching of their boots on rock floor where the tunnel hadn't been plated completely. Every now and again they'd hear mechanical noises and faint howling. It was simply the movement of the limited atmosphere Paisley assured him, no doubt caused by their arrival and opening of sealed chambers. Paisley took samples from the rock and scrapings from the metal walls, placing them in pockets on his legs. He also stuck small devices on the wall, just above the floor, every few hundred yards. They were small, marble sized and wouldn't be easily detected.

'You can stop worrying about something coming up behind us. I can tell from your med-log that you are feeling highly stressed,' said Paisley in his matter-of-fact way. Squire knew the sensors would stop him getting lost. His HUD map was being updated in real time. 'If she were armed, Dee would be the most dangerous person on board,' added Squire, trying to add some levity to how he was feeling.

'I have engaged the motion sensor facility. If anything moves behind us, then we and the ship will know immediately.'

'So, it's only the aliens ahead we have to worry about then.'

## 35

## ZANDER

*Antiope Mining Facility*

They waited until Rebecca had gone to bed before talking. Zander felt agitated, nervously scratching at his patchy white beard and the stubble on his previously clean-shaven head.

'Okay then, Theo, let's have it. I assume all this goes way back, as I don't recall the name "Trike,"' said Jude.

He nodded. 'Yes, was before I was President. I'd just been elected as representative for the American East.'

He couldn't wait to explain everything, so blurted out, 'I think Rebecca must be Scott Arden's daughter. She was abducted years ago, long since presumed dead. That's why they came after me, too.'

Zander knew she was aware of Arden. They both suspected that the ship her father was delivering was for him.

'So, what's your link to Arden…and why would these people come after you so many years later?'

Zander sighed. He'd never really talked about it fully, even in the subsequent Inquiry where he hid, as advised by lawyers, behind legal privilege. He took a while to organise his thoughts before the words poured out of him. A jumble of emotion. Tears came too.

Zander had held these fears ever since Arden's young daughter had famously been abducted from a nursery on board the habitat where they'd been living. Investigations had never quite been able to link it to the attacks on him, however, so long had now passed and it made sense. Arden's wife, who'd been dropping her daughter off, had experienced the attack in which all the staff were slaughtered as well as half the other children. The kidnappers had never been traced. No ransom had been demanded, and the trail went cold. Arden's wife had later taken her own life, heartbroken. Arden had thrown himself into his work and relocated to Neptune to escape his past, where he became the dominant economic and political figure.

Arden had unsuccessfully spent a fortune on private investigators and scout ships to find his daughter. One group of privateers who had seemingly got close were found beheaded, still strapped into their couches when their ship was discovered months after it had gone missing. Its log had been wiped and all efforts to back trace its trajectory had failed.

'It's an unfair thing to put on me,' Zander told her, trying to explain. 'So long ago now.'

He told Jude that back when he was a newly elected senator and attending only his second session, he'd been late to a debate and on arrival was pressured to follow his party line, in order to vote against allowing Earth citizenship to be restored to a habitat whose residents had previously quite publicly revoked it, declaring independence for their new homes.

'It was a huge hab, three wheels, you see. Hence the nickname.'

He'd missed the briefing, and his party has given him firm instructions which, to a very junior representative, left him little choice. On the night it had appeared very dramatic, almost staged (he'd half wondered if a rival had planned it that way) as he'd cast the deciding vote meaning that across the two habitats and one carousel some fourteen thousand people had been refused the right to return to Earth. He'd not been aware at the time of the amendment tucked away that allowed the Earth forces in orbit the right to use lethal force against any protests arising out of the contentious vote where the violence was from those without citizenship.

As Zander talked, he carefully picked his words as he tried to stop himself nervously picking away at his scalp. There was a lot to say, but he kept away from how all this affected him personally most. It had all led to him being later regarded as a monster by opponents.

'So, whilst I can say the timing of my vote was dramatic and just happened to be the casting vote, hundreds supported it, never mind the thousands marching in favour Earthside. The reality I've got to live with is … that I voted against those people being granted citizenship.'

For the first time since he'd started talking, there was an awkward silence. Jude prodded him. 'Why did they even want to return to Earth?'

'The last financial crash. Our abilities to travel the solar system had exploded and led to a rush to colonise and grab land, lots of foolish schemes that ran out of money. It all went to shit at home and people argued we couldn't afford to help those who'd already left. The three we voted against were all vastly different. It can't have been easy for their citizens… with no rights, they couldn't return anyone to Earth or the Moon. Local habitats that were also struggling used the crisis as an excuse to kick them when they were down and stopped trading and co-operating with them, thinking they'd get some sort of advantage.'

Zander looked straight at her. 'Their whole sector collapsed. The neighbouring hab, the Monte Carlo, suffered a catastrophic power failure, and besides a few hundred survivors, all the rest perished. Nobody got there quickly enough. Bar a few nearby barges that saved a ship load, it was a disaster. The Trike took in most of the survivors, but many just vanished or were captured by a group of slavers. It was a huge political scandal.'

Jude slid onto the floor opposite him and reached over to lightly touch his knee. He grabbed her hand and continued.

'The last hab in the sector to fall was the Trike. When I was a kid, it was quite famous for its criminal reputation. It had actually been sold and moved a couple of times beforehand, and one of her wheels was ready for scrap. Even so, I can't believe we rejected their request when I think about it. But nobody briefed us on the safety angle. I only found out a lot later. It just wasn't safe, and in the weeks after the vote, they had to seal off various parts of it due to leaks and part failures. Residents started to disappear; they were being exterminated. Their owners were nasty bastards, their human rights record was awful, so we struggled to deal with them. After threatening to unleash hell on all who crossed and abandoned them, they effectively scuttled their own home. Suicide, or murder depending on your point of view. We had evidence the leaders escaped, killing those left behind in a big show.'

Zander, for only a moment, let the real bitterness in his voice temporarily replace the sorrow with which he'd been consumed. He chewed his bottom lip.

'So that's why they're angry with you? What about Arden?'

'Because of his greed. He enquired about helping. He ran many of the merchant shipping franchises at that time and refused to allow a couple of empty cruise liners to take off those struggling in some of the wings where conditions were at their worst. By the time he realised what he was letting happen and resolved to override that order, the only salvage ship he could get there was simply too late.'

'So, he's been treated unfairly?'

He shrugged. 'In many ways, we were both victims, but that sounds awful, as I say it. Both of us were taken advantage of. I apologised; I haven't stopped apologising. Well, he was such an arrogant man, wouldn't admit any blame. In the media, he criticised the leadership of the habitats, so it all fitted a narrative. He blamed me; that also suited some of my rivals.'

Jude nodded, trying to assess what she'd been told. 'This is all years ago. Why is this still an issue?'

'They swore revenge. Over the years, there's been odd bits of terrorism and attacks on minor officials involved at the time, but the Exiles, as they became known, never really claim responsibility for them. But they've not stopped wanting to punish Arden and I.'

He paused and looked Jude in the eye. 'So here we are. I presume this is their revenge. They have exceptionally long memories. It's also why Arden and I became enemies. Ever since, he has been nothing but provocative towards me, though we have a lot in common, really. We both suffered and became who we are now because of what happened. I only stayed in politics because I had nothing else to live for, and I was angry with everyone. What these terrorists can't comprehend is that there is nothing they can do to me know that punishes me more than what they already have.'

# 36

## SQUIRE

*Inside the Xenos*

Three quarters of the way through Squire's first air tank, he opened a side doorway that Wilding had seemingly missed. Beyond was the first chamber they'd seen that looked anything other than merely utilitarian. Squire believed he was in an engineering and operational zone, however, this chamber looked designed for a completely different purpose. Bar a few metal struts here and there, they were in a short, rocky corridor that opened out into a large chamber. There was no working lighting, though ahead of them one wall sparkled when torchlight touched it. The scout drone flew ahead, updating his HUD and their 3D maps. The chamber was a semi-circular, with a domed ceiling and a flat far wall. The room was devoid of furniture, save a dozen or so thin benches made from metal set out in rows so that anyone using them would likely face the far wall.

They'd been walking in single file in the main, but here Squire and Paisley stood alongside each other, taking in the chamber, peering upwards. The drone headed upwards, lighting up the walls high above them and hovered near the top of the dome.

'When we get this rock back to civilisation scientists are going to be swarming over this room.'

It was the first chamber that gave clues as to the nature of the Xenos's occupants.

Their attention was drawn to a carved relief of a figure. It was three quarters of the way up the flat wall, approximately fifteen feet tall and sparkled when light was shone on it along with the rest of the wall. From their position, approximately two decks below it, they had difficulty making it out. The drone provided close ups.

The harsh lighting from the drone's spotlight made the figure appear more sinister than was probably intended. Almost gargoyle like, thought Squire,. He wondered if it were an accurate representation of the passengers, a caricature, or the depiction of some sort of deity or all of them. Paisley informed Squire he was conducting an analysis that looked for any similar representations of creatures from human history.

The carving was of something that Squire Interpreted as a winged female. The figure wasn't naked, being partially covered in some sort of robe and harness. He presumed the figure was female, as it had breasts. Beyond that, he realised he was being presumptuous. The legs were thin, large thighs betrayed strength, below which the feet contained four toes with sharp talons extending. The torso was comparatively short, with arms spread wide. The hands appeared to hold implements, but it was impossible to work out what they were on a cursory examination. Squire wondered if they were weapons or symbols of office. The head was large and thin, almost horse like, reminding Squire of images of pterodactyls he'd seen in children's books. There were two eyes, perched on either side of the face, the mouth a closed hard line. The top of the head flared outwards to two points where markings indicated potentially the position of ears.

What caught the eye, however, were the wings. They spread outwards either side, beginning at the creature's waist and joined at the shoulder. He estimated a span of circa twelve feet. With this, Squire realised that the benches and balconies were perches. These things could really fly.

Breaking the silence, and for the benefit of the footage they were taking, Squire spoke out-loud. 'Well then, humanity, Santa Claus is real. Meet our neighbours.' Squire hoped he sounded more confident than he felt. This was a huge moment in man's knowledge about the universe.

He turned to Paisley. 'What sort of room do you think the bird people used this for?

Meeting room, church, court room?'

He got the answer he expected from Paisley, a long essay on the usage of such shaped and designed rooms in human history, with the caveat that if the statue was a representation of the shape of the users of this ship, then they weren't human so predictions could not be accurate. He concluded that there were likely other such chambers and if this were a church of some sort, it was one built for those who worked in the near vicinity.

Squire's com bleeped. 'I think you'll want to take this, sorry to disturb you,' said Paisley with the sound of real regret. 'The message has taken rather a long time to reach us and has been routed to avoid being picked up so it's not a live connection. I don't think we can reply at present.'

'Ok, thanks. You make sure our scan is complete. I want complete 360-degree footage and modelling.'

Squire stepped away. He thought about sitting down on one of the benches. To his frustration, his bulky suit made it impossible. He adjusted the mechanical skeleton embedded in the suit to provide him more support.

A small screen flashed up on his HUD, showing an old friend sat in an expensive-looking command chair. The wide angle changed, zooming into the face of Bruce Parynski, who stared into the camera.

'Hey buddy, hope you're well. Important message for you. Before that I'm sending you a spec of my latest ride, just so you can feel jealous. The Skydancer is by far the most incredible thing any of us have ever piloted, not that I've really had to pilot it. I was just babysitting it on the Triton Run before delivering it to your boss.'

Squire didn't have time for small talk right now, though all alone on an alien ship, he did take some relief from seeing his friend. Parynski paused as if expecting an answer, then continued, 'Anyway, I know you've a load of shit on your plate. Let me know what happens when you find Dee.'

'Don't worry, everyone will know,' muttered Squire to himself.

'I just needed to talk to a friend. There's been an attack on one of the space elevators. A group of pirates or terrorists have abducted President Zander and… I think they've got Jude.'

Squire froze, pausing the message to get his head round it.

'Anyway, the goons in charge of the investigation have lost the trail but as luck would have it, I was only a few days ahead of the terrorists, heading outwards so I've looped round the edge of the Belt and am now heading in roughly the right direction. The fuckers are hiding out on an asteroid in a mothballed mining facility.'

Parynski paused. Squire knew he was always the same when sending messages. The timing allowed for a two-way discussion, even if there was never any reply. Parynski grinned grimly. 'It seems as if the authorities aren't really interested in saving Zander, they don't even know who Jude is. I'm going to get her. When I get out, I can find out what's happening with you.' Another pause from Parynski. 'Love you, bud. See you around.'

And with that, the message ended.

Squire turned and looked at Paisley who had finished his circuit of the room.

'Well, that puts a downer on things,' he said. Whilst looking for the corpse of a friend, he'd learnt about the likely death of another. Paisley tried to lift his mood.

'I am so sorry Sir, my knowledge of Parynski suggest he's most innovative, and I hope he is successful. Perhaps now would be an opportune moment to carry on. I've left additional sensors here and we can return another day.'

Welcoming the chance to distract himself from the worry and feeling a long way from the sort of belonging and safety he normally shunned, he nodded. 'Agreed. Let's get this reconnaissance done and find Wilding.'

# 37

# WILDING

*The Dark*

Wilding told her team to turn down the volume on their suit's external mics. The noise of the crowd and the battle on the other side of the compound wall was so loud, and close, that it was influencing their thinking. They were all shouting over the noise. No matter how often you heard it, the sound of death hit you hard, like a punch to the chest, and she needed to clear her head to work out their next steps.

They'd not come with any plan to contact their pickup ship whilst in the Dome for fear of being eavesdropped on and because it was likely that it just wasn't possible. The Government was jamming all com networks, so Mack couldn't even hack into them and get a message out. They were on their own.

Wilding's platoon, with the Ambassador and her family, were all gathered in a loading bay at the bottom of the tower. The loading bay was empty save for a forklift truck and a ground car that was pouring smoke from where a shell must have hit it just before they'd arrived. Dunk had climbed up the outside of the building onto a generator to get a better view and report on the tactical situation.

'We're trapped, Ma'am. The other side of that gate is a war zone, and the war's still going on. The road outside heads right towards the elevators, but they are several hundred yards away.'

# THE TRITON RUN

'Noted. Any ideas for getting through? A diversion?'

There was a crackle on their private channel while Dunk considered their options. She looked back at the rest of the group, cowering inside the garage doorway they had exited via.

The body language of the group they'd rescued displayed their fear. Her men, however, remained resolute.

Dunk said, 'The mob are winning, Government troops are pulling back. I can see a tank that has been damaged. They've pulled the crew out through the hatch and slaughtered them. These people won't stop.'

'No chance they'll listen if we tell them we're not part of the state?'

No delay this time. 'Not a chance. They aren't even listening to each other. They just want blood. The diplomatic status of the Ambassador won't count for shit.'

Wilding looked across at Squire, who stood nearby, weapon drawn and aimed at the gate in case they got through. He didn't flinch as the hammering on the gate, a huge metal structure that was taller than a double-decker bus, intensified. Squire had been listening in.

'Ma'am, we need to make a decision. The gate is solid, the lock isn't.'

She acknowledged him, then spoke to Dunk again. 'Any options for a diversion?'

'Can't see it. They're congregating outside. From my position, there are bigger numbers round at the other side, but there's enough of them here to break through. Shall I lay down some fire and push them back?'

Wilding replied quickly, 'We're on their side. We know this government has been trying to do something awful for a while. We can't fight our way through them.'

She ducked as a volley of gun fire sprayed across the yard, kicking up chips of concrete. Wilding followed Squire behind the forklift as they heard a shout from behind. The Ambassador's aide had taken a shot to the leg. Wilding peered back at the garage. Parynski waved that it would be ok, though it complicated things if the suit were breached and the aide couldn't walk.

She'd not even needed to give the order. Dunk had done what he had to. Two shots from his heavy-duty weapon and the gunfire stopped. 'From a building across the road. Hopefully, they'll keep away from the window now. Not that there's a window there anymore.' He sounded slightly smug.

Wilding stepped out into the yard again, turning a complete circle and peering up into the sky. There had to be another option. Anything that involved going through that gate involved death for either her Platoon or those who got in the way. She pointed back up towards the side of the building they had come out of. About halfway up, there were balconies attached to the accommodation suites. As she spoke, she drew an imaginary line upwards in the direction of a nearby mast that ran all the way up to the top of the transparent dome that was high overhead. 'What about that? Go upwards? Up inside the tower and run a line across to the mast and find an airlock in the roof?'

Parynski replied, '*We'd* be able to do it, but the Ambassador and his entourage would struggle, particularly with the injured and children.'

She was about to challenge him on that when the HazMat alarms went off in all their suits. 'Seal 'em up,' shouted one of her team. As she backed up into the cover of the garage, she checked her own suit was fully sealed and using its own tanks before checking that of the hostages they'd rescued. Parynski was with their medic, applying a sealant wrap to the aide's suit, which had been punctured by gunfire. She received a look to suggest they hoped they'd been quick enough.

'Sitrep,' she shouted at Monk. 'What the fuck is it?'

Monk and two others had slung their rifles over their shoulders and were huddled together, examining a sensor Monk had produced from his backpack. He looked over to her; even through the faceplate, she could see he had gone pale.

'Djikian gas. Shit, shit, shit!'

Wilding jogged to him, indicating to them to switch to a private channel. 'What?'

'All dead. Everyone, including any of us that gets exposed. No cure.' He nodded at the aide on the floor, giving her a look. 'Who the hell would do this? They don't know it yet, but within forty-eight hours there will be thousands of dead bodies out there.'

Observing the scene, Wilding implored the Qarti to understand it wasn't her fault. These people were going to die anyway, no matter what she did.

# 38

## SQUIRE

*Inside the Xenos*

As he continued to follow Wilding's route, Squire wished that Paisley had blocked the message from Parynski until he was safely back on the BSV. He noted that she'd barely explored any of the side passages or doors she'd passed. Squire felt obliged to further investigate the opportunities that presented themselves. He couldn't blame Wilding for not hanging around, anyway. Whilst Wilding had been trying to appear calm and overly confident the reality was that she had known that when entering the alien vessel, she was unlikely to survive, so whilst she did some 'show and tell' for the camera she was distracted, desperately hoping to find some place safe.

Squire moved at a pace far slower than Wilding to allow for extra investigations. Paisley, who had carried an extra bottle of air for Squire, suggested that they postpone their search and return when Squire's mental state was improved. Squire acknowledged his mood was low, impressed as ever by how well his AI knew him, responding that he wanted to get as much done now as they could just in case they did find Wilding alive.

They found no evidence of life. Everything looked like it had been nicely tidied away before the passengers or crew had left, or as suggested by Wilding's footage, had retreated to the chamber that contained all those pods.

# THE TRITON RUN

A few hundred yards deeper, they came across a series of rooms that seemed to be a barracks or armoury. There were dormant screens filling one wall, a set of units that appeared to be a kitchen on another, and a variety of perches set out. There were pipes that appeared to be taps, though the controls near them didn't seem to work. Paisley took some samples by scraping the inside of the pipe and confirmed that it was likely that water had once flowed through it. Its composition was likely close enough to that consumed by humans that, with some filtering, it might have been drinkable. Perhaps Wilding could have found safe refuge somewhere after all.

Off this room was a square room filled with shelves that were lined with equipment. Some shelves contained what appeared to be staffs or batons, whilst others had metal devices that reminded Squire of an old-fashioned machine gun. He picked some up, noting they were remarkably light. They decided against testing if any of them worked. Paisley stowed away one of the smaller weapons for later inspection.

Other shelves contained body armour that would, they estimated, have fitted a creature the same shape as the figure carved into the statue they had seen earlier. They took good images of all they found, put them back into their sockets and moved on.

Squire and Paisley had been using magnetic boots as they were unclear about the gravity situation. There was a weak artificial gravity. They couldn't see what was controlling it and whether it was only weak because it was failing or whether that was how the aliens had preferred it.

As they progressed, and despite Squire swapping air tanks, progress was so slow that Paisley started to express concern about their ability to get back to the BSV. Squire had him alter the composition of his supply, so it lasted longer. Squire could also tell Paisley had also medicated him to help his mood and stress. Paisley had offered to leave Squire and sprint back to the ship to collect more supplies, including oxygen. Squire told him that was no way he wanted to be left alone here, so they resolved to reach the main chamber, and then head back to the BSV.

An hour later, Paisley confirmed to him that they'd reached the opening they'd seen on Wilding's footage. He added, 'I'm afraid that due to the air situation we must set off back after only four minutes. Now we know the route and the air needed, we can plan ahead and bring more capacity next time.'

Paisley stopped Squire's protest in a very human way, raising an arm to indicate he wasn't listening. 'By complaining, you are losing time. It's disappointing we have such little time, but my primary role is to keep you safe. If you don't co-operate, I'll take control of your suit and walk you back.'

And with that, they moved into the chamber. Paisley continued to talk through the data his drone and scans were giving him. 'Residual indications of power. Their technology is better at cloaking it than ours, so we should proceed with the same caution we've exercised so far.'

'With you on that,' replied Squire, realising his anxiety about what might be around the corner was starting to cripple his thinking. He tried to calm himself again and felt a rush of something. Zefyrex. Without asking, Paisley was a step ahead of him. Some restricted what their AI assistants could do without permission, but he'd worked alongside Paisley so long he trusted his judgement.

Squire shuffled forward, trying to keep his feet on the metal floor plates and then reached out to tether himself to the safety rails. Paisley tethered Squire to him once again. Squire didn't complain.

The footage from Wilding's cam hadn't done the chamber justice. It was hardly a surprise because she'd had to film on a low power, single direction camera unit to conserve power.

The size of the open space took his breath away, and he leaned on the rail, concluding it was likely to be a perch, as much as a safety device. He peered out at the strange collection of spires that rose from the darkness. They could see similar levels to the one they stood on, both above and below. Their torches couldn't reach the ceiling, so the drone carried out a short tour of the chamber, revealing a domed ceiling of rough rock approximately four storeys above them. The chamber went double the distance below them to a rough rock floor, out of which the spires protruded. There were a number of tunnels and chambers off the floor.

Squire could well imagine the aliens soaring and swirling around this chamber, flying up to the top and gliding round before landing on the spires or the perches. Perhaps the different heights of the spires signified familial ranking or some other status.

'We only have two minutes left and then we absolutely must leave.'

Squire acknowledged this. Their drone returned to Paisley's side, providing welcome further illumination. They turned so their backs were to the void, their tethers allowing them to move around in safety. As they peered upwards and around at the wall ahead of them, they took in the row of frames or doorways that Wilding had described earlier that ran around the perimeter of the chamber, set into the wall.

Squire jumped as he spotted three lights. Three pods were lit by a dull yellow light, dark shadows within. Two of them were on this level, the third on the level above, around towards the other side of the chamber.

Paisley edged towards the light, Squire following once the tether between them was taut, so he had no choice. He turned up the noise from the external mic, though all it did was make the situation even more nerve-wracking. He was fairly sure the background hum was in his imagination, but the sound of their footsteps and a slight buzzing from the drone were all amplified by the space and echoed slightly.

They reached the first pod that was lit. The creature within it was dead.

At least Squire, at that precise moment, hoped it was dead. That wasn't the likely view of the scientific community, however right now the last thing he needed was the need to try and communicate with an alien life form where his first message was going to be that his air was about to run out and he had to leave right away. Whilst the dozen or so pods they had walked past had been so dark it was impossible to see anything behind the glass this lit one was quite different. It was hard to see where the light came from. It was a dull, dirty yellow glow emanating from within the capsule, from behind the thing within it.

The alien was pretty much identical to the statue, just smaller. It floated in some sort of thick gunge, held suspended in roughly the middle of the pod. Its head was turned to one side, hands across its chest, with a strap tied around its wrists. A thin wire ran out of the strap and vanished into the gunge behind it. It was naked whereas, the statue looked like it wore some sort of harness.

He stepped to one side to let Paisley get a better view. These creatures were either dead or in some sort of suspended animation. The crew being asleep might explain why the ship had been packed up so efficiently, though it was still a mystery why it was drifting when the Scout had the misfortune to hit it. Something must have gone wrong.

Paisley moved towards the second light.

Inside, they found Dee Wilding, dressed in her full space suit with helmet on the floor by her feet. Squire grimaced at the face. Wilding looked like she had choked on the grunge. Her eyes and mouth were both wide open. The eyes were unseeing, blood stains below them. Asphyxia.

'FUCK!' shouted Squire. 'Get her out of there.' He banged on the outside of the pod. Paisley stepped across him to block his view and spoke in a voice that was remarkably gentle for an AI. It knew Squire well and knew what Wilding had meant to him.

'We can't do anything for her now. If already dead, then we will recover her later. If she's alive in there, we risk killing her by rushing. We need to protect you, protect our ship first and then recover Wilding. We'll come back as soon as we can…but we absolutely have to go now, and we will.'

Not for the first time, Paisley took full control of their relationship from his Master. Squire was vaguely aware of the automated skeleton embedded in the legs of his suit slowly powering up and following Paisley back the way they had come. Before they left, Paisley placed a string of sensors. It wasn't long before they were back in the corridor heading back where they had come from.

Squire didn't remember the return journey. They didn't stop. It took a while before the tears stopped. He'd seen corpses before, he'd been at Buchanan. He'd recovered dead that he knew, he'd recovered dead women and children, but this was worse. It was several days before Squire was able to joke that when they came to make a movie of his life, he hoped they edited this bit out.

# 39

# PARYNSKI

*Onboard the Skydancer*

The Skydancer had locked in on Antiope 90 when 200,000 miles out, settled into an orbit near enough to allow Parynski to examine the pair of asteroids as they rotated about each other. Such was their proximity they shared a name. With the Skydancer's silent running capability, he was confident that they were unlikely to be detected unless they wanted to be.

Parynski had located a series of sentinels scattered in the vicinity of the asteroid. Most were antiquated, barely worked, and he had been able to plot a path through them. The binary pair were an equivalent size, both about fifty-two miles in diameter. Records that Roo had sent him before he had gone dark suggested that the interiors had only been partially dug out, but there was still the capacity to house thousands of people.

Antiope had been visited early on during the rush to strip the belt of valuable materials. In itself it hadn't offered much save being located in an area heavily populated with larger asteroids, all part of the Themis family, and so offered a jumping off point for miners. Antiope B was the rock that had most signs of life. One side was scarred with a huge crater from some ancient collision, with a flattened area of over forty miles in length. That was the reason it had been chosen to be inhabited ahead of its companion. The flattened area contained evidence of life, a number of huge metal doors inset in the surface, all allowing access to docking chambers. There were two bays large enough to take the Skydancer. The crater basin spread around the main docking bay and revealed a smattering of small buildings.

Parynski noticed what appeared to be a small missile launcher. Scans told him that it was likely to be inoperable, an antique. There was no other evidence of a defence system, though that didn't mean there wasn't one. Having monitoring equipment itself risked leading to discovery, so these people may have decided to maintain a relatively unsophisticated monitoring and defence set up.

After launching a series of tiny drones, fired off in a pattern designed to look like loose debris from an asteroid collision, he'd spent some time learning about the military capabilities of the Skydancer. It carried an incredible arsenal, as powerful as most military spacecraft. It wasn't designed to engage in a long conflict, though Parynski knew that with some of the Armageddon class weapons available, it wouldn't need to be. It could take apart most of the smaller moons in the solar system and almost all of the civilian habitats. It was no wonder he wasn't allowed to collect it from Earth.

The use of projectile weapons was rare away from Earth, ignoring the war in the Saturn system, and most ships, including those maintained by enforcement agencies, were only lightly armed. Most weaponry was limited to a self-defence regime, designed to protect against space debris. Few resorted to violence because of the risk of major damage being received in response. Even minor damage could depressurise or strand a ship, and the use of sanctions or blockades were far more effective. Parynski knew that if he ended up using any of the Skydancer's weapons, it would be because things had gone wrong.

With no chip, Parynski implanted a temporary speaker in his ear and mic on his throat so he could subvocalise commands to the ship's AI. The Skydancer carried a series of military grade suits, lightweight and perfect for use in battle. He wondered when Arden imagined they'd be used. They were capable of being used in a vacuum and would cope in space as long as there were no major collisions. He'd had it tailored to fit him and kitted out with a backpack that would allow him to carry a whole host of weaponry, tools, and an air tank. A lightweight exoskeleton was fitted to his lower limbs, strapped to his legs from inside the suit, to provide extra speed, strength, and agility. He hung it behind his command seat, the helmet rested on the couch next to him.

On the fourth morning in orbit, he finalised his plan for the rescue. Conscious of what lay ahead, he had a large breakfast, during which time he'd been ready to power up the weapon systems. Indeed, the AI had wanted him to, when a small snub-nosed tug had arrived. Within the hour, it had exited the main docking bay and headed off in a trajectory deep into the belt. Parynski resolved to get on with things before another ship turned up.

'I know it's bloody risky. I know the idea of a Trojan Horse is a bit cliché but give me an alternative!' he argued silently with the AI.

'I've done this before. I'd tell you to look at the Vogue's flight logs, but as I deleted them, I can't! I practically froze to death and survived. I trust you, at the right time, to reboot my suit and warm me. It's the only way I'll get past the sensors. We can put some extra shielding up outside to protect me from the engines, radiation, and visual inspection. I'll effectively be in suspended animation whilst they bring you aboard.'

'What if they don't?' the AI asked.

'They're stupid then. Who'd turn down the chance to get their hands on this bit of kit?'

It took several more days to prepare. A message and data dump for Roo was prepared and Parynski did several EVAs to manufacture his hiding place. The ship was capable of remodelling much of itself and used 3D printers to fabricate a fake hull piece to be placed over where he was going to hide. He tested the suit several times, including one test run at lowering his temperature. He didn't enjoy it one bit and remained conscious throughout before the AI rebooted his suit and warmed him. There were two variations on the plan that would be executed, and it was for the AI to decide which, depending on the behaviour of the kidnappers. Parynski hoped the AI was as clever as it said it was. The AI was also going to have to go into a form of shutdown in order to restrict too detailed a search when boarded.

They'd created fake panelling to keep the kidnappers from certain areas of the ship, not least the armoury. All the consoles that revealed the most interesting capabilities of the ship had been given new dummy purposes that would hopefully pass a cursory examination. After they'd sent the package to Roo, Parynski did an EVA to remove the coms dishes, stowing them whilst putting up a mocked up damaged version. They'd also put some damaged panelling in the area around the dish and radio gear to suggest an impact.

The ship's log was doctored to suggest that following a medical emergency, the Captain and three other crew members had abandoned the ship using the Emergency Evacuation Capsule to get to a passing cruiser. To avoid looting and to back up the story, he'd put most of the gear from the sickbay into the capsule. He'd then launched it on a course that took it away from the area without being noticed and into a holding position where he could return for it if he pulled this off. Parynski grimly noted to the AI that Arden would have his balls if the ship weren't intact on delivery, but then if he didn't get off Antiope then it was unlikely to be too much of a worry. Launching the shuttle would likely encourage the terrorists to go after it and that risked exposing him.

Any intrusive examination of the Skydancer would reveal much of his work was a deception. He just needed to buy some time. Whether they would believe the story about the medical emergency, he just couldn't know.

Parynski just had to hope that those on the Antiope would

take the logs and back up data at face value and accept the Skydancer had been abandoned, subject to several collisions that had damaged systems enough that the autopilot systems were disorientated and the AI offline.

Six hours later he was strapped under a bulkhead he'd bolted tight after himself. He instructed the AI to slowly power his suit down as planned. He tried to relax and drift off to sleep - he didn't much fancy being frozen whilst awake. He barely felt the drugs being injected into him via the suit to help the process and to protect him. Just before he was consumed by unconsciousness, he felt the vibration of the engines as the ship changed course, looped away from its cover and back towards Antiope.

# 40

# JUDE

*Antiope Mining Facility*

They were in the sickbay.

Rebecca had slipped in the gym and hurt an ankle. It had been a good opportunity for Jude to get to know Doctor Howard. He didn't belong. He was one of the few staff members who were friendly, and Jude was aware Rebecca relied on him. He had taken a fatherly role towards her. When the shooting started, Jude resolved to try and not kill him.

Rebecca was walking within a couple of days. An exoskeletal brace protected the ankle whilst it healed and she was, she said, in no discomfort. Jude doubted their captors would have provided the same care if it had happened to her. Compared to Rebecca and Zander, she knew that whatever the Exiles' goals were, she was likely expendable, particularly if leverage were needed over the other two.

Howard checked the ankle, and they'd been allowed to borrow some scissors to cut the bottom of Rebecca's coveralls open so the leg would fit comfortably over the brace. A security guard, never normally on duty here, stood silently nearby, face impassive, keeping an eye on them. He wore the same practical jump suit that most of them wore, with a baton hanging from his utility belt and a taser strapped to his lower leg. His left hand was in his pocket, trying and failing to appear casual whilst his right hand nervously stroked the baton handle.

Perversely, this excited Jude. The Exiles didn't feel totally safe around her. In the weeks she'd been on the base, she'd barely seen any armed staff. Something had spooked them. The guards they saw around the base were all now armed.

Zander finished cutting away the bottom of Rebecca's leggings and stepped back to admire his handiwork. 'Not bad for someone who has his own private dresser back home!'

The guard stepped in and plucked the scissors from Zander's grasp. Jude giggled, and the guard pretended not to notice. He retreated to a position near the door. After thanking Howard, they went for a late breakfast. The canteen had quietened down and Jude enjoyed the smell of artificial sausage and bacon for the first time in a while, wondering where it had come from.

Zander carried their plates on a tray, and they moved near a group of engineers who were chatting loudly. As usual, after being spotted, they slightly lowered the volume of their discussions and were able to relax without too much fear of being overheard. Jude popped a piece of bacon in her mouth, and after checking nobody had come near enough to eavesdrop, jabbed her plastic fork out excitedly towards Zander.

'He's coming, I tell you. That ship we heard they'd spotted has scared the shit out of these people. Why would they have increased security so much for a derelict? And it's the second ship to come here in the last few days.'

Jude waited for Zander's measured approach to try and calm her excitement. There was no doubt that since they'd overheard mention of the ghost ship, there had been a general increase in tension around the place. A modern space yacht had been picked up nearby. It was abandoned without crew. It had been brought inside and orders were awaited as to whether the vessel would be pressed into service for the cause or stripped for parts.

As expected, Zander replied gently, 'It's empty, Jude. There was nobody on board.

I'm sure they checked.'

Jude felt undeterred. 'It's too strange, Theo. Something's going on and they think it too. Howard also said someone really important arrived recently too.'

Zander raised an eyebrow. 'That doesn't necessarily sound like good news for us?'

Rebecca leaned into the conversation. 'Please don't get too excited, Jude, he's right. This sort of excitement has happened before. It usually only lasts a day or so. I'd love to find my family, but it's not going to happen.'

Jude said, 'My Dad is all I've left. He'll come.'

Rebecca's face fell, and she stared at her plate. 'I don't think my family even care anymore.'

Neither Jude nor Zander knew what to say to that.

# 41

# PARYNSKI

*Antiope Mining Facility*

Parynski stirred, coming round as if he had a horrendous hangover. He was relieved to get away from the dream that had been chasing him. It was the regular one when he'd told Mary about his deployment to Mars just as the war of independence was getting out of hand. That had been the first time they'd split up and the dressing down she'd given him in front of his friends had never left him.

A message was being repeated through his suit speaker. Initially incapable of taking it in, Bruce allowed himself to doze again for a while, the warmth of sleep too tempting for his exhausted body. The voice felt like it came from inside him, permeating every cell.

'It's time to wake, Sir. I've been slowly reheating your suit. It'll take a little while before you are ready to move. I've run some checks and there's been no irreversible damage from the freeze and thaw process. I recommend trying not to move for another two hours and I'll prepare your energy drink. You may sleep for a short period again before you move.'

Sleeping longer sounded good. A little later, he noticed that the message on repeat had changed. 'We were intercepted and boarded. The boarders seem to have accepted the log reports as accurate, and I've been towed inside the main docking bay.

We've been inside for three days. They've examined Skydancer inside and out. I started the warming process based on what I could ascertain about their shift system. While the base is operational all day and night, a majority are shifted to live a standard work timetable, so you should have a four-hour window for you to get away from the docking bay.'

Parynski sipped at the drink tube, feeling an almost immediate boost from whatever energy and rejuvenation formula had been put in the water. He realised he had already opened his eyes. It was dark apart from a few lights reflecting on the HUD on the helmet in front of him. The heat visor was currently down. He decided he'd wait until told to raise it.

He tried to stretch his arms and legs, momentarily panicking at his paralysis, before remembering the suit was locked in position and soon, he could feel the suit massaging his legs as they gradually warmed. The warming sensation and the repetitive message from the AI caused him to drift off again.

A further message caught his attention. 'There is increasing activity on the base. I believe that someone important arrived just before we did, and security levels have been increased. I would recommend an early excursion to secure the prisoners.'

'Sounds like this just got harder.'

# 42

# WILDING

*The Dark*

Reliving events on Buchanan vanished from Wilding's mind as two space suited figures appeared outside her Tank. Her heart leapt in anticipation. She was going to be rescued!

Then her heart broke as they vanished. She'd struggled to get a proper view of them as spotlights were shone at her from their suits. She was unable to close her eyes and the bright light burned. As she struggled to watch them, all she could really see was a blur, but the styling of the EVA suits was unmistakable. She also recognised the gait of the figures.

Wilding would recognise Squire anywhere, and that meant the second figure was likely to be Paisley. She retreated into herself to assess what she'd seen. Surely, they'd come back? She had to hold on to that as a certainty. She daren't believe they wouldn't.

The Qarti could feel the emotional rollercoaster she was going through and for a short while metaphorically backed away. After a while, and with no sign that the visitors were coming back, they started to question her, gently initially, then with more force about who the figures were. The Qarti had been aware of the state of their ship from Wilding's description of events that had led to her arrival. This new event concerned them. All Wilding could tell them was that she trusted Squire with her life and that he'd be there to rescue her, and crucially, would be there to preserve the lives of the Qarti. Wilding guessed that Squire was alone at this stage, though feeling it was inevitable that now their ship had been located, others would follow.

For some time afterwards, she sensed an undercurrent of fear from them, an increased level of distrust. Eventually, conversations turned back to Mars. She knew they were interrogating her again, wanting to understand her, to understand humans more. For the first time, however, since she'd woken in this alien environment, she felt as if she perhaps had the edge. Her friend was coming back for her.

Upon the release of the poison gas, Wilding remembered the feeling of panic and confusion well. 'Anything we can do to get our medics in?' Despite her priority being the rescue of the Ambassador, she'd prefer to not leave others dying.

Squire, Parynski and Dunk all shook their heads. 'It can't be cured. Why the fuck would anyone do this?'

She hadn't been sure at the time, now she knew. It had long been thought that the Martian Government had wanted to clear space in the city for more of their own chosen, preferred settlers. The flow of people from Earth was increasing in pace and many wanted to find homes with those of like mind or background. Buchanan had originally been a pioneering base, populated by descendants of the first astronauts and the colony ship that had followed. Those settlers had been picked for their suitability, their skills, and personality traits to build a sustainable city.

As ever, Wilding knew, man had then reverted to its usual prejudices and petty squabbles that developed into more sinister conflict. The plan all along was to create a conflict, then push out those who weren't wanted. If all else failed, she imagined the plan involved deciding to exterminate the enemy in self-defence.

Wilding waved to Dunk, and he pulled her up to his vantage point. The view was nowhere near as impressive as it had been many storeys above in the ambassador's suite. The ceiling of the dome seemed impossibly far away and whilst she could see the near edge of the crater wall, when looking in the opposite direction towards the centre of the city her view extended only as far as a view of nearby, crowded parks, a highway and then a row of towers. One of them had thick, black smoke pouring out of a large gouge in the side. Metal beams and plasteen walls spilled out, hanging like gruesome intestines. The nearness of the crater wall gave her some hope. She could see the silver, vertical lines that were the lifts built into the wall. They'd take them to the surface from where they'd get out onto the Martian surface and await extraction.

The crowd was growing outside the gate, hammering at the lock and the hinges, throwing rocks over and into it. They were having to step over the bodies of their friends and family, cut down by the initial gunfire from the Government troops. They were getting more agitated, desperate to gain control of the Administration centre of the city, unaware that their rulers and civil servants had all long since disappeared.

The battle with Government troops was abating. Dunk pointed out to her various ongoing skirmishes and that many armed vehicles were withdrawing. 'They think they've won the battle and can focus on occupying the HQ.'

'And they've no idea they are all dead tomorrow and it'll be fucking painful.'

Dunk grunted in agreement. Then, 'These poor bastards aren't going to help us whatever. They get through that gate and we're all dead. It'll just be quicker for us.'

Wilding remembered that moment clearly. A moment of horrible clarity in amongst the chaos. She'd never had such a moment in the field before, and she'd never been in a combat situation since. She'd been through the next steps hundreds of times since, during the Inquiry, the court martial, the criminal trials.

The Qarti were here too, she felt them. They didn't judge her negatively. Instead, a cloak of supportive emotions surrounded her. She understood that they'd made difficult decisions themselves. In that sense, they implored her to understand they were all kindred spirits, with much in common.

Despite the clarity round the decision making at that time, the events that followed were a bit of a blur. It was that lack of clarity and control that meant when she was discharged following her appeal against their court martial, she was unable to resume active service. Not that she'd wanted to. The whole process of investigating the events in Buchanan that day had torn her Platoon apart. She'd implored them to forget her and carry on in service without her, not counting on how loyal they were. Though some were suspended alongside her, later reinstated without charge, they'd all resigned in protest. And with that, her closest group of friends, family almost, had broken and gone their separate ways.

She remembered the arguments before it happened, almost all of the Platoon had questioned her judgment and punches had been thrown. Even the Ambassador had offered to surrender to the mob with a view to seeing if that would assist. Eventually, they'd all agreed to follow her leadership and later privately thanked her. She'd made a horrific, ballsy and necessary decision. There'd been twenty-two of them there, trapped in the yard. Outside were thousands of protestors, guilty only of feeling outraged at deliberate government oppression and provocation. She was on their side in the conflict, but the facts were clear. If she didn't act, the gate would be broken down, and they'd be slaughtered by the mob. They wouldn't know who she was and to the casual observer, it'd be assumed they were part of the government trying to evacuate.

The mob were already condemned to death, they just didn't know it yet.

And with that, she took point, putting herself in the line of fire. She'd taken their heavy gunner, Garraway's multi-launcher, and had climbed onto the front of the forklift. Garraway, easily identifiable by the harness she wore that was needed to support the weapon, drove the vehicle after she'd helped Wilding set it up on the roof. On her signal, everyone had backed away to the rear of the yard save Dunk and Parynski, who were standing either side of the gate, ready to open it. On her signal, they slowly released the catches on the gate as Garraway steered the forklift into the gap, blocking the entrance. A sea of people charged forward, pausing as she pulled herself straight, weapon aimed over the crowd. Objects were thrown her way, but she deftly ducked away from them.

She'd patched herself into a speaker on the lift and spoke as calmly as she could. She couldn't remember these moments personally, acquiring a secondary memory based on the footage from her cam and the one on Dunk's suit. Her view now, and that of the Qarti, was based on Dunk's perspective, slightly to one side.

'Hey. Listen! My name is Commander Dee Wilding of the EDFs Expeditionary Force. My Platoon are not with your Government, we're here only to extract the Ambassador and his family. Please let us through.'

She paused for a moment, hoping for any sign of hope. A shout or an acknowledgement. Disappointingly, there was nothing positive. Instead, the mass of people pushed forward at a greater rate. People were being crushed out there, yet still the sea of people approached. There was a guttural growl from the crowd aimed at her, and more objects were thrown. Thankfully, they were not well armed, so for the moment, she felt safe. Once they'd climbed over the front of the forklift, things would soon change. She picked out plenty of anti-government slogans and threats.

She used the muzzle of the rifle she had slung over her shoulder to push some of the crowd back, realising it would only take a few seconds more before they breached the gap. Thankfully, the forklift had a skirt designed to keep the dust out because otherwise, they would have already been under the vehicle and into the yard.

'You've been tricked. You don't know it yet, but you've all been poisoned…'

She gave up. They were in no mood to listen. For a moment,

they were all distracted as a burnt-out tank one hundred yards away exploded, tossing its insides into the air. There were screams as dozens went down full of hot, sharp shrapnel. This only made the group even more animated and aggressive.

Wilding stumbled as her left knee buckled, hit by a piece of concrete. She dropped to her knee, looking out at the direction of where it had come from. Perhaps if she just sprayed some warning shots, she'd thought.

'Ma'am……' Garraway interrupted her thinking. She was sitting in the cab beneath her so would have had a lower-level view than Wilding. 'We've got to do it. I'm sorry.'

Wilding had known then, in hindsight, she realised she'd known earlier, that she'd got no choice. She had to put to one side the suffering she'd cause, telling herself it would be quicker for many and less painful than if they'd been allowed to suffer.

She'd tried once more to get the crowd to move, then fired some warning shots in the air. Nothing worked, and she started to get spooked as the crowd rocked her vehicle, trying to force it out the way.

'Ma'am...' said Garraway again.

It was the presence of her friend that gave her the strength she'd needed that day to save her Platoon and the Ambassador's entourage. Her thoughts became muddled and detached as she remembered the last time she'd seen Garraway. She'd never recovered from what she'd seen and whilst she was discharged as Wilding had been, it took its toll on her. They'd met in a bar where she practically lived, having become an alcoholic. Nothing else would keep the memories away, she'd told her.

Gently, ever so gently, the Qarti brought her back to the events in Buchanan.

Tears had blurred her vision, so she'd hoisted the multi launcher down from the roof and set it up on the bonnet using its stand. She switched it onto automatic fire and turned off her external mics. For as long as it lasted, all she could hear was her own breathing and the sobbing of her colleagues.

Once they opened up a gap in the crowd, they'd all stepped outside the compound, whereupon she was flanked by her Platoon.

Thirty minutes later, she'd reached the crater wall to discover the elevators were all off. She'd led the group up the path and onto stairways cut into the wall by the original settlers. Once at the top, they'd exited the dome onto the Martian landscape where they were collected. Not once did she look back.

# 43

# REBECCA

*Antiope Mining Facilit*

It was the middle of the afternoon when Rebecca was invited to another medical check-up. The guard who took her said her friends weren't to come, wouldn't explain why, making her feel anxious. On arrival at the sick bay, the nurse put her in a side cubicle, before disabling and then removing the exoskeleton that was wrapped around her ankle. She then helped Rebecca up onto a couch to await Doctor Howard.

The Nurse told Rebecca she might have to wait a little longer than normal as they were about to be inspected. A plastic door, with a frosted window set in the middle, was slid across the cubicle. Sighing, she pulled her knees up and rested her head on them. She'd spent forever, most of her life, it felt, waiting for something to happen. Jude and Zander had given her hope, and she prayed it wasn't in vain.

After a while, she could hear small talk between the Nurse and Doctor Howard, who must have come in after she'd been put in the cubicle. She detected a tension she wasn't used to. The base wasn't exactly fun, and it was only after spending time with her new friends that she realised how stuffy and formal everything was. Only Howard had ever gone out of his way to be friendly to her.

The powered external door hissed open and the frosted glass darkened as a large number of bodies filed into the medical suite. She strained to hear what was being said. She could hear the Nurse raising her voice, 'You can't!' There was a loud slap and what Rebecca thought sounded like whimpering.

After a few minutes, the cubicle door slid to one side, and three figures filled the entrance. She recognised Professor Howard, of course; he was dressed smarter than normal and had even combed his normally wiry hair. His normally red cheeks were now positively purple, and he was sweating profusely. Next to him was a tall figure in black, straight-backed, square jaw with impassive expression. Security. The remaining visitor was a slight figure, also dressed in black. Slippers and a business suit. She had short, bobbed hair that framed her pale face. Piercing black eyes looked straight through her and Rebecca felt her skin crawl.

The female stepped slowly and deliberately towards her. Rebecca hugged her knees more tightly, peering through the wispy brown fringe that tumbled over her eyes.

'Hello Rebecca. My name is Chen. I hope you've been looked after.' A statement rather than a question.

Rebecca said nothing. This woman meant her harm. She had come to accept her surroundings and other residents and whilst she resented them, she had been able to get on amicably with most who, whilst keeping her at arm's length, had always been civil to her.

The body language of Chen was so alien to anything she had experienced.

'I'm going to make you a tv star. Your father will be so proud.' Her tone was firm, insistent.

Rebecca panicked and jumped off the bench without thinking, immediately feeling pain in her ankle. Before she could even begin to speak, the security guard stepped across in front of Chen, blocking Rebecca off. He raised his hand and palmed Rebecca away. She collapsed against the bench and crumpled in a heap with a howl of pain. She curled up into a defensive posture, clutching her ankle. Howard started to move to help until the guard obstructed him. Rebecca peered up at her visitors and with the anguish clear in her voice spoke to Chen. 'My father, you know him?'

Chen paused, signalling her guard to step aside. Howard crouched down beside her and looked at her ankle, trying to console her without showing too much emotion in front of his superior.

'More importantly, I know exactly what he and your new friends here did to me and my family. He'll see you alright, I will make sure of that.'

And with that, she turned on her heels and stepped back out of the cubicle. She addressed the Nurse who met her. 'Make sure you get her presentable. I want the brace off. Two days. Without fail, please.'

Chen stepped aside, her guard following and together they left the medical suite and exited into the rocky corridor beyond. Rebecca broke down, sobbing into Howard's shoulder. She didn't know what Chen meant, but it didn't bode well.

## 44

## MULLER

*Neptune Orbit*

Muller was conflicted. Nobody knew about his links to Chen, for which he was relieved. Nobody also knew about the internal battle that was raging inside him, though he suspected Chen might have a suspicion. She knew him too well.

On the one hand, the prospect of first contact, of establishing that there was sentient alien life elsewhere in the universe, excited him. It excited everyone, it dominated the news and conversation. That was the same whether on a Dirigible over Venus, on Earth or out at Neptune. He couldn't believe his luck. He was leading the project to recover and then make safe the Xenos. It was a full-time role, the role of a lifetime.

As such, it hurt him that he needed to see Arden destroyed. Not because of anything Arden had done personally to him, because Arden's existence stood in way of his life with Chen. Chen had stopped asking him to see if he could engineer a situation where he was abducted. That slightly worried him. He hoped that she'd accepted it was unrealistic. Usually, Arden was supported by a large security detail on the odd occasion he left the safety of his home habitat. Muller wished he could go back to being a ship's engineer, on board charter ships between the Moon and Neptune. He'd done that for several years following his escape from the Trike before he'd met and become besotted with Chen.

# THE TRITON RUN

Muller realised that his mind was wandering from the meeting he was supposed to be participating in. He was sat in the cockpit of his own private Tug, camera facing towards him. He'd been in the middle of a shift when the meeting had started, carrying out another inspection of the development work being carried out in preparation for the eventual arrival of the Xenos, as the alien ship was dubbed. The rest of those in attendance were more impressed with the set up for the meeting, so his attention had drifted away to other things. As part of his planning, Muller had taken many VR tours of the explored parts of the Xenos, both internally and externally. He probably knew it better than anyone else. He spent much of these conferences, as well as updating on progress at Neptune, interpreting and explaining to everyone the information that Squire was relaying.

He was expecting Chen to contact him. He had an excuse ready to leave the conference call early. It wouldn't raise suspicion; he was so busy and performing well.

When he'd logged in for the regular conference call, he found Squire waiting on what had become the bridge of the Xenos. As ever with conversations spanning such a distance, and with no Relay ships or Sentinels to boost the signal, there were lots of awkward silences that even the software linking them would struggle to compensate for.

The bridge was towards the rear of the Xenos, a box type area that broke through the

top, or what appeared to be the top, of the rocky exterior. The 'front' of the room was filled with a dead view screen. It was littered with other dead consoles and unresponsive screens.

Instead of chairs or couches, there were perches, as was the case throughout the Xenos.

Muller's VR tour had revealed that with the BSV tethered nearby, Squire had been able to establish contact with Neptune via his own ship. Paisley had run cabling to a nearby exterior entrance and set up a short-range transmitter that was in line of sight to the BSV above. The two men spoke regularly, poring over the data and whilst they'd not yet found any other chambers containing aliens their working theory, based on the apparent internal structure of the Xenos, was that there must be many other similar chambers to that from where Wilding was awaiting recovery. Squire was frustrated that he was so busy that he had only managed to spend limited time in the chamber where Wilding remained.

In the weeks they had been here, Squire and Paisley had managed to map and explore more of the ship, having also found other external entrances. This exploration had covered a tiny percentage of the volume of the ship, though at some point the remainder of the cloak that had hidden the exterior to discovery had failed or been switched off. Whilst unnerving, it was welcomed by Squire and had allowed a complete exterior survey to be carried out and had led to the BSV being moored closer.

More drones had been built and deployed internally, adding to their knowledge of the setup of the ship, however over half of these had only broadcast for a while before vanishing. Paisley believed that they may have contained flaws due to a bug in the 3D printer, though Squire's mind raced with other possibilities. He didn't have the resources on board to create replacements, so had placed motion sensors near the start of the routes that the missing drones had gone down. They'd now been able to identify the engines and locate what was likely the engine room. Despite some cautious tinkering with the machinery, the ship remained dormant. Muller had already passed on all they could get about the Xenos's engines onto specialists he knew. The alien technology was beyond their own capabilities. There was much to learn.

At his suggestion, Squire had moved into the Xenos to save the time and risks of repeated trips back and forth to the BSV. The bridge doubled as his living quarters. A temporary air lock had been built and large units brought across that powered an air supply unit and heating. Paisley had proved incredibly efficient at setting up an area that could house Squire safely. Against another wall was set up a toilet cubicle and a small kitchen unit. He slept on a camp bed that was folded away during the day and told Muller he enjoyed the time he could spend out of his EVA suit. Paisley hadn't been able to bring over a shower, so Squire looked more unkempt than normal. That was commented on by Garcia, concerned that too much pressure was being put on him. Muller could see Roo, her avatar stood alongside her colleague from the Triton observatory, nodding in agreement.

The meeting was about to wrap up, not achieving much save keeping the steering group up to date. Arden confirmed his delight at their combined efforts, with a short summary of how events were being treated by the media in system. Muller made his excuses when the alert from his wife appeared and discretely logged out of all his usual systems, using a private, dark server.

Chen looked serious when her image appeared. Muller sat within a glass bubble, perched on the top of the small, square ship, allowing him 360 views. Whilst travelling between sites, the array of arms and grippers had all been stowed away into the hull. Chen would be able to see, behind him, the pale disc of Neptune, and crossing its face, the dark spidery web of the shipyards that her husband managed. The odd smudge could also be seen, self-illuminating ships or habitats like the one Muller had come from.

Muller had been convinced by Chen to take a job out near Neptune, in the hope that it would allow him to gather intelligence to further the mission. He hadn't expected that once settled and enjoying his new life, he'd want her to give up her political ambitions and come to join him. He wished he felt differently, acknowledging to himself that the anger that burned inside him against Arden and Zander was a candle compared to the inferno that Chen carried deep inside her. He'd risen fast through the ranks, becoming Shipyard Operations Manager, no mean feat as only Earth had a facility bigger and comparable operations at Mars and Jupiter had been under the control of the same companies for decades. There had been an even bigger shipyard at Saturn, though the conflict there made it difficult for anyone outside of the vicinity to know exactly what its status was.

She'd changed, though. Even beyond the surgery and physical changes over recent years, he'd been sensing it for months. The physical change had been dramatic. He understood her reasons, and she was still as attractive to him as ever. It was her personality that was changing for the worse. Muller wasn't sure how that left them. Though the pretence of a relationship from millions of miles away was difficult enough, he clung onto the hope that once she achieved what she wanted to achieve, she'd be happy to abandon her public and private responsibilities. He understood her motivations. He'd felt the same for a long while, but he'd come to realise he was being manipulated and knew he was emotionally trapped by his love for her.

'We are nearly at the end, my love, and then we can take off and spend the rest of our lives together. Knowing our people have been revenged will ensure those who remain are no longer afraid, are no longer in poverty. Our enemies will be wary. Another few days.'

Muller was taken aback. It was the first time she'd ever been definitive with him in terms of timescales. Previously, it was always a dream, pushed away into the future. His heart leapt.

'So soon?'

He wished he hadn't asked by the end. Chen told him her plan and why she was on Antiope.

'I have Zander, I have Arden's child.'

Even the prospect of being with his wife didn't soothe the horror growing within his gut. He felt sick. He'd been committed and had foolishly, in hindsight, told her more than he needed to. He was part of this.

'I don't understand your reaction,' Chen had said. 'This can all be resolved now. Both will be executed as revenge for what they did, and it'll be broadcast across the solar system.'

Muller had been guiding his Tug to the next location on his rounds, and he slowed his speed temporarily so he could focus on dealing with his wife. He wanted her to change her plans, though deep inside he knew he'd never change her mind.

He'd always felt uneasy once he'd realised that his information had led to the abduction of Arden's child, but she'd assured him that the girl wouldn't be hurt and would eventually be released unharmed once Scott Arden had been publicly forced to concede his past demeanours in public and pay reparations. Many years had passed, and the subject had dropped from the news. He'd trusted Chen, using that trust to mask his own guilt. His feelings on Zander were indifferent, but he couldn't live with children being murdered, no matter who they were.

Chen spoke as calmly and firmly. 'Remember the deaths we suffered, your family? You know how painful that was. There was no discrimination between man, woman, and child, and it could have been avoided. But anyway, look forward. This will be the end of the conflict. You've not managed to get Arden, so his closest other family member will have to do.'

Chen had pointedly put the blame on him for not securing Arden. If he had, then perhaps Rebecca could have gone free. That hurt. She had a point. If he'd betrayed his employer and handed him over, the girl might not be in this predicament. Or she might still be killed, anyway. Muller still felt that her actions were futile, but she wasn't for listening.

He didn't know what to say, Chen continued. 'The people of the solar system would know what had happened and would never let it happen again. A new order would be formed. Zander's Party would suffer forever, never be elected again. That's the win here. Revenge and shaping the future.'

Muller noted she had not smiled at him once, or indeed shown barely any emotion that hinted at the relationship between them.

'The party has changed beyond recognition since Zander became leader, we know. And since you abducted him, the government has fallen anyway. We've secured change.'

She gave her stock answer, ignoring the added desperation in his voice. 'It's not enough. I want the elite shaken to the core. And I am disappointed that you aren't willing to follow through to the conclusion of the mission, of our calling.'

She got up, gave a thin smile. 'Once the mission is complete, we can get together again.'

Muller realised that, almost to his surprise, that he didn't believe her anymore.

Chen went to a cabinet where a pot of tea had been brewing. She carried on talking whilst she poured, and then returned to her seat. Her chamber was, by most standards off world, luxurious. All of the stone walls had been covered in fake wood cladding, with soft drapes hung across the ceiling and walls to soften a room that would have been as utilitarian as any. The room contained a large double bed covered in blankets and throws, and the far wall had tall wooden wardrobes and shelves full of clothes.

The conversation changed from talk of revenge onto the excitement Muller was enjoying with the Xenos preparation. He knew she'd diverted the conversation and was a little ashamed to be relieved. He shouldn't be telling her a lot of what he knew, but he enjoyed seeing her reaction to the story as he told it, and it was momentarily a period of respite from the angst that was growing in him.

Muller told her that a flotilla of asteroid movers and tugs had been despatched to move the casualty back to Neptune where it would be secured. It was Arden's view that if he could move the object to a place of safety, then he'd be more likely to be able to claim ownership under the laws of salvage. It was unlikely, Muller argued, that the aliens would be turning up anytime soon to collect their ship.

# THE TRITON RUN

Despite Muller's despair at the start of the conversation, the conversation ended on relatively amicable note, with Chen praising him for his work on the Xenos project and wishing him well. The latter part of the conversation had been a reversal of the norm. It was he who had put on a mask and who tried to fool the other. He'd backed down and wished her well, telling her he understood what she needed to do. He apologised and begged forgiveness. He felt dirty for doing so. He just wanted her off the call.

Chen's image vanished from the top of his dashboard and Muller tried, without success, to focus back on the tasks at hand. He had never even met Arden's child, but he couldn't get her out of his head. He couldn't remain married to someone willing to consider, never mind carry out, what had been revealed to him. Muller wondered if he would see Chen again. He'd have to take the chance she'd blow his cover if he stopped co-operating. He couldn't save Rebecca, but he could stop supporting this evil. He wanted no more of it.

He let his tug drift for a while before resolving what to do. He carefully blocked all access to Chen. All methods of communication were blocked, all her addresses and numbers were deleted, filters set so that nothing from her would get through. Maybe if he knew nothing about what was going on, it was for the best, and he'd be less likely to be implicated. He wasn't sure it would take away the feeling of guilt.

# 45

# JUDE

*Antiope Mining Facility*

Jude was grateful to finally be allowed out of her room. It was more comfortable than many of the cabins she had been allocated on shuttles that ran between Earth and the Moon, though she reminded herself that from time to time she was confined to it, therefore it was still a cell. She had a routine with Zander and Rebecca that was pleasant, and she tried to stay relaxed around them, especially Rebecca.

At some point, she was going to have to do something positive to change their situation. She'd been held hostage before, when an undercover operation in London had gone wrong. Her captors had gravely underestimated her. It had been easier to escape there and once free, she'd vanished into the hubbub of London life to rendezvous with her team before going back to arrest her captors. Here, she was confident she could take down a few of the security staff and escape, though she wasn't sure where to. Rebecca wanted to get away, and that was additional motivation.

As for Zander, he was just so much more complicated. She liked him, actively enjoyed his charming character, though he carried ghosts with him. Like many politicians he'd started as an idealist, later this had been eroded through circumstance. He'd made some mistakes, but the reaction of others to those mistakes, and what they'd done to his family in retaliation, had darkened his world view. Jude wasn't sure if he had the energy to initiate any action here, though he was also driven by a growing affection to Rebecca. It was a strange turn of events that he'd become fond of one of his most public enemy's daughters, assuming their supposition was right. Without a vessel, attempts to escape would be futile, and Jude was also wary of the repercussions for the others if it failed.

Water was again being rationed, and she wasn't allowed a shower, so she dressed and flattened her hair that had gone wild overnight. There was a knock at the door. She shouted 'enter' as she looked at herself in the tarnished mirror. She knew it was one of her friends because none of the crew ever bothered to knock and she couldn't lock the door from the inside. The door slid open, and Rebecca tumbled into the room, throwing herself at Jude, clinging on for dear life. She was shaking, tears running down her face that was pale save for red cheeks.

Jude held her tight, whispering, 'It's alright, it's alright.' Behind her followed Howard, shutting the door behind them. He was also pale, and Jude raised an eyebrow at him. He grimaced before explaining what had just happened.

'Rebecca, it's ok. We'll look after you,' Howard said gently. 'I'll get Zander, so we discuss this together. I promise I'll stop anyone hurting you.'

Jude nodded at Howard, holding onto the sobbing girl who had buried her head into her shoulder. 'Yes, please do. We'll be ok for a minute.'

Howard did an about turn and left. By the time he returned with Zander, Rebecca had calmed herself. When she'd wiped her tears, Howard sent her to get drinks for them all. As soon as she'd gone, Zander stood by the door to listen out for anyone approaching.

'So, what's the deal?'

Howard was shaking and stuttering, so Jude relayed what

he'd told her. 'When Rebecca was in the medical bay, she was visited by a female, someone who is seemingly either very senior or in charge of this outfit. She's just arrived and without saying as much, Howard thinks she's going to execute Rebecca, and very soon. He heard her talking to an aide.' Jude looked at Zander 'You'll be on the list as well.'

Jude could see Zander bite his lip, trying to hide any emotion. Part defiance, part acceptance of his fate. Howard took over the story. He took a deep breath before starting. To Jude, this was a different Howard. Whilst liking him from the first time Rebecca introduced him, they'd been wary of everyone. Now he was putting his feelings for the girl ahead of his loyalty to the Exiles and his own safety. Howard said that he was used to threats to his life, and the base was a dangerous place to be. This, he felt, was more sinister and the fact a young girl was tied into his fate only made it worse. He told them how he'd come to hate what his colleagues stood for, but with no prospect of being allowed to leave, he'd devoted his existence to using his experience to improve the health and lives of other residents. He wasn't even a citizen of the Trike and had been herded off with a gun to his head, under orders to look after the wounded survivors.

When he finished, Zander spoke next.

'I was right. These are the survivors from the three habitats, the Exiles. This is their payback. You think she plans to do it on some sort of broadcast then?'

Jude replied, 'Sounds like it. If she's carried this grudge for so many years, then maybe it's not so much of a shock she's planning something this grim?'

Jude looked at Howard. 'Despite what you say, I can't believe all of these people are in on this. They might be acting as pirates or whatever beyond the law, though I don't see them wanting to publicly execute a kid? I mean, killing the President, I sort of understand.' There was an awkward moment and Jude shrugged. 'No offence, you know what I mean.'

# THE TRITON RUN

They all went silent as they heard voices outside. Zander looked at Howard.

'Describe her again. What was her name?'

Howard was shaking, struggling to be upright and resolute. He described her, this time with more detail. 'Chen something? I've never seen her here before.'

'Fuck, it had to be her!' Zander punched the door in a sudden burst of anger, turning away from them. She could see that hurt. He let the pain subside and then turned back, slightly sheepish. Jude had never seen him lose his temper, at least not least violently.

'After all this time, I knew something wasn't right about her.'

Jude got up and found a towel for Zander to wrap his hand with. He'd taken the skin off the top of his knuckles and blood was pooling in the wounds.

'You know her?'

Zander took the towel and tied it across his hand, pulling it tight and winced. 'Yes, know her well, very well. Not as a friend or even a colleague. She's been a thorn in my side for years, always seemed too interested in what I was up to, lots of information transparency requests and always reminding me about the vote on the habitats. She'd never let things drop.'

'How was she elected?'

Zander shrugged. 'We actually did a lot of checks on her because she came from nowhere in her state election to win. There were allegations of identity fraud … nothing was ever proved. Her record seemed clean. I knew she was a pain, but shit, this is unexpected. Before he died, my personal protection officer, Reuben…joked she was the one senator you wouldn't want to be left alone with.'

Jude saw Zander's face drop as he processed what they had learned. His mention of Reuben stung.

'We need to do something. We've got to stop them killing that girl. I say we try to escape,' said Jude.

Zander and Howard agreed. Howard pulled himself up to

his full height. 'I've got an idea. We can get to the old escape pods and see if we can get outside. Maybe we can steal a ship.'

They paused as someone shouted for the door to open. It was Rebecca, carrying a tray with four cups and four plates. Whilst her face was still streaked with tears, she was putting on a brave face.

'I brought food.'

'Let's eat up, guys. This might be our last good meal for a while,' said Jude.

'It might be our last meal,' muttered Zander.

# 46

# WILDING

*The Dark*

Wilding had been exhausted from reliving the incident at Buchanan. She later gave hints as to the civil and criminal processes she'd faced since, finding the whole process taxing, and she drifted off into silence. Darkness returned, and she was not quite sure if she'd slept or just that the Qarti had left her alone to recover. The one emotion from them that remained was sympathy. They understood that she had made tough decisions and didn't judge her negatively.

After a while, she was aware again of their presence. It was a gentle, furtive feeling this time. Shadows near her. They wanted to tell her something. She'd asked many times how the Qarti had ended up on board the ship, all suspended in tanks. Previously, they had been evasive or gave a response that she didn't understand. She indicated she would be receptive, and they appeared again, consuming her awareness.

There were multiple scenes she was invited to immerse herself in. Realising she needed to focus on one at a time, she tried to concentrate. After trying to seek an order, asking for assistance with no reply she could understand, Wilding resolved to accept at face value what she could assimilate and worry about assessing it later.

The noise was deafening. Thousands, perhaps tens of thousands of clawed feet. All clattering on a series of wide metal walkways

# THE TRITON RUN

that ran up into the depths of a spaceship. Wilding's viewpoint was from a boarding ramp. She was able to spin and take in the scene. As far as she could see, ramps snaked up towards the rocky exterior of a ship, vanishing into its dark belly. There must have been at least a dozen ramps. Lines of Qarti marched past her. They weren't marching in time, or indeed in any organised fashion bar, being in single file. There were Qarti of all sizes and shapes, some clearly children and many infirm, limping and using walking sticks. Many carried packs on their back, a few dragged what looked like large canvass bags behind them.

They were clearly in a hurry and were being directed upwards by other Qarti, who stood at the base of the ramps, waving them on. Wilding could only assume this was an evacuation, and no sooner had she had thought that she felt a gentle approval.

She wondered where they were coming from and turned so she could face the bottom of the ramps. Instantaneously, her viewpoint moved, her environment blurring before solidifying again.

Her view was of something she'd previously been able only to imagine. She was standing alongside the neighbouring companions she'd been communicating with, on a giant flat platform that was floating in space. Floating nearby was the ship she'd seen before. The ramps ran from the platform into loading bays she could just make out in the underside of the ship. She was unable to be accurate, though she guessed the platform could have been several miles long and half that much wide. Sat on it were dozens of small shuttles, and out of their hatches streamed more and more Qarti, most joining the throng at the bottom of the ramps. Others converged near a series of metallic spires that were arranged in a circle. The spires were about twenty feet tall, with small platforms protruding half-way up and on top. There individual Qarti sat. It was hard for Wilding to tell, such was the amount of the noise, but based on their gesticulating, both pointing and flapping of wings, Wilding concluded they were giving out orders.

There was no obvious roof over the platform, though she

could see a few fuzzy patches overhead that suggested they were protected from space by a force field. It was technology that humankind was only just developing. As she watched, she noticed her fellow Qarti observers had retreated into the background, leaving her to take in the scene alone.

From time-to-time shuttles lifted off, replaced by others that spilled their alien cargo onto the landing area. The shuttles that left picked up pace and tore into the dark sky, vanishing momentarily before being picked out as black specs as they moved across the front of the yellow planet that hung overhead. From her position she could pick out patches of greens, blues, and browns, though the majority of the surface was the same colour as the area she'd been in when she'd had her first encountered the Qarti. She wondered if the shuttles were headed for either the canyon she'd seen or the city she'd glimpsed on the horizon. And with those thoughts, her view disintegrated, re-forming elsewhere. She was on board one of the shuttles, she guessed, or at least given the viewpoint from the nose of one.

*We had to run to stay safe.*

She swooped low over a dark blue ocean, gaining altitude over a range of mountains that ran along a coast. Nestled into the lower parts of the far side of the range was a green forest, however at the pace she travelled, she soon left it behind. The sun was away to her right, with the tall trees and lower foothills casting shadows. The colour of the earth became a reddish brown, with fewer and fewer clumps of trees. As the land flattened, she decreased altitude until she was so low she felt she could practically reach and out and touch the ground. She was now travelling too fast to get a proper view and things became a blur.

Whether it was because she felt frustration at the current view or coincidence, her view suddenly changed again. It was as if she had rotated through 180 degrees. She was now looking straight up. The gas giant she had seen previously loomed large however whilst the sky was clear of clouds, it was full of spacecraft that were arriving in orbit. Small wedges, circles, and rectangles. There were hundreds of them. At this distance she couldn't make out any detail, however they were clearly large, and their formation suggested they were part of a co-ordinated force. Wilding could see their arrival was intimidating and appreciated why the Qarti were flustered. She could feel their anxiety and distress. They were evacuating from whoever it was who was arriving in orbit.

As she watched, she understood that there were two levels to the arrivals she could see. Whilst most of the invasion force was still in high orbit, organising itself, some ships were already inside the planet's atmosphere, leading the assault.

Her view changed to show the aftermath of the first wave of attacks. She flashed towards a city, suddenly slowing, and dropping in close to get a better look. It was the city she'd seen that first time she'd encountered the Qarti in this dreamlike state. It looked dead. Skyscrapers reached upwards in strange angles, twisted, and torn as if being pulled down from below or desperate hands reaching upwards for help. There was no evidence of activity. No lights, no drones.

She felt a strong feeling of grief from her fellow observers. She wasn't sure it could be called a city anymore. It was a ruin. Many miles in diameter, it had once been a jewel in a plain landscape. Now it had been torn apart, covered in numerous craters where ordnance had fallen. As she circled, she could see inside the remains of what was once a skyscraper. Other towers still stood with shattered spires, sides shorn off, or collapsed onto the ground below.

Everything was covered in a layer of soot where fires had raged, and metal and concrete had melted. She thought she could see what might have once been a park and a trail where a waterway may have once run. It was a brief sortie, and she felt a pang of disappointment that it was time to move on. She grimly acknowledged that until she knew what was going to happen to her physical self, she probably had a long time to revisit these issues with the Qarti. There was no mistaking what she was seeing. The city that had been obliterated, likely with the majority of its inhabitants killed.

*Our families and friends were lost. Innocents murdered.*

She was on the move again. The shuttle had increased altitude and sharply turned away, heading away into the dusty flatlands. She thought she'd seen a handful of dark figures, away in the shadow of a tower, which were slowly moving across the surface. Perhaps there had been a few survivors. Then she reached the canyon where she'd first encountered the Qarti, swooping down towards the canyon floor, far lower than she'd reached on her last visit. She now believed that their first meeting, if it could have been called that, was simply a misunderstanding. They'd not wanted to scare her. She understood they were worried about an intruder into their collective consciousness.

'I'm sorry,' she tried to message them. She now understood how they'd felt. The Qarti had gone to sleep in what seemed to be desperate circumstances and were disturbed to find an alien in their hibernation tanks with them, and whilst she didn't understand how or why they'd found her intruding on their collective consciousness, she appreciated why it would have made them suspicious.

The canyon had also been hit. A whole stretch of wall had come down, landslides carrying the external surface to the canyon floor, exposing darker rock behind. Many of the spires had been destroyed, only a few thin pillars remained amongst a sea of rocky stumps. The shuttle levelled out, and she flew parallel to one of the external canyon walls, crossing a riverbed and past the shuttle landing area she'd seen on her first visit. A burnt-out shuttle sat there; its roof torn off to reveal blackened figures still strapped into the cockpit.

Compared to her last view, there was only silence, and the air was clear. There was no sign of any Qarti in the air, only many black dots scattered across the canyon floor below.

*We were forced to leave, those who didn't were slaughtered.*

Wilding didn't know what to say.

# 47

# PARYNSKI

*Antiope Mining Facility*

Parynski was glad to finally be on the move. After taking on fluids full of nutrients and running through the strategy he had worked out with the Skydancer's AI, he was ready. The AI had been successful in hacking into the systems that permeated the base and had updated the older plans he had been using.

Assured that the docking bay had been pressurised and was secure. Once he'd unscrewed and removed the insulated plating that had hidden him, he sat up and removed his helmet, taking deep breaths of clean air. It wasn't fresh air, but it felt a lot better than the air in his suit, which had been piped from the inside of the ship. He detached himself and reached upwards. He placed the helmet on the hull and pulled himself onto the top of the Skydancer. All was quiet, bar the hum of equipment and air conditioning. It was dark save for a few odd blinking lights on equipment scattered around the edge of the chamber. He'd been assured there was no monitoring gear in the docking bay except that on the external air lock. Needing the HUD map, he put his helmet back on with the glass visor down, opening vents so he could use external air rather than that in his tank. Parynski engaged his magnetic boots, not because there wasn't gravity but because he didn't want to risk falling off the top of the ship in the dark. His suit was the best he'd used in terms of flexibility, just what was needed for sneaking about and, if necessary, shooting his way off this rock. He reached back into his hiding place and pulled up his weapons out of his hiding place. He checked them over and then clipped them to various parts of his suit, before gingerly clambering over the top of the ship and down towards the floor, several storeys below. He was directed to the side where there were a number of airlocks, and he found a series of rails and ladders he could climb down. Halfway to the floor, he paused, tethering himself to the side of the ship as his head started spinning. The AI told him to slow down as he was still suffering symptoms from the freeze. Parynski couldn't feel it, though was sure the suit would be pumping him full of drugs to counteract the side effects.

After a few minutes, he started to feel better and gently lowered himself to the floor. He crawled behind the Skydancer's front leg, crouching whilst he retrieved his rifle. He put the stock into his shoulder and pointed it ahead of him. The suit automatically synced with the sight on the weapon and a small circular insert was projected onto the inside of his helmet in line with his right eye. He checked it was calibrated and that it vanished when he lowered the weapon. He raised it again and switching to night mode scanned the whole area. As the AI had assessed, there were no signs of life.

The docking bay was square, with a metal plated floor and supporting beams splayed across the walls and ceiling. The ceiling beams held cranes and other loading gear. The Skydancer dominated the bay, though there was also a small repair tug tucked away in a corner.

'Ok then, where's Jude?'

The suit replied almost in a whisper, which suited his mood and the need for stealth, despite technically being unnecessary inside the helmet. 'There are three individuals designated on the list of residents as being prisoners. It's logical that your daughter and President Zander are two out of the three. They have their own rooms allocated and are in a block that is away from the central residential complex. Two of the rooms are very close together so as the President and your daughter arrived at the same time, I would recommend that you go to those two rooms first.'

The map on his HUD zoomed out slightly and an area became highlighted red.

The suit continued. 'At the side of the docking bay is an exit that leads to an internal freight train network. It runs down the side of Antiope and into the accommodation block where they are likely to be. It's the smaller of two such blocks on the asteroid. The other is even further away and more heavily populated.'

Parynski acknowledged the information given. 'And how confident are you that you have the ability to take control of their systems? Seems we might be lucky if they are being held at this side of the Antiope.'

'Completely. I have discreetly tested the systems and I believe I can assist you all the way. I'll be able to disable or confuse their alarms. Their control protocols are antiquated.'

Parynski stepped out from underneath the Skydancer and walked towards the exit highlighted on his HUD. As he did, his stride gained a purpose.

'This should be easy. That's what you are telling me? Take over the suit until I take back control.'

And with that, the AI took over control of the suit and increased his walking pace towards the exit.

'I didn't say it would be easy.'

# 48

## JUDE

*Antiope Mining Facility*

They met in an old entertainment room they'd been directed to by Howard. It was rarely used by the other residents, and they brought drinks with them, trying to look as inconspicuous as they could. Howard crouched, pretending to examine Rebecca's ankle to give him a reason to be there. Jude was the last to arrive. Slipping inside after checking the coast was clear.

Ready for action, she briefed them. Howard had earlier directed her through a door that he'd deliberately left wedged open, just down the hallway from their current location. It led to where some lifeboats were set up for use. Howard had told her that he believed they'd been readied when the asteroid base was first occupied and that the current inhabitants would be barely aware of them, as there was little foot traffic in the area. Nearby she'd found an air lock they could use and some old, working EVA suits.

'We've got to do something, and now. At the very least, we can piss a lot of them off, kill some of the fuckers too if we depressurise this part of the base. I'll go back and see about wedging open some of the local doors onto the main corridor. There're enough suits that we can all get outside, or if it's safe, come back through the base and get a shuttle. I know what I'm doing in an EVA. Theo says he had training in it and the Doc says he has too.'

Howard nodded. 'Back in the old days, five or six years ago, most of us had to take training. They wanted everyone to be able to do everything round here. I just became too useful as a doctor…' Jude glared at him until he paused. They didn't have much time.

'So that only leaves Rebecca. We can all look after her. The suits are old and can't be paired, but we can tether her. We get outside, cause them a load of aggro, and then look for a way to get away.'

Jude stopped, her mind racing. If they didn't act now, Rebecca and Zander were going to be executed, and they would dispose of her too. Getting outside might buy some time, but wouldn't be the solution if they had nowhere to go. The others still looked at her for instruction, so she continued. 'One way or another, if we can get to one of the Tug docks, we can steal one easily enough if we aren't disturbed. Hopefully do some more damage and then try and get away. There has to be a chance we can get a signal out for help.'

They all knew that the chances of passing help was small, but the adults had privately agreed they'd do what they could to stop a public execution. They'd not give their captors that satisfaction, nor political capital.

Jude moved Howard to one side and crouched down in front of Rebecca. She cradled the girl's face in her hands. 'And you need to do everything you are told - if you do, I promise you that you will be ok.' She stared intently into Rebecca's eyes. As usual, Rebecca tried to avoid eye contact, but she eventually caught her eye and looked straight back at Jude with a determination that Jude hadn't seen before. Jude hoped her optimism wasn't false hope.

They set off. Jude ushered them down the corridor she'd explored at Howard's direction, telling them to follow him and that she'd catch them up. She then started a run back along the circular corridor that looped around much of this section of the base. At every arterial corridor she paused, using junk she had salvaged from the entertainment room to jam open every doorway she passed. The doors shouldn't register that they were jammed until someone tried to close them because they were often left open during the day. Satisfied that she'd done what she could, she turned back and caught up with the others, her chest pounding.

Howard had led them to an ante room by one of the lifeboats where a number of EVA suits were hung up. They were trying them on. Howard had one on, bar the helmet, and was now suiting up Rebecca. The smallest suit they had found fit her reasonably well, though she complained about it.

'It's too uncomfortable. I feel claustrophobic in this helmet.'

Jude smiled to herself as she heard Zander talking to her like a parent to their child. 'You've no choice, dear, and there is no time to argue.'

Jude went round the group and checked what they had. The suits seemed to be in working order. There was no time to service them, and all had decent supplies of air. The suit Zander had found for her contained an air supply enough for an EVA of five or six hours.

Jude pulled a suit on and got the others to check it as she connected it up. Whilst waiting for the others to finish off she scoured the nearby rooms for anything of use, returning quite pleased with herself with a set of new tethers that she handed out and also a set of tools that had been left behind by whoever had been down here last.

She looked at the group, assessing them. All were quiet, nervously making small talk as they methodically helped each other dress, ready for their escape.

Zander was calm. He'd told them about the hostage training he'd received and the recent attempts on his life. She knew that he'd not let anyone down. Rebecca looked more determined by the second. She'd looked like she was going to be sick when the helmet was clipped onto her, and Jude was relieved when she regained her composure. Howard, however, looked stressed. His hands were sweating so much he struggled to do up Rebecca's suit and he twice dropped his own helmet. He kept talking about his Nurse, feeling guilty for not having got her in on their plan. Jude was firm about it. They just didn't have time. She had a nagging doubt about Howard, but Rebecca had been insistent. The more of them there were, the harder any escape would be, and she pointed out they didn't have any additional working suits, anyway. If she were within the medical bay when they depressurised the base, the medical bay would automatically seal itself until things were safe.

Once ready, Jude asked Zander to stand guard whilst she took Howard into the various escape pod suites. One of them was empty, having been previously used. They could probably get outside quicker through that airlock, but Jude wanted to create some confusion by launching multiple Pods. She also had a theory that if they launched half a dozen Pods at once, they might just be able to attract some attention from any other ships in the area. If they didn't find a way of getting noticed, any escape they made, even if they were able to steal a tug, might turn out to be short-lived.

# 49

# PARYNSKI

*Antiope Mining Facility*

Skydancer's AI directed Parynski out of the docking bay and into a deserted service corridor. It was hewn roughly out of the rock with metal panels attached to the floor and some of the wall, interrupted by pipes and trunking inside which power cables ran. It was dimly lit with only dirty orange emergency lighting.

The AI claimed to have identified the approximate locations of most residents of the Antiope, helped by an analysis of swipe card usage. The ship was quick to remind him it wasn't guaranteed to be accurate, as it couldn't be sure of the location of those currently in public areas, such as the canteen or the town that was at the far end of the asteroid base. There were several thousand residents, enough for a small army. Fortunately, it seemed that in this area, it was quiet. It was expected that the vast majority were unlikely to be armed and only a small number would be in security roles.

Both asteroids named Antiope were a similar size and only a small percentage of its size was utilised by its residents. Due to its size, the Skydancer had been brought inside a large shuttle bay that was in a relatively isolated position, near a lode that had once been considered a prime area for mining.

The nearest accommodation blocks were built around a smaller shuttle dock and a reactor. That part of the base was more sparsely populated, and since mining was abandoned decades earlier, much of it had been mothballed. The shuttle bay had been built to fit the carriers that would once have carried off materials and brought supplies. It was near here that Parynski expected to find Jude.

The furthest edge of the Antiope contained another docking bay. Near there was the only town as such, where most residents lived. The images he'd seen made it look attractive, but he was not here to see the sights. Linking the various parts of the Antiope, particularly the area that Parynski was interested in, was a railway.

Parynski let the suit take the strain, walking him down the service corridor and then warning him that two guards were stationed nearby, in a side room. This was where, so the ship said, arrivals were held until they were met by suitable officials. The only alternative route into the docking bay complex was via a series of other service tunnels that nobody would ever consider using, and on foot, it would take him days.

Though his first combat lecturer had taught him that the first deaths in any conflict were the worst, he never got used to death. He'd spare everyone he could. He'd been telling himself that these were combatants, were terrorists by all accounts, and had violently - extremely violently - abducted his daughter and the President.

He let the suit do the work, turning the dim lighting off, cutting the CCTV, and then using infra-red to locate and hunt down the guards. They were sloppy, not expecting any visitors. Their weapons were propped against the wall. They sat at a table playing with a games console, complaining at the power failure. He was slightly relieved that one pulled a handgun on him and the other actually got a punch off before the suit had killed them. He moved their bodies away from any cameras so that when the ship allowed it to carry on broadcasting, nothing would seem to be afoot.

Beyond the service corridor, which ran for half a mile with a variety of sealed cupboards and storage areas leading off it, he stepped into what was the railway station. It was a large chamber, with a raised ceiling and dim lighting, manned by a lone engineer sat at the control console. He was shocked at Parynski's arrival, partly because of the fact he was dressed in a gleaming white EVA suit and because of what he was caught doing. He was injecting himself intravenously, into the forearm and upon registering Parynski's arrival, his first thought was to hide the drug paraphernalia, scrambling round into a holdall in front of him. Parynski barely had to do anything. The suit leapt onto him and grabbed him in a headlock. The man passed out immediately. Parynski checked what he was injecting himself and decided to finish the syringe and give an extra dose he found in his bag. If it didn't kill him, then he'd be out for a while. Parynski found some loose cables and tied his hands and legs before dragging him into an empty cargo pallet and leaving him. The man's life was a lie so Parynski gambled that he wouldn't want to report what had happened, as it would expose his drug habit to his superiors and colleagues.

His HUD directed him to the loading platform, where a small train sat waiting. The ship told him it had control of it as he marched alongside it. The rear contained a small cab which Parynski climbed inside, taking the seat next to the control console. The cab contained twelve seats and was open at the front, giving a view of the open top flatbed car in front of it and the direction of travel. The rest of the cab was enclosed, giving the appearance of a tin can that had one side torn off it. It was rusted, in part, covered in dust that clung to everything it touched. He wiped his gloves clean on his chest plate and then cleared his visor. For this journey would push the flat bed out in front of it.

Parynski dimmed his torches and slid into one of the seats. He put his feet up on the back of the seat in front of him and lay his rifle on his lap, ready to deal with any unexpected fellow passengers. The suit estimated he had a journey of a couple of hours ahead of him, so he tried to get comfortable, easier said than done in an EVA suit. The train would stop automatically, and briefly, at only one other stop, records indicated the station there was mothballed. He half wished he had put the Skydancer's AI into a personality mode, so he at least had someone to chat with during the journey.

An internal cabin light came on as the carriage jolted and then gently pulled out of the station. The train was almost silent according to his background mic, running on electric rails. Every few hundred yards they passed side tunnels, most according to the plans leading nowhere. Occasional branch lines went off to areas of the mine that had long since been abandoned. Satisfied that the Skydancer had proper control over the train, and he wouldn't be disturbed on the journey, Parynski allowed himself to relax, knowing he'd be woken at the right time. Still aching from being thawed, he drifted off into sleep.

His rest was disturbed by his suit alarming. He jumped to attention, crouching behind the back of the seat in front of him, weapon raised to his shoulder. 'Ship, what's going on?

Sitrep?' he asked.

Nothing.

The suit told him that contact had been lost with the Skydancer. His mind started to assess the trouble he might now be in. No sooner had he started to worry than the connection was restored. The ship reported that the train tunnel had gone through a blank spot and that there might be other such areas. Satisfied that he was currently at no risk, he settled back into his seat and closed his eyes.

His suit vibrated slightly, disturbing him again. His surroundings were brighter than they had been when he had set off. Unsure if it was his own adrenalin or the suit medicating him, he felt fully alert within seconds. Before leaving the station, he raised his visor and noted that the air here was warmer. Despite his suit trying to regulate his body temperature, he felt hot, his lips dry. He sucked on the water tube in his helmet. The AI told him they were approaching the inhabited areas of the base. The tunnel was far wider than the track here, and he had a good view of what was ahead. The track wasn't completely straight, but using the sight on the rifle helped him get a better view. The improved lighting served to increase his nervousness as the shadows jumped around him as the train slowly weaved its way towards its destination.

The train passed more side tunnels, where there were definite signs of activity. One contained a parked train with a hopper on top and another was partially lit with some digging equipment set up and ready to use. Thankfully, the crew weren't there. As he approached the end of the line, he pulled the visor down so he could see the HUD. From the station, he believed it was only a short walk to the accommodation complex and the rooms where he suspected Jude might be. He hoped to get there with minimum fuss and before any shooting started. The key was to get control over the doors. He re-examined the red lined 3D model projected onto the HUD. Most doors were capable of being controlled electronically, others that were marked were either on a circuit that couldn't be accessed or were old-fashioned manual air locks from the early days of colonisation.

Where the train came to a halt could hardly be described as a station. The track ended at a buffer not far beyond where a branch line had veered off elsewhere. On either side of the train were slightly raised concrete platforms containing lifting equipment and numerous trolleys. The tunnel had opened up into a wider chamber, with a vaulted ceiling fitted with spotlights and a crane. Parynski heard cursing and something or someone banging the side of the carriage. As expected, an unarmed and confused looking engineer pulled himself up into the rear of the carriage, threw a cursory look in Parynski's direction without seeing him in the shadow, before turning to examine the control console. The train shouldn't be here.

Parynski pulled himself up and moved behind the engineer, rifle aimed out in front of him. When he got just behind him, he lowered the weapon and allowed the suit to use its strength to grab the man from behind, choking and smothering him until he stopped moving. There'd barely been a whimper. 'Sorry.' Parynski muttered as he dragged the body off the carriage and hid it away in the shadows behind some long-abandoned piece of equipment. He checked the man's coveralls and extracted a security pass, slipping it into an external suit pocket, just in case. The Skydancer mocked him, claiming it had already secured a higher level of access. Even without personality mode engaged, the ship still knew how to give off an air of superiority.

After taking his time to get here, it was now time to increase pace. It was now a matter of a time before he was spotted, despite the efforts of the AI to control all local CCTV cameras and sensors. Once word was out, it would be a race against time because there was no mistaking someone in a slim line combat EVA suit for a resident of Antiope.

The reception chamber at the end of the platform contained two exits; one an opening that narrowed into a tunnel that wasn't lit and didn't seem to go anywhere, the other a closed metal door, approximately ten feet tall and twice that wide. As promised, the ship opened it for him and allowed him on his way.

Parynski was pleased with himself as he reached what he thought was Jude's room without meeting anyone, only having to hide in an ante room once as a cleaning detail passed. He was confident the first room was Jude's, based on the size of the small number of clothes in the room. The second room, he guessed, was Zander's. As the door slid shut behind him, Parynski felt sick, realising they were both empty.

It was in Zander's room that he was disturbed by a patrolling guard who had seen him enter. Thankfully, the alarm hadn't been raised, as the guard had inquisitively followed Parynski into the room without even drawing his weapon. He was a well-built man, taller and stronger than Parynski, who managed to a get a punch into his side before the suit had taken over. Two blows had put the man on the floor. Blood pooled out of the wound on his face, but Parynski didn't think it would be too serious.

The third room that had been flagged up as a possible location was further away, and he checked the route. The AI set a route that was not the quickest, but a route that made sense as he wanted to try and extract his targets in the most discrete way possible.

He sealed Zander's room with the man in it and set off jogging towards the third room. An alarm sounded, and the lighting changed to a red. He peered round. 'What did I do?'

The Skydancer replied that it wasn't sure, but there was now a security clampdown under way. He increased his pace, bumping into an armed man who was as surprised to see him as Parynski was. The man scrambled for his weapon, so instinctively Bruce shot him and pushed him through an open doorway. He needed to move quickly now. Wherever they were, Jude and the President were likely to be taken into custody as part of any alarm protocol.

He was nearly at his destination when he came across a group of three, two women and a man, who were chatting and laughing. They were armed and were looking through each opening they passed. They were security but clearly didn't take their job seriously. They were walking in the same direction as he was, but far slower. He couldn't afford to loiter behind them, and the map suggested there was no easy way around.

Trying to push any feelings of guilt to one side, he crouched in an alcove and took a bead on them with his rifle, checking it was on silent mode. He took them all down with shots to the head. Only the final victim, the man, realised what was going on before he collapsed quietly. The ship unlocked a closed door nearby, and he dragged the bodies in, adding to the pile of bodies with an unfortunate orderly who caught him in the act. He locked that door and set off again.

The third room was also empty, and he felt crushed. This was going to have to be done the hard way. It risked being a bloodbath.

Despite the suit trying to regulate his temperature, he could feel the sweat inside his suit and his hair was soaked, stuck tightly to his head. He took a moment to open his visor, trying to wipe his forehead on this sleeve. He struggled to get the sleeve in the gap so gave up, grabbing a t-shirt off the bed and dabbed his face as best as he could.

A quick search of the room told him it was someone else's room, neither Jude's nor the President's. He guessed it was the room of a girl. The AI gave him the name Rebecca from the plans, a name that meant nothing to him.

Parynski heard the door lock. The control panel stopped being responsive and the manual override handle wouldn't budge.

He was trapped.

# 50

## GARCIA

*Triton Observatory Operations Centre*

'Are you sure you've enough supplies to last? You won't be back for months, and it'll be a while before anyone reaches you.'

In the absence of anyone else who seemed to care about anything other than preserving and securing the Xenos, Garcia had taken it on herself to ensure that Squire was looking after himself. Though Arden had devoted a huge number of specialists to the project, Squire himself was being treated as an asset rather than a person.

She'd known him since he joined Arden's operation and was aware of his tendency to go off the rails. From what she knew of his past, it was no surprise. Muller had spent a lot of time working with Squire, and she knew their Chief Engineer was all business.

'Yes, should be ok. Could do with losing a few pounds, anyway.'

Squire grinned at her. He was back on the BSV, sat on one of the bunks he'd built when they'd hoped to find survivors. He was now taking them down and recycling materials for use on the Xenos.

'Seriously, will you cope?' She asked in a firmer tone than previously.

'Yeah, if the supplies Arden sent via the unmanned fast rocket arrive ok. They'll get here way before anyone else. I'll have to untether the BSV to get it. It'll give me something different to do, anyway. It'll be a two-week job to go after the package when it arrives and then get back to the Xenos. I should be honoured Arden even agreed to send it.'

Garcia smiled at him. 'Well, you're going to be a celebrity! The only one to survive first contact with these aliens. He needs to look after you.'

'We don't know that Wilding is dead yet, though,' replied Squire.

She gave a sympathetic nod and let him continue.

'Paisley wants me to limit my exploratory EVAs to conserve supplies. That's why I came back to the BSV for a few days. I've been back to the Tomb a few times, and I'd like to do some tests around those capsules they're in. We might be able to extract her, however we need to work out how, or if, they are powered. If it's not power as we know it, then it could be something biological. That gunk those bodies are surrounded in could be keeping her, and them, alive.'

Garcia worried that boredom, or anxiety over Wilding, would lead to Squire doing something rash, something they'd later regret. 'We hope so. We've built up a team of experts, if you can have experts in alien tech, who are desperate to get on board and learn what we can. Please don't do anything too adventurous. If she's still alive, then don't jeopardise any chance we have of recovery. Those aliens might also be alive, but even dead, their bodies are going to transform our knowledge about the universe.'

'I'll do my best not to give into temptation…' he said flatly. Garcia couldn't tell if he was serious or not.

'Please do. The first asteroid movers have some scientists and engineers on board.

They'll take over responsibility for the Xenos on arrival.'

An awkward silence. Garcia was keen to spend time with him, to support him. Being isolated like this would not be good for his mental health, particularly living with a ship full of dead aliens and his old commanding officer. She pointed to the plastic bottle in his hand. 'What's in that?'

He waved it at her. 'Don't worry, it's not alcohol! I have Paisley here to look after me, anyway.'

Garcia shrugged awkwardly. 'Sorry, just concerned about you. You've got to keep yourself busy until help gets there. Please take it easy.'

'As if that's likely. There's so much to do!'

Realising the conversation was going nowhere, she changed the subject.

They both discussed what they knew about Parynski and his diversion to rescue his daughter and potentially President Zander.

'Thankfully nobody knows what is going on, can you imagine the fuss?' said Garcia.

'If I'd not been so far away, I'd have been there to help him,' he said.

'I know, but you can't, so let's just wait and see. If he delivers the Skydancer as ordered, then maybe you can catch up with him in a few months.' The last thing Garcia wanted was Squire distracted at a crucial time.

'That'd be good, if he hasn't taken on more than he can chew.'

To keep him focussed on the mission at hand, she decided it was time to give him the final bit of interesting news she had. It was certainly the most interesting to her. In fact, her whole career had led to this point. She pulled herself up straight in her chair, took her glasses off, and stared at him.

'Anyway, there could be something bigger than the Xenos for you to work on.'

She dangled the bait to catch his interest. He didn't take it. There was another silence, so she decided to plough on, regardless. He swigged from the bottle again.

'I think I've found where the Xenos came from. Not from another system, rather another, larger asteroid or Plutoid even further out in the Kuiper Belt. We've had the whole observatory team on it, and whilst we can't be certain the collision hasn't misled us, it looks like the Xenos came directly from another rock. It might've only used that as a waypoint and it's quite a bit further out than we have ever sent anyone. It's got a peculiar shape, and it could be that the Xenos would have fitted inside it.

With ease too. Sounds crazy and hard to believe, but that's what it looks like.' She smiled awkwardly, hoping he'd react positively.

He stared intently at his bottle, avoiding her stare. 'A lot of things seem pretty crazy right now.'

# 51

# PARYNSKI

*Antiope Mining Facility*

Fear replaced frustration as the AI updated Parynski on its progress of unlocking the door. There were system updates across the base recording a large number of doors that had been locked open or jammed, and in response, the base's own safety protocols were sealing other doors to protect against a crisis. Parynski grimly noted that it would be embarrassing if his rescue attempt ended before he'd even found his daughter and with him locked in a child's bedroom. The station's systems weren't certain what had caused the alarm, though Parynski was sure it was fairly likely it was something he'd done.

All he could do was stand in the far corner of the room, weapon raised and aimed at the door. He'd switched the light off to give him an advantage over any intruder. The smaller pistols strapped across his chest and on his outer thigh were also powered up and ready if needed. He sipped his water again, mouth dry, and waited.

All hell broke loose as the door slid open, engulfing him in bright light from the corridor. His helmet visor slammed shut and automatically tinted itself. He tasted the bottled air within seconds. The suit started him moving and Parynski knew better than to override it.

He charged into an empty corridor and turned left, breaking into a jog as the AI updated him. Alarms were now going off across Antiope due to reports of a depressurisation. It wasn't his activity that was causing the emergency. Security details had been requested to be sent to the area of concern, along with a team of engineers. The area of the asteroid base around the leak was locked down completely, being isolated from the rest of the base and an order had been given that residents return to their rooms and await further instructions. Those in the canteens and gyms were requested to stay where they were.

Jude had to be involved. Once he'd presented this likelihood, the AI concurred and directed him to where the alarm had originated. He hoped that with most confined to quarters, the journey would be quiet, but optimism was replaced by caution as he realised that those he encountered would be part of the security team and, therefore, armed. With the immediate area being closed off Parynski asked the AI to close off the main arterial routes into the more populated area of the asteroid, so that even if the alert were cancelled, he'd still have some extra time before additional militia could get to him.

It was a five-minute run. The corridor twisted round a corner and started to rise as it headed towards the outer perimeter of the asteroid. The AI was already plotting routes back to the train station. He admired its optimism. Even with the support from the suit, he soon started to feel the strain, such was the pace he was trying to make with his weapon held out in front of him, stock firmly pushed into his shoulder. It was years since he'd been in a combat situation like this. He'd have preferred to have had Wilding on point. He was heading into an area that the plans suggested were rarely used, an old entertainment area for the crew and little else save for storage areas and a mothballed set of escape pods installed when Antiope was first mined.

His heart leapt in anticipation. He knew it. Jude was trying to escape. Even if she'd gone in a pod, he could catch up with her as long as the Skydancer could shoot its way out of its docking bay. The AI reassured him that it would not need to be so violent that it could simply open the bay doors. Ahead, up a further steep climb and round another winding bend, the HUD told him were a series of doors that the station's emergency systems had now designated as an air lock, due to the depressurisation that had taken place. There were multiple doors near a crossing of tunnels. Parynski, he expected to find it manned.

It was. He found two engineers, both in grubby, grey space suits and unarmed. Both had helmets on and were studying a screen embedded in a console set to the side of the door. The screen showed the other side of the door, and their radios allowed them to control all the doors. They'd taken control of the airlock, no doubt waiting for security to arrive.

Parynski slowed to a walk to assess his options. The AI confirmed there was a secure room nearby. No sooner had he started looking for it than he passed a dull door to his left. As he approached, the door opened to reveal a cramped storage cupboard containing rolls of cable, pipes, and trunking.

He switched his outward speaker on just as the two men heard him and turned.

Through their visors, he could see their eyes widen in fear.

'Don't make me kill you.' Parynski tried to sound as certain as he could. He knew his suit would do it if it had to. They both turned and backed up to the door, instinctively raising their arms. The larger of the two figures was still dangerously close to the console whilst the smaller held a communicator. Parynski looked them up and down, keeping his rifle aimed at them. 'Don't touch anything or do anything to attract attention. I'm monitoring any chip usage. If you call for help, I promise I'll kill you before anyone gets close.'

The larger man, whose suit looked like it had been extended round the waist, nodded.

'Please don't hurt us, we're just engineers. We've no idea what's going on here.' His colleague nodded vigorously.

Parynski reached into a pocket with his left hand, right hand still on the trigger of the rifle, and pulled out two small pads. A risky manoeuvre followed, but the two were too scared to move, as he dashed forward and slapped a pad each onto the backs of the legs of their suits.

He stepped back, feeling pleased with himself. Both men tried to look down at what he had stuck to them, though neither wanted to move too dramatically for fear of angering their assailant.

'I'll save you time looking. It's a small remote operated bomb. Not hugely powered, as you can imagine due to its size, big enough to take your legs off. It's linked to my AI, so if it goes off, it won't even be down to me. You do anything silly like use your coms, I won't even know about it, you'll both be a lot shorter.'

Parynski stepped back and gestured for them to move towards the storage cupboard, which they did, nervously looking at each other. Once inside, squashed upright against each other, Parynski stepped back and lowered his weapon.

'Well done. You two might survive this. If I were you, once I close this door, I'd shut my visor and rely on bottled oxygen.'

And with that, the door slammed shut on them. Parynski checked with the AI that it was locked. Confused, the Skydancer asked what those patches were because, despite checking, it could not connect to them in light of what Parynski had said to the two men.

Parynski grinned. Another bluff. 'They were patches, simple as that. I think they'd have believed anything I said at that moment. At the very least, it might make them wait until their air starts to run out before they try to escape.'

He moved back towards the doorway with the console and as he did, so the AI proudly reported it already had control of it. Whilst he waited for the airlock to cycle, the AI reported that just before he had arrived, a security team had seemingly passed through from another tunnel and were headed in the same direction he was. He needed to hurry up.

# 52

# ROO

*Triton Observatory Operations Centre*

'Well, I guess if we rescue their President, Earth will be a bit nicer to us.'

Roo knew that Arden was only half joking. Whilst Earth had its own serious problems, it had always tried to maintain a paternal role towards the rest of the Solar System, though it didn't always succeed. Since the Trike incident, Earth citizens were now granted an irrevocable right to return, even if individuals had taken other passports.

Squabbles were more prevalent amongst the other planets, where there was a competition for resources and the movement of the planets meant that economies were strong and weak in a cycle based on the cost of interplanetary travel.

Arden had travelled down to the Observatory Ops Centre for the day. As ever, it was unannounced to keep his staff on their toes. Roo had noticed with some amusement the reaction of her colleagues who'd started running round in a panic when Arden's inter system shuttle had appeared on their landing platform's manifest for the day. Garcia, who ran the base, was also not there when he'd arrived. She'd been away overnight, inspecting the repair of a mobile sensor array that was now being directed towards the projected origin point of the Xenos. She was on her way back, so Roo was dealing with Arden on her own.

# THE TRITON RUN

To most, Arden had a reputation as a tough operator, a reputation that was overly harsh, although one that he was happy to be maintained. The outer areas of the Solar System were tough to operate in and anything that warned off those wanting to take advantage was to be welcomed.

Roo met Arden in Garcia's private room, attached to what operated as the bridge in the Ops Centre. Space was at a premium in the base, so the room was small, with a low ceiling and lighting. It often doubled as a repair shop. One of its two tables was stacked high with broken equipment, all waiting assessment for repair or recycling. They sat at the second table, facing a bank of monitors and 3D displays. A tray before them contained the remains of a ration-based lunch, though Arden had brought with him some extra supplies from orbit to improve morale. Most had been shared round the base, though he'd kept coffee, imported at great expense, for their meeting.

Roo had always got on with Arden. He had high standards, was strict on discipline, and wouldn't tolerate any slackers. With little to focus on but his work, he expected everyone else to do the same. If you worked hard, he was kind. Weak management led to poor performance and in space that was a path that led to accidents, and accidents off Earth were usually fatal.

Roo reflected that she was as happy as she'd ever been. She was occupied with both matters on the Xenos and with Parynski. Though the latter was an extremely serious incident, and the political stakes couldn't be higher, she'd embraced the situation, as had most of her colleagues. On top of that, there was the factor that one of her best friends was involved. She'd forgotten all about days off and had been dumped by her boyfriend for cancelling two dates in a week. He worked on one of the gas mines and had appeared as planned to take her off to one of the social hubs. After she'd told him that she was too busy, he'd had enough. She'd concluded that her actions only confirmed what she'd been thinking for a while, anyway.

He wasn't the right one for her.

They received notifications that Garcia's shuttle was on its final approach, so they talked about events at Antiope. Roo could tell that Arden was concerned about handing over his most valuable purchase to an ex-marine Ferryman for a risky rescue mission at a base likely full of extremists. He put a brave face on it. Such was his desire for discretion he'd not even insured the ship yet. Arden had concluded there was not a lot he could do to stop Parynski from using his ship, and it was better to let him do so with his blessing. Roo had decided not to tell him about the remote-control facility she had discovered hard wired into the AI. If he'd wanted, Arden could have stopped the ship from diverting and direct it remotely to their current location. She didn't think he would do that, but with her friend awaiting rescue, she'd decided not to take that risk.

After listening to him praise the ship and its specifications for some time, Roo concluded that there was no better ship for Parynski to use. She'd suspected as much after working with the Skydancer's AI on the approach to Antiope. Roo had managed to obtain a wealth of material about the innards of the asteroid from when it was used as a mine and as a base for miners across the wider area of the belt. She'd uploaded that for Parynski to use and had developed protocols for the Skydancer to use once it got within range of the base. The new instructions would allow the ship to very discreetly hack into the base's systems and take control over them. She hoped that access to the door controls, airlocks, and CCTV on top of the base wide tracking facility for residents would give Parynski an edge.

Arden was genuinely interested in the rescue mission, so she showed him their plans and timings. If all had gone to plan, Parynski would now be inside Antiope. Roo neglected to tell Arden about the work they'd done on the ship's hull and that the escape pod had been launched already. Roo was able to track it, but without the rest of the Skydancer, it wasn't a lot of use.

# THE TRITON RUN

Arden was pleased with her when she reported on the feedback she'd got from Earth and Mars about a rescue mission. Roo's initial discrete representations had been ignored, so she'd asked Arden to intervene in events at Antiope, just to get the message through. It was far nearer for Earth and Mars to respond, as they actually had forces that could be deployed in space.

'I'm just sorry you had to ask me. They should've listened straight away,' said Arden, interrupting himself to take a sip of coffee. 'Can't believe the response has been so glacial. Suppose it gives Lindstrom time to strengthen her position whilst Zander is out the way.'

Roo agreed. 'That's my impression, too. At least there's a force on the way now, though it'll still be weeks before it arrives. I'm hoping Bruce gets Jude out of there safely before there's a firefight.'

Roo had known Jude since they were young and had met Bruce many times. She was pleased when Arden gave Parynski a positive review, though a nagging doubt remained whether he was just trying to keep her spirits up. 'His record was exceptional. If you had to send one man in to do the job, you'd probably have picked him. Or at least you would've done a few years back before he left the forces.'

Garcia arrived, letting herself into the room and greeting both of them with a hug. Whilst at a business meeting, she was still friendly, engaging, and inspirational. Her hair was tied into a bun. Whilst Roo poured her a drink, and they made small talk, she pulled off the lightweight EVA suit she'd been wearing to reveal coveralls. After brushing herself down, she took a spare seat, reached into a pocket, and put her glasses on.

'So, where we up to?'

Arden filled her in before they turned to the other big issue. The Xenos.

Roo let Garcia take over, listening intently as she updated Arden on the flow of experts on their way to help when the

Xenos eventually arrived at Neptune. The group on board the flotilla that was currently on its way to assist Squire was a mixed bag, a few scientists with genuine curiosity, together with a group of others with mixed skills. There were security and surveillance experts in order to make the Xenos safe, a group of Salvors and a couple of linguists. It was regarding the latter that Roo was most interested.

She asked, 'So what's the view based on the footage we've got? Can we communicate with these creatures? Are the ones in the tanks dead?'

Garcia shrugged. 'Too early to tell, but it's fascinating. We've got reams of footage and images that people are poring over. Roo's taking charge of a group that are running as much analysis as we can of what we've got. Looking for patterns and clues. Even if we don't understand it yet, the more we can do now, the easier it'll be when we do make that breakthrough.'

And with that, they watched a short presentation detailing a host of images of inscriptions on walls, engravings in a chamber that appeared to be a place of worship and symbols that decorated the numerous control panels that they'd all watched Squire have trouble with. At the end she pulled up a 3D image of Squire in the chamber dubbed the Tomb. 'There's also the possibility we might be able to communicate either via Wilding herself or the aliens direct. Watch this.'

Though Roo had seen the footage so many times already, it still gave her a sense of wonder and fear. She provided some commentary to what they were seeing as Arden leaned forward in his seat to get a better view.

The footage was from Paisley's point of view. The Android stood alongside Squire in the chamber where Wilding was, for now at least, imprisoned inside a tank. The footage was far clearer than earlier samples, and Roo pointed towards a shadow that Squire's body cast along the walkway where he stood in front of some of the tanks.

# THE TRITON RUN

'You'll see it's brighter. Squire has set up spotlights to assist. I've sent you some footage, though it's quite long. We've now got a CCTV feed on the chamber.'

Arden got up, went round the front of their table, and perched himself as near to the screen as possible. Garcia winked at Roo; they both knew how enthused Arden was about everything related to the Xenos. After his initial fears for the Kuiper Scout, he'd accepted the fate of its crew and was now focussed on making the best of the situation, a situation that was pushing mankind's knowledge of its place in the universe. And if it could be monetised, the potential was incredible.

'You can watch the full footage, but I've edited this piece to focus on something I want you to see.'

With that, Roo let the footage play. Squire's helmet was transparent, his eyes were firmly focused on the row of tanks set into the wall. As before, two of the tanks were illuminated. The neighbouring tanks were largely opaque save for dark shadows. Paisley moved alongside Squire and Roo could see they were looking into the tank containing the alien. It hung, suspended in the tank, facing out into the chamber.

'If you look at the face, you'll see its eyes are closed. That stays the same here, but the footage from the previous visit that Paisley did on his own shows the eyes were open. These creatures are still alive in there, in some shape or other. Whether, when we recover the ship, we can wake them or get them out of there remains to be seen. Now, look at the right wing.'

Roo put the next few moments on a loop and zoomed in on the creature's right wing and arm. It was barely perceptible, but there was movement. A twitching that started in the shoulder region, from where the wings would flare out and ended at the wrist.

Arden turned and looked at her, a grin forming on his face. 'That's not just movement due to the crap in the tank sloshing around, is it?'

She smiled back at him, sharing his enjoyment. 'We don't think so. It's been checked by some of the scientists on the flotilla and all agree its evidence of activity in the nervous system. We could have found a ship full of thousands of these things.'

He frowned momentarily. 'There's no suggestion they are going to suddenly wake and take over?'

That was Roo's constant concern, and she tried to answer as honestly as she could, without causing a panic. They just couldn't know, even though the evidence suggested that everyone on board was secured inside those tanks and that there was no other life roaming its corridors.

Whilst Garcia shared Roo's concerns, they disagreed over one point. 'There's a huge question over the crew who were piloting the Xenos, or if there was one. We've searched as best as we can and once the support arrives, it'll be searched top to bottom before we move it.'

Arden looked over his shoulder at them both. 'Roo, you think it's too much of a risk to bring the ship back? Is it safer to study it out there?'

She confirmed that was her view. She felt it was dangerous to bring the Xenos to Neptune because it created risks, both unknown from the object itself and political and military challenges it might create from within the Solar System.

'If the Xenos is as special as it appears then every independent state will want a piece of the action and right now, we don't have the defence capabilities to protect ourselves.'

Roo got the response she expected from Arden. 'The biggest defence we've got is location. It'll take a long time and a lot of effort for any of the inner planets to send something out to us, and it'd be a big gamble. In my view, it'll be safer to have the object and our people closer to home. I hear what you say, but I'm not sure I agree.'

Roo moved on. 'Noted. Anyway, the crucial thing I wanted

# THE TRITON RUN

to show you was something that we originally missed from the footage, despite Squire repeatedly making the point. He was right. See this.'

She clicked the footage on, and it jumped to a close up of Wilding. They'd all seen enough images of her now, hair smeared with the gunge that had enveloped her body. Her face still carried the image of anguish, eyes open wide, unseeing. There were smudges below from where blood had leaked. Her body was still, though there had been reports that she'd twitched from time to time.

'The mouth, you see that?' Arden jumped to his feet excitedly, turning to his colleagues. 'She's trying to say something.'

Garcia nodded. 'Correct. Now look closely.'

The few seconds of footage were repeated on a loop. Squire's helmet, visor transparent, pressed up against the outside of the tank, Wilding's body was hanging there, mouth wide open. She'd consumed the gunge that she now rested in, though it was clear that she was trying to say something. They all stared at her mouth as it struggled to form words. After a few attempts, as if she were trying to learn to speak, Wilding managed a pattern that they understood. She repeated it several times.

'Shit. She's alive in there. She's saying "Squire"' said Arden.

# 53

# JUDE

*Antiope Mining Facility*

In hindsight, they hadn't been properly prepared when they opened the airlock in the ready room where there had once been an escape pod secured. Jude privately conceded it was because she was running on adrenaline in her desire to escape Chen, and she had badly miscalculated.

They had hung onto tethers they'd secured as the atmosphere evacuated from all of the open areas, rushing out from not just the reception room but all the way back to some of the communal areas where Jude had been to jam doors open. While she had no idea of what was going on elsewhere, one could imagine the chaos as staff worked to seal off the area.

Despite Jude making sure they were all secured and weren't going to be blown through the gap, she'd failed to factor in the impact of nearby objects that weren't secure. Their plans were immediately put in doubt as a huge as a huge piece of machinery was sucked down the corridor and into the reception area, hitting Rebecca with a glancing a blow, before slamming into the tight airlock entrance. The machine hit the doorway with such a force it shattered, throwing out debris that all blew through the exit after the machine tore through it, taking the frame with it.

With a gaping hole in the wall, there'd be no easy way to restore the atmosphere in this section of Antiope now. It did occur to Jude that if anyone was looking for them, the sudden venting may attract attention, though she hoped the venting wasn't big enough to nudge the asteroid out of its carefully balanced rotation with its twin.

After a few moments, the deluge of debris ended, and calm returned. Jude could hear their heavy breathing through their private com channel. She took a moment to orientate herself. She had been slammed into the damaged door frame immediately after she had opened the airlock manually and her head was ringing.

Rebecca hung limply from a wall, on the far side of the room to her and whilst Jude checked that the anti-gravity system was still engaged, albeit weaker than normal due to the vacuum, she was pleased to see Howard was at Rebecca's side. Now the atmosphere had completely vented, the risk of being pushed outside had abated.

'How is she?' asked Jude as she released her tether. Howard was busy extracting equipment from a pouch in the leg of his suit. 'She's out cold and got a leak in her suit. I think I've got it patched quickly enough. Just give me a few minutes.'

Howard finished his work on her suit, yet Rebecca remained as limp as a rag doll. The whole of her upper left leg was covered in tape and caked in gel, sealing up the tear.

He looked over at Jude, who had now untethered herself. 'Without getting her out of this suit I can't be sure, but I think she'll be ok. Her suit should hold. There's a gash I've sealed. It didn't look like there was much damage to her as her inner leggings seemed intact.'

'Thank god for that.' Jude turned to take in the scene. It looked like a bomb had gone off. The chamber was empty save for furniture that was securely fixed to the walls or floor. Huge gouges had appeared in the walls and floor as equipment had torn through the room.

'We should put her in one of the side rooms whilst we release the rest of the pods. Hopefully, she'll come round.'

Howard raised his hand. 'I'll do it. There was a tool storage room just off to the side that we saw when we came in. I can put her in there and see if I can wake her.'

'No. Just put her safe. Come straight back and do the recon outside as planned. Use the spare tethers and don't forget to boot up your adjusters in case you do drift. Head away from the escape pods, circle round to see if there is anything we need to imminently know about and come back. Be quick.'

Jude could tell Howard was scared. His breathing was fast over the com and his movements were tentative. Howard had completed his EVA training, and it made sense for him to do the scouting outside, though it would be risky if she started launching Escape Pods all around him. Jude was well aware that they were currently unarmed. It was a matter of time before security arrived.

Howard picked Rebecca up and tossed her over his shoulder. He redistributed her weight before standing straight-backed and then setting off carefully, walking in the peculiar way he'd been trained to do that kept at least one of his boots on the floor at all times.

Jude and Zander knew what to do. Zander started with the furthest away and in turn entered each of the ante chambers next to each lifeboat where he would punch in commands to launch them. Jude and Zander had agreed a pattern that might just attract attention from any passing ship. Jude told him to launch eighteen out of the twenty that remained just in case they needed to use any. That, however, was very a last resort.

Meanwhile, Jude jogged around the nearest ante rooms and storage cupboards, collecting all the tools she could find that might be usable as a weapon. It was slim pickings. Jude passed Howard as he headed outside before meeting Zander back in the reception area. She stuffed a few spades into a gap behind a wall unit and handed Zander an object that looked like a gardening fork.

He looked down at it. The handle contained a small series

of buttons.

Jude pointed at the handle. 'It's a utility tool. If you press that green trigger, it'll give off a spark. It's usually used for welding or making small holes, but it'll scare the hell out of someone in a space suit in a vacuum.'

Jude walked back to the end of the corridor from where they had come and peered round the corner. Seeing a shadow play on the wall ahead of her, she turned and ran back, ushering Zander over to the side of the room behind a console where she crouched down. He followed her lead.

'Someone's coming.'

Zander remained calm. 'Launching the pods was bound to bring people here, if the depressurisation wasn't enough.'

'Good. Let's get ourselves some proper weapons.'

As expected, a group of suited, armed security appeared at the entrance of the corridor from the direction they had come in. By their demeanour, Jude sensed they weren't taking the threat seriously at this stage. After all, how much trouble could a child, two middle-aged men and a woman cause? The four of them marched into the space and spread out, examining the mess. The plan was that they would assume the escapees had taken the lifeboats.

Jude wished she could hear what they were saying. The guard who led the group pointed to the opening and raised both hands wide, showing he realised what a big job it was going to be to repair. Two of the guards checked the ante rooms to the launched lifeboats and returned to the reception area. They'd fallen for it. Even through their suits, Jude saw them all visibly relax, shoulders slumping, weapons being lowered.

With their escape now likely being the accepted story amongst the guards, Jude gave Zander the signal. He jumped out at the legs of the nearest guard and pulled him off balance, jabbing him with the utility tool at full power, causing him to spasm. He crashed into the wall, taking Zander down with him. Whilst the others spun, trying to grab their weapons, Jude launched at them. She took the nearest to her and spun him round, throwing him as hard as she could towards the recently made opening to the outside. He floated away at speed, unable to get a foot down, bouncing off the side of the doorway and then outside. The other two were distracted by their friends' fate, giving Jude the chance to grab one of their rifles and leap behind them. Confused, they span to face Jude, who had dropped into an offensive stance, weapon aimed at them both.

Thoughts of Reuben filled her mind and as one of them took a step towards her, she fired a volley at them both, tearing their suits apart. The power of the projectiles the rifle fired lifted them up and tossed them against the far wall where their shattered bodies remained. She was glad that their sun visors had popped down as soon as they were hit. A standard defence mechanism.

Hearing Zander groan, Jude turned to see how he was doing. As she spun, she assessed the situation. She believed it was called a Mexican standoff. She aimed her rifle at the guard who had been tackled by Zander. The problem was that he stood over Zander, his own weapon aimed at Zander's helmet.

# 54

## WILDING

*The Dark*

It was the strangest feeling. She barely had a sensation of self apart from when she consciously tried to close herself off from the others. She still inhabited her body, whilst having little control of it. That, she was told, would return when they were released from the tanks. The material she'd ingested was what kept her alive, even though the prospect of her lungs and stomach being full of it appalled her.

Her viewpoint changed regularly. She was in the tank that, from their perspective, was furthest to the left out of a group of sixteen Qarti housed between two corridor openings. Despite this she could, at will, jump around and take the view of the others. For a while she hadn't even realised she could do it and the switching was happening subconsciously when she was communicating with them. Though they were all able to communicate in a manner which she only knew how to describe as telepathically, she wondered if the gunge was the conduit. Increasingly, she could detect their individual personalities.

She wondered, when Chris Squire appeared, if it had always been him in the space suit or if there were others on board. She didn't know how long she'd been in the tank, but it must have been some time, many months, because of how far from Neptune the Scout had been when the collision had occurred.

# THE TRITON RUN

Squire often stayed for hours, doing tests, and taking samples from the walls and pieces of equipment. He often appeared to simply watch her, having fixed spotlights up to illuminate the area near her tank After a while she concluded that a second figure which sometimes appeared was Paisley, his AI companion, in avatar form. The suit's movements weren't human.

She'd not seen Squire for several years, though he was like a brother, all of the platoon were. They all stayed in touch after being discharged and met on the rare occasion paths crossed, usually at a bar on a habitat, whilst waiting for connecting flights. Even in an EVA suit he looked like he'd put on weight, and she could see his face framed with scruffy hair and a stubble. His whole gait appeared uncomfortable.

She tried to shout to him, struggling to move anything. She wasn't even sure if she could control any of her facial muscles. She tried to track him as he moved along the balcony and perched in front of her, unsure if he'd be able to see any movement in her eyes.

*Who?*
*A friend*
*A lover?*
*No, colleague, we served together years ago. His name is Squire, a good man.*
*Why is he here?*
*Probably trying to rescue me.*

She felt anxiety in her friends as he approached. She could always sense this. They felt helpless, a feeling that was contradictory to the image of power and control they gave her when she was communicating with them ordinarily.

One another visit Squire looked directly at her, placing one hand on the outside of the tank near where one of her hands was pressed against the inside. She strained as much as she could to try and move, unable to produce anything bar occasional twitching that often happened involuntarily. She tried desperately to say his name, though couldn't tell if she'd been successful.

This happened many times, until one day she thought he spotted it. A smile broke out across his face. He started talking back. If only she could hear him. She tried to shout a reply, to no avail. He looked confused, almost disappointed in her for not reacting further.

He then stood tall and looked her in the eye. He mouthed very slowly and deliberately, over emphasising what he was saying.

'Dee, I will help you. You are safe. My ship is here. We are going to take you all back to Neptune and try to get you out of there.'

*Where is that?*

It disconcerted Wilding that they could understand him via her.

*It's the outermost gas giant. We have people there. They must be taking your ship there.*

Squire carried on talking, though he soon sped up and she struggled to keep up with him.

*Are we going to be safe?*
*I trust him with my life.*
*Good, you'd better be right.*

She hoped she was.

# 55

# PARYNSKI

*Antiope Mining Facility*

Parynski hoped his daughter would recognise him and not react as he slowly walked up behind a figure that held a weapon against the head of another suited figure that was on its knees, arms behind head. Parynski guessed that was Zander. Whilst holding his weapon out in front of him, he put a finger up to where his lips would be behind the visor.

He saw Jude look at Zander, urging him through their eye contact to sit tight.

Parynski tried to exude confidence with his walk, even if he didn't feel it. His suit was so much more modern than theirs, a combat EVA hybrid, slim, armoured and with a smaller helmet than their own domed efforts. The Skydancer's AI had hacked into the com channels of everyone in the room and he listened in as the guard switched his secure account to the one Jude was using.

'Lower your weapon now or I'll kill your friend. You can't think you'll escape.

You've led us in quite a dance, caused a lot of damage here, but this stops now.'

Parynski couldn't easily read the guard's body language, predicting it was just typical henchmen machismo. He continued to slowly creep up behind the guard and used his free hand to wave at his daughter. Initially, she didn't seem to understand. He needed her to cause a distraction because at present, even if he shot the guard, then there was still a risk that he'd get a shot off and kill Zander.

It was great to hear her voice.

'Ok, I surrender. I'll put my gun down. Don't hurt him. I'll take you to the girl as well,' said Jude, doing her best to sound scared. Parynski didn't understand the reference to a girl, so had to follow Jude's lead on that. The tease was aimed to interest the guard and to pass on the information to Parynski.

'Good. Do it…slowly.'

The man tried to sound firm. To Parynski, it seemed fake. The guards on the base may have had security or military training. However, he assessed it unlikely they'd seen much action. Just bravado. Jude placed her weapon on the floor and then, to the surprise of the guard, gingerly turned towards a side corridor where, presumably, this girl was.

'Don't move.'

Jude turned back to him. She spoke slowly and evenly, whilst trying to provoke the guard to move.

'You won't shoot me until I've shown you where the girl is. Your boss wants her.'

'What the?' shouted the guard, and gunfire sprouted from his weapon as he spun away from Zander.

Parynski feared the worst until he realised the guard wasn't shooting at Jude. Another suited figure had appeared in the opening that had once been the doorway to the airlock. Having immediately established the situation was precarious, the figure immediately partially pulled back outside. Anyone the guard was shooting at was likely to be on his side, thought Parynski.

The guard fired a few salvos at the doorway and started to move towards it, momentarily forgetting about Jude, who he would have known was unarmed. Zander rolled away and presented Parynski with a window of opportunity. He cleanly shot the guard, puncturing his suit in the middle of his back

His weapon tumbled out of his grasp as he slumped forward, feet still clamped to the deck.

Parynski spoke on her circuit. 'Sorry I was late.'

'If I didn't have a space suit on, I'd hug you.'

He grabbed his daughter, nonetheless. 'Ok, what's going on?'

Jude introduced him to Zander. 'I told you he'd come.' She sounded relieved. She explained their plan for escape and why they had expedited it.

Parynski got down to business. 'Let's get off this base while we can. It was you who kept opening the doors I wanted locked then?' Parynski lamented, only half joking. He explained how he had traced them, used the Skydancer as bait.

He helped Zander up and told him he'd fill him in on developments at home later, but it wasn't good. Jude went to the opening to the surface of Antiope and signalled to Howard that it was safe for him to come back in. He had been cowering behind an outcrop. Howard reported that a tug had been launched to retrieve the lifeboats, apart from that it was quiet outside. He was visibly shaking, even though he had an EVA suit on, after the guard had fired on him.

Parynski paused for a moment, receiving an update from the Skydancer. 'That was the ship. We've got to move quickly. It's been cut it out of the network for this part of the base, we can't rely on help for a while. They seem to think it's you lot who've done the hacking so fortunately the ship is untouched. Not sure if they've realised, I'm here yet. The ship has just switched us all to a secure channel.'

He pointed towards the room where they'd told him Rebecca was. 'Someone will need to help the girl. If we can get to the internal train system, we can grab a ride. It'll take us the fifty kilometres we need to go to the docking bay. It's safer than going outside.'

Howard turned to go. 'I'm going to be the least use with a weapon. I'll get her.'

# THE TRITON RUN

'Be careful with her,' commanded Zander, 'Or I'll help.'

Howard stuttered that he was fine and set off.

Parynski briefed them on the route to the train. It was a different, but more direct, path than the way he'd come via. This route would lead them to where they could use a maintenance chamber as an air lock and then hopefully get access back to the train without coming into too much contact with security, at a time when due to the air breach most residents were still in lockdown. Parynski's suit alarmed, detecting movement and heat signatures nearby.

Howard had just gone for Rebecca when the lights went out. Immediately, Parynski's suit automatically powered up torches that cast light across the chamber. He switched them off, waving animatedly for the others to do the same.

Zander's suit struggled to comply, so he briefly turned to face the wall, minimising the light spread from his suit. After a few seconds, it went out. 'Sorry,' he whispered.

Unable to run for it before Howard returned, Parynski moved off to the side so he could ambush any intruders.

His HUD gave him an infra-red view on the inside of his helmet. He could detect a moving series of smudges nearby. They were coming from two directions. As he counted up eight figures, he cautiously slid along the wall towards the corridor he had come in via, noting that the bigger group were coming that way. Parynski then realised that Howard was, en route to Rebecca, likely to walk straight into three guards coming that way.

Across their channel, he heard a grunt and a moan. Howard shouted out in pain, begging for help.

'We need to help them,' said Zander.

'Hold your positions,' Parynski whispered. Despite Howard's plea and Zander's shout, nobody moved. Parynski was expecting a firefight. Jude could hold her own so he could focus on the rest of them. Several minutes passed, Parynski assumed the new attackers were talking on a private channel he couldn't currently access. Then there was a crackle as someone else joined their channel. Parynski cursed. It was supposed to be private.

A quiet, though powerful female voice. 'Former President Theodore Zander. Please don't run or we'll hurt your friend. I just want to talk to you and Rebecca before we decide how we complete what needs to be done. I'm going to come through there with my colleagues and we'll meet your friends. I presume one is Judith Parynski. I'm afraid I don't know who the other is. My suit is shield enabled, so don't waste your time with those laser weapons you have. They'll only bounce back and cause you all a nasty injury. Please confirm.'

Zander shouted that he'd comply. He didn't mention Parynski, confirming that Jude would also comply. Parynski started playing scenarios over and over in his mind, trying to work out the best angle here.

The lights came back on, temporarily blinding them all at the same time whilst their eyes adjusted, their visors not reacting quite quickly enough. Once his eyesight had stopped blurring, Parynski gave a discrete thumbs up to Zander. Jude stood next to Zander, her body language suggesting she was resting, waiting for a signal from him.

Parynski didn't know how this would play out, especially if their weapons wouldn't work against the woman who he presumed, based on what they'd told him, was Chen Yang. They all noticeably tensed and came to attention as the figures appeared. Parynski backed further away, trying to push himself into a crevice alongside a wall unit to minimise the chances of him being seen in the first instance. He feared it was likely Chen's suit might be able to detect him. He'd engaged a 'dark' mode even though he wasn't sure how it worked.

The security team gathered in the middle of the room and fanned out. At the front of the group came the smallest figure, barely five feet in height. Chen Yang. Her guards were all taller and bulkier than her. All had their visors opaque. Zander involuntarily retreated a step, intimidated by their

# THE TRITON RUN

aggressive outlook and the weapons they all carried. Bar the two immediately flanking Chen. Their suits also looked antiquated, as worn out as the ones Zander and Jude wore. Zander and Jude initially stood side by side, weapons facing their new visitors.

Chen's visor was transparent, her face emotionless. A skullcap inside the helmet covered her hair and framed her face. Sculpted, arched eyebrows rested on top of two piercing eyes with jet black pupils. The nose and lips were both thin. Scrambling in front of her was Howard, cowering from the pistol she held in her right hand and the stick in her left. Every time he started to straighten up, she prodded him with the stick, causing him to lose his footing. His body language showed he was terrified.

Zander composed himself and stepped forward ahead of Jude in a statesmanlike manner, rendering his visor transparent so Chen could see him. Parynski thought he was a brave man, or maybe he believed he was already dead.

Howard was sent sprawling, pulling himself into a crouch position so his boots were in contact with the metal plated floor. He turned himself sideways so when he looked up, he could look in either direction to Chen or Zander, who stood above him. Initially, he looked away from Chen, who maintained her pistol aimed at his helmet.

Parynski watched Chen focus her attention on Zander whilst her guards fanned out.

They also had their weapons raised. It occurred to him that the girl wasn't here. They must have got to Howard before he'd reached her.

'Former President Zander. It's important that we talk. Be aware that this is being filmed for broadcast.'

Chen again laboured the word *former,* and Parynski was pleased to hear Zander cut her off. 'Chen, I have to say I'm surprised to find you behind this. In hindsight, I can see some of your behaviour in the senate would suggest your support for the Exiles, but this amazes me.' He shrugged, encouraging her to reveal more, no doubt awaiting Parynski's intervention.

Her response was calm, firm. 'That sums you up, no empathy. You just can't understand what could drive several thousand people to seek revenge and to build new lives. You just shrug. Did you do the same after voting to support the bill that abandoned three habitats?'

Parynski knew Zander's shrug hadn't helped, but it was so hard to express feelings without speaking in these suits. Chen continued, waving her stick around, pointing at all the corners of the room before slapping it down again on Howard's shoulder as he crouched in front of her.

'If only you'd have been as resourceful back then as you have been now. Though perhaps that's down to your young friend.' She pointed her stick at Jude. Jude stood impassive; her own weapon remained aimed at Chen, who appeared oblivious to it.

'I have to say I'm disappointed in my station surgeon.' She prodded Howard again in the shoulder. 'But this is about me and you, Zander. The girl is here somewhere. I know you brought her with you, so unless she was sucked out of the airlock…what were you thinking, by the way, on that? Anyway, perhaps it's best if she doesn't see what I do to you.'

In a stage managed and planned move, the second group that Parynski had detected filed into the room, moving alongside Chen, setting up what was a large, professional piece of kit, a 3D camera. She slightly turned to it and began a pre-planned speech. 'What I'm going to do is legal…'

Parynski zoned out of the speech, assessing his next move. Chen talked and talked about what happened all those years ago and the fall out. She set out a legal basis for an execution, explaining how the Government that Zander had led had now collapsed and new elections were imminent. Chen finished her speech and kicked Howard so firmly he shouted out in pain. She prodded him and pushed him out of the way. Her weapon followed him, though her eyes never left Zander. Howard

# THE TRITON RUN

was whimpering in fear. He was probably regretting getting involved in their crazy escape plan.

'It's time to carry out the sentence I have lawfully handed down.'

She let the comment hang in the air. They knew what she meant.

'We can do this quickly or have a fight, which will result in more suffering. If you cause me any inconvenience or hurt any of my men, then rather than killing you quickly, I'll make you all suffer more. I can edit the footage later to suit our purposes.'

She chuckled. 'We don't really need you to generate the footage, but I need this for closure. I want to see you suffer like I did, like our families did.'

She used her stick to point for Zander to move next to Howard. Zander didn't move, adjusting his stance to confirm his defiance. Amazed that he'd not been spotted, Parynski knew it was time. He raised his weapon and squinted at the sight that he could see on his HUD.

'I'm not going to wait-'

Chen staggered back as her pistol was shot from her grip. A second shot deflected off her suit helmet into the ceiling, bringing down some trunking and showering the room in debris that floated all around them. A further spread of blaster fire knocked her down. Zander threw himself to the floor alongside the prone Howard.

Above them was a blur of blaster fire. Parynski stepped out from his alcove, raking Chen's guards with fire. Assisted by the combat tech AI his suit contained, he shot and moved rapidly across the room, moving from target to target. Their focus had been on Jude and Zander and the direction of fire caught them out, giving Jude time to start firing her weapon as she too dived for cover behind a nearby console.

Three of the guards went down from Parynski's fire, their suits not being up to the standard of their leader's equipment. Parynski switched to a projectile firing pistol, taking down another with a shot to the knee that tore open the suit the attacker was wearing.

Suddenly not feeling so invincible, the remaining four, realising they were exposed in the open, returned fire whilst retreating for the corridor from where they had come. Parynski kept the pressure on by striding forward, firing more selectively. His projectile weapon was potentially more of a risk in space due to the increased risk of shrapnel. He didn't have time to assess risks, so pulled a close proximity grenade from a pouch on his suit and tossed it round the corner after them. A cloud of debris indicated it had exploded, and he paused. There was nothing further from that direction, but he had to be safe.

He looked over at Jude, who was finishing off one of the guards who had tried to rush her. 'Jude, cover the corridor. If anything moves, kill it…or shout me and I'll do it.'

She took the projectile based weapon from him, checking it. 'It's got half a clip.

Should be enough.'

Parynski patted her on the back and turned back to the others. The suit had rolled back his years of rustiness in a combat situation, improving his accuracy and speed. Expecting to see Zander and Howard getting up, he was horrified with what he saw. First, he was distracted by a floating corpse and a plume of blood that had come out of it and formed a frozen cloud.

One of the bodies still held the camera in its hand. He wondered if it was still filming. Then he saw her.

Chen was crouched down, staring up at him. Her two arms were held out to either side, both holding weapons that had been dropped by the dead, aiming at Zander and Howard. Howard was still curled up in a ball, clearly terrified. Zander was now sitting, knees on the floor, arms folded defiantly across his chest. 'Just get it over with Chen. I've been dead since you killed my family. I'm just a fool for not working out that you must have been involved in that. So, fuck you and your cause. You are as barbaric as anything I was responsible for.'

Chen didn't respond to Zander. Parynski slowly walked

towards the three of them until Chen told him to stop. He told Jude to stick to the securing the corridor.

'I'll edit your little speech out, Zander, and perhaps I will have to fabricate some of the footage. Zander, I hoped you would pay your debt. Your thug over there has killed some of my men. We'll have to wait till more backup arrives. Don't worry, it's coming. You'll have seen your beam weapons deflect off my suit and your crack shot friend cannot shoot both my weapons out of my hands at the same time.'

Parynski decided it was time to introduce himself.

'My name is Bruce Parynski, you won't know me. I'm a nobody. I don't particularly know you either, I've little interest in politics, though I seem to remember a friend of mine is still traumatised from trying to save all the people you killed to make a political statement. I came here for my daughter. She's no part of this and I'm going to take her and get off this shithole of a rock. What you do after I get on my ship is not my problem.'

Parynski hoped he sounded confident, because despite support from the suit, he felt exhausted from the exertions of the shootout.

Chen's voice remained steady. 'Ah, you came on that ship. I told the retrieval crew it was too good to be true. Well, you shouldn't have come. Justice must be served, but I'm willing to negotiate.'

Remaining in her crouched position, she shook the gun aimed at Howard and continued to talk. 'I can't tolerate this coward's traitorous behaviour; however, you and your daughter have shown some good skills. Maybe once this is resolved, we can talk about a role with us?'

'You won't be surprised to know that's not an option. And remember you are outgunned now,' Parynski said on behalf of them all.

'Then the only option is that none of you leave this room alive.'

'You seem quite confident of that. Who says you'll survive?' Parynski asked.

# 56

# MULLER

*Orbital Shipyards*

Muller ended the call to Arden and Garcia and turned his focus back to the task at hand. He was in his office at the Shipyards, a screen on the wall taking on the appearance of a porthole, using software to enhance the view which otherwise would be largely hidden in darkness.

Two huge carriers were now looming over Neptune's largest ship dock, waiting to unload their construction materials. Arden owned one of them already and had diverted it from another project. The other had been bought from Uranus, in exchange for early access to the Xenos for their political leaders. Arden had overruled everyone's concerns; said he'd give a personal tour himself. He made it clear it was the only way to get the materials needed to build a cradle as designed by Muller and his team. Their space dock was empty for the first time in years, surrounded by dozens of small tugs and groups of engineers buzzing round in EVA suits. The frame of the dock was being cut apart so it could be extended.

Muller had enjoyed the last few days, solid progress was being made, and he was arguably, or definitely when Arden asked, ahead of schedule.

He had other worries, however. Arden had updated him on the Skydancer, not because Muller had been involved in its purchase or fitting out, but because he'd reminded him that if Parynski was able to complete his mission then a private, and discrete, docking berth would be needed, despite the capacity problems Triton One currently suffered. Parynski had updated Arden on the news about Antiope, and ever the cynical pragmatist, had privately commented that even if Parynski's mission failed, he hoped to still recover his ship when enforcement got there.

Bar keeping Arden happy, Muller hadn't been particularly interested in the initial story about the Skydancer, however when he was told of the ship's destination, his heart sank. He'd been struggling to lock away his thoughts about Chen and had once been on the verge of removing the filters and secure measures he'd put in place. She was going to haunt him. He shouldn't care anymore about her, but their relationship might yet be exposed before investigations lead his way. He wasn't certain that Antiope was where Chen was. She'd kept the location of the base secret from him, though it was too much of a coincidence.

'Roo's got these bastards pinned down. There can't be that many who can hold a grudge so strongly and launch such an audacious kidnapping against the Pres. You see the footage?'

Muller told him he had.

Arden had continued. 'Ruthless bastards. Hope they get what's coming to them.' And with that, he explained what Parynski's plan was. 'Anyway, I just want Parynski and his daughter out of there safely with my ship. They can leave Zander to his fate if they want.'

Arden then reflected on things, and the edge that usually appeared when discussing Zander faded. 'Though we can't have crooks like this doing what they want. It's bad for business, its unstable out here as it is.'

With news that there was going to be some sort of incursion against Antiope, Muller wobbled. Momentarily, he considered the potential to warn Chen, before accepting it was too late, would be too obvious and he just didn't want to be part of her plan.

The call between Muller and Arden ended with some of the most exciting news. 'Squire was going to tell you tomorrow when you speak, but fuck it, I'm excited. We've had Paisley doing some deep scans of the tank where Wilding is and doing some tests on how their systems are wired up. Looks like we might, just might, be able to move some of those tanks so we can get a proper look at saving the girl. Might need you to look at getting a separate reception facility built for a dozen or so of the tanks. Just think, we might have our own live aliens to study?'

Muller had to admit, even though distracted, that this sounded positive. He resolved that before going off shift, he'd pin down a shortlist of suitable local habitats and moon bases that could house the most unique of guests. He also was determined to work out arrangements at Neptune so he could be spared by Arden and go on the excursion to the origin of the Xenos. His level of interest in that was only matched by the fear he needed to get away.

# 57

## CHEN

*Antiope Mining Facility*

Chen wished she could meditate at this point in order to clear her mind. She needed to carefully calculate a solution. The adrenaline pumping through her body made it difficult. She gave a sub vocal command to her suit to lock itself in position, so it supported her arms whilst they were pointed outwards at Howard and Zander. Her eyes flicked around the scene, expecting an attack at any point. Her suit could take a bolt or two of laser fire, despite that she wouldn't risk a firefight on her own. Chen knew they'd be unlikely to take the risk of shooting her whilst she had two of them at point blank range. She tried to ignore the chatter from the man calling himself Parynski and her thoughts wandered, briefly alighting on Muller. He'd not replied to recent messages.

This was unusual. Usually, he replied within minutes like the lap dog he was, despite recent complaints from him. She wasn't sure whether his silence was because he'd lost faith in her or because he was simply too busy in his project to house the Xenos. She'd spent years looking internally, seeking retribution for the crimes committed against her people, and once this situation was resolved, she would have a clean slate.

First contact with aliens interested her. It interested everyone. She'd made peace with the reality that she'd be unable to return

# THE TRITON RUN

to Earth or even Mars, but Chen was confident she could head to the outer planets with many of her people. With Muller's help, she could try to secure some of the alien technology to give her people an advantage. She took the positivity from Muller's love for her and the opportunities he provided before putting them in a box in the corner of her mind whilst she tried to focus.

For a while, nobody spoke. The only noise across the common channel was the sound of breathing, some heavier than others, along with Howard's gentle whimpering. He was, rightly, terrified.

From time to time, the lights would come on and then go off again. Chen couldn't tell if it was a systems failure or by design from those coming to rescue her. The effect was to make everyone anxious.

'I wonder whose air will run out first?' Parynski said, breaking the silence. Nobody replied.

Chen remained crouched, assessing those she was to execute, if not now, then later. Howard was curled into a ball, arms pulling his knees towards his chest. He really was pathetic. Zander sat cross-legged, facing her, staring into the muzzle of her pistol. He'd set his visor to be transparent so she could see his face, his jaw set. The slight shake told Chen he was struggling to remain in the awkward position he was sitting in. He didn't seem afraid.

Chen was positioned facing the direction from which she expected her backup to come. The female prisoner, Judith she was called, stood near that exit, where the chamber twisted away into a corridor, weapon aimed. She kept glancing at Parynski. He was the pivotal figure in the situation. He stood, legs apart, rifle aimed at her. He was half the distance between her and Judith at the back of the room.

Parynski was still talking. 'You can live through this if you let us go. Just let us get off this rock and we won't fire another shot. I came here for my daughter, but I'm taking her friends too.'

# 58

## PARYNSKI

*Antiope Mining Facility*

Parynski wondered if Chen could tell he was trying to sound more confident than he felt. He'd not dare shoot her without a diversion. Even if he took her head off with a shot, the chances were that one of the weapons in her hands would still discharge.

After a period of silence, she spoke directly to him. 'You misunderstand the situation.

My life isn't important here. Making sure we get justice is all that matters.'

Parynski rocked slightly towards her, wanting to reply, biting his tongue. He knew how these things worked. They'd been here so long now that all anyone could do was bluff. Better to wait for something to change. The Skydancer reported it was primed for a quick launch and had recently deterred a boarding party. He flashed a look towards Jude, who was still focussed on the corridor entrance.

The lights went out again. And stayed off. Suit torches kicked in again. They all jumped as a hail of gunfire tore out of the corridor entrance, scarring the wall near Jude and creating a cloud of debris that spread across the room in the vacuum. Jude didn't return fire, instead taking a knee and sliding slightly away, getting a better aim.

'Drop all your weapons now.' A new authoritative voice was heard. 'You are outgunned.'

# THE TRITON RUN

As previously instructed, nobody moved. They all switched their lights off. Bruce wanted to assess the backup before he reacted. There were only limited options available to the new security team to gain any sort of advantage. Changing the light was one of them, so he wasn't surprised at what they'd done. Parynski was, he guessed, the only one with a suit that had infra-red capability, but that didn't give him a huge advantage. The new team also faced the risk of their leader being killed and even if they did have infra-red, any sudden incursion was a risk. The initial volley of fire from the corridor was a warning, a bluff. They needed to do something else to gain the initiative.

'Anymore and your leader gets even shorter,' he shouted back. The only light came from Chen's helmet beam, fanning out in front of her, illuminating Zander and Howard.

Replacing the dark came blinding light. A stun grenade must have been tossed into the room, exploding on impact with the wall, creating a wall of white that burned the backs of their retinas. Parynski was blinded momentarily as his visor reacted. He guessed his suit was quicker to respond than most. The pain was excruciating, and his eyes filled with tears, blurring his vision. Quite a problem in a space helmet. The lights remained off, and the darkness returned, save for Chen's suit.

It was hard to know how long had passed before Parynski could focus on the infra-red display clearly enough so he could fire without hitting Chen's captives. Everyone had remained in their positions, though they'd been supplemented by four new figures stood just inside the room, pointing rifles out in front of them. They had torches on their weapons, but the beams didn't extend that far, not touching Parynski or Jude. He was confident they didn't have infrared. If they had, they would have acted to take him and Jude out. These guys weren't professionals, likely more scared than he was. The grenade had been used to get them into the room, and he guessed that their plan went no further. There must be more of them on the way.

In their shoes, Parynski would have waited things out. He knew that if instructed, his suit could take all four out with ease, but that wouldn't stop Chen from shooting Zander and Howard.

Through the darkness came Chen's voice. 'Whatever happens, we win. Even if we have to fake some of the footage, we'll get a blockbuster out of this. I can still show everyone your corpses. This constant changing of the illumination is boring me. Cassidy, I'm disappointed you haven't brought more help, but I'm sure it's incoming. We can resolve this as we want.'

The guard, now known as Cassidy, was who had shouted before, acknowledged her.

In the dark, Chen's voice took on a menacing tone.

'Mr Parynski, if everyone fires at the same time, then theoretically, we all get shot, though some of us have suits with better armour. I suggest you don't miss and fire lots.

Except you might still hit your friends, and even if you do hit me, I won't miss them, and you can't be sure your weapon will pierce my suit. You don't have the nerve. None of you do. Surrender.'

Parynski felt an emotional kick in the gut. She was right. There was nothing he could do to break the deadlock without Rebecca and Zander being at risk. He'd messed up.

Just as he was considering bluffing a surrender, his suit's motion detector flagged someone coming in from one of the side corridors, his HUD detecting only a vague heat signature. He didn't turn to look or say something for fear of giving Chen the initiative. In hindsight, he wondered if she had thought the same. After a 'thwump' across the com channel, Chen's beam tilted to one side as she collapsed, her left hand fired, missed Howard, and she lay still.

The moment of confusion was all he needed. Parynski spun on his heels and dropped to his knees, firing rapidly. The gunfight was surprisingly brief, and the guards were despatched. Despite his state-of-the-art suit, he took a shot to the leg and swallowed down the scream he wanted to give out, taking some relief

# THE TRITON RUN

from the suit immediately pumping him full of pain killers and confirmation it was self-sealing. He hoped the others didn't spot the wound for now. Jude put her spotlights on. Others followed and surveyed the scene. 'Is everyone ok?' she asked.

The scene was clouded with blood from the bodies of the four guards. One of their suits was torn to shreds and the area around Jude was temporarily filled with blood and innards. They spilled out before freezing as a macabre sculpture, floating between them all. Her beams swung over to the fallen woman and saw that crouched over Chen's helmet was a small figure in a space suit that didn't seem to fit that well. Rebecca looked up at them and put her own torch on, grinning. She was still tethered to the wall, the rope taut as it had reached its limit. If Chen had moved a few inches, the girl might not have got there.

'I had the nerve.'

In her right hand she held a nail gun, presumably found in the storage room she had been left in. From point blank range, she'd discharged a dozen nails into Chen's helmet, killing her instantly. She lowered the tool she'd used and looked at her friends. Howard climbed to his feet whilst Zander reached over and hugged her. Sobbing came across their channel as Rebecca came down from the adrenaline rush of her sprinting across the room to save her friends.

'Can we please go now?'

# 59

# JUDE

*Antiope Mining Facility*

Once through a series of doors the group were able to use as an airlock, they removed their helmets and clipped them to their backpacks. Parynski kept his helmet on so he could use the tactical information the HUD provided. He reported increasing problems accessing systems due to a security lock down and that the Skydancer's AI was engaged in a battle with the facility's own computer defences. The AI was creating a false trail to a shuttle bay on the far side of the base with the intention of drawing security that way. It had even managed to power up a shuttle in a different docking bay to add to the confusion.

They all hugged each other in relief that they had got away. Jude was conscious she n needed to take the lead where possible, concerned about her father. He'd initially not mentioned it, but he'd taken a shot in his lower leg. His suit had sealed itself and was providing emergency pain relief, injecting nanobots into the area to get on with the repair process, though the fact he had to remain active was going to hinder his recovery. She also thought that being thawed recently was still affecting him, not that he would admit it.

Jude let him lean on her for a moment. He was peering closely at the map on his HUD. 'We can party once we get to the ship. This is not the same route I came in on, so I'm trusting this map.

We've got to cross a crop facility to come out near the train station.'

The next section of corridor was largely downhill, heading into the depths of Antiope where some larger caverns had been excavated. They set off at a run, though soon slowed to a jog. Most of their suits, even with the assistance from exoskeletons, were heavy in artificial gravity and they were all sweating profusely. With her father's injury, Jude took point, acting on directions he shouted from time to time. Between them, the other three stayed close together, Zander and Howard flanking Rebecca, who still held onto the nail gun. She was still groggy after being hit when the atmosphere had been evacuated.

Where the Skydancer couldn't help with locking doors after them, Jude vandalised circuitry and door furniture, shooting out lighting and any CCTV units. They only came across one person, a maintenance worker who seemed oblivious to the emergency that had been called. Jude shot him before realising he was unarmed. She dragged the corpse into an alcove filled with ancient machinery, ignoring the disapproving look from her father.

Eventually, they gathered by a door. Jude leaned to one side so she could see past the others, to her father who was lagging behind. She worried about his leg, but until he got the suit off, they couldn't check it properly. She took him to one side when he arrived. His voice was hoarse, gasping, 'This is the crop room. We need to go left once inside. Stick to the wall for two hundred metres and then head for the far wall.'

Jude nodded. She opened the door, which was controlled by an old-fashioned wheel, and pulled the door open. She stepped inside, followed by the others, waiting for her father before pulling the door to. They stripped some supplies off Howard's backpack and jammed them into the wheel to stop it being turned from the other side.

Jude couldn't help but admire the view. The chamber was huge, though appeared larger than it was. As far as the eye could see, there was a wheat field. The crop, Jude could tell, was approaching the time for harvest. She'd grown up on a farm her mother had shared for a while with her parents, whilst her father had been away, which was most of the time. They could all feel the warmth of the room, noting the lighting simulated a summer morning and a breeze that caused the crops to gently sway from side to side.

The crop swept into a shallow valley ahead of them and she could just make out the far wall containing a huge metal door that appeared incongruous amongst the projection of a further valley. The image of a small hamlet could be seen tucked away by a copse of trees. Howard confirmed that this was the smallest such chamber and that deep within the asteroid there were two others that were in better repair, one of which even contained a sports field. The ceiling was high above, a bright blue with only the faintest hint of clouds drifting overhead. The scene wasn't perfect, however, there were plenty of signs of decay. Close by was a piece of abandoned farm machinery that was rusting. The wall image and the ceiling showed signs of wear as scattered across the moving images were gaps where projectors had failed, and the beautiful scenery was replaced by black pixel squares.

Looking round, she could see they were all exhausted. 'Come on, we must keep moving. Dad's AI is buying us time, but we need to pick up a trail that'll get us to the exit on the other side.'

Telling them to wait, she jogged ahead to check that the path they wanted was available, before beckoning them all to follow her.

Jude felt it a surreal moment as the four of them in space suits jogged, shuffled, and limped their way across the chamber, following a path that had been cut into the crops to allow for machinery to pass. Parynski remained at the rear. They came across two farmers who weren't armed and Jude knocked one out with a swing of her weapon whilst Zander shot the other on a setting. He said he hoped was designed only to stun. They didn't stop to check. As the path dipped through the valley, the wall behind them vanished from sight, the tall reeds of the crop blocking their immediate view.

'The ship has that door under its control for now, so when we get there, we should be ok through it. The train I came in on is still parked in the station, which is the other side of a garage and storage bay. It should be a straight run back to the Skydancer. The ship doesn't know how many friends we might have waited for us as security is en route. We need to be going before they arrive.' As Parynski spoke, his strained voice failed to disguise his pain.

Jude had an idea. She waved an arm around, indicating the crops. 'We could put up an extra hazard for any followers, you know. I reckon we could set this lot alight. Not only would that slow them down, but having acres of crops on fire can't be good in a pressurised area?'

Her father looked at her with the same expression of distaste that appeared on Zander's face. 'I'm here to rescue you, not endanger the lives of the other residents that have nothing to do with this shit. Most of them are innocent, I imagine.'

Trying not to feel too chastened, she dismissively waved them away and turned back to lead the group on. 'Fine, whatever you say, let's hope we get away without anyone else getting hurt. I've seen how ruthless these bastards are and they've massacred thousands of innocents, most of which were so they could capture you, Zander.'

She knew that hurt Zander. He stopped, took a deep breath, and then continued, clearly trying not to rise to the bait. Seeing his reaction, Howard slapped him on the back. 'She's fine. She knows that not all of us were supportive of what's been going on off the Antiope.

She's just stressed at seeing her dad like this.'

Zander looked at the Doctor, his face grim. 'The trouble is, she is right. A lot of people died with Chen trying to get revenge and she hasn't done it all alone. You are pretty much the exception.'

Howard looked away awkwardly, pretending then to check

Rebecca's suit. Jude decided to pretend she hadn't heard the conversation and pressed on ahead.

They reached the door, which was wide enough to allow large vehicles through it, looming high above them. When Parynski caught up, he motioned for them to take cover whilst he opened it. Jude made them fan out away from the doorway, hiding amongst the nearby crops. Howard had grabbed Rebecca by the hand and led her the furthest away. Parynski limped up to the door, which had a complicated console embedded in the wall next to it. His suit told him it was also the controller for the room, responsible for lighting, temperature, and the weather. Jude saw him playing with the controls, as directed by the ship before cautiously retreating, weapon aimed at the entrance as the thick metal door slid upwards with a squeal.

Silence. Jude lay nearby in the shade of a small, abandoned generator. She had a clear view of the opening. She gave a thumbs up and pointed that she'd cover her father. She watched nervously as he stepped cautiously round the doorway and swung his weapon across the large room. There was no activity, and he waved everyone in. The garage area where they found themselves was partly lit, shadows thrown down from where vehicles and machinery blocked out the spotlights above.

'The ship says though there is nobody ahead of us, we are in a race. The ship's going to lock this door, though I don't think there is anyone actually following right behind us. They are coming in from the route I originally took.'

Before they set off, Jude was given directions. They made good progress with Parynski's suit, keeping them up to date with the progress of the group who were on an intercept course. The AI predicted they would arrive at exactly the same time as they did, so where it could, it locked doors, turned off lighting and generally tried to be obstructive.

Her father swore. 'Whoever's now in charge of the base is aware of the Skydancer's presence within the network. They are working hard to restrict its access. We are going too slow.'

With the extra fear of being cut off from the train, they upped their pace again.

# 60

# PARYNSKI

*Antiope Mining Facility*

When Parynski caught up with his daughter, she looked exhausted, sweat running down her face from her soaked hair, but looking pleased with herself. From a distance, he'd heard her take out two technicians who'd manned the control room, plus three guards. He felt happier when she told him that, as asked, she'd slightly lowered the power rating to hopefully just disable or knock them out. She was less bothered than he, whether she'd miscalculated or not. Parynski understood her bloodlust. She'd not had time to grieve those mercilessly killed on the elevator, but he couldn't let her become a murderer. And this wasn't a situation like at Buchanan.

Parynski directed them all towards the station and was relieved to find the train waiting for them. The entrance through which he'd originally left the station was away to one side. The Skydancer told him the door was locked for now. However, it believed that the incoming pursuers would be able to override it. They were close.

Jude climbed the ladder onto the rear of the train where there was a flatbed surrounded by a lip. It was raised about six feet off the ground. Everyone passed up their helmets and weapons and then climbed on board. Parynski watched as she went towards the front of the cab, taking a seat at the control console. The others sat on the open flatbed, peering back into the station.

Parynski shouted instructions to Jude. 'Stay near those controls in case the ship loses access. The manual override switch is that big one right at the top of the console.'

After seeing her give him the thumbs up, he turned to look back into the station, where he noticed a spotlight playing across the floor, emerging from the main entrance corridor. Their pursuers were being cautious, expecting an ambush. The train was now humming with power as it slowly came back online. It felt like it took a lot longer than it had on the way in.

The suit around his wound had now turned pink. It hurt. A lot. It was going to be grim when he got to the medical bay on the Skydancer and had to take the suit off. The pain was manageable, no doubt due to the drugs his suit was pumping him full of. He wondered if the drugs would affect his aim.

A figure appeared, and he squeezed off a couple of shots, forcing them back. Moments later, three appeared, one crawling and the others crouching against the wall. He fired again and two of the figures went still. The third retreated. He looked anxiously round. Jude was sitting at the control desk, patting it impatiently. Zander was away to one side with a weapon aimed in the direction they had come from. Howard was sitting alongside Rebecca, their backs to the lip that ran round the flatbed with their helmets and spare weapons. Howard was protectively holding her down.

Barely perceptibly, the train started to move, then stopped. They all looked anxiously round. Parynski queried it with the AI.

'Shit, bad timing. It's a pre-planned self-diagnostic check before we set off.'

Parynski fired a few warning shots into the gap in the hope it would hold their pursuers off. A moment later, a smoke grenade was launched into the station. It landed near the buffer where the train rested. It poured its smoke out, obliterating the view Parynski had of the station area. Shrouded in smoke, his suit was still able to pick up figures based on their heat signatures. He fired another volley at the figures his suit could identify, but was unable to tell if he'd hit his targets. As the smoke billowed, he couldn't tell how many attackers were in the station due to the haze, but he feared it was now at least a dozen. It might be more if they were wearing more advanced suits.

The first shots back at them weren't that accurate. The attackers were also hindered by the smoke they had deployed, though it was a success in allowing them to get a foothold inside the station. Part of the ceiling nearby came in, showering the roof of Jude's cab with rubble, and the tailgate took a hit, throwing up sparks.

The train started to move again, slowly at first and then settling initially into what was little more than walking pace. Parynski knew that once it had cleared the loading area, it would increase speed. They all ducked down as laser and projectile fire enveloped the tailgate and cab. Jude threw herself onto the floor, taking refuge behind her seat. Parynski was the only one with a view over the lip and kept popping off shots. The train wasn't gaining any ground on their pursuers, whose numbers were swelling. His gun was more of a precision weapon, so whilst he was picking off those, he could get a bead on he wasn't able to put down a blanket of fire to slow them down. In hindsight, he'd have had Jude alongside him because he couldn't rely on Zander or Howard.

They were forty or so yards from their pursuers when Parynski was hit. The laser bolt hit his rifle, blowing it out of his hands. He recoiled as the glove of his left hand took the brunt of the shrapnel, which also flashed up towards his face. The suit saved him from losing his sight and the hand. His visor was pitted with marks and his hand burnt. He howled in pain at the AI to pick up speed. Slowly it reacted and as he looked over the top again, he realised it wasn't quickly enough. The nearest pursuers were breaking into a charge, encouraged by the lack

# THE TRITON RUN

of suppressing fire.

Parynski flicked his scarred visor up and yelled across at where Rebecca and Howard were crouched down, huddled together. 'Doc! Throw me those weapons you have,' he implored. Howard nodded and reached across Rebecca to grab a pistol. He slid it across the floor to where Parynski sat cross-legged, back to the lip. Parynski waved in frustration for the other weapon, the machine gun, to be passed over too. Howard couldn't reach it and, to everyone's horror, Rebecca decided to help. He screamed at her to keep down. The noise of the train engine and the chatter of gunfire shattering the walls and ceiling meant she didn't hear him. Howard tried to pull her down, but it was too late.

Rebecca half-stood to lean over and pass Parynski the gun. As she did, a direct shot hit the rear of the train, and the tailgate's hinges shattered, half breaking and falling away to expose the back of the train.

Parynski shouted at everyone to stay low. He instinctively collapsed flat into the floor of the tailgate, grabbing the weapon Rebecca passed him, but she was not so lucky, tumbling out of the back of the train as the train rocked with the impact of the fire, beyond Howard's despairing grasp.

Rebecca fell to the ground, bounced, and curled up in an unmoving ball. Parynski screamed at the AI to slow the train down, which to his relief immediately worked. He slid towards the open rear of the train in order to drop off the back and go to get her. His legs swung down, and he brought his weapon round, spraying the air above Rebecca to try and deter their followers. Having now moved away from the smoke cloud, he was pleased to see it work as the security team, following them all, temporarily at least, dived for cover.

'No! You'll never manage it with that leg.' Howard pulled himself up, pushed Parynski aside and slid to the rear of the trailer. Zander beat them both to it, scrambling past them and dropping as gently as he could onto the track.

Parynski cursed him. Howard was right. All he could do was try and cover them. Zander sprinted towards Rebecca, keeping his body as low as he could. Dust clouds appeared in his wake as he sensibly chose a weaving path to make it harder to hit him. As the older man ran, he limped heavily. He'd his own wounds to contend with.

With Parynski laying down a barrage of fire with his new rapid-fire weapon, their pursuers were unable to get out into the open to hit him. Instead, they remained lying low, taking cover in recesses or behind old boxes left abandoned on the trackside.

Parynski could sense Zander might have regretted his decision as soon as he hit the ground. He wasn't cut out for this and was out of shape. He reached Rebecca, who was now coming round, blood running from a wound on her forehead from where she had landed on the track.

With no time to say anything, he scooped her up and threw her over his shoulder. He pulled himself straight and turned back to the train. Parynski could see the fear in his eyes, but also determination and acceptance of his fate. Howard waved Zander on as the train came to a halt. He set off in a staggered run, gritting his teeth, and headed directly for the back of the train. He was unable to weave due to the weight of Rebecca. Parynski hoped Zander didn't look over his shoulder as the pursuers were getting closer. They'd started to come out from their cover, realising that whilst the train was stopped, they had their best chance of re-capturing the escapees.

Zander focussed on Howard, who had slid across the tailgate and was lying with his arms outstretched towards him.

'Quickly!' Parynski yelled. He told the ship to start the train's engine again. It started to gently pull away again as Zander got to within twenty feet. Zander seemed to find it in him to accelerate and he sprinted to the rear of the train, keeping pace with it. He reached up whilst running and half passed, half threw Rebecca into Howard's arms. The doctor grabbed the girl under the shoulders and pulled her away from the edge. As he swung back to reach for Zander, they all watched on in horror as he stumbled in the effort to pass Rebecca to safety.

He got back up and started running again. 'Help, grab me.' The gap had grown and Parynski could see increasing number of pursuers getting closer. More laser bolts were striking the train and the chamber walls that were now closing in as the storage area ended and became a tunnel.

'Come on! One last push.' Parynski shouted, waving Zander on. Parynski pulled himself into a kneeling position to see if he could help, in between taking shots at the nearest pursuers.

Zander got close again before he was hit. The first shot in the back went straight through his stomach, burning a hole in body and suit alike. Surprisingly, he kept running for a moment as his face turned pale and he looked down in horror. A second and third shot caused him to stop in his tracks, staggering to one side. He looked up at the train, eyes wide in desperation. A further two shots took him down and he fell face forward onto the rocky floor, arms and legs splayed out. Within moments, those who had taken him down were past his body and within touching distance of the train.

Parynski noted later that Jude had saved them, overriding the AI, and pushing the train to increase to maximum speed as quickly as possible. Parynski angrily raked the attackers with fire. As they pulled away, he fired so much the weapon overheated, so he threw it off the train. All those in the lead group went down and even as the next group became smaller and smaller as they pulled away, he kept shooting with his pistol until Howard gently put his arm round him. 'It's done. There's nothing you could have done. Let's do what he wanted and get Rebecca off this station.'

# 61

# ZANDER

*Antiope Mining Facility*

He was dead. He knew it. He'd been dead for a while.

Zander tried to lift his head, catching a glimpse of the departing train vanishing into the haze, hearing the slight clanking of the train as it pulled away and the noise of gunfire overhead, shouting and an occasion explosion. There were footsteps getting closer.

There was one thing left for him to do in these circumstances if he could remember and didn't die first.

The breeze coming through the tunnel took him back to the moment that defined his life, ended it as he knew it. It made him who he became, reinforced all the prejudices and intolerances which he'd tried to ignore.

The helicopter's vanes slowed; the gale being whipped up around him eased. He was back in an oasis of green, a safe distance from his now silent government helicopter, wearing a white-buttoned shirt and khaki pants with flip-flops. His arm protected his eyes from the glare as he peered across the pitches towards the school buildings. The school had been renamed in his honour, as their most famous alumni. Senator Zander, being pushed for President too. He dabbed at the sweat on his forehead, noting the changing positioning of various security drones that circled the school.

A group approached from the school buildings, flanked by

some of his security detachment. The male teachers looked like they'd been forced to put on ties for the visit, the females dressed in bright flowery dresses, some with equally colourful headscarves. They knew they'd be on the news tonight.

The central figure, a short, stout lady of about sixty, broke into a jog when she spotted him. Principal Radebe was panting in the heat when she reached him, but still managed to leap up and embrace him. He waved his security detail back. Ignoring all the etiquette that usually surrounded him, she looked him in the eye, not letting go.

'Thank you for coming! It's been so long. We are so proud of you but so worried! Next time give me more notice!'

She let go of him and stepped back to inspect him. 'Are you ok?'

He laughed. 'Good to see you too, Mrs Radebe. If it wasn't for you, who knows where I would've ended up?' He always felt guilty for not finding enough time for one of his foster parents.

'And sorry for the late notice, typical security being cautious.' He gave her a wink.

Whilst Mrs Radebe introduced him to a number of other senior members of her teaching staff, Zander knew that his wife and children were being escorted around the school buildings. They'd never experienced where he'd come from before and were as excited as he was.

'Well, Mrs Radebe, are the children ready for us? It's hot out here in the midday sun, but I understand the reception area is well shaded? After the formalities, I hope we can at least squeeze a cup of tea in before I have to go.'

He gestured for her to take the lead and they strolled back across the grass towards the school buildings. They made small talk as they crossed the area, flanked by security guards, and followed by the rest of the reception committee. Zander was relieved that she didn't ask him anything about politics.

They reached the buildings and followed a path along a whitewashed wall. The main building of the school had been there at least fifty years, and despite the lack of investment at times, it was in rather good condition, largely due to donations from Zander.

The area in front of them opened out until they were facing the open end of a 'U' shaped single storey building. The open area was large, perhaps fifty metres across. Within it was a reception area, encircled with trees and over a dozen palms. Their leaves provided some shade. Within that circle stood a small wooden pagoda. Cowering under the shelter away from the heat were the parents, all crowded together, trying to get a better view. He waved at his son, who wasn't yet old enough for school.

Assembled in front of the pagoda were what he assumed was the whole of the school. Approximately four hundred children lined up, standing proud in their school uniform. Some wore the whole uniform; others had clearly just done their best, as they always did. He expected no more.

Their smiles always made him happy, and he beamed back at them, giving them a wave as he was pulled to one side for yet another round of introductions to staff and parent governors. Zander was keen to get on, to hear the children sing for him, to meet them and then to see the new building that he was here to open. Behind the Pagoda was a two-storey rectangular building. It closed off the open end of the "u". He glanced over at it and felt excited for the pupils. At last, a fully functional science and technology suite, connected to the Unet. It was built of tinted glass, with its metal and concrete supports hidden carefully. Across the front, he could see the entrance with a customary ribbon strung across it, awaiting his attendance to cut it.

He was ushered to the front row of benches just inside the Pagoda, in front of the children. His family were sat nearby. All enjoyed the show. They sang, danced, and read out carefully written speeches. Mrs Radebe introduced each segment and at various points addressed Zander and his entourage. His mind began to wander, curious about the new building. He hadn't had time to consider it properly, so he called up its plans on his pad

# THE TRITON RUN

and directed one of the drones to give him a feed of an aerial view. It looked magnificent. Whilst his charitable foundation had funded some of it, he had not been able to play any role in its design or build. He called up information on the architect and builders. He'd never heard of either of them. Zander reminded himself that he'd been away a long time. He looked forward to meeting them. He checked the manifest for approved guests for today. They had no representatives here. He thought it unlikely that they'd been invited but had been unavailable.

Not again. Not here. He suddenly felt a feeling of dread wash over him. Trying to remain calm, he started to discretely look round, smiling at those children whose eyes he met. His security team all seemed calm.

On his pad, the security assessment of the site was all clear. He checked again what he had on the building. It had actually taken a year to build, had been used for months. This was merely a formal opening ceremony. They'd cleared it out and cleaned it from top to bottom just for him.

And a special reception is what the Exiles had planned.

An explosion nearby shook Zander, and he opened his eyes. He blinked repeatedly as rock and dust covered him. Bar the asteroid floor on which the track was laid there was not a lot to see. There was still the same noise as before. Perhaps he'd passed out only for a few seconds.

Then another bang, the breeze.

It was like a hurricane blowing through the school site. The new building shattered with an explosion that rushed through the structure like a volcano erupting from beneath it. The roof was pushed into the sky and the sides were blown out. Glass and metal ripped through the crowd, killing dozens in an instant, not distinguishing between the proud parents, the teaching staff, and the children. The shockwave flattened the crowd as shrapnel tore many limb from limb. A second fireball followed as the gas supplies in the building went up. The Pagoda was shredded into sharp splinters of timber.

When Zander came to, he had no idea of how long had passed. His clothes were torn, covered in shards of metal, plastic and glass mixed with the blood and flesh of others and his own. He couldn't hear. The ringing in his ears was severe, but he managed to hear the noise of death. Whimpers, last breaths and screams from survivors.

He raised his head and tried to look around. Debris rained down on him and smoke obscured the scene. He was sick at the sight, heaving onto the floor in front of him. He could see dozens of bodies, some moving - writhing in agony - many not.

It was later that he discovered his wife and their two children had died. Not in the explosion, but in the assault that followed. The school was swarmed by a group of militants, linked later to the Exiles. Anyone who hadn't died in the explosion was put down with a shot to the head.

Zander was rescued by his head of security, Crosby, who'd dragged him away and hidden him amongst the rubble, underneath the corpses of school pupils. He'd never seen Crosby alive again after that.

He felt someone grab him roughly and lift his body. He burned all over, his body full of holes and punctured by shrapnel.

This time, he wasn't found by a rescuer, twelve hours later. He was staring at a solider, one of the many who'd been pursuing them. An Exile. His head was spinning, but strangely, he had moments of clarity. This man was older than he was. Had he been there at the school?

There was no way out now, only one thing left for him to do. Something to help Jude and Bruce escape, to allow Howard freedom, and most of all, to give Rebecca Arden a new life. It was strange how things worked out. He'd have reacted very differently if her father had been here.

His ears were ringing from the sound of gunfire and explosions, so he couldn't hear what the man was saying as he leaned close to his face. A pistol was waved in his face. The search he'd been subjected to when he was captured had missed his own weapon.

Zander considered goading the man, but it would make no difference. He was the executioner, not there to be executed. Closing his eyes, he ran an internal protocol he'd never had to even consider before and detonated the small explosive device hidden inside one of the bones in his right leg, blowing himself and the attackers in the vicinity to hell.

# 62

# JUDE

*Antiope Mining Facility*

Barely a word was uttered for the rest of the journey, spent largely in the dark. They heard an explosion behind them and once they picked up speed, they knew they would not be caught by those on foot.

Jude dragged a box from the cab into the trailer and was leaning against it with her weapon resting on top, in case it was needed. There were so many miles to travel, it simply wasn't possible to keep it raised all the time. Howard sat holding onto Rebecca, who had come round after her fall. She sobbed into his chest while he cleaned her head wound using a first aid pack. Bruce was drifting in and out of consciousness. As the pain grew, she'd told him to increase his pain relief. Jude prayed he'd be alright once they got to the sickbay on the Skydancer. At least they now had a doctor with them.

Apart from two mechanics who came out of a side tunnel as they passed, they didn't see anyone else until they reached the ship. When her father awoke, he told her that the ship had confirmed that it maintained control of its immediate vicinity and that all doors would be controlled to ensure safe passage.

The ship was right. They were relieved to arrive at the home station and disembark from the train. Rebecca and Howard helped support Parynski whilst Jude took point again. Doors opened before them, and they followed Parynski's directions to the docking bay.

As they entered the bay, the smell of burning and death hit them, though Jude's eyes were drawn to the gleaming shape of the Skydancer. Parynski had boarded it in orbit and told her he hadn't appreciated the beauty of its exterior until now. When he'd disembarked in the dark, he'd been concentrating on avoiding security. It was a thing of beauty, designed to look good as well as being superior to all other vessels of its size and class. The Skydancer filled most of the docking bay, wings that weren't even needed in space, slung back alongside it. It was a dark red colour with black wings and undercarriage.

Jude then spotted the bodies. The floor was littered with them, ripped apart from weapon fire. Hanging from underneath the hull was a cannon, almost proudly rotating slowly. It paused ever so briefly at their approach before continuing its scan. Parynski pointed out two bodies on the top of the wing that jutted out in their direction.

'The ship wasn't kidding when it said it had taken care of the local trouble.'

Parynski's leg had given way again, and he was hobbling, using his good leg to push off from and a rifle as a crutch. As they approached, an open cage lowered itself from underneath the rear of the ship. Parynski allowed himself to be lowered to the floor of it. Jude watched him look up at Rebecca, whose tearful and dirt-stained face stared at him. She was pale, and a bandage had been wrapped around her head with her long hair tied up out of the way. She nodded at him, exhausted. 'Thank you.'

As the cage was pulled upwards into the inside of the Skydancer, Jude broke the silence, putting her arm around Rebecca and squeezing her tight. 'Let's get out of here and see if we can't get you home.'

'This was my home.' Rebecca spoke quietly as they all went first, through the darkness of the lower storage deck and then arrived at their destination, the brightly lit main reception area.

'But I meant what I say, thank you. Theo sacrificed himself to save me. Let's get your dad to the medical facilities.'

Parynski released his helmet and dropped it onto the floor alongside him. He was lying flat on his back, looking up at Jude. 'Get me to the bridge first. The ship said it's ready to depressurise the dock and open the doors. Once we are away from here, we need to collect our lifeboat, as it's got most of the medical gear on it. Then you can get me fixed up.'

# 63

# PARYNSKI

*Onboard the Skydancer*

For the first few hours after the Skydancer successfully opened the outer docking bay doors and navigated its way out of the Antiope mining facility, they all remained nervously huddled together on the bridge, waiting for an attack or the signs of pursuit.

Bruce Parynski felt awful but was trying to keep his spirits up for the sake of the others. He was confident they'd now be able to get to Neptune. 'The rock just isn't armed in a way that could touch us from out here and I didn't see any evidence of them having any sort of vessel that could pursue us.'

He was still in his combat EVA suit, slumped in the command chair. Jude sat on the floor at his feet while Howard was at the helm console, with Rebecca fast asleep, leaning on him. She had flaked out almost as soon as they had launched.

The bridge was dark with only a minimum level of running lights on, the only other illumination came from the glare from the main viewing port. That currently showed the view behind them, a dark field punctuated with occasional stars and the faint shadow from an odd asteroid here and there. Despite the mythology from movies, Parynski had explained, most asteroids were actually so far from each other that you'd not be able to see a neighbouring asteroid. The ship had highlighted a small smudge in the centre that it said was the two parts of

Antiope rotating around each other. There was no movement that suggested a response to their escape.

'We need to keep dark for a few hours. I've put us on a course to collect the escape pod with the medical gear in and then head out of the belt into clear space. That's going to take us several days, and hopefully lose any tail we may pick up. We aren't anywhere near most of the main trade routes, so hopefully nobody'll notice us for a while. Then we can consider who we contact first and what we're going to say.'

Howard looked over to him. 'There'll be a lot of media attention. Imagine the amount of crap that's been written about us, never mind Zander?'

Parynski agreed. 'And once we are safe, we'll stick to the original plan. I have this ship to deliver, and Rebecca is to be reunited with her father…'

Jude shushed him. 'We haven't told her yet.'

His head was so muggy he'd forgotten. Parynski lowered his voice. 'Sorry, plus we need to get you both safe.'

'I might be arrested, swapping one prison for another,' said Howard.

Parynski shook his head. 'Not with Arden. You'll be a hero. Like Zander.'

After a while, he pulled himself up. Jude jumped up to help. 'While we wait, I think I need to spend a day in the medical suite. Jude, the Doc has Rebecca to look after, so you need to make sure your old man gets there without falling over.'

# 64

# MULLER

*The Orbital Shipyards, Neptune*

Whilst concerned about his own state of mind, Muller was increasingly concerned for Squire's mental health.

They were engaged in one of their regular discussions about the salvage arrangements for the Xenos. It was the biggest engineering feat attempted away from Earth and to Muller's frustration Arden, as ever, was only half paying attention. He was an ideas man and easily distracted. He faded in and out of the conversation, making it very frustrating and difficult to get decisions out of him. The other engineers sitting in on the conversation had no authority without Arden. All of the huge facilities and habitats that ringed the Neptune system had been pre-built or planned to such a degree, that printing of parts and structures made putting them together fairly straightforward before the fitters had to move in, but what was being proposed here was unique. Nothing they had at the shipyards was remotely big enough to house the Xenos and the work was complex.

Muller was disturbed that recently, more often than not, Squire was hosting these discussions inside a simulation he was running that showed a live feed from inside what some had named the Tomb. None of them knew if it was technically a tomb, increasingly it appeared that Wilding and the aliens were alive. For now, the nickname had stuck.

# THE TRITON RUN

Squire appeared, as usual, near the capsule that held Wilding. She looked the same as when Squire had found her. She wore her EVA suit, less the helmet, which was on the floor by her feet. She was stood up straight, suspended in the same substance that filled the capsules where the aliens were housed. Her face was calm, eyes closed, with mouth slightly open. Whatever the liquid was, it enveloped Wilding, inside and out. He'd seen the footage of her twitching and attempting to speak. Whilst seeing the aliens was fascinating, the constant reminder of Wilding's fate was upsetting.

Muller had obviously heard of Wilding. However, her friendship with Squire was new to him and, with an open mind, he had listened to Squire's version of events. Buchanan was a situation for which he had no skin in the game. The man was clearly suffering.

Muller could tell this was a simulation was because Squire hadn't tethered himself to the railings that ran around the inside of the balcony and because he dressed simply in his coveralls. After investigation, the real chamber was deemed too big to pump a breathable atmosphere into it at this stage.

Muller and Arden were projected, facing him, other engineers nearby. The simulation was relatively small and only covered the immediate vicinity of Wilding's location. Whilst not a desperate situation, they were carefully working with Squire to manage supplies and to use the materials he had sensibly. The conversation had been going on for over an hour, stuttering along due to the distance and interference from a storm in Neptune's atmosphere that had slowed down all work in near orbit. Most logistical issues had been covered when, for the first time in a while, Arden suddenly looked excited. The other two looked at him in surprise, interrupting their conversation mid flow. Arden grinned.

'Sorry we've finally had word from the Skydancer…it's safe and back en route.'

Most of the engineers looked confused. Arden raised a hand, acknowledging their confusion. 'Sorry, it's not a conversation for now, but this is great news. Let me leave you to finish off and I'll catch up later.'

And with that, Arden's figure vanished. Squire took a long swig from a cup, wiped his mouth on his sleeve and yawned, his face dropping. 'Yet again, he proves he really does not give a shit about any of us!'

Muller was frozen, barely heard Squire. Though it was the news, he'd strangely been expecting it still hit hard. Chen taken her own path. Now he had to hope he wasn't ever implicated.

'He's just busy Squire, you can't imagine how crazy his job is.' One of the others filled the silence.

Squire laughed. 'Don't make me laugh. Anyway, we were talking about extracting the capsules from the Tomb. I've spent far too long there with Wilding; Paisley's been putting together a schematic that shows how these capsules are linked and powered. He took apart one of the capsules from a lower floor that was empty, and he's been seeing if we can take our own portable power supply over and move the capsules one by one. We might be able to extract Wilding and see if I can get her on the BSV with me.'

Muller's mind remained elsewhere, but he tried to follow what Squire was saying. Every conversation they'd had went the same way once the basics were out of the way. Squire was the best salvor around, with a reputation for being stubborn and single-minded. When he'd first started to worry about his behaviour, Muller had checked out Squire's records. He surmised that his love for his solitary role was little more than a way of escaping his problems.

Muller tried to get back on topic. 'Stop! I've seen your plans. If you keep tinkering with the capsules, you risk killing her and all these creatures… if they aren't already dead. Wait till the flotilla gets there. We've got a whole load of gear and some very clever people who are going to be there to help.'

Squire's voiced cracked. 'I can't wait. I need to help her. I arrived too late once, not again.'

Squire was wobbling. Muller had his own worries about

Chen, but he had to sort out Squire. He thought he could see his eyes welling up.

'Trust me, Squire, we've been doing great work so far. This is man's most important development since we got to the Moon. You're the man who survived first contact. Your knowledge and experience are needed by us all. Just try to step back. We need you fit and well. I've been promised a slot on the trip to the source of the Xenos and you'd be the obvious man to lead it.'

Muller felt guilty as his own excitement temporarily took over. Getting out on a ship away from Neptune might prove to be the safest place for him. Muller filled the silence, trying to rein things in. 'So please try to take it easy.'

Squire shook his head, took a deep breath, nodded. 'I'll try. I need a break.'

Muller looked down at the pad in his hand and scrolled through the agenda. He wanted to get Squire offline, though safely. His own mind was all over the place. He waved the pad at Squire. 'Look, we've done all we can. There's nothing hugely important scheduled for the next forty-eight hours. Go back to the BSV and get some sleep. Proper sleep? I'll square it with Arden.'

Squire's shoulders slumped partly in resignation, partly in relief. He looked away, avoiding looking Muller in the eye.

'I'll try.'

# 65

# HOWARD

*Onboard the Skydancer*

Howard felt that, compared to the others, he had got away lightly, with only a small number of wounds to recover from. His cowardice had probably saved him. Parynski was in a bad way. Even whilst being attended to by the on-board medical AI, Parynski had spent some time monitoring news feeds before he allowed anyone else access to the coms. He reminded them that he'd run dark until it was safe.

Howard was full of mixed emotions. He was relieved and excited to be free, and wondered whether any of his family or acquaintances from his previous life were still around. Whether they would want anything to do with him remained to be seen if he wasn't locked up. He knew he could hold his head up; he'd never hurt anyone during his forced employment for the Exiles. He did, however, feel guilty for what had happened to Zander. Nobody had said anything, but he couldn't shake the feeling that he should have been the one to jump off the train.

They were all relieved when Parynski declared them on a safe trajectory to the outer planets. As soon as Parynski opened up the coms, he had a ping from the Neptunian Shipyards, so Arden knew his ship was intact. Parynski had been joking that he expected Arden to complain about the delay and refuse to pay him. Parynski said that if Arden wanted his ship delivering and not just dropping off somewhere awkward, the original price should stand. The surprise of being reunited with his long-lost daughter should also seal the deal.

Jude was frustrated with her father for the coms blackout and paced the ship, also angry that he failed to take the time to recover properly. She wanted to find out what was going on back home and find out what was going on with her job.

Today, they were going to break their silence.

Howard brought Jude and Rebecca into the suite Parynski had taken over and routed all coms through. Rebecca looked brighter than she had previously. She'd found a bedroom that had clearly never been used before, yet which contained some clothes that fit her. It might have been a coincidence, Parynski said he hadn't even been in the room before, and he wondered if Arden had carried on all these years preparing for his daughter's eventual return. Rebecca was smiling, had colour in her cheeks and looked proudly like the young woman she was becoming, something that had been repressed on the Antiope. She'd slept for several days after boarding, initially sharing Jude's bed with plenty of tears shed for Zander. Howard was relieved to see her, even if for a brief time, looking relaxed. Her face fell slightly, partly at seeing the state of Parynski and realising that she had no idea what this was about.

Parynski looked rough, though Howard could see gradual improvement. He was out of his EVA suit and was dressed in an orange coverall. His injured leg was covered with a protective case and his injured hand by a protective glove. His neck and cheek were black from bruising that showed through his stubble. He'd not washed his hair yet because of a head wound, and his hair was matted and greasy.

Howard smiled as Parynski read their minds. 'Don't be afraid, my good looks and athleticism will be back to normal soon enough…'

Howard took a deep breath, excited and nervous for the girl. It was time to tell Rebecca who she was, and that they were now en route to a reunion with her father. Parynski indicated that they all sit at a table next to his coms console. Howard nodded to Jude, indicating "after you". They'd all agreed that Rebecca may respond better to the woman.

Jude grabbed Rebecca's hand and squeezed it. 'Remember how you said all you wanted was to know about your family? We've found your father.'

# 66

# ARDEN

*Triton One, Neptune*

Arden took the call when he was on his own. When Parynski had closed the link, Rebecca's image had faded, and he'd collapsed in a heap on the floor. He was consumed by a mix of happiness and grief. Happiness to have seen his daughter again after so many years, relief that she'd somehow survived, yet this was matched by grief at the years with her that had been lost and the loss of his wife. He'd never allowed himself to be seen as weak, always expecting a ransom demand or bad news. But she was alive, and nothing else mattered. He was getting his little girl back. He sobbed and sobbed, struggling to take it all in.

After what felt like an age, he sat up, wiped his eyes, and went to his drinks cabinet. He started to pour a drink, stopped, and pushed it away. No more. He used to drink himself into oblivion to hide the pain. He didn't need to anymore. He had to be as healthy as he could be for Rebecca.

Later, as he sipped a tea, he turned to the window. The shipyard was slowly rotating into view. It was, for the first time he could remember, empty, though there was a whirl of activity around it. A structure that looked like a set of ribs, inside which larger vessels would be moored whilst repairs and servicing took place. Coming off that structure were a whole host of smaller bays and a habitat where the servicing crew lived when on duty and where guests could stay whilst their ships were being processed. Now, one side of the skeletal structure was surrounded by small tugs, all cutting away at the frame. The Xenos was far too big to fit inside the original bay, so the plan was that with one side opened up the alien ship could be brought alongside it and then a new exoskeletal structure built around it. A carrier loomed nearby, storing the materials being used for the new build. He'd purchased or hired all the shipyard facilities he could get his hands on. A new space port would be constructed in record time, based on a mothballed facility that had been shut down years previously.

It had belonged to miners who had been taking advantage of the trojans in Neptune orbit before being abandoned once they'd plundered all the resources in the vicinity. That structure was being moved so that it could be nearer to Arden's facilities and provide additional capacity. There would be an increase in incoming traffic. In addition to the experts, engineers, and scientists that he was inviting, there would be a huge amount of media interest and likely also many political figures would be wanting to come and engage with him, to either vicariously bask in the glory of the find or to try and manipulate the situation for their own benefit. No President Zander, though. Having heard of how Rebecca had been rescued, he didn't know what to think of that.

He resolved to change his priorities with Rebecca en route, telling himself he would work out the logistics of handing over day-to-day control to his able deputies. This was a chance of a new life, and he had to grasp it.

Within an hour, he'd made progress.

As the image of Garcia faded away, Arden momentarily allowed himself a moment to reflect. His wife would have been pleased to see him willingly delegate. He wouldn't have space in his life for Rebecca whilst micromanaging all aspects of his business. Garcia was going to take control of working out where the Xenos had come from and co-ordinating the scientific projects that would arise. Whilst the news about the Xenos had broken across all the news networks, it seemed nobody else had the data that had allowed her to trace its potential source.

It was clearly important to secure and study the Xenos itself, as there was the possibility that there were more of these aliens not that far away. Garcia had been delighted for him, though he suspected that was because it now meant she'd be more easily able to follow her dreams with less of his interference.

The conversation with Muller, who attended in person in between shifts three days later, began much the same way as with Garcia, though there was an edge to it that Arden couldn't quite put his finger on. Muller was delighted to be told that he was effectively being given a promotion, with far more delegated authority to get things done. Arden could see that to Muller, the idea of more authority appealed.

Muller smiled, but there was something bothering him.

'All sounds great, Scott; I'd be honoured to take on whatever I can handle. How often in a career does one get to be responsible for hosting an alien spaceship? But why this change now?'

Arden was slightly confused at Muller's reaction, though he was so excited he had to tell his engineer about recent events. He'd now spoken to his daughter and Parynski on multiple occasions. Arden told Muller about the kidnapping of Zander, how Parynski had been able to locate the Exiles on Antiope and how the rescue had been executed. It was clearly going to be huge news all across the solar system. Arden told him that as they spoke a team of space marines were rumoured to be en route from Mars to secure the Antiope base and investigate.

After some small talk, Muller apologised for not being up to date, that he was delighted at the news. Muller said his only concern was that he still wanted to be on the mission to trace the origin of the Xenos. Arden admitted he'd forgotten about Muller's request but that he'd sort it. Good men needed looking after. Arden slapped him on the back and sent him on his way.

Things were going to work out.

# 67

## PARYNSKI

*On board the Skydancer*

Parynski woke as Jude entered the sick bay. The pain he'd been in from his leg and hand were nothing to how he felt emotionally. The room was dark and Parynski had been lying on his back on the bed. He'd slept in there for the last few days because it was easier to administer pain relief and change the wrapping for his burnt hand. He was sure he had offended Doctor Howard, only asking him for advice on treatment from time to time. He swung his legs off the bed and sat up, pulling the blanket around him. His leg poked out from underneath; frame still attached. He wiped the sleep from his eyes and blinked at Jude as the lighting came on.

His voice was croaky, and he reached for a cup of water. 'So, we did it. Saved you and the girl.'

He'd sounded harsher than he intended, but Jude didn't react. He knew that she knew how he felt. Jude didn't say a word.

'Couldn't save your mother, though. Some fucking hero I am.'

He tried to keep it together. These feelings had been building again since they'd escaped Antiope. He carried guilt with him. He shouldn't have been away when Mary had been killed. Silence. Parynski was the first to burst into tears. Jude came over, hugged him. and she followed, sobbing violently.

After a while, Parynski withdrew and wiped his face on his sleeve.

'You need to get back to the bridge, check everything is ok?'

She shook her head, deliberately not taking the hint that he wanted a moment to clear his head. 'No, it's fine. Howard saw me on the way here. He's keeping an eye out for us.'

She shook her head again. 'Dad. What do we do now?'

He shrugged and passed her a tissue from a box beside his bed. 'We do what we always did. We keep going. We both spent all our lives trying to keep moving and now the only reason not to has gone. I'm so sorry I wasn't there.'

'Dad, it's ok about Mum. It's done and nobody blames you but yourself. She'd be dead proud of you, what you just did. Stop torturing yourself. Practice what you preach to me, you know?'

He reached over and hugged her again. 'There's no point going anywhere apart from Neptune. We can return Rebecca to her father and arrange for Howard to get himself sorted. I won't get paid if we don't deliver the ship, anyway. This whole alien spaceship thing might give us a distraction.'

Jude didn't say anything. Parynski's worry about her is what was keeping him going right now. Deep inside he knew she was using Rebecca as a distraction, frankly she didn't care about any alien spaceship. Right now, she didn't care about her job either.

'The Force will take you back after the Inquiry, you just need some time,' he tried to reassure her. 'You've done your bit here. You saved Rebecca, tried to escape with the President. They'll be kissing your ass to get you back on the front line.'

'We'll see. I'll stay with you and Howard for now and take some time to think…'

He smiled and gently kissed her forehead as he had when she was young. 'Yes. I didn't want to speak for you, but I'm glad we're staying together until we get to Neptune at least.'

He hoped he could help her keep it together. He just wasn't sure if he could do so himself. The last few weeks had brought home how fragile life was.

The tears came again for both of them.

# 68

# WILDING

*The Dark*

Wilding was convinced that Squire knew she was trying to communicate. To her frustration, she never succeeded in making a connection again, though he continued to spend a large proportion of his time with them, just watching or working alongside the AI in the space suit. She tried to speak whenever he came near, encouraging the Qarti to do the same, getting nowhere. They'd told her that the point of the tanks was that those in them were supposed to be completely unconscious and that what had happened to her was unforeseen, possibly due to the different makeup of a human compared to the Qarti.

She came to understand Squire's routine. He was working nearby when the lights were bright and lowered when he was off-duty or working elsewhere. The lights remained on now, so she knew he, and others, were watching from somewhere.

Wilding was mentally fatigued by her status. There was only so much that she could learn about the Qarti when in this predicament, and she knew they were keeping a lot from her. For the same reason, she held back, pretending she didn't know the answers to some questions they posed for her. She was slightly concerned at questions about the technological capabilities of humans, the extent of their exploration outside the solar system, and even their military capacity. A lot of it was moot anyway, there was not a lot, it seemed to Wilding, that the Qarti could do to be a threat to Earth whilst they were all trapped in tanks on board a dead spacecraft.

One day, it all changed. She saw less of Squire, but was never alone. There were dozens of space suited people in the Chamber all the time, scouring every part of it. They filmed her, tried to communicate with her. Frustratingly, she still couldn't reply.

*What is happening? Who are they?*

She was as sure as she could be, as hopeful as she dared.

*We've been rescued.*

# 69

# PARYNSKI

*Triton One, Neptune*

It didn't take much for Parynski to get drunk. He'd drank with purpose that afternoon, lying to himself that his head was clear. But it was what he wanted and needed at this moment. He was sure there were people looking for him. It wasn't that easy to vanish in a facility in space, even on one this big. He was also a bit of a celebrity now.

He ached all over now. The pain relief was starting to wear off, and he reminded himself that was why he'd spent so much of the time since their arrival in the medical facility. Deep inside, he knew it was why should go back there. His wounds were rapidly improving, but he was still suffering the aftereffects of being frozen. He looked pale and gaunt, having lost quite a lot of weight. But it was the mental pain hurt most.

He couldn't do this anymore. It was his fault she was dead.

None of his recent heroics mattered compared to what had gone before.

After discharging himself from the medical facility, he'd headed into the main commercial hub, had spent time in one of the less salubrious bars and had rented one of the smaller VR suites. He was sitting on a stool, a rucksack on the floor in front of him. The footage he'd been immersed in had been an AI mix of the footage Jude had obtained from Roo of their home, after the assault, mixed in with the few bits of footage he had of Mary. He'd started the afternoon revisiting the broadcasts that Jude had gone through, just in case. He then pulled up a sim of the town as it was before the attack, taking a stroll round the streets, ending back up at Mary's place. The AI had generated an avatar based on his own files. It wasn't as accurate as some sims, but it was her.

Mary looked younger, wearing jeans and a jumper. As ever, in the mountains, she had a scarf wrapped around her neck and wore sunglasses. They'd sat on a bench and talked about trivial things for what felt like hours before he'd tried to talk about their relationship and his future. The avatar didn't respond sympathetically to him, being as harsh as Mary was when their relationship was at its worst. He was being selfish, she'd said, like he always was. He was needed by their daughter and others. Parynski had argued back before realising he was arguing with himself. The avatar had too much of him in it to be realistic. Frustrated, he'd said goodbye, and the figure had hugged him before fading away.

He felt numb. He'd hoped Mary would give him a purpose; it was a fool's errand. He paused the interactive elements of the footage and took in the view. The bench was high up on a hill overlooking the rest of the town. Mary's house was several hundred yards away. It was summer, the trees were all full of leaf and green. There were only a few cotton wool clouds here and there and the sky was blue. The sun was behind him, casting shadows out ahead of him down the hill. He could see lots of activity down at the town centre and the nearby lumber yards.

He reached down into the bag in front of him and produced the nail gun that Rebecca had used to kill Chen. He checked the cartridge. It was half full. He would only need one nail, anyway. He felt the weight of the tool in his hands, passing it from one hand to another. It was far heavier than the weapons he'd used over recent years.

He powered the device up. It hummed slightly, belaying the power it held ready for use. He raised it, looking down the barrel as a sharpshooter might, then turned it on himself. He initially struggled to get his finger on the trigger, aiming it towards himself. He started sweating and shaking profusely, struggling to aim straight.

He cursed. He was so ill enough that he risked not succeeding. He'd not be waking to see Mary and live happily ever after, if an afterlife were a thing, rather in a hospital bed with an eye missing.

Parynski was pleased he'd rescued Jude, but she didn't need him anymore. The attention he'd received for leading the rescue mission was phenomenal. Journalists had posed as patients to get near his suite. If only he'd been there to save his wife, just as they were rebuilding their marriage.

He raised it again and then nearly jumped out of his skin as the com unit in his bag chimed. Shit.

The moment passed, temporarily. He put the nail gun down and rummaged inside his bag to find the com. He should have turned it off. He pulled it out and saw it was Rebecca. She was a lovely kid. She'd taken to Jude as if she were a big sister and he realised that his daughter was enjoying having someone looking up to her. Rebecca distracted Jude from her own grief and anger.

He took a deep breath and answered, selecting voice only.

'Uncle Bruce, it's me Rebecca. Where's the visual?'

He smiled inwardly at the familial title she'd given him. On the rest of the journey to Neptune, they'd got close, and she'd visited him daily in hospital since. He didn't want her to see him looking so bad, nor for her to get a sense of what he was up to.

'Oh, sorry… What's up?'

He tried to control his breathing, which he realised was out of control, hoping she'd not notice. She didn't. She was too excited, her voice speeding up as she struggled to get the words out quickly enough.

'Dad said I could give you the exciting news. Once the Xenos is fully secured, whilst the scientists are all over it, he wants to launch an expedition to its source. He wants us all to go on the Skydancer, to Propylaea. And he wanted me to persuade you to lead the mission.'

Parynski didn't know how to respond. He wasn't fit enough right now to do anything. He didn't want to do anything. He didn't want to be here.

But maybe he'd left his com on deliberately? He barely got an 'Ok…' out before Rebecca continued.

'It'll be great. He wants you, me, and him, Jude, and Doctor Howard to come as well. He's picked a good team to help too. He's spoken to most of them in person, as he couldn't find you, so I said I would try.'

His head started to swim. He just wasn't in a position to have a conversation about the future. 'But I'm busy, I'm not well, and I need to…'

She had all the answers.

'No, it's fine. You'll be recovered by the time we get there. I'd love to have you along with us. It'll be something to look forward to. I know you are, well, Jude said, still upset after Mary…'

Rebecca realised what she had said and went quiet. Out of the mouth of babes. She was right. He'd known that he had nothing to go back for. That's why he was here. He couldn't remember the last time he had been wanted, or needed, so badly. It all fell into place.

He could keep running, keep exploring, hide from his past whilst being with Jude and Rebecca. It kind of made sense.

She spoke first. 'I'm sorry, I didn't mean…'

He cut off her off. 'It's ok Becca, and thank you. I'm glad you want me along. It sounds interesting and if your dad is paying the same rates, tell him I'm in.'

And with that, the conversation ended with the girl excitedly saying she'd go and tell him. He slumped back on the bench and at his command, the surroundings all vanished. He was back in a small, square cubicle. He looked at his hands. The nail gun was resting on top of his bag where he had put it down. He looked it again, reaching down. He paused for a moment and then tucked it back in the bag.

# 70

## JUDE

*Neptune Ship Dock*

It hadn't been planned that way, but the event took on a slightly formal tone. As well as a celebration, it was also a wake. Arden had invited all the arrivals from the Skydancer, who had now been with him for several months, plus a whole host of senior staff from across his business empire, together with odd political and media figures who'd descended on Neptune recently. After a meal and drinks, more for some than others, there were informal speeches, some favourite music, the sharing of anecdotes and pictures or holovids. President Zander, the crew of the Kuiper Scout, Reuben Volchik, and others recently lost all dominated the conversation. To everyone's amazement, Rebecca had prepared a short speech to thank Howard for filling in for her father, and to thank the others for rescuing her. She spoke well about Zander. Jude was proud of the girl; she'd written it herself and they'd rehearsed it together.

Everyone broke into small groups after a final toast, a toast to absent friends, and to those they didn't know who'd lost their lives as a result of recent events.

The chamber was a hastily constructed viewing room bolted on the front of the engineering block that sat at one end of the new temporary ship dock that had been built in Neptune' orbit to replace some of the capacity lost by the arrival of the

# THE TRITON RUN

Xenos. There were about two dozen tables spread across the room, and once the formalities had concluded, almost all of the guests had stood to mingle.

Many faced the wide panoramic window which had zoomed in on the view ahead of them in orbit. Stretching out in front of them was the metal lattice work of the original, now reconfigured dock, its spindly frame disappearing into the distance. Like a spider clinging onto its prey, the dock contained the alien craft. Drones chased each other across the rocky surface. Occasionally, they caught glimpses of small tugs and shuttles that buzzed around the outside.

Jude had one of the seats nearest the window and had remained seated. Tears still filled her eyes following Rebecca's speech, and she'd kept her eyes on the Xenos, pretending to be distracted by the view. Her blurred vision tried to focus on a stream of black dots on the surface of the ship, likely a mix of security personnel and investigators. She cried not just for those she'd lost over recent months, but for the situation she'd found herself in, the victims of crime she'd dealt with and a general frustration at herself. All she could do now was focus on the future, and their planned expedition would be a welcome distraction for them all. A chance to reboot her priorities. Beyond that, the future would have to take care of itself. Her Father likely felt the same.

Jude had only heard stories about Scott Arden, and not many of them were positive. Everyone she spoke to about him at Triton One had said that he'd changed with the rescue of his daughter. For her own part, Jude had enjoyed seeing him build a relationship with Rebecca.

The girl had originally been housed in a private block with Howard, Jude and Parynski because the whole process of extracting her from the Antiope had been so traumatic. The plan was to slowly introduce her to other people and the wider world. Arden had accepted this, visiting regularly. Rebecca had been increasingly spending time with her father, following him around and even sitting in with him on his reducing number of work commitments.

Jude had been following the media frenzy that had blown up when news of their escape had been publicised. There was interest primarily in Zander's death, but also interest in Rebecca because of her father's relative celebrity status. Jude had felt obliged to do many interviews to shield everyone else. She made sure she sang Zander's praises as a leader and a man, while declining to get involved in commentary on how quickly Lindstrom had deposed him.

She was relieved that coverage of the Xenos recovery eventually pushed Antiope out of the headlines. Jude avoided politics generally, though noted that the discovery of alien life and the Xenos, particularly the fact that Earth had no control of it, had generated even more controversy.

Arden had told her he was worried that Earth might send a task force to seize it. They both also wondered if other private organisations or Planet states might consider such a move. For now, Neptune was in a state of lockdown. They'd shut down many of the public refuelling centres to keep tourists and anyone who might be inclined to try and seek control of the area away.

In the Neptune system, there was a focus on security and investigation. Under tight control, swarms of scientists and experts in every possible discipline had been invited in to work on the Xenos and to seek answers to the hundreds of outstanding questions, including the status of Wilding and the aliens.

Her own personal future remained cloudy, though she was optimistic. The inquiry into her conduct had been adjourned generally, and there had been back-channel communications implying that she could use her service helping the President to get the charges dropped. Her Union had gone on a PR campaign to protect her, and people had generally been supportive. Yes, the public were happy for their police to shoot criminals when necessary. She'd said she'd be in touch when

# THE TRITON RUN

she was back from Propylaea and left it at that. Money certainly wasn't a worry at the moment. Everything was on Arden.

Jude had been left to her reverie by most diners, and as the event broke up, she set off down the corridor back towards a shuttle bay where most of them would be transported back to their accommodation.

They had to queue for the elevator, Jude eventually sharing it with her father, Muller and a few engineers who kept themselves to themselves. Parynski told her he was worried about Squire. She remembered him from when she was young and knew what he'd been through. Squire had arrived with the Xenos eight weeks earlier and he'd kept himself isolated. Parynski and Garcia had both tried to spend time with him, struggling to get him to open up.

'He's bound to be fucked up. He was suffering PTSD anyway; from the stuff I went through with him. God knows how he reacted to finding Wilding's body.'

Jude talked in a low tone. Nobody else needed to know. 'Can you not persuade him to take a break? He's completed his mission.'

Parynski shook his head. Also spoke quietly. 'Says he wants to keep working, won't even see Arden's medical staff. Arden couldn't even force him off his ship. Chris owns the BSV.'

He shrugged. 'Apparently, he forced Arden to agree to let him help clear some of the debris that's accumulated near the shipyards. I've tried to have a word, but he won't have it.'

There wasn't enough space on the next shuttle, so Jude let others go whilst she waited for the next one with Muller and some of his team. She wished her father a good night. Let him go first as he'd promised to take Rebecca to the sim library before bed.

Jude got into a conversation with Muller about the imminent departure of the Skydancer, planned for a week ahead, to Propylaea. Within moments, she regretted it. Muller hadn't been made aware of it. Jude had no idea why Arden hadn't entrusted him with the information. She could tell that despite trying to remain cool, Muller felt both disappointed not to have been told, and angry.

'Sorry, I probably just overlooked the news. I've been so focussed on finishing the cradle and then getting a backup shipyard into operation.' His attempt to look nonplussed failed.

She tried to change the topic of conversation, but it was difficult, and they kept returning to the expedition. Eventually, Jude decided to tackle the issue head on.

'Are you ok, Hans?'

Muller paused for a moment, gathering his thoughts.

'I'm not sure. I now know how much I am respected. Scott promised me a berth, maybe he forgot or I'm too important here. The departure is sooner than I imagined, so I need to decide on my priorities.'

# 71

# PARYNSKI

*Triton One, Neptune Orbit*

'Dee is the first one we lost since we were all discharged.'

It was the most obvious statement Parynski could make. They both knew. Parynski stared into his beer and waited for a reply from Squire. They'd been in the bar for a couple of hours and had talked about everything, including Mary's death, bar the elephant in the room.

Squire nodded, rubbing at his unkempt beard. He didn't say anything. They were the same age, though Squire looked older, largely, Parynski knew, because his friend wasn't looking after himself. His weight had increased dramatically, his hair was a mess, and he wore a dirty coverall. Parynski gave him more slack than most. He knew how tough it was spending months alone and his friend had been through a lot.

'This is the first time I've left the BSV. In fact, the first time I've not been with Paisley since we set off home.'

Parynski found meeting him face-to-face more painful than expected. Squire was in a worse state than it had appeared when they had spoken over recent months. His old friend just wasn't the same, and it was difficult to get much out of him, bar basic factual details about his time on the Xenos and an update on Paisley's capabilities. He didn't seem remotely enthused or aware of the importance of his role in boarding an alien space craft. Parynski had been like a child at Christmas during the tour of it he had made with Arden and Zander. For the first time in a while, he'd felt that he was recovering from the damage the Antiope rescue had done.

Eventually Squire spoke, a hint of defiance in his voice. 'We may yet save her. She's not gone, yet.'

Parynski waved to a waiter to bring another round over to them. 'Yeah, hope so. Would be a shit way for Dee to go out. We were a good Platoon, just a pity she was a scapegoat back then. I think many of us might have made the same call she did.'

Squire nodded but didn't respond.

Parynski filled the silence. 'We're setting off in a week, and we'll be away for at least six months.'

The bar was getting busier. A shift handover had just taken place and those off duty were taking the chance to fill up on locally brewed beer. Clouds of smoke were also filling the air, blurring the tacky blue neon signage that hung from the ceiling.

He looked straight at Squire. Squire looked away. 'There's space on the Skydancer for you to come along, you know? We could do with your help.'

'No, I'm not leaving the BSV. She's too big to hitch a lift with your ship and if the Skydancer is as fast as you say, I'm too slow to accompany you. You'd be on your way back before I get there. And Dee might need me.'

Parynski decided there was no point asking anymore. Perhaps he was right. Someone should be around for their old platoon leader. 'Ok, stay in touch. We may need your input, so we'll keep a channel available and when they get her out of that tank, say hello from me.'

Squire sipped his drink before replying. 'I will. And look - I appreciate your concern. But my life is the BSV. I have nothing else right now. The contract to clear the debris round the Xenos housing will keep me occupied. And I can't leave my ship behind. Paisley wouldn't let me anyway…'

His chuckle didn't convince Parynski. Squire just wanted to be alone. He knew if he pushed him too far, he'd just cut off contact altogether, so he went along with it.

'Ha, well, that old AI is worse than your mother was. You'd better stay in touch?'

Squire nodded. 'Have you been to see Dee?'

Parynski's view, despite what Squire told him, was that the odds of Wilding being alive were slim, that hope, however, gave Squire had a reason to look after himself.

'No.' Parynski felt slightly ashamed. 'I can't face her yet. And we still don't know what'll happen.'

'You'd find it interesting. Her unit is rigged up with the pods that powered the other nearby aliens. There are a fair few of them on the same circuit, apparently.'

Parynski shook his head again. 'I still hope something can be done.' He just couldn't see how it would work.

Squire looked down into his drink again.

'Me too.'

# 72

# MULLER

*Triton One, Neptune*

Once Muller learned that the expedition was going without him, a dark cloud followed him round. He kept telling himself it wasn't personal. After all, he was one of the few people left behind that Arden really trusted. And at worst, it was an oversight.

The timing could not have been worse. For weeks Muller had convinced himself that the best way to avoid any fall out from events on Antiope was to get away, and travelling millions of miles into the outer edges of Solar system suited him. The Antiope rescue remained in the news, the public furious that a proposed assault on the base had been abandoned. Lindstrom had said she was not willing to risk hundreds of marines' lives because as soon as the base on Antiope B was boarded, its residents might just scuttle it. Muller had no idea who was now in charge, but the new President was probably right.

He'd stopped sleeping. At night, he tossed and turned, expecting a knock on the door. When at the edge of the Solar System, it wasn't possible to run. He'd be implicated even though he had always been careful when contacting his wife, using bogus and proxy accounts. He deleted traces of his contacts and ran a decimator application to clear his history as best as he could.

The next morning, he was due back on the rig, working on the skeletal framework of the shipyard that housed the Xenos and as he sat on the bench in the back of the transport ferry, he realised how tired he was. Carrying on with work was, however, the only answer. There was much to do.

As he left the transport he tried to focus on work, looking inward at his feed. He could feel a subtle, but important, change. All the usual blockers and supervision subroutines were gone. No longer did he need to request authority from Arden for most things. They had all cleared. The two people in his life who had previously governed his every move and thought were no longer there.

His feeling of being liberated didn't last long. At the top of the morning's task list was the need to approve a request for a landing permit for a team of investigators. They were coming to interview Howard, Bruce, and Jude Parynski, as well as Rebecca. At least that was what their public remit was.

They weren't due for several months, but Muller felt that time was nearly up. He enjoyed working on the Xenos project so much he resolved to do what he always did when events with Chen got to too much, he'd throw himself into his work and hope a solution showed itself.

## 73

# GARCIA

*Onboard the Skydancer*

Most of the crew and passengers were gathered on the Skydancer's bridge. Those that couldn't fit were holed up in the canteen in front of a big screen. Arden sat alongside his daughter on a plush couch that had been fitted along one of the walls. Garcia watched them for a while, enjoying seeing how happy they both looked. She had feared that after years apart, they would struggle to bond. For most of their journey, she had barely seen them. They'd spent a lot of time in the VR rooms, watching footage of Rebecca's mother and getting to know each other. Rebecca was also monitored by Howard to ensure that mentally she was coping with her newfound freedom. Arden was a different man. No longer controlled by his loss and an anger at the universe, he'd become fun to work with rather than someone she just had to tolerate.

Garcia could feel the tension building in the room. She could barely contain the excitement herself. This was the mission she was born to lead. Those on the bridge had either grabbed seats or were fanned out against the walls so that they could all see the large view screen. Garcia stood at the front, slightly off to one side, ready to speak. She stepped forward, in front of the screen, which was still blank.

'Okay, let's have some hush.' She spoke firmly, and as usual, people listened.

The room went quiet, save for occasional noises from the consoles and the fans that formed part of the life support systems quietly whirred in the background.

'Thank you. We gather at this time to celebrate something really important. We are now only a week away from our destination and we want to thank you all for your hard work and good spirits. This moment is an interesting one as we are about to go through the first boundary, or first layer of cloud that is, I think, partially intended to disguise Propylaea.'

Garcia knew, as did her close team and the crew who were piloting the Skydancer, that in fact the footage they were about to see had, in fact, happened about an hour ago. There was no way that any of the senior members of the party would have risked going through the barrier they had just passed without being fully focussed. She knew that Arden loved drama, so she'd had the images they were about to see, slightly enhanced and manipulated for effect.

The footage would be sent to the media in due course.

Garcia reminded them all, conscious she was being filmed for future broadcast, that whilst they had left behind at Neptune a hugely exciting discovery, their immediate future could be even more important. The Xenos seemed to be evidence of alien life, and after the initial excitement it was likely to be in lockdown for some time whilst it was examined, particularly with focuses being on the potential life forms on board and with securing the advances in technology that the ship might provide. As of yet, there were no developments with efforts to extract Wilding from her tank.

Ahead of them, she said, was an object that might prove to be the origin of the Xenos, or somewhere it had been in the period before it had headed in-system and collided with the 'Scout. They were about to pass through an outer cloud that had previously partially obscured the target, reflected back many of their scans, and made it difficult to get a decent image. Initial observations were inconclusive as to whether the barrier had formed naturally out in the cold depths of the solar system or had been put in place deliberately to disguise their destination.

The screen lit up to reveal an image of an object obscured by a cloudy material that blurred the image. Tendrils of grey, yellow, and blue cloud snaked out towards the edge of the image.

With a smile, Garcia continued. 'So, we are about to crash through the lead edge of what we think is a cloud of ice particles.'

She'd seen the footage before, so paused for effect, as after a few moments, the image cleared. They were through the other side. There was a cheer and a round of applause.

The object solidified. A planetoid sat there in the darkness and their sensors had to use various bandwidths to create an accurate image. It was surrounded by another cloud of the same blues and yellows they had just passed, though sensors suggested there was a lot of rock and ice rotating around her.

'As you can see, it looks like a giant potato, but look at that side that opens out like a mouth. Our initial theory was that it's a volcano crater that extended many miles into a funnel shape. We believe that the Xenos would have fitted inside with ease.'

As she revealed that theory to the crew, Parynski gave her a wink as the crew gave the excited reaction they both expected. They were headed somewhere very important.

# 74

# MULLER

*The Xenos Cradle, Neptune System*

Muller resented the Xenos and the surrounding hullaballoo. It was an incredible discovery, and he should have felt honoured to lead the management of the logistical exercise that surrounded its arrival and examination. He'd spent as much time on or around it as anyone, though primarily he'd been on the outside leading the operation to secure it in the extended ship dock that had been constructed.

His excitement faded when his thoughts turned to his future, a future where it was inevitably revealed that he was the secret husband and co-conspirator of Chen Yang, a figure now regarded as a monster across the Solar System. He knew she had her faults, but she was a victim of circumstance, what had been done to her.

He took in the scene as his one-man tug orbited the alien spacecraft, angry at what it stood for. Angry at Scott Arden, the Parynski's and even Arden's daughter. The Xenos was now encased in a cage, a structure that appeared like a set of ribs extending out of a chest piece and curving round the exterior of the rock. The chest piece was essentially the administrative centre of the ship dock. It was an oblong block that ran about half the length of the Xenos, containing accommodation blocks for both those working on the ship dock and those whose ships were visiting. It contained dozens of cargo holds,

# THE TRITON RUN

launch bays, and other facilities. There had previously been an entertainment block including a casino, hotel, shopping mall and bars, but Arden had closed them to convert their use for the influx of media, scientists and engineers arriving regularly for a chance to contribute. He charged a high rate for the media and other observers, only encouraging those to come who could actually drive every last bit of learning from the ship.

Muller approached the Xenos with a feeling of finality. Better to be his own man, make his own decisions, and decide how things ended before that opportunity was taken from him.

His tug looped over the bottom of the administrative centre and through two of the ribs. As the small craft swung back around, he got a glimpse in the darkness of the BSV, flanked by two security craft. Today was the day that they were moving the tanks that contained Dee Wilding and over a dozen of the aliens. He hoped his arrival wasn't too late.

Muller had been inside the Xenos to see the pods twice. Shortly afterwards Arden had instructed the scientists in charge of the habitat to restrict access, even to Muller. They were too worried about infection or interference with the pods and the leaking of images.

Muller had been in little doubt that Wilding was dead, though he understood the need to examine her. It would only be following months of investigation that they would attempt to open up the pod and extract her body. Though the aliens also looked like they were beyond saving, the scientists had said until they knew what the substance the bodies were suspended in was, they couldn't be sure. The current theory was that it was the substance that made the bodies twitch and that Squire's report of communication from Wilding was down to an emotional reaction from him. Nobody else claimed to have elicited such a reaction.

Muller wondered why the aliens had seemingly willingly climbed inside the pods. They looked so peaceful. There must have been a malfunction at some point. Their figures had been unlike any form of alien he had seen described in books or movies, thin and tall with long thin faces with eyes either side and tucked up wings attached to comparatively short upper limbs. Based on what they knew about the inside of the Xenos most assumed they could fly.

Whilst he was musing about Wilding, the tug swung back towards the Xenos and gently slowed, coming alongside the end of one of the rib pieces. Docking clamps slid out and grabbed the tug, pulling it slowly towards the airlock. With a satisfying clunk, docking was confirmed. Muller stayed seated whilst the ship did its checks before the airlock would be opened. There was only an atmosphere in selected areas of the Xenos in order to preserve resources and try to minimise the risks of contamination from outside.

He watched Chen's message to him again, her last will and testament. She must have updated it before leaving Earth for Antiope. He didn't delete it. He wanted those who followed to fully understand why the things that would happen did happen.

The investigators had recently arrived, and his name was on a list of interested people they wanted to speak to. He'd missed the appointment they'd made with him and had been covering his tracks for the last few days, deleting much of his personal history.

One of the reasons he'd wanted to go to Propylaea was to give himself time to think, to escape, but it was too late now: they had him in their sights. Every time his chip pinged that a message had arrived, he feared the worst. He'd not been back to his own apartment for a week. If they wanted to stop him, then they'd have to physically come and find him.

The link between Chen and him had not been public yet, though he presumed they knew now. He'd lost everything, including all he stood for and his wife. He was about to lose his freedom. He'd be a scapegoat. If they didn't shoot him on sight or make him suffer an accident, an air leak on the way back to

# THE TRITON RUN

Earth perhaps, then he was going to spend the rest of his life in prison. He just couldn't face that. He'd shut himself off from Chen to save himself, not this. He wondered if she had known what was likely to happen to him. If she cared.

Muller reflected that his biggest regret was that he had allowed himself to adapt to normal life. He should have acted years ago when he could have just killed Arden and made it appear an accident. Chen was so determined that he wait until all the pieces were in place. She wanted Zander and Arden to suffer before they were killed. Muller understood why she felt like that now and the one thing he could do was to at least have the last word. He had believed in her mission, the mission on behalf of so many of them. He couldn't finish the mission as she wanted, but he concluded he could honour it and finish it as best as he was able. It was either that or spend the rest of his life in a cell in orbit round Earth. He'd have preferred a normal life with Chen, though with that no longer possible, this was the alternative.

When he was ready, he shut his chip down. He sat back in his seat and took a deep breath, enjoying the peace and clarity that isolation from the Unet brought. He couldn't take too long. Even going offline might set some alarm bells ringing. He got up and opened the airlock as his suit came online. Behind the airlock was a guard in a space suit. He knew him.

Jimmy Canon. They had both started working for Arden at the same time.

'Good morning, Sir. Hope all is well. Is there anything I can do to assist you?'

Muller paused. For a time, they had been good friends, sharing the same apartment before their careers had gone in different directions. Muller briefly thought about asking him to move the shuttle in an hour or so, but it just wouldn't make sense and he couldn't risk alerting anyone.

He looked Canon in the eye and smiled through his transparent suit visor. 'It's been too long Jim, hope all is good with you? Give me a call when you get over to the Indigo bar next and we can have a catch up.'

The other man grinned enthusiastically. 'That would be great, Sir. Thank you.'

And with that, he purposefully strode towards a walkway that would take him down the corridor in the centre of the rib and towards one of the entrances to the Xenos.

# 75

## JUDE

*Onboard the Skydancer*

'You said I'm always right?' said Roo.

Jude and her father faced a screen talking to Roo. They were too far from Neptune for a full 3D conference. They'd managed to get decent coms with Squire when he was at the Xenos, but they were now even further away, and Arden had decided not to authorise the extra expenditure of dropping off signal boosting Sentinels because he didn't want to attract too much attention and lead a trail of breadcrumbs to their target. His attitude was that they should let the Solar System focus on the Xenos whilst they investigated potentially an even bigger prize.

'Yeah, maybe not always, most of the time. You sure about this?' Her father sounded worried about what he was hearing. His features were screwed up in thought and he ran his fingers through his hair as he tried to digest what they had just been told.

Roo grinned at the false praise, despite the seriousness of their conversation. She'd known Parynski since she'd met Jude at school. Her tanned face filled the screen as she spoke quietly. 'It all makes sense. It's what the grunts on Earth are reporting back. They've already been through Chen's personal data files. A court order is awaited to get her records from her position as a Senator. Her personal stuff has already been cracked.'

The smile left her face. 'I don't need to remind you what Chen's motivation was, but I'm telling you that she was in regular contact with Muller. I don't know how much the investigators know, but if I made the link, they should be interested. I've tapped what they have. If we'd known to watch him, this could all have come out a long time ago.'

Jude leaned across the desk so that Roo could see her, her hair tied back out of her face. 'You verified this from Muller's side?'

'Yes. Though he's been trying to cover his tracks, I got proof. They were a married couple long before Chen changed her identity.'

Whilst they spoke, hundreds of files were listed on a second screen as they were transferred from Roo to the Skydancer. Jude pointed at them and mouthed to her father that she would review them later once they'd been received.

'OK, what's the current concern? Zander is dead. Her other target is here; Arden is with his daughter in a sim suite down the corridor and we are millions of miles away on the best ship in the solar system with a squad of troopers on board. Shouldn't we just let the authorities get on with it, or maybe you could tip them off?'

Roo looked frustrated. 'I just think something big is about to go off. I don't know what the investigators think, though they've asked to see him. And even left alone, do you trust this guy now? Muller is on the loose, with increased authority levels and likely bearing a serious grudge against Arden's operation. Who knows what he could be up to? Jude mentioned that he seemed pissed that you'd gone off without him being informed.'

'Was he still close to Chen? They can't have seen much of each other?' asked Parynski.

Roo looked off screen, as if checking some notes. 'They were still very much in contact. Their last conversation was in the last few hours before her death.'

Jude spoke, glancing at her father. 'Neither of us knew Muller was side-lined by Arden. I doubt it was deliberate. Arden is so distracted with Rebecca; I doubt he intended to upset him. He spoke highly of him.'

Parynski agreed.

An image of the shipyard surrounding the Xenos appeared on the monitor. Roo controlled the view, swooping low over the rocky surface and beyond the spike that was the remains of the Kuiper Scout and into part of the metal skeleton that surrounded it all. A flashing dot was marked as being Muller.

'Good, so you can even track him when he's on duty. Just keep an eye on him.' Parynski sat back into his comfy chair, hands behind head and swung his feet up onto the unit in front of him. 'It's got to be good if the investigators want to see him. They might arrest him and at least he'll know he's being watched.'

'He's not on duty. He's taken a tug and flown it to the deserted end of the Xenos docking facility.'

'Well, what's he up to?' asked Parynski.

'He's just gone offline. We can't track him any further.'

Jude suddenly got it. She looked grimly at her father. 'We need to speak to Arden now.'

# 76

# WILDING

*The Dark*

Wilding had no real sense of time, however she suspected they hadn't been in the new chamber long as she and the Qarti collectively already knew every millimetre of the view, observing even specs of dust that blew across of the room, tumbling across the front of their tanks. After a while, the dull grey storage area became tiresome.

It had been a traumatic period of time, and they were all anxious. Wilding was feeling more optimistic. As long as she was alive, she had a chance, even if a small one, of somehow getting out of this state she was in. To the Qarti, developments felt a threat.

*What have they done?*

*Why are we being moved?*

Sheets were draped over the front of the tanks. They couldn't see anything, exacerbating fear amongst her new neighbours. Next, the vague illumination from some of the tanks failed. Their working theory had been that there had been power problems with the Xenos post collision anyway, but now all internal tank lighting had gone. They were trapped in darkness. It was that which scared Wilding the most. Whilst she could see people, she had hope.

Whilst they couldn't see what was going on, the Qarti reported a sensation of being moved. Wilding couldn't feel it, though she knew they were far more sensitive to such things. As their fear grew, she sensed some anger and aggression towards her. If she weren't in a separate tank, she'd have feared the worst.

*If Squire is behind this, it's ok. They want to help me, and they will want to get to know you too.*

*Why are we being separated from the others?*

Wilding obviously didn't know but understood there had been a breakdown in communication with the rest of the Qarti. There were sixteen of them now, closer than ever.

*Maybe they think it's going to be easier to extract me.*
*What about us?*

Wilding understood their fears. They were so tightly bonded that she couldn't lie to them. They'd know immediately. They knew that Earth hadn't had any contact with intelligent alien life before. The Qarti feared being specimens in an exhibit. There was not a lot she could say to that.

Eventually, the sheet was pulled off. They were in a new room, no longer on the Xenos. It was a fairly utilitarian storage bay. It seemed strangely familiar, though she didn't know why. That was until, wearing just a set of coveralls with a bushy beard and hair tied back, she saw Squire staring in at her. He looked unkempt, but he managed a big smile and a wave.

Maybe things were going to work out.

# 77

# ARDEN

*Onboard the Skydancer*

'How sure are you that he's on the Xenos? His last ping was at an airlock on the skeleton. He can't just vanish. Has nobody seen him?'

Arden was troubled by what was happening back at Neptune. Garcia had linked up a conference with Roo back home. She'd been trying to investigate discretely, but it seemed as they'd run out of time. Communications were more difficult since they'd gone through the cloud that surrounded their destination, and Roo's voice crackled.

'I can only assume he switched his Chip off. Security spoke to him on arrival, but after that he's dropped off the grid. None of the local grunts can trace him at all, but Muller would have override authorities.'

'So, what now? He's supposed to be in charge!'

Roo had clearly already taken on responsibility for the situation, and for that Arden was grateful. 'I've ordered a temporary withdrawal of scientific staff back to the dock. Lofgren has told them it's a routine review and head count. He's diverted all security he can into the area where Muller was headed.'

'Which was?'

Roo hesitated. He could see from her wrinkled brow that she was worried. 'The Tomb. I'm working on the assumption he's following Wilding's original route to that chamber.'

Arden slapped the desk. 'We've got enough going on here. Find him. Tell Lofgren to divert anyone he can and to send any internal drones he has. I'd rather a paparazzi get through and get some images they shouldn't than Muller does something crazy that damages the Xenos. When he's found detain him for the investigators.'

Roo nodded. 'Will be back with you when I hear more.' She ended the call.

Arden sighed and looked over at Jude, who had followed him into the room, curious. She had been listening.

Jude raised an eyebrow. 'We don't know what he has planned, do we? Might be a fuss over nothing. He could have even fallen ill or got lost. Thought you trusted him?'

Before Arden could reply, one of the screens flashed. He reached out to swipe open the message. 'It's Squire. What the hell has he been up to?'

Arden knew that Jude had known Squire from when she was a child. He moved his seat so she could be nearer the screen.

There was no image, only audio, and it wasn't Squire.

'Please forgive me for communicating in this way. I am permitted to contact interested third parties in the event of what I class as a risk to the health of Mr Squire or if other emergency protocols are engaged.'

Arden spoke over the AI while it tried to introduce itself. He knew all about Paisley 'Where's Squire? What've you been up to? I need him.'

'I'm afraid that for medical reasons we are unable to resume our duties in the vicinity of the Xenos. Mr Squire has become unwell. I understand that you're not in the Neptune system. Is there somebody more local you wish me to liaise with? I'm grateful for you taking this urgent message.'

Arden looked at Jude, rolled his eyes. 'He's being polite. Squire has overdosed or something again, I bet.'

Arden had a bad feeling about this, and felt the calm, affable man he had become in recent weeks become diminished. 'Get on with it. Your AI grade is banned on half the habitats this side of Mars. Don't make me extend the ban!'

Paisley ignored the comment. 'I have moved to safety in a wide orbit and will update you when we are ready to resume work. We have your cargo on board and will deliver it in due course, once the reception area is ready. The reason for this communication is to urgently let you know that one of the security measures that Mr Squire set when he was onboard the Xenos has been triggered. This information was set as being of the highest priority, so should be investigated.'

Arden's eyes widened. 'What sort of security measure?'

'Due to the considerable number of potential approaches to the chamber that contained Dee Wilding and the alien creatures, a number of digital trips were set up to identify any movement. Our accommodation on the bridge was quite some distance away. I am sending, embedded into this communication, the co-ordinates.'

Arden glanced at Jude, who nodded back in agreement. 'That's got to be Muller?' whispered Jude.

Arden cut Paisley off with the briefest of 'thank you' and a request for a full report on Squire's health within twenty-four hours. He knew the AI wouldn't co-operate. Squire had him well programmed to protect him.

He decided to focus on the Xenos, and called up a 3D plan of the vessel, marked where the chamber Wilding had reached was and the co-ordinates of the trip wire.

It all seemed obvious. 'Yes, he's heading to that chamber. He's trying to avoid any personnel we have on board. What's he playing at, though? I think Wilding has already been moved.'

Arden called Roo back up, and while she was online, called up his head of security. He gave instructions to direct security teams after him. Roo indicated it was unlikely they would get to him before he reached the Tomb.

'Of all the times for this to happen. Is our shuttle ready?'

# 78

# PARYNSKI

*On approach to Propylaea*

'Scott, stop worrying about the Xenos. There's nothing we can do right now except wait until security catch Muller. You don't even know if he's going to do anything.'

Across the channel, everyone could feel the tension.

Parynski piloted the shuttle Runaround that had been added to the Skydancer before they left Neptune orbit. It was a small, green oblong shaped box, in complete contrast to its sleek mother craft. Arden's head of security, Jim Aska, sat alongside him in the co-pilot's berth. Strapped into seats behind them were Garcia and two other security personnel. They were all suited up save for their visors, which remained up.

'I know, sorry.'

They all understood Arden's anxiety, but they were in uncharted territory now and needed to focus. They'd not expected any drama back at Neptune whilst they were away.

'Let's stick to the plan. The drones have been deployed. We've one more orbit to ensure external 3D mapping is accurate and then I will take us in.'

Arden, in a temporary Ops room back on the Skydancer with the rest of the party, sighed 'Just keep it efficient, take no risks. You go in, see if you can land and if you can, you take a quick look inside. Not much more than that. We've got sentinel drones in place now so we can keep this place secure if we have to abort.'

Arden closed the connection.

Parynski and Aska looked at the 3D image that glowed on the console at the front of the dash. Parynski pointed at the side that appeared volcano like, where the rock opened up as if blown out from the inside. The opening was many miles in diameter and inside it narrowed slightly before opening out into a far wider chamber. Of particular interest were the shelves that had been cut into the sides of the chamber. They were unlikely to be naturally formed, as they were of a rough uniform length and parallel. There were over a dozen on each side. The shelves were wide and flat, most wide enough that the Skydancer could have landed with relative ease. Parynski had agreed with Arden not to take that risk and decided that the shuttle would be used.

The chamber was large enough to hold the Xenos, with room to spare. Caution was being exercised because sensors were detecting some faint traces of energy fields, though the rock was impervious to most of the scans the drones were capable of. Exterior mapping presented nothing obvious of interest, save the overall unusual shape of the object. It wasn't a space craft like the Xenos.

The 3D image of the interior highlighted half a dozen spots in red, and Parynski zoomed in on the nearest one. It seemed likely they were entrances into the rock of some sort. The doorways were based on the footage they'd got, three storeys high, many times as wide. They appeared to be cut out of the rock and had a metallic looking surround. The door itself was covered in lines that Garcia was convinced meant the opening could be adapted to open to suit the size of visitors.

Parynski completed his pre insertion checks and moved the shuttle into close enough proximity to plot a course into the interior of the rock. The exterior required careful consideration to navigate the random selection of rocks that circled Propylaea, some disguised by the whisps of blue and yellow smoke that were wrapped around its surface.

To supplement the real time footage, Parynski provided a commentary for those listening.

'Right, we've got all the mapping we are likely to get so we're going in… igniting burners and letting the computer take us into the opening…I'm ready to take over if things get choppy inside or we have trouble setting down on that shelf.'

It was an impressive sight as the Runaround looped back over the top of Propylaea and swooped down along the outside of the cone, heading towards the opening. Software enhanced the views because of the dark.

'Visors down and suit air on, please. Let's not take any chances. There's a lot of debris floating around. Once inside, we will do a circuit of the chamber to fill any gaps that the drones have missed before heading towards the shelf.'

The view through the cockpit window was enhanced. The shuttle had multiple spotlights and scanners playing on its surroundings, and there was also a pinpoint light from the drones that were tracking them.

Parynski struggled to keep his mind clear of the historic nature of what he was doing as he monitored the Runaround's course, almost instinctively reaching for the joystick as the shuttle looped outwards and then turned into the dark maw. He wondered how close this was to how Wilding felt when she boarded the Xenos, immediately feeling guilty for such thoughts. Wilding had approached the alien ship in the knowledge her colleagues were dead and that she had little chance of survival. He had people back on the Skydancer rooting for him and providing backup. Dee didn't even know if anyone had seen her messages.

They were being genuine explorers in the same way as the famous settlers he had read about at school, those that both explored Earth and later the solar system. He wondered if Mary would have been proud of him. Perhaps for something as important as this, she might not have minded him being away from home.

## THE TRITON RUN

Parynski went silent as the main burners cut out and the shuttle glided through the opening, jets firing out of the front to slow them.

'Good luck everybody.' It was Garcia in the back.

'Stay safe,' said Howard over the com. They could hear Arden stressing about Muller in the background, Rebecca telling him to enjoy this moment.

Parynski was used to flying in dangerous situations, often with ships that had developed major problems or were flying way beyond their normal capabilities. It was that experience he relied on as he tried to resist the urge to take manual control. There was currently no indication of anything that was about to surprise them.

He caught a glimpse of Garcia out of the corner of his helmet. She was leaning forward as far as the straps would let her, and despite her helmet being on, he could clearly see her face. Her reaction brought a smile to his face. There was no fear, just wide-eyed wonder. They'd spent a lot of time together on the journey from Neptune. This was what Garcia had worked all her life for.

The shuttle moved out into the centre of the roughly oblong space, a chamber ten of miles wide. After holding their position for a few minutes, Parynski tried to think of something appropriately profound to say, blurting out, 'So, here we are! We can see nothing, but it feels pretty amazing, yeah? Was going to say it looks man made, you know what I mean?'

'We do Bruce, we do.' Arden was first to reply over the circuit. 'Your signal is a bit weak, though please keep talking. We should be outside the entrance in a few minutes, whereupon we will go into a holding pattern and match the rotation.'

Garcia was quietly talking to herself. 'This is alien, it was made by aliens. It was in our own backyard all this time and we missed it.'

One of the security team sat next to her and put his hand gently on her arm. 'We didn't miss it; we are here aren't we? And it's hardly our backyard.'

The shuttle pulled off to the left and headed towards the interior wall. After moving through the darkness, they eventually reached and then followed the interior wall all the way round before repeating a similar circuit of the chamber by heading up to the roof of the Chamber. The orientation of the object was decided by reference to the direction of the shelves. Parynski noted that Aska also seemed distracted, staring intently at an image on a display on his side of the dashboard. 'You ok?'

Aska took a moment to respond. Judging by the temporary way his face went blank, Parynski guessed he was trying to assess was he was seeing and assimilate it with a data feed into his Chip. The moment passed and Aska threw the image he was looking at onto the main view screen before them.

'Look, we've just gone past it. All the way round the inside of the chamber, about twenty-five percent of the way in, is this groove. It's about twenty metres wide and the sides are all parallel. Our drones didn't get a good enough look, but I'd guess it's some sort of door frame?'

Garcia shouted from the back whilst staring intently at the screen. 'Great spot, you might be right. This place must be an artificial construct. Can't see the door, though thankfully our landing target is going to be on the outside of it. Can we get a couple of the drones to take a look?'

Aska gave her a thumbs up. 'Already in hand, will get two of the internal ones to take a look at opposite sides once they've completed their current assignments.'

Parynski rotated the Runaround, so it was facing and drifting slowly towards the left side of the interior wall where they could see the series of huge shelves been cut out of the rock, each parallel with the one above and below. The gap between each shelf was about three hundred metres, large enough for a reasonably large space craft to land. The shelves were several miles long. Each shelf was about two hundred metres wide. Following its pre-arranged flight path, the shuttle slowly came into land. The gateway their drones had identified came into sight, spotlights confirming that the door itself, if that is what it was, was not made of the same rocky material as the rest of the object. They moved in, hovering above the shelf whilst trying to get as close to the entrance as they could. They set down with the slightest bump and for a moment there was silence as they all took in the importance of what had just happened.

Everyone cheered, shaking hands, and patting each other on the back. It was a feeling of relief. Shouts of celebration came over the circuit from the Skydancer. Parynski waved everyone to sit still whilst he ran some checks to ensure they had landed securely and that the grappling hooks on the landing gear had taken hold.

When he was ready, Parynski turned to Aska. 'Ok, we're secure. Over to you with the docking tube.'

'Aren't you supposed to say something inspirational at this point, Parynski?'

# 79

# SQUIRE

*Onboard the BSV*

He'd lost all appreciation of time. Squire sat on the floor, propped up by a cushion against the wall, opposite the tanks in the hold of his ship, desperate for another indication that Dee Wilding was alive. They were in a holding orbit around the Xenos and its entourage of supporting craft and drones. Paisley was running the ship at present, waiting for confirmation that their destination was ready to accommodate his valuable cargo.

He stared intently at Wilding. He guessed he'd been there for several days, drifting in and out of sleep. He wore coveralls, his left leg rolled up over his knee. Left on the floor nearby was an empty vial which had been drained of Zefyrex that morning. The syringe and driver lay by his foot. His anxiety had lifted since he'd taken it. All he had to do now was wait for a sign. He'd seen Wilding move once. If he waited long enough, there might be another. The biggest risk was that he'd miss it while asleep. He had cameras running, but the movement, when seen through the filter of the material in the tank, might be barely imperceptible. The sheets that had covered the tanks whilst they were wheeled through the Xenos and through a transit tube to the hold of the BSV remained scattered on the floor between them. It had been suggested that he should leave the covers on, so as not to distract him. There'd been a lot of unease that he'd refused to allow anyone else on board. He didn't want anyone poking their noses round his ship.

Someone had to be there for her. He wanted her to know, as had happened during the trial, that there was someone waiting for her. She'd saved the Platoon enough times, and they still owed her. There was nobody else here to help. Parynski had gone off to lead the search to find the origin of the Xenos and might be gone for six months or more. There was nothing urgent for him to do. He'd subcontracted some of his clearance work out whilst he'd been en route to the Xenos. He'd therefore been delighted to accept, in truth, he'd insisted, responsibility for ferrying the tanks around the Neptune system and to their new home where scientists could focus on saving Dee.

He was relieved that it seemed as if extracting Wilding had worked. Her tank and three others stood alongside each other, next to a series of generators. A host of cables and wires snaked from the units, disappearing round the back of the tanks. For a while, his anxiety had taken over, after learning that the first two trial extractions had all failed. The power connections hadn't worked properly and after an hour, the gunge had turned opaque, and the lighting had gone out. The alien corpses, still stored in the tanks, had been removed for eventual post-mortems and dissection after a period of quarantine.

Another dozen tanks had been successfully removed and were stored in the on-board gymnasium. He didn't use it half as much as he should, anyway.

Still, she didn't move. Her position had adjusted slightly during the move. Drifting in and out of sleep, he was aware of an alert from Paisley. He couldn't think of anything that would concern him right now. Paisley would have to deal.

She might wake any moment.

# 80

## MULLER

*Onboard the Xenos*

Muller didn't spot the digital trip wire. Frustratingly, his suit alerted him to the device after it had been triggered. Before he put a boot through its control box, he briefly examined the object and decided it wasn't of alien origin. More likely used by Squire to protect him when alone for all those months. As a result, Muller reassessed his route and quickened his pace.

As he let his suit walk him to his destination, he tried to put his thoughts in order. He'd watched Chen's final message over and over, reminiscing over their good times together. It felt a long time ago and whilst she'd changed, Muller realised, contrary to how he'd felt recently, that he couldn't imagine life without her. The possibility of things working out had kept him motivated for so long. He'd not been keen on the surgery she'd undergone, but his hope remained that by becoming a politician, she might've been influenced and inspired by public service, the same way he had when working for Arden. However, it wasn't to be.

Her cause, *their* cause, was more important to her than her love for him. It hurt, but he didn't blame her. She'd lost all her family at the hands of Arden, Zander, and the Earth Government. He sympathised. He admonished himself that attempts to break contact with Chen stemmed from his own fears and complete cowardice at a time when she needed him.

# THE TRITON RUN

He'd betrayed her. He wondered if she knew.

The tears came again, never good in an EVA suit, so he paused for a while, calling into the room that appeared to be either a church or a school. A temporary air lock had been attached, such was the interest in examining the space, so he was able to remove his helmet. He wiped his eyes and the inside of the helmet before staring up at the statue cut out of the wall, musing over what could have been. There was so much to learn from the Xenos.

He continued, satisfied that interception was unlikely at this point. He'd been able to briefly monitor the internal network chatter and was aware that an alert had been raised. Ironically, it had made things easier for him. The security personnel now looking for him were too far away, nor would they even be sure why they were looking for him.

Eventually, he reached the Tomb. The chamber containing the pods had changed since his last visit. Muller stepped through an open temporary air lock door frame. They'd tried a second time to introduce a temporary atmosphere before the idea was abandoned, unable to maintain pressure. Both ceiling and the floor were obscured by the darkness beyond his suit's spotlights. As he investigated, he repowered the abandoned spotlights, casting shadows across the walls, serving to further highlight the darkness of the chasm. He cast the two cameras and their tripods over the railings. Additional fencing had been secured to the railings to stop people falling from the ledges. While metal plating was welded to the floors so suits could remain magnetically secure without the need for additional tethers. Muller stepped over boxes and scattered pieces of equipment, abandoned by the crew when the call to withdraw had come. He was glad they had gone, so now he could conduct the plan without discovery. It was cowardice not to face those he would hurt, but the peace allowed him to do what needed to be done.

## 81

## PARYNSKI

*Inside Propylaea*

Parynski deliberately slowed their preparations to leave the shuttle Runaround, ensuring all safety checks were followed. Everyone was impatiently desperate to explore as quickly as they could, aware that they the call to return to the Skydancer could arrive at any moment. Eventually, Aska stepped back from the hatch, letting go of two small joysticks perched on top of the control console. He gave a thumbs up.

'We're securely attached with a seal. Even though I'll pump some atmosphere into the tube, we'll stay suited up. Fingers crossed those markings are an opening.'

Despite remaining suited since they'd left the Skydancer, they double-checked their equipment again. Their modern suits were the kind Parynski had used at the Antiope. With sun shield visors, up Parynski could see their HUD displays. They all had spotlights mounted on their helmets and shoulders, with illuminated pads running down the side of their trousers to ensure they didn't tread on anything they shouldn't.

Parynski and Aska carried weapons, Garcia a portable sensor kit. A more powerful camera replaced one of her spotlights, superior to the standard issue suit cams. One of the security team, Turtal, always remained with the shuttle and looked perpetually disappointed at missing out.

# THE TRITON RUN

'Skydancer? You there?'

There was silence for a period, and before Howard was heard across the open channel. 'You're good to go. Scott's awaiting an update from home, so I suggest you move fast.'

When the outer hatch slid aside, they peered into the tube extending from the shuttle to what they hoped was a way inside. There wasn't much to see. The tube wall was as grey as the surface and a matt black wall was some twenty metres away. Lighting strips ran along the ceiling and the floor of tunnel, allowing them to power down their torches. The tubing was designed to create an airtight passage for loading or unloading. This time, they had done it to make sure they didn't lose anyone.

Parynski stepped aside to let Garcia through. Desperate to be the first person to set foot on a new planet, and this was likely as close as she would come.

Garcia grinned at him, briefly grabbing his wrist in thanks, before bounding forward as best as she could while still tethered to a rail along the inside of the tube. Everyone followed. The shuttle extended its temporary gravity field into the tunnel, but coverage was patchy and faded the further they went.

Garcia let Parynski come alongside her. They both peered at the surface of what they hoped was a way in, looking for any sign of an opening mechanism. Indentations and grooves curved off in various directions. They had chosen this part of the wall to inspect as a combination of the grooves formed an outline be big enough for them to pass through safely. Parynski gave Garcia a moment to inspect her sensors.

'Can we touch this without getting electrocuted or anything?'

Garcia replied in an animated manner. 'Oh lord, I'm getting power readings from behind the door, if that is what it is. Doesn't seem there's anything on the door that should cause a problem.'

Parynski looked at her. 'Shall I knock?'

She ushered him forward. 'Please. I hope they are welcoming.'

Parynski swung his rifle over his shoulder, sticking it to a patch on his back so it wouldn't float away and hit anyone. He reached inside a pocket on this chest and produced another sensor and reached out tentatively to place it on the wall. Just before he made contact, the dark grooves in the wall became illuminated in a white glow, tracing the pattern across the section of the wall in front of them.

It startled them all. They'd hoped to find signs of life, mechanical or biological, but weren't ready for one so soon. The guard at their rear lost his grip on the tether and momentarily crashed into the back of Aska, who, in turn, knocked Garcia. Parynski sharply raised a hand, signifying they all freeze, which they tried as best as they could in almost zero gravity. He reached round and grabbed his weapon again as the wall dilated in front of him. The surface slid away, withdrawing into the grooves, until a gap large enough for them to pass through had opened.

Bright white light spilled forth from the room. Within the glow, they struggled to make out various colours, shades, and hues. No immediate source of the light could be established. Their HUDs all blinked off and when they returned, began to alarm as sensors failed to cope with the onslaught of a vastly different environment, with light and energy readings they couldn't parse.

Parynski became suddenly aware of a horizontal beam which seemed to rake up and down across them.

'We're being scanned?' Parynski stuttered across their channel.

'Bruce, this is Skydancer. We're watching. Keep calm.'

After an indeterminate period, the beam vanished, and in the glare ahead of them, they perceived movement. Inside the space, floors formed, walls sliding into place, a ceiling lowered. It was too bright to make out anything definitive and their suit cams had long since given up trying to cope. Their suit's priority was to ensure their wearers weren't blinded. As abruptly as it'd started, the light blinked off, and momentarily, they were plunged into darkness.

'The fuck…'

Parynski didn't know who'd said that, but he understood the sentiment. He cursed himself, wishing they'd thought of sending a drone ahead. He started to calm as the room before them became illuminated to a level comfortable on the eye. He raised his weapon in front of him, out of habit rather than any instinct of any danger which lay ahead. He stepped forward, suddenly realising that the new room either attracted their boots or was level with the artificial gravity aboard the Skydancer. He raised a hand to wave Garcia to follow, and one by one, they entered the new space, staying close to each other for safety, despite their training to fan out.

Garcia broke the silence. 'I was not expecting this.'

# 82

# MULLER

*Onboard the Xenos*

The spotlights added a sinister ambience to the tomb, further illuminating the fluid in the pods which lined the walls. A whole section of pods had been removed, including the one containing Wilding, an empty one and a number that contained alien specimens. The gap had been covered with sheeting to stop contamination or accidental interference with the exposed pipework and circuitry behind it. Muller had seen the schematics, and his engineers were trying to develop a full understanding of them. They didn't want to do anything that might damage the other aliens, though some had died during extraction or were already dead.

He walked the full circuit of the walkway, reaching into his backpack as he went, extracting small devices and sticking them to the walls. A few moments after he walked away from each, his suit notified him that they were powering up and syncing. Occasionally, he paused to examine the aliens, all suspended in similar poses. He wondered what they had known about their destination. When he'd completed the lap, leaned over the barrier, peering into the darkness at the walkways below and above him. There was no certain way onto any other levels, confirming the common theory that the aliens could fly. A team of engineers had been planning to climb up onto the floor above.

# THE TRITON RUN

Muller checked the simulation he'd ran before setting off and satisfied himself that all would go to plan. His suit pinged an alert. There was a team less than ten minutes out. It didn't matter whether they captured him now or not. Muller found a suitable sized box to sit down, breathing deeply, contemplating what was to come. He was angry with himself for missing the chance to punish Arden, which only fuelled his current attempt at revenge. Even if he hadn't always agreed with her, Chen had honoured their colleagues with her actions. She had led a fightback and kept them safe for so long. Muller knew he'd failed to meet what she had asked of him. At least he could be comforted in knowledge that the repercussions of what he was about to do would be felt for decades. It was now or never, because he'd soon be arrested.

In one moment, Muller could destroy Arden's business empire and unleash anarchy across the Neptune system. Anarchy would lead to the Earth swarming the Neptune system, competing with Jupiter and Uranus if they got their act together.

None of it really mattered, ultimately. Ready, he shut down all but the vital functions of his suit and called an image of Chen up onto the HUD. Not the Chen he'd barely known over the last few years, but the girl he married and loved for over a decade. Her features had changed, hardening what was a beautiful soft face, framed by shoulder length dark hair. Sarah was her name, and he did this for her.

A simple command from his suit detonated the ring of explosives and Muller was no more. The Xenos cracked like a quail's egg and the shrapnel tore apart the Neptune system.

## 83

## PARYNSKI

*Inside Propylaea*

'I don't think anyone was expecting this.'

Parynski cautiously stepped forward, weapon sweeping the room, whilst he kept an eye on his sensors. They still hadn't begun to understand what they were seeing.

'Skydancer, you got this?'

The only thing he heard was the sound of breathing from his colleagues across their mics and the noise of their suits air supplies. Then Aska spoke. 'We've lost the Run'. I've got nothing bar the readings from our suits on our close circuit.'

Parynski turned back to him. 'Step back outside, see if we still have a signal there.'

Aska nodded and slowly retraced his steps, swinging his weapon round to cover his retreat. The entrance they'd passed through remained, the sheer white and clean lines of their current surroundings stark against the exterior rock floor and the walls of the tube.

Whilst waiting, they made small talk, cracking poor jokes and trying to kid each other, that they weren't equally terrified and amazed by where they found themselves.

Their speakers crackled. Aska was back.

'-signal is struggling to get through. Once out the doorway, I was back online. I uploaded all the footage and readings we have back to the ship. Arden says he's waiting for an update from Triton, so we're to continue for now.'

Parynski lowered his weapon and tried to feign a casualness he didn't feel. 'Ok, Aska, stand guard, keep stepping through the barrier and checking in. Sounds like we could use a signal booster next time. If the door does *anything*, please shout.'

Parynski spun round, his free hand gesturing at the surrounding room. 'So, what do we all think? Teresa, is this tech the same as the Xenos?'

She seemed to shrug, though it was hard to tell through her suit. 'All bets are off, Bruce. I've a feeling this is something bigger, something more advanced.'

He still hadn't been able to take in what was going on around them; none of them could translate what they were seeing into words. 'Agreed.'

Parynski noted they were all running suit self-checks. What he'd thought was a steaming up of his helmet was, in fact, happening in the room. The chamber was cloaked in a peculiar fog, with clouds that moved around, flitting from place to place, constantly changing shape. Parynski could see it, could sense what it was doing, but was unable to focus on what the cloud was. However, when the cloud drifted away from an area, the space it vacated was clearly visible. The sensors on their suits couldn't detect anything.

He pointed at the nearest cloud. 'What is it?'

Garcia stepped alongside him; her eyes wide. 'Some sort of nanotechnology? Way beyond what we've got. Or maybe it's organic?'

Parynski hadn't considered that. 'Yeah, perhaps. Maybe this is the second alien life form we've discovered this year. It seems to be clearing. Shall we take a look round? Avoid walking into it, though.'

'Ok, it doesn't seem to mean us any harm,' replied Garcia, who, while excited, didn't sound quite so certain.

Parynski noticed that the gravity had increased. They didn't need any support from their suits. Nearby were a series of white consoles, which Garcia peered at intently. Parynski turned to take in the scene. Completely alien, yet vaguely familiar. It was clinically white, yet hospitable.

The far wall was still obscured, millions of motes swarming around in a cloud, building their surroundings. The room almost seemed designed to be friendly and welcoming. There were rows of comfy benches, various clusters of tables and chairs, and a facility that might've been a kitchen. The far wall contained a number of closed doors, and in the centre a wide stairway curved out of sight, heading upwards. Curiosity as to where the steps went triggered something deep in Parynski's memory. He took a moment to assimilate and accept the conclusion he'd reached before continuing. Garcia leaned over the console, engrossed. Parynski nudged her arm, startling her.

'I know this place. I just can't place it. This is a less friendly, more… white… but the layout is so similar.'

'Holy shit,' Aska had stepped back inside again, listening in as more of the room formed around them. 'How can this just have been built?'

Garcia looked over at Aska, pointing to the far corner of the space which remained cloudy. There was activity in amongst the fog that hung in the air.

Garcia spoke as she thought. 'What do you think is going on there? It's definitely being built as we watch. We've all seen the room becoming sharper as these things finish their job. Those lights when we opened the door were scanning us, perhaps reading our minds. Maybe they're building what we want or need? Bruce was first to step inside, so we get the pleasure of his subconscious?'

Parynski laughed. 'Lucky you!'

Aska suddenly straightened, coughing to get everyone's attention.

'Sorry. We need to go. Arden has called us back. Said it's an emergency back home, and he wants us docked with the Skydancer within an hour so we can be back on the road in two.' The urgency in his voice told them he was serious. Garcia showed disappointment in her body language, shoulders slumping. Parynski felt the same.

'So far for this!' Garcia looked heartbroken, voice breaking as disappointment verged on anger. 'What a waste. What good can we do setting off now?'

Parynski agreed that leaving now was plain cruel. 'Tell Arden he can wait a bit longer. This is ridiculous. Nothing can be enough of an emergency for us to turn around.'

Aska approached the two of them so they could see his face. He looked pale.

'There's been an explosion on the Xenos. It's gone. Vast amounts of damage have been caused to all neighbouring habitats and ships. It's grim. Not much is online, Arden says it doesn't look pretty. Any survivors are going to need all the help they can get, even if it takes months to get there.'

Parynski looked at Garcia, her face now devoid of colour. She later told him that she regretted failing to ask if there were any reports of damage to her base on Triton, but it didn't occur to her at the time. She was so focussed on her surroundings. The slight nod Parynski detected showed him that Garcia understood the change in situation. He'd enjoyed the journey. It had given him time to recover, to grieve, to spend time with Jude, probing what mysteries the object might hold. He resolved that they would have to use their limited time the best they could.

'Right. The clock's ticking. Let's not waste the time we have.' He pointed to Aska. 'Tell the shuttle to make the pre-flight checks. Run it warm so we can take off immediately. We can leave the tunnel behind to save time. Then scour this room. Every single inch of it. I want footage of the lot. I want you to touch every object, so we can scale it later. Go.'

Aska nodded and turned on his heels. The other member of their party, Foss, swung his weapon over his shoulder and headed to the corner furthest from them to start work.

Parynski patted Garcia on the back. 'Let's do what we can. Nothing looks a threat. If this place - these things - wanted us dead, they could've done it a long time ago. You get what you can out of that console. I'm going to try those doors and that stairwell. I'll pipe across a live feed to you and will shout if I find anything worth seeing.'

She smiled. Parynski knew she was trying to hide her disappointment. As he walked towards the wall containing the stairwell, Parynski looked back at Garcia. 'We'll learn all about this place, don't you worry. We'll be back.'

'I hope so.'

Parynski approached a section of wall consisting of a patchwork of grooves. A combination of hand movements along the grain caused the wall to ripple and dissolve into an opening. He leapt aside as bunks and loungers rapidly disgorged from the wall. All were the same pure white and, unlike the hard surfaces they'd encountered so far, he discovered bedding and cushions.

He reached the staircase that had caught his eye, bounding up the steps he arrived upon a garden path of sorts. Clear blue sky sprawled above a stone path which meandered between hedgerows along the rise of a hill. Parynski peered upwards, assessing it to be a more advanced, immersive version of the crop room on Antiope. Birds flew overhead and the collision detector on his suit registered a light breeze.

Parynski paused as his boots sank slightly into the grass before a further step put him onto the stone path, wide enough for two to walk abreast. It seemed too realistic to be a sim.

He knew this place.

Conscious the clock was against them, he started to jog up the hill. The hedgerows were thick and well maintained, so he couldn't see over or through them. As he reached the crest of the hill, some one-hundred meters or so away from the entrance, he turned to look back. He could still see the door he'd come through, but above and around it was a view of rolling hills. Nestled at the foot of the adjacent hill was a grand, old-fashioned building. There were a number of vehicles which he could see parked out the rear, as well as an illuminated logo up above the entrance. It was a hotel, the one he had stayed in with Mary, after his last visit here.

Parynski turned back the way he was originally heading as he reached the brow of the path. He strode out onto what became a fenced area enclosing a carefully manicured lawn. Immediately before him was a white, wooden bandstand. It was empty. Vastly different to the last time he had seen it. Beyond the bandstand, another fence could be seen, and beyond that, cliff tops fell away to reveal the ocean. His suit mic could just about pick up the sound of the waves breaking on the shore out of sight. Parynski climbed the two steps to the bandstand and leaned on the rail, taking in the view, unsure how to react. Garcia's voice interrupted his pondering.

'Bruce, where are you? I need to show you this console. I've got it working. What've you found?'

He looked once more out to sea, wondering if it were his imagination or if he could see a small fishing boat out near the horizon. 'Not much. Coming.'

He decided not to explain, or at least not yet.

## 84

## SQUIRE

*Onboard the BSV*

Squire was still in the hold when the alarms rang, and he felt the sudden change in thrust. It was so powerful he should've been strapped into his couch. Even the internal dampeners couldn't hide the effects of the acceleration, violently throwing him against the tank he'd been facing. He grabbed onto it and held on, winded by a toolbox launched from the floor, striking him before emptying its contents across the deck. He'd have to pick everything up before he next shut the anti-grav down.

His face was pressed flat against the front panel of the tanks. As the hold shook, he could see the alien inside twitching. Movement wasn't particularly unusual since their extraction. Eyes flickered open and closed, arms moved up and down, giving the impression of wings in flight, and the thin, horse-like head moved from side to side. Despite being seemingly asleep, they were subconsciously reacting to what was going on in the BSV. Gradually, they'd grown more animated since their removal from the Xenos, but this was another level. The creature lurched forward; face turned to one side with one dark eye staring out at him.

Before he could catch his breath, he heard Paisley. 'Sir, the Xenos has exploded. I'm increasing thrust and maintaining an outward course at maximum thrust.'

'What about the science crew on board? And turn the alarm off.' Squire shouted. The alarms promptly ceased.

'Nothing Sir. The Xenos and its cradle are gone.' Paisley paused, even an AI knew to give him chance to take this in. 'I'm sorry.'

Whilst clinging onto the alien tank, he could feel anxiety and guilt rise in him. The BSV, Paisley told him, due to its precious cargo, was forbidden to return and retrieve any crew from the Xenos during the evacuation. He needed more Zefyrex, but he tried to clamp down the instinct. This was not his fault, not this time.

Finally, the dampeners were able to compensate for the acceleration and Squire stepped away from the tank. Scooping up the scattered tools and stowing the bag, he set off to the cockpit at a run. Before he left the hold, he glanced back at the furthest tank. Dee Wilding remained there, both eyes open, yet seemingly unseeing. Her arms now outstretched, fingers splayed against the inside of the glass as if trying to escape.

On the way to the cockpit, he shouted for Paisley, 'Distance?'

'Ten thousand miles and rising.'

Squire realised Paisley had it all wrong. Whilst incredibly intelligent, the AI still struggled to make what were, on the face of it, counterintuitive steps. He sprinted down the main hallway from the hold, swerving around a corner towards the largely empty accommodation area. Taking a shortcut, he leapt up onto a pole and pulled himself up through an opening in the ceiling onto the command deck. The BSV continued to vibrate all around him; she wasn't designed to go this fast.

Squire dashed into the cockpit and secured himself into his couch. 'ETA for debris?'

Paisley responded immediately, projecting diagrams onto nearby monitors. 'Two minutes. Triton One has taken most of the impact from the initial debris wave. I'll update you on the effect of that as soon as I can.'

Strapped in, Squire pulled a control console across his lap

and pored over the data.

'We aren't going to make it; it's coming too fast. Turn us round, full stop.'

Awaiting Paisley's complaints, Squire manually took control of the external shields, fanning them out as quickly as possible.

'Sir, that would put on a course with the debris wave?'

'I know! That's our only hope. We won't outrun it. Open all shields. Every single one flared as wide as we can. Prime point defence cannons, too. I want a decent spread of fire. Let's try to break up some of what's coming.'

Fresh alarms flared, his suit's bioscanner warning of his elevated heart rate following the record efforts of returning from the hold, combined with the shuddering frame of the ship as it pulled to a "stop".

'Understood. In hand.'

Squire was pinned back into the bottom of his couch, the ship still moving forward under its own momentum. The engines disengaged, save the manoeuvring jets down the sides. They were lit to full power on one side to try create enough spin while the ship rapidly decelerated. As it spun, the nozzles died, and the other side ignited to slow the spin, nudging the BSV into the required direction. Squire's fingers danced across the control console, even as he struggled to lift his head from his headrest.

He knew the ship inside out and could pilot it blind. Even though he'd not put up any external views, he knew how the BSV would respond. It was now an ugly, industrial peacock, with its external deflectors splaying out in all directions. It wasn't the most attractive shield, pieces composed of hundreds of mechanical fans, in any array of colours. Pushed out in front of the shield was an invisible energy shield that would, if not deflect, slow down a substantial amount of the incoming assault. Squire knew that it was the only thing that might keep him alive. Had the wave of deadly shrapnel struck the BSV from behind, it would have gouged straight through the engine blocks and reactor, completely destroying the ship. The titanium coffin at the heart of the BSV, designed largely to protect against radiation, wouldn't be enough.

There was a brief respite from the chaos. The ship ceased shuddering, and he asked Paisley to alert him once the wave reached the maximum range of his PDCs. They certainly weren't manufactured to take out anything like that, but they'd help, even if they only broke up or dispersed some of the larger pieces of debris. He set them to automated fire, designed to spread fire across a wide area of space. Disappointed, Paisley advised Squire that there was no time to deploy the compliment of the mines or missiles they carried to assist in salvage or clearing work.

'One minute, thirty seconds until maximum firing range is reached. Make sure the magnetic shields are at max strength.'

It was going to be close. He couldn't see it yet, but approaching at great speed was a shattered wall of stone and metal. He tried to pull up an image of Triton One. Usually, he'd have a choice of dozens of angles from all local ships and habitats with publicly accessible cameras. There was now only one option, which he dialled into.

It was barely recognisable and as he watched, Squire could see the central core spinning away from its usual holding orbit around Triton. If he survived, which appeared unlikely in the circumstances, he'd check where the remains were heading. Triton One had been a tremendous feat of engineering, a central habitat acting as a core, from which had run dozens of tubes, leading to accommodation, offices, and storage blocks. Docking bays and eruptions of antennae once sprouted from it. Now it was almost entirely gone. The core remained, but its superstructure was shattered, its central cylinder crushed.

Squire switched back to his own situation. Triton One had been directly in between the Xenos and the BSV's current position, the old station stopping some of the debris in their tracks. He counted down the clock until it was time to start firing on the oncoming tide of death. He switched off his coms board as it became lit up with dozens of SOS messages. The Xenos' remains were bouncing round the Neptune system like a macabre game of stellar pinball.

At the right time, he felt the ship kick a little as the forward PDCs engaged, spraying projectile and laser fire at the on-rushing wave. It only took a few gnawing moments for Squire to realise it wasn't likely to be enough.

# 85

# ARDEN

*Onboard The Skydancer*

The feeling of excitement that had consumed him as they'd arrived at the object had transformed into grief, frustration, and fear. The situation at Neptune was the most serious, but the situation he could do least about. Based on the messages he had received, it looked bad. There were likely to be thousands of casualties and it didn't seem feasible that the survivors and others that just happened to be in the vicinity would be able to step in and save many. Neptune, as far as the shipping lanes were concerned, was the end of the journey. The Triton Run. There was no passing traffic.

Propylaea would have to wait. He just couldn't stay away to examine an alien artefact at the edge of the solar system whilst his people died back home. After giving the order for the shuttle to return, he cursed Parynski for not immediately replying. Some of their footage received looked incredible, for now it would have to wait.

Jude had been with Rebecca, watching developments with some of Garcia's colleagues. Most on board had come to accept their trip was now in vain. They weren't going to get to explore the object, not this time, anyway. Frustration and disappointment were now shrouded in fear and grief. Despite the paucity of information from Neptune, everyone was now aware of what had happened, with most of the crew having family, friends, and colleagues back home.

The Xenos had exploded and taken much of the neighbourhood with it. Projections suggested debris would cause considerable problems for any habitats or ships in the vicinity. Some of the high sitting gas mine units were at risk, and the scientists who Garcia had brought feared for their colleagues on Triton. There had been reports of surface installations going quiet.

At least Rebecca was with him, and safe. Whilst waiting, they watched the live feeds from the shuttle and the drones inside the object's internal chamber. They'd both sat open-mouthed whilst the barrier slid from the wall in the main chamber, quickly interlocking its panels into a solid wall that cut off the inner area of the chamber from the outside. The barrier, or door, was miles in diameter. Rebecca spotted quicker than he did that thankfully the shuttle was on the outside of the barrier and could, at present, still get away.

'Aska, get out of there now. Power up the thrusters and get strapped in. If anything else happens, you may need to launch.'

'Understood. But I can't just leave them. They are coming. If needed, I will go back and extract them.'

Arden then looked at Howard and his daughter. 'We can't lose any more people today.'

# 86

# SQUIRE

*Onboard the BSV*

Silence, save for his own laboured breathing and the reassuring background whir of pumps inside his suit. It had been the same inside the BSV. Paisley was gone, for now at least. The main brain of his ship was dead. Extremely limited operations worked that didn't require manual input.

Squire was relieved that his last order before impact had been to close all the internal doors and seal them. That had probably saved him, as the ship's hull had been punctured in multiple places and the auto repair systems had failed. The difficulty that had presented was that he'd been unable to open many of the doors since. Some, he believed, would have been open to vacuum whilst others were just jammed shut, due to structural damage to the integrity of the ship or systems' failures.

He took a deep breath and resumed his EVA, carefully pulling himself along the outside of the BSV. His first excursion had revealed that half of one side was gone, the whole shielding cradle had been torn straight off and the ship underneath had been peppered with shrapnel from the Xenos.

He'd tried for hours to find a way to the hold via internal means with no success. The only alternative was to go outside and cut his way in through the external cargo door if it wouldn't manually open. He was desperate to find out what had happened to Wilding and the aliens. The internal CCTV was down. His route was longer than it needed to be, and more awkward, but it was around the side of the ship that faced away from where the Xenos had been. Even now there was buffeting of the BSV by rubble that orbited Triton. If he was hit by any object, he was pretty much certain to die. As he climbed the last few dozen metres, Squire wondered if the Xenos and the ruins it created from other orbital platforms might even create a small ring system for Triton itself.

Whilst the ship's AI was gone, its SOS had broadcast. He'd received a message, to which he was unable to reply, that suggested help was on its way. He'd been warned he might have to wait though, as a lot of help was needed by a lot of people and it was extremely dangerous in the vicinity of Triton. It was as if the whole area had been mined. All non-emergency traffic round Neptune had been grounded and any ships capable of participating in a rescue attempt were being diverted to help. Bases were all being locked down, with some reporting they were being subject to dangerous showers from the debris. Fortunately, many of the planet's atmospheric mining facilities had been on the far side of Neptune, so had escaped the initial explosion. Their heavy-duty transporters were used to rough conditions, so were all being sent to assist. Squire cautiously glanced over his shoulder. There were a few pin pricks of light moving, though he couldn't tell if they were here to help or were like he was, stranded and disabled.

Whilst crawling from handhold to handhold, he grimly told to himself that this would create a lot of work in the clean-up operation. If only he had a ship that was well equipped to deal with that, he'd make a fortune. At this point he knew the BSV was in bad shape, she was possibly a write off. That in itself didn't worry Squire too much. He'd be able to afford any repairs. He wasn't short of cash and had nothing else to spend it on, anyway. Alternatively, he was sure someone would be willing to give him a scooper if he volunteered to make Triton orbit safe again.

Upon reaching the external loading hatch to the hold, he took a break, exhausted at his exertions. He was as much mentally exhausted as he was physically. His ribs ached from where his harness had saved him, though he could sense wet from around his ear where he'd been hit by some equipment. The wound must have re-opened.

As expected, Squire's suit was unable to talk to the door. Fortunately, it had a backup, a manual opening mechanism. Squire crawled across the cargo bay door and found hidden away, underneath a piece of shielding, a small hatch. He cursed as the whole hull was buckled and the hatch was jammed shut. He tried to use a wrench that was strapped to his backpack to open the lid. He hammered on it in frustration, trying to assess his options. The longer he was outside, the more at risk he was of being hit by the wave of shrapnel that was now sweeping round Triton in a wide orbit.

Realising he had no choice, he crawled over to an external storage bin that, to his relief, opened and returned with a laser cutter. He knew the cargo doors were far too thick to cut through, but this hatch was only a thin, protective cover. As he set about cutting open the hatch, he realised how tired he was and how rough the collision had been. He hurt all over, an extreme form of whiplash. His vision was blurred, not helped with sweat pouring from his forehead. It stung even more where it mixed with the blood running from behind his ear, pooling on his face. He was relieved to make short work of the hatch as the cutter failed just as he was able to prise it open. Breaking every rule on orbital safety, he tossed the dead tool away from the BSV into the dark.

He paused to get his breath, nervously looking over his shoulder for fear of another shower of deadly rain, before twisting the manual control and being relieved as the cargo door slid toward its recess. It juddered to a halt halfway open, but there was enough space for Squire to get through.

Nervously lighting all the spotlights his suit carried, he swung round the door and grabbed for a tether point he knew was on the ceiling near the opening, intended usually to assist the stowing of awkward cargo. He pulled a tether out from his belt and clipped it on before moving inside the cargo hold itself. His suit's beams only ventured so far into the cargo hold, so he pulled himself across to switch on a static light set near the tether point.

The cargo hold glistened with frost. If it wasn't so dark and scary, it might have resembled a Christmas grotto. All the surfaces sparkled silver. His stomach yawed, and he had to hold back the urge to vomit inside his helmet. At the far side of the hold, partly hidden in shadow, were the tanks successfully extracted from the Xenos. To one side sat a large generator. Whilst it was also frosted over, Squire could see from the lights that it still worked. Winding their way from the generator were a number of tubes, pipes, and trunking, snaking behind the rear of the tanks. The science team brought by the flotilla to help him recover the Xenos had been good, and Squire was relieved when some of them were moved, without hurting any of their residents. The tanks on transfer had been undamaged.

That had now changed.

Most tanks appeared intact. Figures could be seen within them, consumed by the gunge that scientists presumed was keeping the inhabitants alive. One tank had lost its integrity. A pipe had been pulled down from the roof as the ceiling had buckled and its sharp, torn end had speared itself into the tank as a Knight might use a lance during a joust. The sharp end had gone straight through the tank, shattering the glass exterior, and allowing the gunge inside to spill out whereupon the loss of atmosphere had sucked the material out through a gap in a side wall into a neighbouring chamber, whilst smearing much of it across the surfaces of the hold. The alien inside had been ripped apart.

The other occupants of their tanks were far more animated than normal, twitching and moving as if they were zombies trying to escape. Carefully using the tether, he pulled himself towards Wilding. She looked terrified, eyes wide in horror. The mouth was open as if she'd tried to cry out. Her legs shuffled slightly, and her right arm moved up and down against the tank. The monitoring unit on the generator suggested that the survivors were still as healthy as before and that the tanks were still working.

Satisfied the tanks were still working, Squire wasn't sure what he should do next. All he could do was wait to be rescued, and he was better off doing that back on the bridge. There was nothing more to do here, though he wondered if, or rather hoped, that his visits had reassured Wilding.

Before he set off back on the hazardous external route to the bridge, he decided to try to tell Wilding what had happened. He slowly tried to speak aloud, exaggerating his mouth's movements as he spoke. When he reached the part about the Xenos being destroyed for a moment, he was sure those in the tanks understood. Their bodies shook before becoming still. Squire was never sure if it was a trick of the light, but he later swore he saw a tear run down Wilding's cheek.

# 87

# GARCIA

*Inside Propylaea*

Garcia barely noticed Parynski at first. She was so engrossed in the readings from the console in front of her that when she did finally acknowledge his return, she didn't even look up. 'The other two have gone back. I've assured Arden we're on the way, but before we go, I just want to show you this…'

The console in front of her was lit up, a dark background behind dozens of colourful touch displays. Garcia's eyes didn't leave the console as her hands worked it. Most of the time she struggled to get a reaction out of it, trying to press different pads in different combinations only generated what were presumably red error symbols. Parynski leaned in close but said nothing.

'It's so frustrating. I've been trying to get footage of all the different symbols and combinations to see if we can work out some sort of language here. We can probably do a better analysis back home when we have more time.'

She took hearing Parynski's sad sigh as a nudge, so she looked at him. 'Sorry, I just want to stay, that's all. Anyway, just before we go, watch this.'

She reached forward and pressed a coloured square on the console. As she had a few minutes earlier, Parynski jumped as above the console, a 3D hologram appeared. It was recognisable as a star map. The image was intense, full of thousands of scattered glowing dots that rotated slowly.

One star in the centre was illuminated green, whilst the rest were golden with odd whites, reds, and other pale colours.

'Obviously, a star map. Have you worked out where?'

She shook her head. 'No, nothing in there is recognisable to me. It could still be part of our local neighbourhood, viewed from a different direction, but I doubt it. Not even sure of the scale. Now, when I have this up, only a few controls work.'

Garcia moved her right hand to a lit panel and traced a finger up and down. As she did so, the star that was illuminated brighter than the others changed, the light jumping from star to star. It didn't jump from all stars, rather it appeared to cycle round about twenty before coming back to the first one.

'So here I can select a star whilst the only other thing I can get to work is this one. I was waiting for you so that if it blows us all up, at least I'm not alone.'

She pointed at a circular display.

Parynski laughed. 'That's reassuring. Ok, well, at least if you kill us all now, we can't be shouted at for being late. Go on, be quick.'

She swiped her hand in a clockwise direction, stopping just before a full circuit was reached. She lifted her hand and looked at Parynski.

'Just do it.'

Garcia used her finger to drag the dial round the full circuit. The display went green and froze before going out. On the hologram, the star that had been selected flashed green and then the image faded.

They looked at each other again. She felt let down, but it was something for another visit. If only she had time.

'Well, that was good.' Parynski laughed. 'Come on, we really do need to go.'

As he spoke, there was a slight tremor. In their suits, they barely felt a thing as their balance was adjusted for them, but alarms went off, flashing on their HUDs.

'What was that?'

Garcia felt a sense of dread. 'I don't know. Let's get back to the Runaround.'

# 88

# JUDE

*Inside Propylaea*

Jude was feeling helpless, struggling to hear the chatter across the com circuit. She was still angry with her father for not taking her on the journey. It sounded like an experience, and one that she would now have to wait for.

'Shit! You feel that?'

Aska was talking to the others on the shuttle.

'What is it, Aska?' Arden asked.

'It's ok, it stopped. We just felt a slight rumbling…sensors picked up a slight earthquake of some sort. It only lasted a few seconds.'

Aska continued, 'We've also got some readings of a power surge behind that shield or wall or whatever it is. But it dipped within seconds. Will review it all on the way home.'

Those on the Skydancer listened intently as the shuttle readied itself for launch. The shuttle's external cameras showed little bar darkness and the rocky floor on which they rested. Soon after, they heard Parynski radio through that he was now in the boarding tunnel, and they were being as fast as they could. Jude buzzed the Skydancer's docking team and told them to prepare to receive the shuttle.

Jude watched the cameras as Aska lifted the shuttle away from the shelf, relieved to hear her father and Garcia were safe. As the shuttle gently moved towards the exit, they, on Parynski's command, undertook a short loop in order to get some images of the wall, or doorway, that had closed whilst they were inside trying to look for any evidence of what had caused the tremor. The door had closed before the tremor and logic suggested they were linked.

They all saw it at the same time, on the enhanced imaging. The wall that had closed whilst the landing team were inside suddenly opened back up behind them, folding up and sliding away in different directions into the groove from where it had come.

'We can see that, too. Keep moving.' Arden said as he thrummed his fingers on the console impatiently, wanting to get the Skydancer moving.

Garcia, ever alive to the potential for collecting information, spoke up. 'Make sure the drones are all recalled. We'll want to examine them inside and out, especially the ones that were trapped behind the door.'

A pause.

'They aren't there.'

Jude didn't know what that meant and looked over at Arden, who shrugged. 'What do they mean - they aren't there? Can't you get a fix on them?'

There was a short silence whilst both the shuttle crew and Arden's analysts tried to check his systems.

'There were two of them trapped on the inside of that door. Both have vanished. I can see nowhere for them to have gone. I have no sign they crashed. In fact, there is not even any residue from their engines. It's as if they were never there.'

## 89

## SQUIRE

*Near the Triton Observatory Mobile Operations Centre*

Squire sat nervously, strapped into his command chair, waiting for news from his AI, Paisley. The ship vibrated slightly, power engaged and ready to launch urgently if necessary.

Despite this now being part of his regular routine, it remained just as dangerous as when he had first landed on Triton after the explosion of the Xenos. Whilst his shields were on full power, he knew that if a sizeable chunk of debris hit the shuttle it would likely be obliterated. The shuttle itself was the best he'd been able to get hold of. He owned a share in it anyway, but it was limited in comparison to the BSV. The BSV had been put into a hopefully safe, wide orbit round Neptune and awaited a slot to be taken for a refit and rebuild.

His temporary craft already showed damage from a minor hit that had torn off a whole area of plating and had taken a sensor array with it. The replacement panelling was, to anyone who gave it a cursory examination, only a quick fix.

Squire tapped into Paisley's optical feed, something he rarely did as it felt intrusive even on an AI and was pleased to see the avatar he was using was quite close now to getting back to the ship. The EVA suited figure was sat astride a snowmobile of sorts, slowly traversing the ice and rocky surface of Triton between the Ops base and the ship. His vehicle was towing a large sled that was empty save for a space suited figure. On the way out, the trailer had been full of supplies, as this was now the only way to service the base since it had been forced to move location to evade the worst of the bombardment from the Xenos. The bases landing platform had been abandoned after taking a direct hit. The base was now tucked up against a tall cliff. It wasn't the most useful place for it, but it had been hoped it could ride out however long it took for the bombardments to settle down and for Neptune orbit to be cleaned up.

Paisley messaged ahead, seeking permission to come aboard. Squire opened the rear.

cargo bay, its large door swinging down to create a ramp up which Paisley could ride his snowmobile.

'No other passengers today?' Squire asked.

'No, only Roo. This should speed our progress onto Nereid, as we won't have any other drop offs or errands to run.'

'Agreed. Let me know when your gear is stowed, and she's buckled in for launch.'

Squire clicked off the com and turned to his controls, starting pre-launch checks. After checking his scanners, he sighed with relief. There was nothing incoming from above, so they should be able to take off safely. He waited whilst Paisley closed the loading bay and restored the atmosphere. Once notified, they had strapped into launch couches, and he lifted off. He'd catch up with Roo once they were out of harm's way.

The thrust of the shuttle lifting away from the scarred surface pushed him back into his seat despite the ships dampeners and he gently swung the ship around and headed away from Triton's surface. After a few minutes he swung the nose around and the blue disc of Neptune revealed itself rising above Triton's surface, its rings sparkling. Triton was tidally locked so that the base, with its nearby Observatory facilities, were based on the side permanently looking outward.

Within minutes he became aware of Paisley's presence, now

fully integrated again into the shuttle's control system, assisting with plotting a course. These days, even a regular route needed to be planned carefully due to the presence of space debris. They monitored the latest reports and Paisley plotted a safe course.

Leaving Triton and Neptune behind, they headed out into a wide orbit to circle the planet before heading onwards to Nereid, its outermost moon. The enhanced view screen he had up presented a view that reminded Squire how lucky he had been to avoid being killed, as thousands had been, when the Xenos had been destroyed. The enhanced view of the screen showed their projected course, sliding in between both functioning and dead habitats, abandoned gas mining towers, derelict ships and millions of pieces of debris, all rattling around the orbit of Neptune. The pieces ranged from flecks of metal or rock that could still cause severe damage if a ship or habitat weren't shielded to huge pieces of machinery or rock. The flotsam wasn't just from the Xenos, so many nearby habitats and ships had been hit that their remains also violently tore around Neptune causing havoc.

The screen highlighted a few of the mining facilities in Neptune's upper atmosphere that had restarted work. It was a much-needed development as efforts were made to restore Neptune's previously prosperous economy. They swung around the largest remaining piece of the Xenos that had survived. Whilst most of it had been obliterated; a large chunk - several miles square, had survived ejected from the initial explosion. It had been kicked into a path that was to take it out of Neptune orbit and only recently had it been recovered. That had caused a lot of controversy, critics arguing that the focus should have been on assisting those in need rather than securing the alien remains. An empty, cylindrical habitat that eventually would house a team of scientists hung nearby, for now dark save for collision beacons.

After an hour, they turned away from Neptune and headed outwards towards Nereid. There was half a day's flight to intercept her today.

# THE TRITON RUN

The moon was the third biggest of Neptune's, but one had that previously been ignored due to its unusual orbit. It had, however, avoided any damage from the explosion and aftermath, so Arden's organisation had taken control of it and imposed a more regular, and human friendly, spin on it. They were headed to the small base that had been established just under the surface, a base that was intended to be the most secure in the system and one which was home to mankind's greatest secret.

Later, as they approached the moon, Roo joined him in the cockpit. She was still limping, and her head still covered by a skull cap from the injuries she'd suffered when the module of the Ops base she had been in had suffered a direct impact. Whilst busy with the clean-up efforts, and Squire was perversely grateful for the distraction of the work, he and Roo took these trips to Nereid as regularly as they could, usually at weekly intervals, staying there for a couple of days at a time. Such was Nereid's erratic orbit that this commute had taken longer as the moon was nearly at its furthest distance from the planet. It ranged from being less than a million miles from Neptune to almost six million.

They orbited the 200-mile diameter moon twice until the signal was received that they could land. There was no evidence of any other ships in the vicinity, and as ever, they were going in dark. They could barely make out the moon as he killed all its external lighting. Sensors put up a simulated image and Paisley fed Squire additional guidance.

At the very last-minute Squire held his breath as he always did when suddenly the planet's surface loomed in front of them. And then they were inside. Squire's shoulders relaxed, and he released the control stick, reversing their thrusters to bring the ship to a halt. For the first time in a while, Squire remembered to tint their scanners before the lights went on. Usually, they were temporarily blinded as the lights inside the docking bay came on.

Today they were prepared, but he was always impressed at the view as suddenly dozens of bright spotlights came on, illuminating the grey rock walls. Out of one of the walls in the square bay, a crane arm extended, its grabbers opened up to clamp around the shuttle. Despite previous experience, the sudden shake and rumble always disconcerted him. The crane gently lowered the ship on a wide metallic landing pad. Above, a ceiling slid out from the walls and sealed them in. It was designed to make it harder for external scanning to discover them and to allow for an atmosphere to be pumped into the bay.

Squire and Roo made small talk as they unstrapped themselves and secured the shuttle, talking about the predicted arrival date for the Skydancer.

As they exited the ship down the ramp, they said hello to the regular ground crew who came out onto the bay floor dragging with them fuel hoses and other servicing gear. A squad of troopers also met them, using scanners to check them for contamination and weapons. It was a familiar, but necessary routine. Others boarded the shuttle to check for stowaways.

As they waited, Roo broke the silence. 'So, what do you think? Will we make any progress today?'

If she'd been facing him, Squire could have seen her face, though her shrug told him all he needed to know. 'I hope so. I certainly think she's starting to try to communicate more often.'

They were interrupted by a beep, and the wide door in front of them slid open. It was wide enough to carry two standard storage pallets and a cart to pull them. They stepped in and nodded to the operator who was inside. In silence, save for the clanking of the elevator mechanism, they rode downwards for several minutes, both feeling the uncomfortable effects of the change in pressure on their ears.

At the bottom, the door opened again, and they were taken into a spartan reception area. The area was busy with construction workers continuing to finish the building of the facility. They were escorted through the throng and down a corridor, where they waited to pass more security checks.

# THE TRITON RUN

At their destination, another trooper, Joe McNabb, welcomed them with a smile and handshake, taking their bags and putting them on a trolley to be taken to their rooms. Squire had got to know him over recent months. He'd been one of Arden's most trusted security advisors and had jumped at the chance to take control of his own facility. He'd lost his family when Triton One had been shattered by the Xenos explosion and he'd welcomed the chance to be given some focus, even if just temporarily.

The room was plain, three walls were hewn out of the rock with no decoration. The floor had been tiled with polished black tiles. Also reflective was the fourth wall, which ran the length of the chamber.

'Is she awake, Joe?' Roo dropped into one of two chairs that had been placed facing the reflective wall. The three of them had spent many hours here.

McNabb shrugged. 'You know what it's like. She doesn't say much to me. We should get some more experts in, seems you two are the only ones who get anything.'

Squire stood alongside the spare chair, alongside Roo. 'OK, let's light it up.'

'With pleasure,' said McNabb,' I'll leave you to it for now. Buzz me if you need anything.'

And with that, he was gone. As he left, the lights dimmed and the reflective wall became transparent, flooding the room with an eerie light. The room on the other side of the window was as large as the one they were in, hermetically sealed. Against the far wall were a row of fifteen empty pods. The room was akin to a tank you'd see at an aquarium. It was full of an orange material. Towards the rear of the room were many dark shadows that were hard to make out. Sat at the front of the room was a woman. Naked, cross-legged, head in hands.

Squire spoke out loud, knowing his voice would be pumped inside the tank.

'Evening Dee, how are you doing?'

# 90

# PARYNSKI

*Onboard The Skydancer, Approaching Neptune*

Parynski had explained to Arden that traditionally, on long cargo voyages across the solar system, a crew would enjoy a feast in the last few days. They ate whatever supplies were left, leaving the spacecraft ready to be serviced and replenished. Captains justified it in terms of the benefit to morale, a way of thanking a crew that were often underpaid and forced to survive in poor conditions as well as seeing no need to increase profits for either the current charterer or their new clients. This tradition had spread to other ships where journeys of more than two weeks took place. Inspired by this, Arden had called a 'celebratory' dinner on board the Skydancer, though the mood was far more sombre and business like.

The dinner was a week before they reached home, designed to draw a line under the journey back and to allow time for the crew to prepare the ship for the tasks ahead. A refuelling tug was due to meet them in two days and after that they were to get down to work. The meal itself was no more than the simple rations that everyone had voted to take. There were reports of people starving on some of the damaged habitats that still had life support operating. Any leftovers would be used to keep them supplied for the days ahead and were not to be wasted.

The Skydancer would arrive just before a second wave of help was due from Uranus. It remained to be seen if any support would arrive from further afield, though most of the Planets were saying the right things.

Arden was the host of one group in his private dining room. More of the group were established in the galley. Parynski sat opposite Garcia, with Rebecca and Jude alongside them. As usual, conversation turned to the same topics on everyone's minds. Garcia updated them on a chat she'd just had with Roo, who had survived a damaging shower of debris to the Triton base. Others there weren't so lucky. Roo and Squire had been visiting Wilding and the BSV's precious cargo that had been recovered.

They'd been debating the location of Propylaea and its link to the Xenos. Garcia had already formed some strong opinions, ones that, for now, at least the others couldn't disagree with.

'Yes, it's a long way out from Earth, but that's probably deliberate, isn't it? Two reasons for that. It must have a big source power inside, because it uses a lot of power, so it'd be a potential safety risk if something went terribly wrong. The most likely reason is that whoever put it there, whenever they did put it there, did so because if we were to discover it, they wanted us to be ready for it. We needed to have, at the very least, system-wide travel?'

Jude was slightly more uneasy about it all. 'What if it was put there to allow some other alien race to invade more easily? Could the Xenos be part of that?'

Garcia nodded and smiled. Parynski could guess, based on his own tour of the Xenos, what Garcia would say in response. 'If the Xenos was the first wave of an invasion, then it didn't do a particularly good job, did it? It crashed into one of our ships, doesn't seem to be armed and all its passengers are trapped inside tanks full of gunge. I think they must have been here with some different purpose.'

Parynski interjected, 'And if we can get Dee out of that tank, then maybe we can find out what that was?'

The topic then moved back to what happened inside what

they now called the reception chamber inside Propylaea.

'So, come on, Bruce. Spill what's been on your mind ever since we left. You said you thought they'd read your mind when they scanned us. Why?'

He decided it was time to reveal what he knew, even if he felt it was slightly unbelievable. He sipped his drink and leaned forward slightly, speaking quietly so the whole table didn't hear. Jude knew and had been pushing him for weeks to tell everyone.

'That machine that scanned us actually read my mind. I've been wondering ever since where I knew the reception room from. It wasn't identical, but it was remarkably similar in design to the departure lounge we waited in when we were waiting to be shipped out to Mars after I signed up. That room wasn't all white. In fact, it was quite dark. The shape and design were the same, especially the pull-out bunks. Also, and this is the bit I've struggled with…'

He took a longer sip from his glass, looking upwards for inspiration, hoping Garcia wouldn't notice the slight glistening in his eyes.

She did notice. 'I'm sorry. It's ok, I didn't mean to upset you. What is it?'

After taking a deep breath, he continued. 'Sorry. It's Mary. The footage you've seen of me heading up that path to the bandstand on the cliffs? A bit weird, some sort of advanced simulation, well that's where I married Mary. Ever since…we heard the news about her passing, she's been on my mind a lot. That had to have come from inside my head. Not sure I like that. Those nanobot clouds, everything they built, came from my subconscious.'

She grabbed his hand across the table.

'Ok, I understand. And I know you've found these last months tough. Please let me pass on this information. It'll affect how we behave when we go back. Maybe they might just want to make us feel welcome?'

Jude nodded. 'That was my view when he told me. Those nano bots were trying to tailor the reception areas and controls to what we'd expect. It just happened they scanned Dad first.'

# THE TRITON RUN

Parynski pulled away from Garcia's hand as he regained his composure, aware that some of those sat near had gone quiet to listen in.

'The more I think about it, the more it all makes sense. That room was set out like a departure lounge...somehow, they were looking in my head for such a chamber. A room linked to departure? Yeah?'

He could see Garcia didn't understand what he was getting at, so he carried on.

'Well, when you were messing with that console and you could choose a star, that's when that door blocked off the central chamber. And when you selected a star, that's when we felt the tremor and power surge?'

She raised her eyebrows. 'Go on...'

'Those drones went somewhere, didn't they? After the door opened, they'd all vanished. Maybe the whole object is some sort of transport device?'

Garcia gave him a smile, eyes lighting up. 'That would explain why we couldn't even find any residual trace of the drones or their exhausts. Maybe the whole space in there was transported elsewhere? God knows how! Maybe that's where the Xenos came from. It arrived via the object.'

Bruce sipped his drink, feeling relieved his theory wasn't rejected out of hand. 'Exactly my thinking. Rather than just an alien rock or another spaceship, maybe we've found a gateway to another part of the galaxy?'

Jude had been having these thoughts since her father had discussed it with her a few weeks earlier. 'Well, we've got nothing to go back to Earth for, not for a while, anyway. Once we've helped with the relief exercise, fancy going back and doing some exploring?'

Parynski's eyes flitted between his daughter and Garcia.

'Things will never be the same again, you know. What if the next alien ship to arrive isn't friendly?'

## 91

## WILDING

*The Dark*

Wilding felt strong emotions from the Qarti, emotions which showed no signs of fading. Grief, fear, and anxiety dominated, while she herself felt excited.

It had been stressful being removed from her tank and deposited in a larger one, but it was a development of sorts. She didn't know where she was, though after events on Squire's ship, she was relieved to feel vaguely safe. The Qarti feared the worst.

For now, at least, Wilding decided to focus her mind on her own situation. This was the closest she'd been to returning to normality since first entering the tank. She didn't regret it. The alternative was death, but increasingly, she yearned for freedom, both physically and mentally freedom from the Qarti.

They were now in a large tank, effectively a cell. It was spacious enough that their original tanks now stood at the rear, doors open, with plenty of room to move around.

The remaining Qarti were considerably larger than Wilding, but they usually huddled away to one side, suspiciously staring at both her and the screen which filled one wall. They communicated their fear, and she attempted to reassure them that these were good people; how she knew some of them, and why this must be the first step towards their collective release from the tank. Squire appeared at regular intervals, and she could see he was trying to read her lips. She wasn't convinced that this was what the Qarti wanted.

The substance which had consumed them all filled the chamber. She wondered if scientists could replicate it, or whether it had somehow self-expanded to fill the required volume. Originally, Wilding had been terrified as the tanks migrated from the wreck of the BSV and were transported down a lift before arriving in this room. Whilst at times it felt like being a zoological exhibit, she was reassured by the attention she received. There were always people on the other side of the semi-transparent glass.

Wilding had more movement than previously, but still not much. Although her mind operated at a million miles an hour, her body still felt like it were in slow motion, swimming in treacle. The substance was keeping her alive, even though she'd not quite gotten used to not breathing or being unable to swallow.

One side of the tank contained a wide door. Since the EVA suited figure who opened the tanks had left, it remained sealed shut. She was fairly certain there was an airlock on the other side. The figure had taken all her clothes and those of the Qarti, seemingly for analysis. Her preferred position was sitting cross-legged, arms covering the scars and wounds which covered her body.

Even as they were being released from their original tanks, the suited figure had tried to communicate with her using a laminated pad. Wilding had been physically unable to write a response, but the last card she received remained on the floor in front of her.

For now, it was enough.

The message read: 'Everything is going to be ok.'

She hoped that was true.

# ACKNOWLEDGEMENTS

TBD

# THE TRITON RUN

Printed in Great Britain
by Amazon